Praise for *Grace*

'A thing of power and of wonder…Paul Lynch writes novels the way we need them to be written: as if every letter of every word mattered. This whole book is on fire.'

Laird Hunt, author of *The Evening Road*

'Passionately lyrical…*Grace* belongs to several great traditions – the picaresque novel, the coming-of-age novel, and the orphan novel… [this] is a relentless novel, but Lynch allows his heroine a true complexity of feeling – about her brother, her mother, Bart, and what she sees happening around her – that allows the reader to empathize even as we wring our hands. *Grace* is not only a gripping tale about an appalling period in history – although that would be quite enough – but also, sadly, piercingly relevant.'

Boston Globe

'Lynch's wonderful third novel follows a teenage girl through impoverished Ireland at the height of the Great Famine…In Gaelic-lilted poetic prose, Lynch evokes nearly five years of misery: the Samhain (end-of-harvest festival) after flooding destroys the harvest, wintry deprivation, endless days on nameless roads, starvation, and desperation. Heart-wrenching images include Grace's pregnant mother dragging Grace to the killing stump to chop off her hair, Grace eating stolen seed potatoes, and much worse. Lynch's powerful, inventive language intensifies the poignancy of the woe that characterizes this world of have-nothings struggling to survive.'

Publishers Weekly (starred review)

'A gifted Irish author offers another take on his country's Great Famine through the eyes of a teenage girl as she travels through a land wracked by want.... This is a writer who wrenches beauty even from the horror that makes a starving girl think her "blood is trickling over the rocks of my bones."'

Kirkus (starred review)

'In these pages Lynch has deepened and refined his art considerably – there are entire sections of the book that are unforgettable.'

Open Letters Monthly

'*Grace* feels as though it has already claimed its place among great Irish literature.'

BookPage

'*Grace* is fierce wonder, a journey that moves with the same power and invention as the girl at its center. What Paul Lynch brings to these pages is more than mere talent – it's a searing commitment to story and soul, and in witnessing Grace's transformations, one can't help but feel changed too. This novel is faith, poetry, lament and triumph; its mark is not only luminous, but it promises to never fade.'

Affinity Konar, author of *Mischling*

'*Grace* is a masterful sequel to *Red Sky in Morning*; a beautifully written, lyrical portrait of a young girl coming of age during the Great Famine. Lynch's Ireland is a land of sadness, harsh reality and starvation, yet there is beauty found in the air, the sky and even the insects. The prose flows like good Irish whiskey and compels readers to keep drinking in Lynch's words; sometimes so poetic they read like a James Joyce novel.'

RT Book Reviews

'If you took the most overwhelming and distilled moments of a life – those instants when even a small brush of the wind over a stream seems to speak to the whole problem of living – and scattered them along an Irish riverside during that country's great famine, you might arrive at *Grace*. This is a major work of lasting, powerful feelings that might find a place amidst your memories of *Light in August* and *Huckleberry Finn*.'

Will Chancellor,
author of *A Brave Man Seven Storeys Tall*

GRACE

PAUL LYNCH

A Oneworld Book

First published in Great Britain and Australia by Oneworld Publications, 2017

A CIP record for this title is available from the British Library

ISBN 978-1-78607-305-1 (hardback)
ISBN 978-1-78607-306-8 (eBook)

Printed and bound in Great Britain by Clays Ltd, St Ives plc

Oneworld Publications
10 Bloomsbury Street
London WC1B 3SR
United Kingdom

For Louise Stembridge, who has left us
For Amelie Lynch, who has joined us

My life is light, waiting for the death wind,
Like a feather on the back of my hand.

—*T. S. Eliot*

Who, without death, dares walk into the kingdom of the dead?

—*Dante Alighieri*

Time dissipates to shining ether the solid angularity of facts.

—*Ralph Waldo Emerson*

I

The Samhain

This flood October. And in the early light her mother goes for her, rips her from sleep, takes her from a dream of the world. She finds herself arm-hauled across the room, panic shot loose to the blood. She thinks, do not shout and stir the others, do not let them see Mam like this. She cannot sound-out anyhow, her mouth is thick and tonguing shock, so it is her shoulder that speaks. It cracks aloud in protest, sounds as if her arm were rotten, a branch from a tree snapped clean. From a place that is speechless comes the recognition that something in the making up of her world has been unfixed.

She is drawn to the exit as if harnessed to her mother, her body bent like a buckling field implement, her feet blunt blades. A knife-cut of light by the door. Her eyes fight the gloom to get a fasten on her mother, see just a hand pale as bone vised upon her wrist. She swings her free fist, misses, swings at the dark, at the air complicit, digs her heels into the floor. Will against will she pits, though Sarah's will now has become more like animal power, a secret strength, she thinks, like Nealy Ford's ox before he killed it and left, and now her wrist burns in her mother's grip. She rolls from her heels to her toes as she is dragged out the door.

What comes to meet them is a smacking cold as if it has lurked there just for them, an animal thing eager in the dawn, a morning that sits low and crude and grey. Not yet the true cold of winter though the trees huddle like old men stripped for punishment and the land is haggard just waiting. The trees here are mountain ash but bear not the limbs of grace. They stand foreshortened and twisted as if they could find no succour in the shallow earth, were stunted by the sky's ever-low. Beneath them pass Sarah and her daughter, this girl pale-skinned, fourteen, still boy-chested, her long hair set loose in her face so that all her mother can see of her are the girl's teeth set to grimace.

Her mother force-sits her on the killing stump. Sit you down on it, she says.

It seems for a moment that a vast silence has opened, the wind a restless wanderer all times at this height is still. The rocks set into the mountain are great teeth clamped shut to listen. In the mud puddles the girl is witness to herself, sees the woman's warp standing over her grey and grotesque. The spell of silence breaks, wing-flap and whoosh of a dark bird that shoots overhead for the hill. She thinks, what has become of Mam while I slept? Who has taken her place? Of a sudden she sees what the heart fears most—pulled from out of her mother's skirt, the dulled knife. And then out of her own dark comes her brother Colly's story, his huge eyes all earnest, the story of a family so hard up they put the knife to the youngest. Or was it the eldest? she thinks. Colly, always with the stories, always yammering on, swearing on his life it was true. Quit your fooling, she said then. But now she knows that one thing leads to another and something has led to this.

She hears Sarah wheezing behind her. Hears the youngers creep open the door to peep. She thinks of the last living thing they saw put to blood, the unfurling of the goose into arching white as it was chased, rupturing the air with shrill. The eerie calm of that bird with its long neck to the stump and their sister quiet now just like it, the same blunt knife that made such long work. And Boggs that time waiting. The way he picked them clean. She sees the blade come up, becomes an animal that bucks and braces against her mother.

The rush of Colly then, this small bull of a boy twelve years old, his cap falling off, yelling out his sister's name. Grace! She hears in his voice some awful desperation, as if to speak her name is to save it from the closure of meaning, that as long as he is sounding it no harm can be done. She feels the swerve towards an oncoming dark, Colly tugging at his mother, the way he gets an arm around Sarah's waist until she makes light work of him, puts him to the ground. Then she speaks and her voice is shaking. Colly, get you back into the house. Grace turns and sees her brother red-cheeked upon his sit-bones, sees the knife in her mother's hand as if she were embarrassed of it. Eye to eye they meet and she is surprised by what she does not see in her mother—any sign of madness or evil. Hears when the woman speaks a knot twisting in the cords of her throat. Enough, please, would ye.

Then Sarah moves quick, takes a fist of the girl's hair to lay bare the porcelain of her throat, brings up the knife.

All the things you can see in a moment. She thinks, there is truth after all to Colly's story. She thinks, the last you will see of Mam is her shadow. She thinks, take with you a memory of all this. A sob loosens from the deepest part and sings itself out.

What she meets is the autumn of her long hair. It falls in swoons, falls a glittering of evening colours, her hair spun with failing sunlight. She sobs at the pain in her scalp as her mother yanks and cuts. Sobs as her hair falls in ribbons. Her eyes closed to their inner stars. When she opens them again her mother has circled her. Colly on his knees holding fistfuls of hair. The wind-cold licking bitter at her bare neck. She raises her hands and puts them dumb to what's left of her head, her mother stepping in front of her, the knife going into the dress. Sarah looks frustrated, breathless, wan and exhausted, the skin on her throat beginning to hang loose as if to wear it well requires effort she has not within her. Her collarbone a brooch of banished beauty. She rests her hands on her seven-month swell, bolds up her voice to her daughter. What she says.

You are the strong one now.

The shard of looking glass holds the world in snatches. She snares the cloud-tangled sun and bends it towards her feet. They are long and narrow feet and though unshod are unmistakably hers—as delicate as any girl's, elegantly formed, she thinks, and if you washed the dirt you would see beneath the nails a perfect rose-pink. She is proud of her slender ankles, not swollen like Mam's. The knobbly jut of knee with its moony scar. She turns and reflects the sun towards the back of Colly's head, the boy in a sulk, snorting fumes from his clay pipe. She hears the padding of speedy feet inside and then a child falling, knows from the cry it is the youngest, Bran. Colly muttering a curse, then getting up in a flop when the crying does not cease. She cannot bear to look at her head. Swings the looking glass to see gossamer strung between two rocks—a cobweb that swings a gentle arc on the breeze and the way it pulses light makes it seem alive with the sun. She reaches her finger and severs it, wipes what sticks off the rags of her skirt. If her finger were a blade it would be as sharp and pointed as her hate. She thinks, the things I would do with it.

Movement by the door. She angles the looking glass so she can see her mother step out of the house with her red shawl, a fisherman catching a shoal of daylight as she swings it over her shoulders. Sarah pulls a chair to the middle of the road, sighs, sits red-faced as if awaiting somebody—awaiting Boggs, Grace thinks—Sarah's hands fumbling on her lap. She sighs again, then stands and steps wordless into the house, emerges with the ash pin and fastens it to her shawl, sits down on the chair. No one dares talk when Sarah is like this, though Colly and Grace keep their eyes fixed on her. She knows that Colly sees the makings of a witch in his mother, wants to lay her cold with his fist. She watches the way her mother sits watching the road on top of the hill, pokes her eyes into the holes of Sarah's dirt-white skirt, each hole as wide as two or three fingers. The way the skirt fans down from the waist like the warped pleat of a melodeon. And then, for a moment, she sees her mother as someone different, thinks that by seeing Sarah in the looking glass she can see her truly as she is—a woman who might once have been young and wears a glimmer of it still. The way this fifth pregnancy is greying her. And then like light the awareness passes and she grabs hold of her hate.

Of a sudden, Sarah is standing and bunching her skirt. The way she sets off up the road that rises to the pass, her arms folded, her body leaning into the weight of the hill, into the deadening void of colour but for the total of brown where nothing good grows, the land unspoken but for the wind.

She knows the youngers are made every part of them innocent but still they bear the mark of Boggs. That same scald of red hair. A hang of earlobe like a polished coin. That bulldog nose. How he has stained all his children. In the town last year she saw two boys just like them the same age as well, though Sarah kept on walking as if blinkered. She thinks of this as she rebuilds the low fire. Sizzle-spit of moss and then slabs of turf that sit valiant to the embers as if for a moment they were the equal of it. She settles the youngers down with tin cups of water, watches the fire come to judgement. For too long she has watched her mother's descent—down and down into some inner winter vision. Her eyes taking the glaze. Went that way after Boggs's last visit. The man sweaty, calm-as-you-like in his manner. That backward-leaning walk. That sprawling red beard as if it were its own majesty. The way he sits in the room twirling his knuckle hair while pinning you with his stare. Never gone from his heels those greyhounds lunatic about the place. Every time he comes there is what he does. What sounds at night. Sarah's whimpering. During the day even, when Sarah sends them all outside. And then that day when he asked to see Grace alone in the house and how Sarah straightened up to him, told him he had no business with her, but as soon as he was gone how the change came over her mother, her eyes becoming black and unseeing like Nealy Ford's ox, the way that ox stood a philosopher to its own stillness before taking off across the field in a run, as if startled by a vision of its own end.

That was before Nealy Ford left the cabin next door unannounced and took himself off, the place empty, the land he'd limed and reclaimed — another one gone, Mam had said.

She steps outside and fixes the latch, sits beside Colly on the hammer rock. He curls his dark toes while a hand burrows to pull loose plug tobacco from his pocket. They sit in his palm like question marks. He is still slit-eyed with anger. He tamps the pipe with his thumb then shouts a loud fuck and slides off the rock. He returns a moment later with the pipe lit, his hand swinging a broken umbrella. She watches the top of the road for her mother, draws her skirt over her feet and puts a hand to her head. What lies unknown is a sickening thing like the slow knotting of rope inside her. Colly sits beside her hanging the pipe from his lip. He is trying to fix the umbrella with string, though the mechanism is broken. She can feel the look that reads her as if she can see herself. The awkwardness with which she sits, knees to chin. The weirded shape of her skull and what it does to her ears. The shame she cannot hide at being undone of herself. Being unmade of her beauty. I look like bad pottery, she thinks. A wretched blue-eyed cup. A kettle with two big bastarding bools for ears.

She turns and catches him looking. What? she says.

Listen, muc, who gives a fuck about that auld bitch.

She puts her hands to her head. Thinks, there is shame now in just being looked at.

She says, my head is sore and frozen with the cold. No one will look at me now.

He takes off his cap, throws it at her. Here, put this on. I don't feel nothin of the cold anyhow. His smile becomes broad when she puts it on. Hee! You look like me now. That's not so bad, is it?

She brings the looking glass shard to her face and sees the soft under each eye is puffed. Examines the crust of blood that has formed over her left ear. She adjusts the cap but her ears are huge under it. She forces a smile. Says, she has made me look like you with your big lug ears.

His face creases in mock anger. Get away, you bald goat.

They sit in easy silence, watch the land become shadow, an enormous cloud passing low overhead like a weightless mountain. They sit dwarfed in this rift between the earth and the sky, trying to see into what lies mute and hidden. In the crosshatch of a tree a blackbird sings and she decides the bird sings for her. From this bird's flight she will determine an augury. She thinks about Sarah's far-cousin, the Banger, a blacksmith on the bottom of the hill. What he said. That these are dangerous times, Grace. That it rained frogs in Glásan and what have you and that's what done it for the lumper potatoes. A sign from the fairy pooka, he said. She knows that after the failed harvest, men from the big houses in the land below began carrying guns to protect their shortages. That Sarah is worked up about it even though she and Colly are good foragers. What a strange year it's been, she thinks, the rain and the storms that upturned summer into winter and the heat of September and then that bilgewater stench that came from the fields. Now, this flood October. The rains like something biblical and everything dead. And this the first dry morning in weeks.

Where do you think Mam's gone to, Colly?

Like I give a toss.

There is a bloom in his cheeks that never whitens. He is always thinking, tinkering with things. His latest are the bird traps, though Sarah scolds him—you'll eat no such thing, not ever. But Grace knows he has eaten one or two, dirty crows probably. She has seen the ashy bones in the fire. She thinks, unlike the youngers, we two are the same blood and now one face is the same as the other.

She turns to read what is foretold by the bird but the bird has gone and left behind mystery. And then it comes to her, the answer so clear she is startled. She whispers it to herself, over and over. Thinks, do not speak it aloud.

Colly says, anyhow, what in the hell was Mam on about? Cutting your hair is hardly going to make you strong. Wasn't it Samson came to weakness because of it?

She thinks, he hasn't yet figured it. That might be as well.

Everybody around here knows I'm the strongest. Look. He rolls up his sleeve, squeezes his fist and pops his scrawny biceps. This is what I mean by power.

Colly, yer twelve.

She watches him toke too deep on his pipe and struggle to contain a cough. She wants to cry for herself, at the pain-cold of her head, at this dumb-tongued feeling that has settled inside her. At this future she knows is being fixed without her consent. She chooses instead to laugh at him.

Just you watch, he says. He sucks and shapes his mouth into a pout, tongues through the mouthcloud of smoke. What emerges are not smoke rings but little grey tuffets. There, he says.

There what?

His voice drops to a whisper. I think Mam has got the tunnies.

The what?

The tunnies.

What's that?

It's when they get into your body and eat into your brain and put you out of sorts with yourself.

Where did you hear that?

I heard it off some fella.

He falls silent. Then he says, do you think Mam is gone for good?

She thinks, Mam will return, but then, what of it?

He says, I think the tunnies have got her good this time. I think the auld bint's rotten for good.

She stares into his eyes until she sees the fright he is trying to hide. Says, she would never abandon you lot.

He sucks thoughtfully on his pipe. I can look after myself anyhow.

She says, don't you realize? Boggs is coming back. I know it like I know the day is turning. That is why she is frightened. That's why she has gone strange like this. We have nothing for him. The way things have gone now with the harvest all rotten. She doesn't know what to do.

She wets a finger and puts it under her cap, rubs at drying blood.

Colly says, I know what it is. It is the way that Boggs looks at you.

She slides off the rock and bloods it with her finger. C'mon, she says. We need to go gleaning.

Hold on, he says. His hand to his chin like a man in boy bones, always puzzling something out. What's fat as a cake but has nothin to ate, is ten times tall but contains nothin at all?

You told us that riddle last week.

How could I? he says. I just made it up.

Colly!

What?

She means for me to leave.

She stands in the shade watching for her mother, the creeping sun stirring strange colours in the far-off. The land has become manifold, stretching itself in darkly different forms, shadows that reach and consume and dissolve into the one dark as if everything were just play to this truthdark all along. The wind low like a snuffling animal bending unseen the grass. This wind an accompaniment to all her days here, Blackmountain, a rock-ribbed hill road used by travellers, sales folk, drovers herding livestock to the townlands by the sea, or farmers carting lumpers before they went black and liquid in the earth. Men who took a meal and sometimes stayed the night if they were late passing, left the odd coin but most times bartered. But this last while, the road has risen few travellers and those who pass bring nothing to eat. A knock on the door now is more often the open hand of a beggar.

She sees her mother's relief coming over the pass, steps quickly into the house. Colly on the stool, his body bent over the yellowing book of sums. The youngers tangled together on the straw. The older, Finbar, is making rope of Bran's hair until the younger wails and she swings the child onto her shoulder. She hushes him and the candle beside Colly flickers as if something unseen has entered, though something unseen has already entered, she thinks. It sat itself down and spoke in secret tongue with Mam and it is you now who has to deal with the consequences. Footsteps and then Grace turns to see Sarah standing ill-sainted between the jambs of the door muttering about her feet. What is held in the woman's hand.

Hee! Colly throws the book and leaps from the stool.

Sarah says, don't you even think about looking.

She turns her back, takes the knife, and unsleeves the hare from its skin with a slowness the watchers inhabit. She drops it into the pot and fills the pot with water and hangs it over the fire. Then she takes the jug outside and laves her hands and cools her feet with water. Colly pretending again at the book but he is sly-watching the meat as if it could leap from the pot back into its skin and hare out the door. Grace sits rubbing at her head but Colly takes no notice. It is still strange to her, this bareness of scalp. Having hair now that tufts like tussock grass. Hair like fir needles. Hair like the blackthorn robbed of its sloes. She thinks of what the hare looked like headless and skinned, how it glistened gum-pink. The shine of its inner parts as if the mystery of what brought it life gleamed with revelation. And then the shock of a thought. What did Mam barter for this? She watches the woman carefully. She says, we gathered some charlock while you were gone. Cooked it up with some nettles and water.

Sarah sits and beckons for Bran. She opens her clothing to the hang of her breast and puts the child to it. My feet are broke, she says. Pass me that creepie for my feet.

The child takes the nipple but cannot draw milk.

Tongues thicken to a meat smell that can be tasted. She cannot remember the last time she had meat. She thinks, the spit-taste of lead. That man with the wolf face, telling stories over the fire, left hanging two wood pigeon full of shot. How he told them he was raised by wolves, said he could bark before he could speak. Started yapping at the roof, leaping about with two fiddling elbows. Mam telling him to shush, you'll stir the youngers. The way his eyes shone while telling his stories as if they were not just true but had happened to him. Then he quietened down, hunched like an animal when he told them the story of his birth. Said, my name is Cormac mac Airt and I was found in the woods by a wolf. I was left there by a mammy that didn't want me. The wolves raised me up as their own, so they did. Learned me to lap at the river with me tongue. I did everything the way of the wolf but they weren't impressed later on, when they saw me do a man's business standing up. How everybody had a laugh at this but Colly, the entire time giving the man a funny look. Cormac mac Airt's not yer real name, he said. You're Peter Crossan. And the wolves died off, so they did, in Ireland before you were born.

How she had wished Colly would shut up. Wolfman pawing at Colly with his eyes. You be careful, *buachalán*. Too much knowledge will make a tree grow from your neck.

It was two days later when Boggs came to visit.

All eyes at the table are upon Sarah as she piles the meat into a bowl. Colly's elbows have expanded, his eyes eating the meat. He shoves at his sister as Sarah carries the bowl to the table. She slides it before Grace. Colly reaches to grab at it but Sarah cuffs his ear with a quick hand. Sit you quiet, she says.

She speaks to her daughter. All this is for you.

Grace blinks.

Eat you all of it.

Her stomach tightens as if with sickness. Question and confusion alight her eyes as she looks at her mother, looks at Colly, the faces of the youngers. She eyes the meat again and slides the bowl towards the centre of the table.

She says, the others are hungry too.

Sarah pushes the bowl back towards her. I got this meat specially for you.

I won't eat it. Here, Colly, you eat it instead.

She does not see the hand that strikes from darkness, her cheek scalded. She closes her eyes and watches the fire burn out. It is Sarah who begins to shout. Yer just like your father. You with your stubborn head. Her voice drops and then wobbles. If only you knew what I went through to get this. Now eat it. Eat every part of it. And what you cannot eat you will take away with you.

Salt tears in her mouth flavouring the food she eats with her fingers, heaven's taste though she cannot enjoy it. She hears only the words her mother has said, wants to ask what she means though in her heart she knows. Colly has gone quiet, his eyes squished with anger. She eats until she can eat no more, pushes the bowl into the centre of the table.

I feel sick. I feel sick with it. Let the others eat some.

You will take what is left with you. You need it to make you strong.

Sarah stands away from the table with Bran hanging from her arm. She points to Colly and Finbar. Take a look, Grace. Take a good long look at their faces. The harvest is destroyed, you know that. I've tried all over but nobody is giving alms. I am too far gone with child. You have to be responsible now. You must find work and work like a man, for nobody will give but low work to a girl your age. Come back to us then after a season, when your pocket's full. This meat will get you started.

Her mother's words reach her as if by some foreign tongue. The measure of what is known of her world stretching abruptly and beyond what a mind can foresee, as if hills and valleys could be leveled into some sudden and irrevocable horizon. She will not look her mother in the eye, is trying not to cry but she is. She looks around the table, sees the way the youngers stare at her, sees what is in Colly's eyes, the whites of all their eyes and the who they are behind that white and what lies dangerous to the who of them, this danger she has feared, how it has finally been spoken, how it has been allowed to enter the room and sit grinning among them.

* * *

She wakes wet with tears knowing she has grieved her own death. A dream-memory of herself lying broken after some fall, a strange witness to her own passing. She touches her wet cheek, feels relief to have wakened, listens to the others. The way it seems each boy's breath entwines one to the other like rope. The arch of Colly's foot warm to her shin. His mind off on some night adventure. She wonders how far he is traveling in his dream and hopes he is happy. How each mind, she thinks, is held in its own husk, a night-drift more private than anything you can see behind a face by day.

And then it comes. Grief for what has changed. Grief for what is.

The whispering breath of Sarah tells her to change out of her clothes. Soon she is out of bed, stands naked before her mother, covers an arm over the small of her breasts. Sarah grabs Grace's hand and yanks it away from her. Weren't you naked the day you were born? She produces cloth to bind Grace's chest, stops and says, you've no need of it. Hands her a man's shirt that swallows her. It smells like rocks pulled from a river. She holds the breeches in front of her and studies them. The fawn fabric is patched tan at the knees. She thinks, they look like a dog has had them for slumber. From whom did they come? Into the first leg she steps and then the other and she looks down at herself—such a sight, wishbone legs snapped loose into two gunnysacks. The breeches go past her ankles. Sarah rolls the ends up, stands behind her and loops the waist with string. A jacket that stinks of rained-on moss. A frieze coat ravelly about the neck and yawning at the elbow.

I might as well be wearing jute.

Sarah whispers. Here. Put on your boots. And try this cap. Your brother's cap is too small for you. Pull it lower. Plenty of boys go about dressed in a father's old clothing.

Grace stands staring past the door at the world held starless by a flat dark. Leg-skin strange in these breeches and the cold whittling her head. Sarah hands her a candle and the light falls from her mother's face so that it seems she is not herself, stands masked to her own daughter. She fusses over Grace, puts a satchel over her shoulder, rolls up the sleeves of the jacket. Then she looks towards the sleeping children, holds Grace with a long look, and whispers. Get to the town and don't dally on the mountain road. Ask for Dinny Doherty and tell him you are your brother. He has always been kind to us. He likes the boy's humour, so try and sound a bit like Colly. Tomorrow is the Samhain, so stay indoors with him and keep from going out. The streets will be full of trouble.

She sees a memory of a man passing by stringing heaps of ponies and a huge laugh out of him. Dinny Doherty is that wee man who takes over a hill with his laughter.

Sarah says, go now before the others stir up.

She turns, finds the centre of Sarah's eye, holds it. She says, what are you going to call the wean?

Sarah holds her eyes closed and then opens them again. If it is a girl, I'll call her Cassie. Now go.

Cassie.

A hand on her arm the last moment of her mother.

Of a sudden she knows. That these old clothes belonged to her father.

The sun's breaking light traces the mountain's solid dark. She steps into that first light, the track cold to her feet, her legs weirded. She cannot stop sobbing. Cannot understand how it has come to this. Her life as if it were just some rock hurled by someone else. She wades up the hillside path and stops at the vanishing point. When she turns she sees her mother has been watching, an indigo streak that steps into the house. By now the dawn has fanned its bluing light to brighten the stone house made small but held within it a universe. The chair on the road with its shadow is a twice-empty shape. She thinks of Colly and what he gave her before they went to sleep, his hand spread open in the dark so she had to see it with her fingers. His box of lucifers. The matchbox cindered at the edges where one time he tried to flame it. Now it is filled with strands of her hair. Just so you can keep your strength till it grows back. And then his whispers. Let me go with you. Please. Let me. And she answered. I wouldn't know how to care for you. How he lay there sulking.

She is about to turn when she sees the small shape of Colly come running out of the house. Her heart leaps to meet him, Sarah out the door after Colly and she takes a hold of him by the shirt, tries to pull him back. Something sad and comic in their distant scramble and then Colly hurls a heart-full shout that rises and then is gone into the sky's all of sound.

She waits all day out of sight of the house until evening fringes the moss. Knee-bent and in stealth she returns among shadows down a different hill. The heather brushing off her breeches whispers, do not get you caught. She steals by the back of the house, can hear Sarah chiselling at the youngers. To the side of the house and what she hopes to see—Colly is toking on the hammer rock. She wants to tell him everything will be all right. That she will be back soon enough. That it will be a matter of months. That he has to be strong for the others. She fingers a small rock and flings it at his leg, misses, throws another. He springs off the hammer rock like a jacked-up dog. What in the fuck? he says.

She whispers. Would you ever shush.

He steps forward. Grace? Is that you?

I said would you shush.

His voice comes to her luminous and then his face appears and he is bright with the sight of her. He pulls her into a hug. Are you back for good?

I'm still gone.

Then what are you doing here?

She hears herself speak as if another has stolen her mouth.

Do you still want to come?

Everything is still wet. Where can she wait for him but by the windbreak of a peat trench cut by who knows when and dry just about. The night enfolding all into the one. She thinks, he did not come when he said he would. He did not come because to do so would be mad in the head. He did not come because Mam will be watching—she knows what he is like. He is so giddy he would not be able to hide it. You are on your own now, wee girl.

She lies and listens to the pulse of all things. The closing song of the birds. The air stitched with insects. The wind's voice and how it speaks over everything. Closer still, the sound of her own body. The sound her blunt head makes as it scratches her cradling arm. The breath held short in her mouth. When she squeezes her ears there is a sound like distant thunder, loud enough to drown out her heart. Closer still, and what lies beneath her heart's thudding, the silent screaming of fear.

She awakes with a start when Colly finds her. She is sullen with tiredness, wants to slap him. The night has almost swung through.

She says, why didn't you stay at home?

Colly can manage, it seems, with the shortest of sleep and his mood never darkens but she can tell at once he is different.

He says, Boggs came back like you said he would. How did you know he was coming? Came in the door as we were off to bed. I had to wait till they were asleep and then Bran was crying and when I finally got out, the hounds followed me halfway up the hill. I had to keep telling them to shush their yapping. He's in a wild temper. Said everything was gone to fuck. That some cunt up in Binnion clubbed one of his dogs dead. Kept giving out about the rents. I was sat at the fire. He asked Mam to feed him and she gave him the soup and he fired it across the room. It went all over my legs and the bowl rolled at my feet. I'm still wet with it. He said to her, what is this? Charlock? After all I done for you. Putting a roof over your head. All I ask is that you look after me now and again. You want me now to treat you the same as any other spalpeen? It was then that he saw you were gone. He asked after you and laughed when Mam said she sent you off to get work. He said, what's the use of her? There's only one use for her, and then he laughed again, a great laugh to himself. Mam said you cut your own hair and would go at it like a strong lad. He answered her back that you could work all you like but there's no lumpers for a hundred mile that can be bought or sold and that means what it means. And she said, what does it mean? And he said, I'll tell you what it means. It means she'll be coming right back with her tail between her legs. It means everything is beyond dire and getting worse, for there are men sitting about hungry and idle and they'll grow violent because that is the way of it. It's simple economics unless they do something about it—the Crown, he said. And it was then that Mam said the strangest thing I ever heard from her. This is the truth. She said, let her steal for us, then.

They walk all day deeper into the deep of the world than they have ever traveled alone. Colly gushing as if rivered with words, walks swinging his arms like a soldier. She has begun to notice how she holds her breath as she walks. She thinks, he sees all this as sport, but my heart beats out of my chest like a fist. They walk through the mountain bogland along rough track, the place vast-seeming, almost treeless, a mean wind scolding from the east. The cloud shadows drifting against the moss. She thinks, there is no memory in this place. A slab of lake and a lonely tree and a sky that foretells the worst kind of rain. They sit under the tree and she unwraps for Colly what's left of the meat. He sucks and slavers on the bones while her stomach sounds out as if something is being ripped leisurely from it. Colly looks up, says, would you listen to the unholy yelling in my gut.

That was my tummy, eejit.

He looks at her dumbfounded. Twas not.

Twas so.

Tell me this, then. What's thin as a rake but looks fat as a cat, is bald as a coot but wears a black hat?

She pinches him in the ribs. Says, shut your bake.

She wishes her mother had not made her eat the way she did. Her appetite had grown dormant, had settled into a low ache you could live with. Now it is alert — the tearing teeth of an animal inside her, or a knife with a twisting point.

Colly reaches into his pocket and produces a clay pipe. This was lying about, he says. You'll have to learn to smoke it.

She rolls her face in disgust. I will not.

Do you want to be a man or not?

I can be a man without smoking.

No you can't. Anyhow, I keep telling you. You can stave off the appetite with tobacco.

He tries to teach her how to walk like a boy. Yer doing it all wrong. Like this. Hold the pipe in your mouth. Let it hang like so. Aye, that's it. Now say something to me.

She sucks on the pipe. Says, can you gimme some plug, please?

Jesus. Whatever you do, don't speak.

What's wrong with my voice?

What's right with it?

She adjusts her voice, says it again. What's wrong with it, I said?

You've got to stop sounding considerate. Your voice needs to sound like yer always telling somebody to do something even if yer not. Like there's a dog listening, waiting on your command. That's the way men talk, so they do.

Gimme some plug, she says.

He smacks his hands together. That's it. Say it again.

She fills the pipe and tamps it with her thumb and he leans in and lights it with a dirty smile.

Where did you get them lucifers? she says.

I stole them.

She tokes on the pipe, fills her lungs, and blows the smoke clean out, does not cough once. He stares at her with a slack-jaw mouth, realizes he has been wound up. She drops her voice low and husky as if it has been worn out from excitement. You smoke like a wee girl, Colly.

You sound like a man, he says.

The rain comes yoked to a hooded sun, unfastens and falls like a cloak. This continuing warp of season and its slurs. You must ignore the rain. You cannot tense, otherwise the cold enters your bones. You must walk like it is not a bother to you—like this. You must think that you will be dry again, for you will. The way it has rained this October murders the memory of warm September. And tomorrow it is November the first, the quickening of winter, though hardly worse weather will come of it. The fairy pooka have come to pluck November from the calendar and corrupt another month.

Colly has produced from his coat the broken umbrella. It is useless and raggy against the rain but still he persists with it. In the lowlands they pass lazy beds that lie in ridges along the pale hillsides, like the rotting ribs of some dropped-dead beast, she thinks. The ruined stubble fields are but a memory of green. Now they suck uselessly upon the rain. Everywhere there are great puddles like stoups, holy water for all the tin cans in the world if a priest had want to bless them.

These roads are too quiet. Perhaps it is the rain, for it is not usually like this. Even children and beggars are keeping indoors under leaky roofs. The townlands beginning to thicken with cabins filled with peat smoke to burn the spying eyes that watch them pass and sometimes a curious face leans out. Not a turnip head on a stick to be seen among the poor this Samhain. By the bridge in Cockhill they are accosted by a woman who stands threadbare to the rain and drunk by the looks of it. She mutters some curse at them or perhaps what she asks is for a coin but Grace pulls Colly along by the wrist the moment he begins to chat with her.

She says, don't be telling people all our business.

He says, I was only having fun with her. She stank like a dog.

She says, you can tell a wild lot from the eyes of a person. The who of them and what they want and how mad they are.

When they reach Buncrana town they are dark with wet. Colly cupping the lucifers to his chest, for they have gotten soaked in his pocket. She takes them off him and puts them in her satchel. Who would want to be a man? she says. The way breeches stick to your legs and make you cold, it is worse than being in a skirt. And a hat just sends drip into your eyes. You are better off with a shawl over your head. A man's clothing is so ill-considered.

Colly shakes his head at her. You canny run in a skirt.

The sky is slate and sits so low upon the market town she thinks of the lid of a coffin, then tries to unthink the thought. Everything under these clouds is sodden. A horse trough is overwhelmed and sputters. A bill on a yellowing wall announcing some public meeting is folding over itself. She sees a man in a doorway with his eyes to the ground scratching at himself and there are others, people who look like they have stepped out of their bodies to become their own shadows tight to a doorway or wall. The town, it seems, is held in a kind of stupor. And such a shush. She hears some angry voice rise up, it seems, against the rain but the rain beats the voice down. It is a quiet she does not remember. You would expect to see more going on, the movement of booley cattle through the streets after being taken down from the hills for the Samhain. People taking to drunkenness. But the main street keeps a Sunday's quiet. She tries to hear what hides behind the rain but it is a mask over everything. What is held within that sound are all things but it is the rain that decides what is and what isn't.

A scrawn of donkey tethered to a post turns its head with curiosity. Colly leans in as they walk past, swells up his teeth. Hee-haw! he says. Grace points to an awning that hangs over the street and pulls him by the elbow until they are under it. Colly takes off his cap and hammers it off his hand. She pushes him. Quit shaking your wet all over me.

You can't get any wetter.

The church rings the quarter hour then twice upon the half hour. A dark hound steps onto the street with a lowered head as if it has taken a beating. It is then she sees a bone tied to its tail. She pinches Colly's elbow. She says, do you think it is some kind of omen? Or perhaps it's just a trick.

A door opens beside them and the bristles of a broom sweep outwards and stop. A whistling male voice roars across the street. Would yez quit tormenting that dog. The head of the shouter leans over the broom and takes in the sight of Grace and Colly bit down on their pipes. He shakes his head. Yez look like a pair of wet weasels. Are yez here for the traveling holy man?

Colly says, what holy man?

She thinks, it is the gap in his teeth that makes his words whistle.

The man nods down the street. In the town last night, he says. A man came through here with the hat of a bishop dead two hundred year and said to cure everything from the pains to the hunger for the wearer. They made a long line for him.

Colly eyes the man up and down. We're looking for Dinny Doherty. The pony man. Do you know where to find him?

The man leans thoughtfully on the broom. His cheeks look freshly razored but he has missed a salty streak of stubble under each eye. He looks like he is growing a set of eyebrows on his cheeks, she thinks. Auld Fourbrows, so he is.

The man says, yer looking for Dinny Doherty?

Colly says, we're after walking from Urris Hills.

In this weather? And yer looking for Dinny Doherty?

That's what I said. Are you not listening, sir?

And who are your people?

We're the Coyles.

The Coyles? You must know my cousin, then. Tommy Thomas?

Colly looks at Grace and she shrugs.

How can yez not know him? Everybody knows Tommy.

The man pauses as if chasing a thought. Wait, now, Tommy's dead this two year. It's hard to keep track of everyone, so it is. You pair aren't here scouting for trouble?

A horse and carriage pull up farther along the street and Colly stares at it. A man is stepping down and helping a woman alight and both are immaculate, she sees, the man with his black-bright top hat and the woman with her cuffs of white lace. There is no rain where she walks under the man's umbrella. She seems to glide on her toes.

Auld Fourbrows juts his jaw in derision. You'd think he owns the place, the way he goes about. Then he turns towards them. Get yerselves back home to Urris. More and more are coming to the town same reason as you are and all they're doing is hanging about. There'll be nothing here but trouble and you'll get yerselves sucked into it, mind my words.

She turns as if to go but Colly says, our mam is dying.

The man gives the boy a soft look. He says, sorry to hear that, wee man. What is it that ails her?

Colly eyes the man with great seriousness. He says, she's got the ass cancer. She canny sit right or lie down or stand up or do nothin with it. She's dying slowly whilst lying sideways. The doctor says she must have caught it sitting down someplace.

An arrow of laughter shoots from her gut to her mouth and she cannot pinch it quiet. Auld Fourbrows shakes the broom at Colly and they turn and run as one into the rain, its immensity, its ability to gather all things into its expression, and she thinks she can hear Auld Fourbrows's laughter huge and hoarse behind them.

She shakes Colly by the arm. Where did you get such talk? I never heard nothin like it. Could you not come up with something simple?

What's wrong with it? Auld Benny died of the ass cancer, so he did.

That was just banter, Colly. Auld Benny died from the bad lungs. Did you not hear his coughing? People said it as a joke because in all the years nobody ever saw him leave the bed.

Colly is silent. Then he speaks. How was I to know if nobody told me?

The dog with the tail-tied bone appears again, its face bent against the slap-rain.

Colly says, that is the saddest looking creature I've ever seen.

She sees in the dog's eyes a look of both sorrow and regret and wonders if a dog can reach an understanding of such things.

This night is different from all others, Samhain, the night of the dead. Before it grows dark they must find refuge, for the spirits are allowed to roam the sky tonight. She believes if they leave the town it will be easier to find some unused shelter. It is one thing to face another night in the open but another to be out under a sky filled with demons. They leave the town and in the far-off the hills are hunched against a bullyragging sky. Over a bridge they lean and watch the waters writhe with the spirit of the rain. In the creeping dark they walk past large farmhouses that send out the feeling of being watched with the burning eyes and burning mouths of sentinel turnip lanterns lit to fend off the dead.

Look! It is Colly who shouts and points to a rough-stone byre. Built onto its side is a rickety lean-to. They climb a gate and meet oozing mud-grass, step soft-foot towards the hut with their ears cocked. Colly points to the flash of a rat that vanishes into a ditch. Her hand goes up and she mouths silently for him to listen. Just the bellow and bump of cattle inside the byre and the rain scattershot upon the roof. And then the dogs come, four, then five, raggedy creatures of every size and hue. They are wild in the eye and fang the air with their barking. Colly bends down to one of them. Here, girl. The dog sidles skinny towards him and does not mind being patted.

The byre is bolted. The lean-to is half rotten, its timber run with mildew. A corrugated roof so rusted you could drop a pebble through it, she thinks. Not even a spalpeen would sleep here. Not even the pooka. Mouldy straw and old rags laid down by someone for the dogs and the stench of micturate so strong it is almost physical. They build a firepit out of sight of the road and gather wet tinder.

She watches Colly make a wriggling sit. What are you doing?

I'm trying to warm the tinder.

You cannot warm it with a wet arse.

What do you suppose, then?

We need to leave something out for the pooka. We don't want to upset them on a night such as this.

They search a wild field and find a bush stripped bare of its blackberries but for a few late bloomers almost unreachable. Hold on, muc, Colly says. He slides his small shape under the bush and reaches out his hand towards the centre, plucks one and then another, gets all of them. Six unripe berries, the last fruit of the year. As he slides out a thorn catches him on the cheek. Ach! I've been got by a witch's fingernail.

She rubs his cheek with her thumb. How many did you get?

A few. I dunno.

It will have to do.

That man never told us where to find Dinny, did he?

We'll try again tomorrow.

Hee!

What?

Didn't Dinny Doherty do a doo-doo? He did, did Dinny!

The sides of the hills have begun to wink with the glow of Samhain bonfires. They can't get their own fire lit. She rips some bedding from the dogs and lights it in the firepit and finally there is small flame to build on. Later, they watch their hands colour pink over the small fire.

Colly says, I heard that some people turn hairy about the face when going hungry for months. That'll be us yet, turning into monkeys.

Stop that.

When the fire burns out they warm together amid the dogs and the stench of piss. The dreeping outside and the rainwater that drips inside from the roof a steady torment and the worry that is building inside her. She whispers to Colly, give over the berries so I can leave the offering out.

Colly is quiet. I'll put them out myself in a wee while.

You won't know what way to put them.

How is there a way to put them?

It's just that you don't know it.

She puts out her hand but he offers her nothing. She begins to rib him with her finger.

Finally, he says, I don't have them anymore.

What do you mean you don't have them?

I couldn't help myself.

What did you do?

I ate them and now I have a pain in my belly.

She is silent a long moment. She wants to scream. The long night ahead and so unprotected. Lying here in the dark and what could come of it. This night in particular and its thousand sounds and soon its thousand eyes and she is afraid to look skywards, for in her mind she is afraid she might glimpse their spectre light, the dead winging the dark, whistling by on fields of air, making their lamentations as they wander the world tonight. Plunging down on top of them like huge birds to carry them away into the place of the dead. This is what will become of us, she thinks.

Then she remembers. She says, we must turn our clothes inside out. That will protect us. But it's your fault if it doesn't.

She turns her back and she slips out of her clothes. He does the same. Afterwards, they share a laugh. This is wild uncomfortable, he says. He falls silent. Then he says, do you really believe in them? The pooka? The dead? Has anybody ever seen them?

I think so. I dunno.

Where do you think they come from? Do the dead live in the middle of the earth? And how do they get out? Is there a mouth to hell? I've often tried to guess what lies at the centre of the earth. If you dig a hole there's nothing but rock and mud, so there is. So where would there be the room for them? Maybe they hide in the woods or in the waters. Or inside secret caves in the mountains. You wouldn't see them there so you—

A sudden creak drawls from the gate. The dogs sit up and one of them woofs a welcome or warning. Somebody—or something—is stepping towards them. Her voice sharpens into a shush. She feels Colly tense and grabs his wrist and squeezes. Now she sees they are damned anyway, that a dead soul will come because they have no protection, that a dead soul will swoop for them because they are fools. And then the stepping sound becomes the sound of a man coughing into a fist. The rattle of a key in a lock. A man opening and closing the byre door. They sit tense for a long moment and she can hear the man come out again. Then she is standing and Colly is pulling at her to sit still but she has to see who it is, wants to know what he is doing. She continues out, closes her eyes to the night sky and then allows herself to peep. There is only darkness, great and flat and fallen upon everything and she flat-foots to the corner and peers around, cannot see much but can hear the sound of piss-fall by the door. Then she sees the man's outline move, sees him pick something up from against the wall, then return into the byre. She can hear him coughing, imagines him settling down into straw.

She creeps back and says to Colly, it is only someone come to watch over the cattle. Protect them from the spirits. I think he had a gun.

A dog yips as she steps on its tail. She stands very still a moment and then whispers to it an apology, slides into the heat of Colly.

She wakes sudden into the dark like dream-fall. Awake to the echo of a man's roar. The way terror trebles the size of your heart but keeps you stock-still. There is still the tangle of a dream and for a moment it seems she is both in the heat of that dream and the night that is cold and actual. She wonders if what she heard came from some blind cavern of dream, her ears reaching out as if they have power to travel beyond her physical self, reaching around the hut, expanding into the dark, seeing her hearing. What she hears is that the rain has stopped. That Colly has not woken. That the stranger in the shed is murmuring to himself and then a minute later he is snoring. The cattle man is having bad dreams, that is all. This long night and the stretch of it like the longest day turned to dark and anything for it to be over, anything at all, Mam and all this trouble she has caused, this place we have to be sleeping. She looks towards the hills and sees the Samhain fires have gone out and her eyes close and seek that same dark.

A hot stubbled tongue wakes her and she blinks and sees the sticky eyes of a pup. He is all slather and stench. Eeooowwww! She pushes away the dog and sits up. The dogs have scattered but for this one, a flap-eared mongrel that leaps about or studies them from the vantage of its front paws. Two circles on its inky feet like daubs of lime. Everything is better this morning, she thinks. Everything in the world washed clean. The rain has gone. The spirits are shut back to wherever they come from. Even the watchman has left.

She wakes Colly. Says, you can change your clothes back around now. We're safe.

Every part of her stinks of dog stench.

Colly says, naw, I can't be bothered.

You'll look ridiculous.

I'm used to it now.

Then turn you around while I change.

She stands behind a whin bush and he talks to her as she strips.

Usually when I dream I remember nothing of it. But last night I remember heaps. I dreamt about some strange city that looked like that picture of London I seen one time in the school. Big buildings set along roads that stretch forever and so many people. I remember all I wanted was to see the machinery they were making. So I asked and this man took me to them. Wild strange, so he was. Kept scratching his arms like a monkey. He was dressed head to toe in red, even his boots, and he said his name was Red Hugh. He took me along to this building and he opened the door and let me in and it rose to the ceiling with every machine and mechanic that has ever been thought of, contraptions and levers and swinging pendulums and giant screws like the noses off unicorns and wheels and planes and things accelerating and balls dropping and I knew if I thought about it I could puzzle everything apart and then put it back together again into something even better. It was the best dream I ever had.

How did you dream all that in this place?

I don't know where it came from. I dreamt also that I knew how to make it so no umbrella would ever break again. All I needed were the right materials. Only I can't remember now how to do it. It's annoying my head. I'm going for a piss.

A crow wings down and scratches the air with its caw. She has heard that after Samhain the dead travel in the likeness of such birds. She thinks about what Colly said last night. Where do the spirits come from? There is so much you can't know. Like where the rain really comes from. Sarah says the rain is God's sadness at the world but she heard once it is something to do with the sea air reaching the mountains. Perhaps that is so. And what is the weather anyway and why has it been so fierce this year over all others? Storms in the middle of summer and whatnot. And why does she hear about all these different sorts of animals in different countries but there are no dangerous beasts in Ireland but for the pooka, who you cannot see anyway and which nobody has ever seen except in stories that involve people you have never met and aren't likely to? And what is taking Colly so long?

She scatters the remains of the firepit with her foot. Puts her hand to the ashes and there is not even a breath of heat. She stands waiting for Colly. Another minute and she goes around the building, walks out towards the road.

It is then that she sees the long back of Boggs. The shock red of his hair. It is him, all right, dragging Colly by the scruff, the boy wriggling with his pants around his ankles and his heels trying to get purchase on the ground. Then Boggs turns and drops Colly with his fist, hauls him up over his shoulder like a sack. Says, I'm taking you back to your mother. That jut of red beard and the backward-leaning walk like some hunter happy with his kill. Colly's fists hanging useless. She does not think about any of it. What she does. It is something later she realizes that just happened, as if she turned mechanical or became possessed by some spirit. Or even that there was another person hiding inside her all along. The way she plucked from the wall a tooth-shaped rock and came up behind Boggs, put it to his head. The way she felled him, the big man turning around like some slow animal to the blow, hinging down onto one knee and then the other, and how their eyes met as he turned to fathom what struck him, the unexpected composure in his eyes, the poison boiled to those darkly stars and behind that dark the light she saw of an understanding, a communication between the two of them that terrified her to the place of her innermost—and then Boggs is just sitting there on the road with a hand to his head, muted, stupid, bloody, and Colly is on his feet trying to hitch up his trousers that are inside out, the flesh of his right eye sprung red, and she is shouting at him—run! Colly, run, for fuck's sake! But he is fumbling to get his trousers up and buttoned—cannot—and then what he does. He steps out of them, slings them under his arm and runs bare-bottomed into the fields, chased to his heels by one of Boggs's hounds.

* * *

They run until their hearts no longer beat but shatter into jags that swim the blood to stop every muscle. They drop to the ground, floppy useless shapes, lie gasping under poplar trees that stand aloof whispering to themselves a different story of the world. Colly lying holding his pants over his modesty, an indigo bruise flowering uneven on his face. She sees that Boggs's fist struck the cheekbone. Colly is crying from shock, exertion, and pain, no doubt. Keeps pressing at his face as if he is in wonder at the novelty of hurt. Leave it be, she says.

They did not think where to run. Ran blind through a field of winter wheat that met a flooding bourn, then flatland, a planted forest, a puddling dirt road. They sent up the birds, ran swift like swallows last of season, all breast of white neck and their coats flung behind them like tails. Behind a settlement of limed-white houses came towards them a shooting blur, something demon-black that barked itself into dog and ran alongside them, party to the fun. And now they are here, this quadrangle field with two piebalds and a bay that group together to watch these wheezing visitors and snicker at the intrusion.

Colly turns his trousers the right way around and steps into them. He doesn't care that she sees his pizzle.

She thinks, what is it I have done?

She says, lie down. Listen.

Colly whispers. That bastard. He didn't say a word. Came up behind while I was having a piss. I could hear him. His breathing. As he was coming behind me. And then I could smell him. But I was halfway through the piss and couldn't stop. And then when I got it stopped and I got it back in and I was trying to get the buttons done but the breeches were inside out and I couldn't button them. It was like I knew something bad was going to happen. But also I didn't. I don't think he knew you were there. He lumped me with his fist and threw me over his shoulder like a straw man. Like a bag of sticks. Like a—

Would you ever shush a minute, she says. Just for once? Do you think he is kilt? Do you think that I kilt him?

Colly shakes his head with vigour. Then he rubs at his face as if he has shaken new pain into it. You winged him is all. He was breathing fine when we left him.

I hit him hard with that rock. If he is not dead he might be mortally wounded.

She can see the shape of Boggs growing pale on the road, sitting there with his knuckle hair turning grey. Having to lie down with great slowness and his hands grown weak and his face whitening as the blood leaks out—

I have to go back, she says. I have to see if he's dead.

She is already on her feet. I'll be back, I promise.

You can't go, he says. What if he gets you? His eyes reach as if to seize her by the heart. Don't you leave me here on my own.

She studies him, the way he sits folded over himself, unmanned into the boy that he is. One side of his face popping out.

I must.

She will pass through the air like the wind itself, secretive and invisible. Like light as it passes over all things without noise or touch. As delicate as the butterflies that flit her stomach. If only it would rain again to quieten this noise in her head.

She has to think her way back, for the path is unfamiliar. It is as if it wasn't she who had passed by here earlier but somebody else. A shadow. That secret other who hurls rocks from walls. She sees Boggs's face everywhere she walks, hears the silence of his death and the gathering of a hunt. She walks past the woodland and stares at the spangle of wet prints they stamped fresh into the track but has no memory of making them. Then she sees it, the boundary wall along the road. Creeping towards the wall on hands and knees, like some cud chewer, she thinks. Afraid to look over, to witness the unalterable fact that sits in this moment of which there cannot be any other. She crouches and waits a long moment counting each breath. You will rise at ten breaths and not a breath before. On her sixth breath she suddenly rises.

There is no body. There is no sign of Boggs at all, not even a drop of blood.

The rock has been put back in the wall.

The cabin stands an abandoned hump, the roof caved in or destroyed. Its mud walls slowly returning to earth but it will do for tonight. There is a dead vegetable plot that looks like fire was set to it and they kick through it in search of an old tuber. She gets a match to spark tinder alight and they make a small fire and lie in an alcove where the bed used to be. She huddles with Colly, above them the mouth of the world wide open and the stars tongued out, a sky magically quit of rain. Nearby they can hear a river roaring. She rolls dock leaves and puts them to his face. Here, she says. There is a loose look in Colly's eyes, a tremor in his voice. His body looks wrung out of shape.

She is almost asleep when he whispers to her. I have a plan, he says.

What?

I will become a poisoner of horses. You will travel town to town behind me and fix the horses right again.

But I don't know the first thing about horses let alone unguents. Has that blow made you gone silly?

His sleep comes quick like a candle quit smokeless to dark. His head resting upon her. She sleeps under a skim of dreams that scatter like birds and she wakes to the vast night, the fullness of cold, the long tooth of hunger. The dread weight feeling she has not slept one bit. We are like dead bodies, she thinks, with a past but no future. I have died and climbed into the earth of my grave. When she was alive there was heat and food and laughter and all the old familiar things, the faces of the youngers and Mam who still wanted her. But now Mam is done with her. To be so unwanted but yet

Colly is wanted and isn't that why she sent Boggs to take him back home? It strikes her now, how in the morning she must say to him, you are going back home because you must, because this was all a mistake. A great adventure to remember. She will take him back as far as the bogland and send him on alone. She will send him home to save herself from Boggs.

They are cold-stiff when they leave the hut, numb to the tips of their fingers. The truth of the world, she thinks, is that cold is the truest state of all things and heat is a temporary nature. The cold does not burn itself out in rush like fire but waits with unlimited patience. She stamps her feet awake, claps her hands as she walks, Colly trailing sullen behind her. She keeps asking what he dreamt. She tells him she dreamt about a man with missing fingers following her, but Colly isn't listening. Come here, she says. She puts her arms around him and he is so small against her. The way he goes on, she thinks, you would think he is almost a man, but his shoulders are like angel wings that could snap in your fingers.

The river sound comes to meet them like a roar of the world. It is the sound of rain and anger pleated into rush. They see it is in freshet, a turbid brown spate traveling eyeless and white-tongued and tasked with all the flood rain from the hills. It is a clamour that fills up their ears and damns the sounds of all else. Colly whistles in awe. He has to shout for her to hear him. It wasn't this bad yesterday. Then his look becomes serious. Will we try for a fish?

She shouts, the trout are all fished out.

She thinks, this river would strip the very rocks it rests on.

The river travels through bogland and will guide them back to town. Her mind tangled with Boggs. What he will do with the sore head she gave him. Perhaps he will be done looking for them, will return to Blackmountain and roar at Mam instead. This angry river sound is the sound of Boggs roaring in her head.

They shadow the river's edge, meet places where it has risen over its banks to swarm at trees and grab at thickets or reach for low-hung branches that fly back from the current as if stung.

It is when the river has returned to its banks that Colly sees it. He turns and points at the river behind them.

She has to shout to be heard. What?

Are you blind or what?

Where am I supposed to be looking?

He steps towards the bank and wags his finger. There.

I don't see it, she says. And then she does. Drifting slowly towards them is a sodden white rump, the remains of a sheep that slopes headward in the water as if staring into some deep wherein lay an answer to the truth of its death. It seems to her the river is carrying the body at the noble pace of a funeral.

He shouts, how long, do you think?

It must be dead recently otherwise it would have been fished out.

We have to get it.

There is so much hope in his voice she doesn't know how to answer. She thinks, the thing will be rotten, poisoned, or worse. And what trouble if they are found carrying it. And yet she can see in her mind the meat in the pot.

She follows him towards the bank. He nods towards her pocket.

Gimme the knife Mam gave you.

He leaps upon a young ash and hangs off a branch until it splinters. The secret soft of its flesh revealed and he begins to saw at the rupture. By the time it is cut free and carved with a point, the carcass has disappeared downriver. They run along the bank, Colly charging with the stick like a lance. She hears him shout. Hee! And then, there it is! An old hawthorn like twisted rope leans out over the river in a statement of bitterness. Colly begins to climb it and she shouts, be careful. He sidles out along the bough and begins making stabs at the animal. The carcass passes with its head blind in the water. She helps Colly climb down off the tree and they follow the sheep to a place where the riverbanks begin to hunch and narrow and she holds him as he steps down onto the leaf-rot by the water's edge and reaches his arm out, tries again to catch the animal.

Don't poke at it, she says.

I'm trying to catch the wool.

You're going to send it to the other side.

They watch the sheep travel onwards as if to meet some grim appointment. It disappears behind rows of whin and high ground that fence the bank. Colly walks shaking his head. He says, we could have had it.

She says, we weren't thinking straight. Anyhow, how in the hell were you to get it home with you?

I'd manage it on me back.

The weight of it and it might have been smelling. And people would think it was thieved. You wouldn't be able to answer for it.

She tries to put the sheep out of her mind but her stomach continues to dwell on it. Colly stops to light his pipe.

She nods at it. Gimme a wee toke.

He smiles. I knew you'd like the taste of it.

In the sky she sees all things are considered. The northwest is bruised like Colly's cheek but elsewhere the sky is like good cloth, clean and white, and the sunlight promises warmth. She thinks she can hear the sound of Colly's mind coming up with a plan. The way his eyebrows gently knit when he is puzzling something. But all he comes out with is a riddle. What is always traveling but stays put, has a bed but canny be slept in, and a mouth that never eats nothin?

Ugh, Colly. That's an old one.

Through trees she sees the return of the river. Wonders what kind of animal it looks like, its restless hide sleek and brown. Of a sudden Colly is running and she sees the sheep alongside them as if it has traveled all along in quiet accompaniment, listening to their talk, waiting to be fished out. She sees it is caught on a thicket of bramble. She is running towards it before she can think. The river's bank is low to the water and covered with sedge grass and leaf-rot. Colly reaches for the sheep with the stick, pokes until the stick catches the wool, begins to pull the animal towards him. He has become a fisherman, swollen-cheeked and puffing as he leans out over the water, shouting at the sheep — come on, would you! — and she starts to shout too, the pair of them hollering at the animal's dead hearing. And then, as if they have willed it, the carcass comes free and stays stuck to the stick, ceases to travel downwater. Colly yells in satisfaction. He is puff-faced holding on, has not the strength to pull the carcass towards him. She gives him her strength but the stick bends as if to break and Colly roars out, go get another stick!

She sees that every ounce of him is holding on to the sheep, his body pulled into a sickle.

I can hold it, he says. But hurry the hell up.

Her mind crackles with panic and excitement as she runs. Anything at all she would use but along the bank there is nothing but whin. A stand of trees farther back and she runs towards them, hears Colly call out, the sheep's head is rising up! She shouts over her shoulder, I'm coming. But she is not. Under the tall trees the ground is a puzzle of rot and she can figure nothing from it. She grabs at a stick but it is soft with decay, thinks of the trees as some huddle of old women watching scold-faced. She hears Colly's roaring voice weak above the river. The sheep, he shouts. The sheep is lifting its head! The sheep is staring right at me!

Deeper into the trees. She runs with her eyes the flit-wings of bats in a hurry to see everything. The way the trees shut out the sound of the river so that she can only hear her thoughts. Just one stick. Just give me one stick. She thinks of the pooka, hiding everything from her, the way they are always playing tricks. She bargains with them but the ground yields nothing of use. Now she knows their haul will be lost. That Colly will be angry with her and sulk all the way to Blackmountain. She turns and runs back towards the river, the roar of it as she breaks free of the trees is the mouthblast of some huge animal. What comes to her then is sensed before she can grasp it, like the changing of air before great weather. A feeling heard like whisper. How the air has changed because something is wrong—towards the riverbank she runs but she is met by confusion, this part of the bank she cannot remember—she has run to the wrong place, for there is no sign of Colly, and where is the sheep? She looks to the riverbank in both directions but Colly has gone, and then it hits her, the precise nature of what is, of what must have just happened, and she starts to scream out his name, screams it at the river, stands helpless by the bank where the leaf-rot sits disturbed, and it is then that she knows what has happened, sees the mud scar that has been made by Colly's foot slipping into the brown water, the river that reflects nothing but itself. And it is then that she sees Colly's stick floating deep amid brambles and beside the stick, the sheep, its eyeless black head grinning at her.

II

This Boy Called Tim

She is lifted off rocks. There is no will now to fight this old man, his smell when he carries her of brine and dogs, finds herself placed in damp wickerwork shivering under his coat. What she sees of the sky is a cowl pulled low as he rows her across the estuary. The old man with his flashing eyes and beard. Don't you worry, wee man, he says to her. Aren't you lucky that Charlie has found you? Sea-lap in her ears and plashing oars. When she looks up she sees those oaring hands huge and red-knuckled, fisting towards her like some languid play of drunken violence. The ferryman whistling to himself between grunts. There is nothing now to the will but that which craves the dark of a beneath and she sinks down into the down, finds herself lifted out, put to his shoulder, carried towards a house, a dog bounding beside them. She hears the bird-chatterings of an old woman. Charlie says to her, quick, Theresa, I found this boy near drowned on the lough, lying by the mouth of the river. Like a lump of seaweed there he was on the rocks. Would you look at the colour of him. Go quickly get our blanket. He is light, light like a feather in my arms.

She is rested on a stool in front of the fire. Sits in the nothing of herself. What forms for thought a void wind without light. When the old woman goes to remove her wet clothing she is able to summon sudden strength to stop her. Smell of carrageen off the old woman's hand that rests uncertain on her shoulder. The woman says, never mind your modesty, wee man. Didn't I raise up three boys? And yet the old woman steps away from her.

Later she learns she is near Rathmullan, a townland she has never heard of. How Charlie laughs when he hears this. How could you never have heard of it and it here all this long? Twas here the old gaelic order was put to a stop. It was from here the earls took flight. Anyhow, I will row you back across the water when you've got your colour back.

Later, he asks, who are your people? Where are you from? Will they be worried for you?

She shakes her head. Says, my mam died, so she did.

The old man shakes his head. The old woman leans forward and asks, do you not have anybody else? A sister? Or a brother?

She has not given them her name. They call her wee fella. The old woman comes to her with clothing that will fit better but she will not wear anything else. The old woman left standing in the room with her lips pursed holding on to the clothes, the old man taking the clothes out of her hands, putting them into a trunk, a strange noise out of her like sorrow.

Days pass like drift-clouds unseen in some unwatchable night. She spoons seaweed soup, the occasional fish, spits bones into the fire. The old man and woman try not to watch the dead-staring eyes, eyes in the hell of herself that see the private animals of darkness, animals that roam in grotesque shape as if watched in shadow light. Her mind echoing soundings from an older life. The voices of Blackmountain that ring and dull. She hears the voice of her mother strange to her, Sarah's voice without words just the sound of it, hears it without feeling any tenderness. And then comes a night when she wakes sweating from a dream so lifelike it haunts her for days. A baying crowd of hundreds of people carrying torches and slash-hooks shouting for her. Sarah among them. What it is they shout. Murderer. At the head of them is Boggs, his eyes lit, the man's image morphing into the shape of a wolf that moves in its own anger-light like a mill wheel at full violence if she could even explain it. When she wakes from the dream she walks in a daze and cowers in a corner until daylight. Charlie finds her and lifts her back to bed. She sees that ghost image of Boggs-as-wolf as if she has witnessed it in daylight's fullest expression, wonders if such dream power is prophecy.

She thinks, I could stay and live with these people and eat their seaweed soup. Charlie has said as much. He has pawned all but one of his fishing nets, he tells her, because he no longer has the strength to fish the channel on his own. But she knows they have pawned the nets for food. And so the wintering has reached even here, she thinks.

Charlie wants to teach her his tricks with the net. In the boat he tells her that all three of their sons died at sea in a single evening some years ago, a storm of great violence, he says. One day they were here with us and the next they were gone. She repeats the names of his boys in her head. She thinks, the old man's voice is kindly, not done in by bitterness like his wife. He gives her plug, talks to her as if she were a son while the pair of them sit smoking. When they are outside together she secrets her pee into a tin cup standing up, her back turned to him. The old man tells her, your piss makes a wild lot of clatter. The old woman always watching her, giving her strange looks. She dreams of Boggs-as-wolf and she dreams of the old woman until night-long she is wrought by their faces that together snake and loom from that mind-dark, as if what glimmers there portends her own end, and she begins to think of the woman as evil. And then one evening as she sits smoking on the step, the old woman steps past her and stops, leans down, and pulls her by the lobe, puts a question into her ear.

Who is it, girl, you are always talking to?

It is December when she leaves, a morning sleeved with blue-cold and the stars a silvery dust. She takes nothing for her satchel but a smoked herring wrapped in brown paper. From his bed the old man has risen silent on his elbow to watch.

She will drift southwards for days, expectant of the gnaw-tooth of winter that has not yet come, the weather mild for December. She thinks, you can try this place or that and then you will find something to do with yourself, some type of work, and then everything will be better. The flatlands by the sea are seasonally numb and scrubbed of their colour, the roads thickened with bare footers. She thinks, they are the kind of folk you would see passing through Blackmountain—wretched souls, Sarah would call them, the kind without even a hut. There seem to be more of them now, some looking so troubled even the pooka would not bother them. They slouch about the byway as if waiting for someone, roam the roads with eyes that poke and yearn. They look at her as if they can smell the fish in her satchel. She thinks, there is no winter yet because the wintering has entered inside them. Their eyes drink in her strength.

She climbs down off the road to eat her fish in private, for who knows who'd be looking at you. Stands in the underside of a stone bridge, unwraps the fish and gobbles it, chewing to the steady plink of drip-water from the span above. She turns to the river, hears the whispering water's shallows and grows dizzy with it, begins to feel sick in the gut, maybe it is the fish, maybe it isn't, balls the paper and throws it behind her.

Of a sudden she hears Colly's voice.

Watch out, muc, behind you!

There is movement in the shadows and she sees what she thought was a rock shape-shifting now into some form rising darkly upon legs and advancing towards her. A person. The rustle of the paper being picked up. Backwards now in slow steps and then she turns and runs for the bank, crabs sideways up it, loses her footing and finds it. Her head turning to see a stooped man footing stupid into daylight, naked but for a cloak, his limbs a filthy white and the man all eyes, searching her as she climbs. When she reaches the sedge at the top of the bank the knife is held ready but hidden behind the wrist. She is a single shape on that road, a single shadow that moves away at a run and then slows to a breathless walk. Can see in her mind a clear picture, the white of the man's cock and his long tongue licking at the fishy paper. His eyes fucking at her with hunger. She checks over her shoulder but nobody has followed.

There is just the sound of her breathing, her feet on the road, her body parting the breeze.

She says aloud, that man near frightened the heart out of me.

Colly says, I caught you, Grace, looking at that man's dong.

I did not.

You did, you dirty wee bitch. Now get that pipe lit and give me a toke.

She has taken to the soothe of the pipe. The way it settles a racing mind, for the roads are making her anxious. It is not the long-faced beggars that worry you, the men trying to sell you their ravelly frieze coats, their pokey-holed shirts, one fellow giving a great talk trying to sell a pair of men's boots, their soles undone like wagging mouths. Or that half-blind woman who she helped drag a peeling dresser onto the verge of the high road, how it threw a shadow like some man stooped beside her, the woman asking if there were any carts coming in the direction of town.

It's the others that are the trouble—the youngers you don't see rising from the road. Raggedy little shapes that follow you, walk alongside you, say a prayer for you, ask you your name, hold a cupped palm out. One boy walks silently alongside her for an hour or more, his eyes on her like a dog. Colly says, tell that boy to fuck right off. By eventide the boy continues alongside her until she turns and screams at him to stop, to leave off from haunting her, for she has nothing to give, has nothing for herself. And she can still see him many miles later, his body like a ghost.

She sees the youngers in every child's turnip face. Sees tiny Finbar sentry on a wall, watching her come, stepping out and dragging behind him a bed tick full of straw onto the middle of the road. The child no more than four, flame-haired, bulldog-nosed, the little hand held out, the voice so tiny it is like the sound that escapes from a hug. For the price of some meal, the boy says. She eyes along the wall for a watching adult, for she knows there is one. And then she thinks, perhaps there isn't, perhaps this child has dragged for miles this tick on his own. She holds the knife ready, just in case—will run it through flesh if she is so much as troubled.

She thinks, I will run the knife through Boggs if I so much as see him again. The idea of him, even. That brute idiot of a man. A bully and no better. I am no longer one bit afraid of him. And yet the next morning when she wakes wrapped in dawn-cold, she is haunted again by that dream image of Boggs-as-wolf. That mind picture of inexplicable and circling violence.

She walks into south Donegal because here things might be better. Sees men on the bigger farms keeping guard over their animals. How they have a way of stopping what they are doing to watch you. A good many with rifles slung on their shoulders or resting on a rock. She thinks, if one of them were to shoot me now I wouldn't mind so much. For what would be the difference?

One small town and then another, they are all the same, she thinks. There is always a bridge and people with long eyes idling on the stonework. Always the day hanging heavy on half-empty streets. Eyes whispering behind windows watching for trouble. On a clothesline outside Convoy some fool has hung a wet wool blanket. She steals upon it like dusk, finds it crisp with cold. When it is dry she begins to sleep better. In another town she is drawn to the window of a dress shop, sees Colly dim and wild-haired staring back from the glass. She takes out the knife and cuts at her hair. Sees the reflection darken and take the shape of a woman inside the shop. Cut your hair someplace else, she shouts. What must this woman see? she thinks. Some wild creature in men's clothing too big for him. The woman raps her knuckles on the window and calls out until a man appears hunched and reluctant. He shouts at the glass. Go on, would you. Cut your hair someplace else, you little caffler. She leaves at the crown of her head a crest of hen hair. Brings the knife up to the angle of violence.

It is Colly who shouts at them. Riddle me this, what's frightened as a sheep but fattened as a lamb? Will run away soon as look at you but would eat out of your hand?

The days are shortening to a distant sun that sits sister to the moon. She walks southwards or some days she just sits, the world without size, sun and moon clocking timeless around her. In an early dawn she awakes to see a bolide shower light the northern sky. Each star blinking out of an illimitable dark and falling in silence for a blazing brief moment. Her mind startles at the imprint of such beauty. Racing to count—six or was it seven? Quick as a wink and such good fortune, she thinks. In the whole of the world, I am the only witness, am alone to all this. To the tip of her tongue come seven wishes. I wish I was in my bed. I wish I was by the fire all warm. I wish I had a bowl of lumpers. I wish I had my long hair. I wish I had never left Blackmountain. She meets a thought, sees Boggs-as-wolf torchlit and circling towards her. I wish Boggs was dead.

She counts them up. One more wish, what is it? She thinks a moment, chews on some berries, then says it aloud.

I wish I was home with Mam.

She closes her eyes and Colly whispers.

Sure, what would you want to be doing back with that auld bitch, she is the cause of all your trouble—listen, muc, I say keep walking because farther ahead you'll find something better.

Colly warns she is becoming reckless but she prefers not to listen. It seems to her now there are more people following the roads. There is nothing but cadgers and bother. The things you come across. In the declivity of a field she is startled to see the head part of a horse lying as if to sleep it went and its body ran off like some headless spectre. The horse not even stripped of its meat but taken whole, swiped perhaps by some huge and ravenous animal. And yet she knows it was butchered by thieves, neck-to-tail to be eaten. Better off away from the roads, passing through fields and homesteads. People are watchful but they are also careless. They might keep an eye on their livestock but there is chattel to be had if you are quick about it. She develops an expert ear for dogs. She fills her pockets with nuggets from a coal bunker though she has no matches to light them. In one farmyard some fool has left out the butter churn. She scoops her hands with gold, leaves a black-smudged signature, licks catly at the slow melt. She is becoming reckless, all right. There are times when she looks at her behaviour and asks who she is or what she is becoming. The best part of you, she thinks, the part you have known all your life, has gone missing.

She is chased by men from the backyard of a farmhouse into a dark that knows no moon and falls away like a precipice. Shouts noose the air for her neck. Gunshot travels unseen and soundless but for the report behind her announcing what has already passed. Grunt noise and the thunder-plod of footfall and a flaming lamp like some demon eye fixed in the dark upon her breathless singularity, and the way she runs into that cavernous night with nothing but her blanket and bobbing satchel, the accompanying report of a second shot, and how as she runs she tells herself to stop. And she does. Feels herself overcome, realizes in this moment she doesn't care anymore, about any of this, whatever you would like to call it—life, if you will—and so she stops running, stands awaiting the first fist to strike her head or for the shot to strike the kill. She closes her eyes but what happens is this—the two men chasing her like dogs to the perfume of violence run past her sightless into the dark.

Days like sleep drift past her. She hears the New Year has passed from a newspaper reader days later in some Bally-o village. A fellow on a wooden crate announcing aloud and in mechanical fashion the days-past news while dabbing at his reading glasses with a digit. He reads about the celebrations in London and Dublin to a motley gathering. Some *dailc* standing beside her unshoulders a sack of turf to listen, wipes at his filthy face and red eyes with a cap. He turns to her and says, he has that newspaper read every week in that drone and I never know what he's on about. She watches the people around her, the same clatty children and some woman who is beyond old and talking spittle, a hand on her shawl, the other pulling at the reader's sleeve, trying to pull him towards her cocked ear. Speak up, man, speak up.

If this were another time, she thinks, you would be asked the who and what of you. You would be offered straw and put beside a fire. But there is so much movement on these roads nobody troubles to look at her. She thinks about the things she heard from the newspaper. Guns going off and fireworks and the grandest celebrations and the people in great numbers and the dignitaries gathered. She cannot imagine the look of such excitement. Can only conjure bright and strange colours, people as glittering effigies that move through some shapeless yet shining light, the brightest of hues like the purple-blues and the yellow-reds of flowers.

Later she thinks, where has all the time gone? She feels she has not been present for most of it. And yet this winter drags on like a leaden sack pulled by some dumb and sightless mule up an impossible hill. The pale sun hidden. The trees in their bones standing penitent. Everything, it seems, waiting for the earth gravid with spring but not yet. She is luck itself, she knows. The way she has evaded the worst of winter. The year previous, the frost came furtive into the house like a long hand under the door. Icicles on the jambs and Colly licking at them. And now the days are almost warm if you keep moving. Just the rain and the way the clouds swell with dark purpose, there seems no end to it. She walks down-headed and internal to the rain, her eyes turned to chatter.

So riddle me this. It weighs no weight and cannot be seen. But when you put it in your stomach it makes you grow lighter.

That's the worst one yet, Colly, but I know what you're getting at. Oh, boy, do I know it.

For two days Colly has been singing the same line of a song over and over.

Hó-bha-ín, hó-bha-ín, hó-bha-ín, mo ghrá.
Hó-bha-ín, hó-bha-ín, hó-bha-ín, mo ghrá.
Hó-bha-ín, hó-bha-ín, hó-bha-ín, mo ghrá.

Shut up. Shut up. Shut up. You are driving me demented, she tells him. I hate them old songs. Why won't you stop?

But now in the bruising dusk upon this wet hill he goes silent. She has come to a crossroads and there is a commotion ahead. A carriage has parked on the side of the road and its lamp falls upon a gathering of people. She thinks, the coach is being raided, but Colly says, it is not, look! She sees scrags of people gathering around some woman standing on the coach step. It is like a public meeting. There are shouts, prayers, and pleading and one young man is chanting the names of old saints and crossing himself over and over. Above the carriage woman she sees a scowling coachman in his boxseat with a blunderbuss on his lap. She does not care for all this racket, continues on past them. She craves the company of herself and no other, for there are secret feelings that darkly gleam. It is not that she wishes to be dead in a direct manner. It is that she wants to disappear without consequence to herself. To break from the tree like the autumn leaf. To fall the way dusk falls into its deeper colours without thought of its falling self. To drift from the self like the moment of sleep.

But Colly starts up again and will not stop. Hee! Would you look what she's handing out. Look! And then she is pushing through the clamour, sees the carriage woman is old, long-nosed and appointed in her dress, is putting something into their outstretched hands, the woman's eyes seeing her and not seeing her, a piece of biscuit that meets her hand and then the taste of it—gingerbread, somebody says—oh, lordy. Never has she put into her mouth anything like it, wants to cry with the taste.

Hee! Colly shouts. I told you so— leave me some, you greedy bitch.

It is like everything sweet on earth all at once and when it is gone she sucks from her teeth the memory-taste. For a long while she does not notice the wet road, cannot stop thinking about her gratitude. About that woman. The way she stood as if she owned the road, that look in her face that was a look that didn't see you. And it is then she realizes the power of food this woman had over them and of a sudden she feels hateful. She would like to hurt that woman if she could. Take that fox stole from around her shoulders and wring her neck with it. Why are all these people standing in such wintering while she parades about in her fancy coach? It is only when she tastes salt on her lips does she realize she has been crying.

Donegal town, a road sign announces. The clatter and clamour of a town fair. This place redolent of better times, more than half full. Mouths, shouts, hands, coins, purses, the bleating and bellow of animals, high-to-the-heavens this dung smell. She hears more people here talking in Irish than English. She has not met a town as busy as this.

She says, it would make you hungry just to look at it.

Colly says, you must go among the mill.

What would I want to be doing among them?

To be stealing things from under their noses.

I will not.

You will.

A bagpiper catches her eyeing the coins at his feet. She pretends to be studying the ground. His knees are as wrinkled as his face and when the cheeks release his skin maps his skull. She goes to the stall of a tin-woman and handles a cup, sees a shapeless dull version of herself but drops it when the tin-woman rattles at her to clear off. A fruit dealer's table is guarded by some man and a half who is tree-tall, his arms knotted and his eyes leaning out as she watches the last of autumn's fruit she can taste just by looking. She knows she is hungry but not yet hungry enough to risk prison. Over there is a policeman watching and there is another. What they watch is the hungered drifting through the square like shades. They are marked out of the crowd by their winnowing. Their watchy eyes. Their watchy feet. The way they slow over the street—children, men, women—eyeing for scraps and refuse, dallying over an item, picking it up with their toes. Or those that sit by the building fronts, under awnings, upon steps, hardly reflected, it seems, by the windows. The way they hold perfectly still as if it were possible to disappear in plain sight, every part of them dead but for their alert eyes, eyes like wolves, she thinks, wolves concealed in human clothing wearing stringed masks of badly painted faces. Such wolves are waiting to seize the town with their teeth. Only they are not, she thinks. These people are sheep. They stand in plain sight and do nothing but beg.

Colly says, it's better not to look pitiful, better to pass seen but unseen, better to look happy among them.

She practices holding a smile the perfect look of an angel. She whistles though she cannot find a tune. She is glad her father's clothes are not in rags. The belling of the church tells her fifteen minutes has passed as she circles the square. All the time she has been eyeing a jute bag of horse apples left under the nose of a piebald. There is a way of getting it without being seen. She watches without watching, smiles without smiling. It is then she sees a strange man eyeing her from the bottom of the square. His stare is fixed, cuts through the people between them, races her heart into her ears. She watches with dread as his hand comes out of his pocket. The hand becomes a wave or perhaps a warning. He lets loose a shout and begins towards her. She stands rooted in bewilderment, does not notice how the bawling noise of the town has flattened into soundlessness, the way all points of light are suddenly upon the carriage of this man, an appalling presence coming towards her. Their eyes at full communion and her mind grasping for facts she cannot fathom, the who of this man and the what of his intent, if what is approaching is evil. It is then she knows it. This man is an agent of Boggs.

Colly shouts, run, you stupid bitch.

And now she can see it. Her rank stupidity as if she has lived blindfolded. As if you can leave things like breaking Boggs's head behind you. As if you can just run away. She thinks of her knife but her hand cannot move for it and then the man is upon her.

The man calls out. Is it yourself?

His voice is high, unfettered. His tobacco smile all toothsome like a donkey. The hand held high is a greeting but her legs are soft and then he pinches her at the elbow, his breath reaching in warm, sour and whiskeyed.

I knew you were the son of Marcus by the look of you. And that blanket rolled and ready. You'd better come along, the others are waiting. I told them you'd be here a half hour ago. What has you so late?

Her mind is flung and it is Colly who answers. I couldn't get any sleep. There was an owl hooting all night in the chimney.

Donkeyface man hoots a high laugh and frowns at the same time.

There flashes the memory of a story of the pooka, a young woman led astray by some dark visitor—a man wearing black clothing with a donkey's pointy ears hidden beneath his hat. How the pooka man called to the woman's house, the story went, in the late hours of evening, asked for help with his horses. And when the woman refused and did not invite him in, he stepped inside of his own accord and took her off for seven years to hell. She searches now for Donkeyface man's ears but they are hidden under his hat. He is sallow, stooped at the shoulders, swelled with teeth. His frieze coat is only patched here and there. But his eyes are the devil's red or perhaps he is soused.

She thinks, is this a trick? Am I being put under a spell?

Colly says, let's make friends with this devil.

Donkeyface man frowns. What's that yer saying?

The hand to her elbow is its own answer and master. She finds herself being marched alongside him, away from the square. He asks something about Marcus and her mouth grunts an answer.

Colly says, steal your hand in his pocket.

* * *

She is taken to a street choked with dark cattle. Donkeyface man pushing through the animals and in her mind she meets a vision of Boggs. Instead they meet some stringy young fellow who sits on a box with a priest's crooked back. It is then she sees the blunderbuss on his lap, the sunlight caught in its brass.

So this is it, she thinks. She finds herself wishing it would happen quick.

Donkeyface man says, look, Mr Soundpost, I found the hireling.

Soundpost fumbles the gun as he goes to stand up, almost drops it, his face reddening, and Donkeyface man winks at her, then turns upon Soundpost. Be careful, now, Mr Soundpost, how you hold that gun.

What she sees is a mule laden with a sack of meal, a butter churn strapped to its side. A man-boy called Soundpost red in the face with a bucktooth. But for that he could almost be good looking, she thinks.

Soundpost says, tell me, Mr Boyd, where might that Clackton fellow be? He grabs at a golden pocket watch on a chain and squints. Mercy, mercy. Where has the time got to?

Another lad appears from among the cattle. His face bursting with freckles, his hair a shock of red. She studies him a moment as if he were the child of Boggs. His face weathered beyond his years and yet this boy must be her own age. He eyes her up and down with a grin that pulls his eyes into preternatural wrinkle. You look nothing like your brother, he says. Then he winks and leans towards her in whisper. So you've met Embury Soundpost, have you?

She mutters something inaudible and watches Soundpost talk to himself. Mercy, mercy. We have wasted too much time as it is. Here, Wilson, get that mule ready.

She thinks, so it is he who is in charge, this Embury Soundpost fellow. These ribby black cattle are his. The others are here for his bidding.

She watches the way he sucks his lip over his bucktooth. Wonders what a well-to-do man is doing roughing it with animals. He is eighteen at most, as stringy as rope, but his stovepipe is new and not done in like most others. His hair cut square over his eyes like the toes of his boots.

Donkeyface man turns and bows. I will leave you gentlemen to your booley. She watches him walk up the street without turning around, ignoring Soundpost, who is still asking after Clackton.

She holds her breath and eyes the sack of meal again. Her mind grasping through dark to what might lie ahead, waiting for the moment when she steps into the fall and the inevitable upside down of it. She imagines the howling laughter of the pooka. Such is the way they play tricks on you.

Wilson leans in. I've not booleyed with cattle this far before. Have you?

She shakes her pipe out of her pocket. Drops her voice gruff as a dog. Says, I hope you boys brought plug because I'm all out. Soundpost stares at her and does not answer. She turns as if to see up the street but instead she is trying to hide a blush. She thinks, if he comes, whoever I'm supposed to be, I'll run off down that way or this. Her mind replaying the names of the others. Embury Soundpost. Wilson. Some Clackton fellow, who has not appeared yet. The Donkeyface man called Mr Boyd, or maybe he is the pooka after all, gone back up the street looking for devilment.

She thinks, how have they mistaken me?

She turns and Soundpost is still sizing her up. He says, what kind of look is that you got going on for a hireling? You could pass for a hen in a gunnysack. I would hope we do not have to share the same haircutter.

She hears the words leap out her mouth before she has thought them. They are not her words and yet they sound from her voice.

Who died for that tombstone in your mouth?

Soundpost's mouth hangs open but his voice has vanished. His lip snaps over his tooth. Wilson slaps her on the back. Ho! The quick mouth on you, Tim. Never mind him, Mr Soundpost. They're a strange lot, them cousins. His brother is the— look, there's Clackton.

She waits for Soundpost to send her away but instead he turns and glares at this fellow called Clackton. He shouts, so, Mr Clackton, you have been shirking on us. We have not the charity for any more time wasting as it is.

Her eyes seeing inwards to this new self, to what is held in a name.

Silently she speaks it, tongues the mouthfeel.

Did you hear that, Colly? My name is Tim.

The road becomes a wailing river of cattle bumping the ditches. Their grave and heavy footing amplifying with the sound of lowing until the sky is full of thunder and lament. They consume the high road outside the town and everything upon it, carriages and jarveys and work carts and a party of dragoons faceless in blood coats high upon their horses.

People stop to watch the booley pass as two dogs yap and circle. She learns they are Wilson's dogs, two black collie sisters. Both are white-socked with blazing white faces. Soundpost heckling at the rear of the group with the blunderbuss loose on his shoulder. Wilson with his gentle woahs and whistles. He walks with a cudgel in his hand, wears on his back a satchel and a melodeon. Clackton in tweed up front, though she has not seen much of him. A man, it seems, of little talk, his combed-back hair oily and yellow-white. A rifle resting loose over his shoulder.

Keep your mouth shut and do the work, she thinks. You might even get coin for it.

Colly says, Wilson is the one to watch, he's a natural with the animals—move your arms like him, shout at them like he does.

She puts her fingers in her mouth and tries Wilson's whistle but no sound comes out. Still, she thinks, this is easy enough—just keep the cattle together and stop them from wandering. And yet in a blink the animals spook and wander. They are hardly out of the town when one cow leads three others into a winter oat field. She runs after them through the soft muslin rain with Soundpost's high and charmless voice following after her.

Mercy! Mercy! Drive them back out!

She flails her arms but the cattle stare beyond her as if she were but a bird, some coal-coloured thing flapping frantic wings. It is the collies who come to her rescue. They circle the rogue animals and then Wilson with his big hands is beside her. Into the air he slices a whistle. She watches the cattle march back out.

She thinks, that Wilson has the power of a spell over them. I will be found out now for sure.

Soundpost is staring at her. Mercy me. Patience! I thought you knew cattle.

After the rain the glittering treetops. A benign and shining winter as if the world is witnessed through glass. The flatlands fall away behind them and it is slow work walking these cattle up hilly roads, how the animals want to wander among firs or nibble at the moss. She watches Clackton, sees when he turns to give some instruction to Wilson that a scar cuts the side of his mouth. He is midsize, clean-shaven, easy-fisted. He makes Soundpost look like the man-boy he is. He shows no interest in talking to her. As he walks he sometimes takes a quick sup from a flask.

Colly wants to know why they are booleying these animals through wintered country when there's so little grazing to be had. She has no nerve to ask them. In dusk it takes a good hour to find the booley hut hidden behind gorse on a hill. Soundpost chiding at Clackton. This is your fault for keeping us in the town so late.

The hut is sound enough, made of stone with a door that swings into the earth as it opens. The slope walled with stonework to enclose the cattle. The animals come to rest blank-eyed and haggard. Soundpost stares at her and puts his hands on his hips. Mercy! Patience! She looks about for something to do and Wilson points to the cow kept for milk and winks.

That's your work, hireling.

She unties the bucket from the mule, watches the men step inside the booley hut and goes to work with her fingers. Wilson steps behind her. He sits on his haunches and fingers the grass, then leans in and speaks quietly. That Soundpost! He's in some rush to take these beef half-breeds back to Newtown McFuck or wherever he comes from. Some of them are carrying calves. Wouldn't wait until the spring. You'd think he was a great farmer the way he goes on, yet I heard he's in training to be a solicitor. Got these beef for half nothing off some poor fella. He's only an auld rich grabber.

She cannot remember ever eating so well. A tin cup of milk and mealcakes burned to a crispy black that sets Soundpost chiding at Clackton. Mercy! Mercy! It's not peat you're cooking, Mr Clackton.

Clackton turns around, his features very still. Finally, he says, might I ask, Mr Soundpost, how old you are in years?

I'm eighteen and three-quarters to the month.

Colly says, you'd think he's an old galoot.

Clackton says, let me tell you, Mr Soundpost. I've been cooking these mealcakes since before you suckled on that tight teat of your wet nurse.

She watches the mouth snap shut and then the suck of the upper lip. Wilson tries to sit on a snicker. Soundpost looks so helpless, she thinks, like a child roused to anger. He grabs the lamp and steps outside and throws the door closed, leaves them to the fire's glow. They can hear him counting the cattle, stalling for a moment, starting up again. Clackton and Wilson trade laughing glances.

She nods towards the door, says, is he a strange one or what?

Clackton quits smiling and stares at her.

She sits tickled under her blanket against the booley hut wall, relishing the aftertaste of the mealcake. Even if they found out now, she whispers, even if the real Tim turned up, it would have been worth every moment.

Colly whispers, how would they ever find out? It was Donkeyface man who mistook you, they're nothing but fools—that Wilson with his slap-red hands is only a gobdaw, you can tell him anything and he believes you—and that Clackton is a drunk, sipping on gin when he thinks nobody is looking, he nearly got us lost, so he did. Now, if I were in charge I would have drawn up maps and I would be taking account of the—

She cannot stop thinking of Embury Soundpost. A kind face but for that shame of a tooth. The strange way he has of looking at her. She is not used to being looked at.

She says, he's a funny sort, that Soundpost.

Colly says, he's lost in his head all the time with his notes and calculations, he doesn't suspect a—

In the corner on the wooden bed Soundpost stops murmuring and looks up. Clackton and Wilson are asleep on the floor. For a moment she watches the outline of Soundpost, the lamp on the bed angled to illumine his notebook. How his shadow rides up the wall a dark and flickering other-self, his truer self, she thinks, the part he guards from others. She thinks of a story once heard of a man who lost his shadow to the devil, the trouble he had after it. She turns quick to see her own shadow snug to the wall. You lost your shadow a long time ago, she thinks. This shadow belongs to Tim.

She continues to study Soundpost in the half dark, his gaze fixed on his notebook. Recording, no doubt, every minute detail. Already he knows all his cattle to the hoof. When a cow wandered into the trees at near dark he was the first to know. Stood staring at the dusk squeezing his hands. She knows now why they are armed. Soundpost with his blunderbuss, Clackton with a rifle, Wilson wielding a cudgel that would bring light to the dark of a man's brains. How tense Soundpost got when Clackton almost steered them through a large village. How he made straight for Clackton. We had an agreement to stay out of them, to use the back roads. We don't want to make a show. Clackton inscrutable, oiling his hand through his yellow-white hair, his eyes saying one thing but his mouth another. It's impossible to get where we're going without meeting places. The days of the Whiteboys hiding in the hedges are long over.

Right now, Clackton is not so much snoring as snarling. It is as if in dream he has shape-shifted into some beast and is trying to make good of it. Soundpost puts the room to dark. She can hear him make a long settling breath. He keeps turning to get comfortable. She tries to sleep but cannot, listens instead to the sound of the world after the rain, the trees slowly releasing their drops, how it sounds like a rain shower brought to a great slowing of itself. The slap of each rain bead as it falls onto the sleeping cattle and the stones and the earth, the ring of each bead unique. And if you listen hard enough you can almost tell the distance between each drop.

Colly whispers, that Clackton—there's something of the dog about him, don't you think, and Soundpost with all his calculations is like a cat.

She is silent a moment, then says, wasn't it the dog that swallowed the cat?

She awakes to the din of men and scuffling animals. A vision of Sarah returning to the obliquity of dream like rainwater seeping through earth. Wilson outside shout-herding the cattle. Then Clackton's face moons above her and she stares at the scar cornering his mouth, sorrow carved with a knife. Clackton grimaces and he grabs her wrist and slaps into her palm a mealcake so hot she struggles not to drop it. He says, eat up, young hireling, and get a move on.

That dream of Mam. She feels there is something her mother was trying to tell her. Yesterday she had hated her but in the dream today she is love and comfort. How a dream can leave you so unsettled.

In the hoarfrost outside everything that trembles in nature seems to hold still. A far-off bird does not fly but is held numb under a struggling sun. She rolls her blanket then stops and ties it into a cape instead. Soundpost is walking past her holding the blunderbuss and reading from his notebook. Of a sudden he trips, falls face-forward, the moment of his falling slowing, it seems, to the tempo of stillness, the minds of all expecting the gun to go off. Soundpost then upon his face and he utters a groan. He lifts his chin and stares blindly for a moment as if he cannot register what happened. Wilson stands with a comb frozen in his hair then hinges into laughter. Clackton reaches a hand to Soundpost and hauls him up. Says, you're lucky that gun didn't blow your brains out. Soundpost violent with his hands, dusting himself down, juts his eyes about for the notebook. Kicks at the ground that tripped him. An arid tree root like a warning finger. He turns upon her then, begins to shout. Mercy! Mercy! Get a move on, hireling.

They shout the cattle into ponderous march up the bogland slopes. The cattle keen in unison grief but then quieten when they meet the all-sky of the bog. The land near treeless and how it sends thought shooting in every direction. Shadow-clouds like enormous animals grazing the brown slopes as if the sky were trying to mirror the booley. When a cow stops to test the bog sedge Grace gives it a push. Finds herself studying the dead-time of the bog, how it seems as if great violence were struck in the long-ago, imagines a land razed by fire.

This place is like Blackmountain, she thinks. The silence and how it is held. In the far-off she sees a cabin. A drawl of peat smoke. A person outside it reduced to shape and movement. She thinks, that place could be home. That person could be Mam. She sees herself walking towards the house and stepping in, her heartbeat rising to Bran and Finbar. The songs she used to sing with them. And then she wonders how she could have forgotten. Or perhaps you didn't. The child born by now. A girl called Cassie, or Conn, perhaps, if it was a boy.

She says, you know what, Colly? I have slid out of my life. I've lost who I was. I am as stupid as those cattle.

Colly says, I'll tell you who you are, you are Tim—now get me a smoke.

He has begun to whine like an upstart pup. He says, there's an ache in my mouth something terrible, Grace, are you listening?

Ugh.

Everybody else gets to smoke their pipe as they walk, I canny walk any further unless you ask Soundpost for plug.

I was given a pinch already.

He'll give you more, so he will.

Mercy! Mercy! That's what he'll say. The way he looks at you when you ask him for something. He'd drive you demented.

If that is so, why are you always staring at him?

I'm only staring at that tombstone tooth.

You are dripping your eyes off him, you are doing it now, so you are.

The way Soundpost half smiles when she drops back and yet his eyes are frozen in their looking. Mercy! Mercy! From a leather pouch he pulls two pinches then lights his own pipe first. He says, my tobacconist in Newtownbutler imports it especially.

She tokes her pipe, does not know how to answer. Says, that's smoother than down, so it is.

Soundpost does not smile but says, never a truer word.

He nods towards Wilson. That fella there couldn't tell the difference.

Wilson turns and scratches his underarm. Baccy is just baccy, he says.

She is learning to mirror Wilson's behaviour—the carefree disposition, his easy laugh and lope. The way he sits on his honkers wrapping his arms about his knees. His general assurance with the animals. Already she has mastered his whistle—two fingers in the mouth, loud enough to command the dogs, though they don't yet respond.

She also studies Clackton, walks sucking on her pipe for he does it best—the pipe easy on the lips, shouting at the cattle without moving his mouth, swinging an ash switch. She puffs into the sky a perfect smoke ring.

Colly says, I can do them as good as that.

Show me.

How the cattle never tire of their lowing and yet there is peace to be had. A gap has opened in the trembling place of herself. It is a quiet she has not heard for a long time. It is like being nowhere for a moment, each step like stepping into an absence. Like holding in the closed cup of your hands the settle of a frightened bird.

Soundpost calls to shore up the cattle. He points towards the lee of a heathered hill that holds some sun. A rough circling of rocks to sit on. Wilson whistling and shouting at the dogs, go bye, go bye, that'll do. Clackton scratching furiously at himself, grumbling for all to hear that the cattle can't feed on bog sedge. Wilson as usual bursting with talk after the morning's march. His chatter is light-hearted until Soundpost and Clackton begin disagreeing loudly again, this time on some political matter about the Crown, talk of coming relief in the newspapers. Wilson casts them a mocking look.

Soundpost says, the shortages are none of my business.

Clackton says, you're making them your business.

Soundpost says, I don't see you out of pocket.

He picks up the blackened pot of water and drops it on the fire, sits on a rock and turns away from them. Clackton continues to scratch himself. He is trying to reach an arm to foreign parts of his back. When he draws up his shirt there is a rash of red as if in sleep he has been wrestled and clawed by some demon. Christ in the manger, he says. Any of you men scratchy after last night?

Wilson guffaws and points a large finger. He says, looks like somebody caught beasties on the straw.

Soundpost stares at Clackton's back and says, I have some lotion in my bag. My mother made some up.

Clackton nods towards the fire. He says, tell your ma to get that tea on.

They eat their provisions and smoke and drink tea. Afterwards, she lies belly-warmed, her eyes closed and listening to the all. Clackton soft-snoring. Soundpost muttering into his notebook. Wilson stretched out on the bog grass with the collies pawed out beside him. The shuffling and lowing of cattle. The sound of the wind as it rubs the long necks of the grass into an infinitude of voices, the whispering at once of every person on earth.

Colly says, tell me, where do all the different winds come from—I've been thinking they must come from the gulf, wherever that is, the gulf of the four winds, it must be a great hole, I suppose—

Footsteps and then she blinks upon the upside down of Wilson.

He bends down and whispers. Who are you chatting to? Then he summons her to follow and they step over the hill, find seat on springing heather. He looks over his shoulder and whispers. Word is that brother of yours got himself caught.

Colly? she thinks. Then takes quick hold of her tongue.

She says, he has a wild big mouth on him, that's for sure.

Take a look at this.

He pulls from the satchel a heavy-looking pistol.

Hee! Colly shouts.

Wilson tries to hand it to her but she recoils from the touch.

She says, what do you want with that thing?

Wilson says, it's a flintlock horse pistol, eejit. A right man-stopper.

Colly says, let me have a go.

Wilson says, it's not loaded, at least not now it isn't. It belongs to a pair. If I had the other half I'd give it to you.

His eyes smirk though he watches over his shoulder again, then slides the gun into his satchel.

She says, what are you planning to do with it?

He says, the others have their guns, don't they? Just like them Whiteboys.

* * *

Clackton empties his tin cup and stows it in the packed mule. He squints into the distance and spits. Looks like heavy rain, boys, he says.

Soundpost measures Clackton with one eye. That's a curious pouch you got hanging around your neck, Mr Clackton. Do you find your tobacco dries out? That material, you see, is not so desirable.

She watches how Clackton's upper body seems to tighten. He stands with his lips pursed. Then his hands drop and he speaks. That pouch was made by my mother a long time ago. Wilson, pass over that cup.

What you need, Mr Clackton, is something like—

She does not know why but she shoots the dregs of her cup close to Soundpost's head. He shuts right up, stares at her, and she stares at him back, sees an island of blue lost in the sea-brown eye.

She says, did you say it is likely to rain all day, Mr Clackton?

Clackton turns and eyes her. All day? he says. Hard to tell. Could be just a shower.

Soundpost has turned to the willing ear of Wilson, who is pulling bramble from a cow's ankle. He waves his pouch, the leather red like dried venison. See how it's lined with oiled silk, he says. I read about this particular make in a newspaper. It's a Hungarian design called Kaposvar. Everybody in London has it. The oiled silk helps maintain the proper humidity. Look here, Clackton. See this—

She watches Clackton scratch at himself as if Soundpost were an annoyance, a horsefly nicking at his neck. He half shouts. Wilson, your cup.

Wilson has that sly smile again. He reaches out a ruddy hand for Soundpost's pouch. Let me touch, let me touch.

Mercy, you with your filthy hands. If you want one I'll get you the address when we get to Newtownbutler.

She has heard mention of it before by Soundpost, three or four times. Newtownbutler. This must be where they are going, she thinks. She is afraid to ask what kind of place it is. It sounds like a great town, the way Soundpost goes on, though Colly says it is probably some hole of a place. Soundpost's brother the eminent doctor. How he will become the town solicitor, he has said. His cousins own half the businesses on Main Street. And then there is the young woman he has mentioned. Some Mary Black or was it White whom he plans to marry soon as his studies are complete and the farm sufficient. She has pictured the young woman with her hair nice and dark and ringed with curls. The certain way she sits, her legs crossed, her ankles in fancy stockings, and she is smiling coyly at Soundpost, leaning towards him in a lace dress—no, white taffeta—her sleeves are lace, smiling softly, soft gloves that travel to the wrist and young men asking you to dance and the dancing and the way they smell and whisper to you and the smell of them you inhale before you pull away—

Wilson stands up and shouts. Right, boys, pissing contest. I'll bet you from here I can put out the fire.

She watches him unbutton his breeches and does not know where to look, Wilson pulling it with his hand—his cock, Colly says, and don't you dare look. She turns abruptly, studies a rock and its lichen.

Wilson leans back and sighs himself into an arching yellow piss that reaches the edge of the fire.

Clackton says, you couldn't strike a daisy with that thing.

Wilson leans back and stands shaking his organ with vigour. He stares at Clackton. Go on, you, then.

Clackton stands with his almost smile but says nothing.

Wilson turns to her. Your turn, Tim. That man is hung like a newborn. Couldn't even piss his own pants.

Soundpost sits muttering into his notebook and refuses to look up.

Colly says, I could piss on his boots from here.

She grunts her voice down at Wilson. Would you ever quit. I only had a piss five minutes ago.

Clackton's throat throbs as he swallows from his flask.

Bunch of small-cocks, he says.

*   *   *

A slump of hill rises in absolute peace with itself. The wind seems to blow from all quarters and yet so little stirs but for the sounds of their passing. The mule's burden that squeaks in rhythm to its walk. The hide-slap and hoof-thud of cattle. The soaring horns. She watches Wilson hang a pipe from his mouth. He is humming a tune to himself, fingering with his right hand an invisible melodeon. Past the brow of the slope the track leads down towards a shallow river that cuts through it at a cross. Clackton leading the booley near to the water when of a sudden she senses some alarm unspoken and her tongue moves to shout but already the cattle have splintered. A sudden surge and then hoof-thunder in every direction and the men yell and follow and she hears Soundpost issue some curse. He follows downhill after the others with his body strangely loose as he runs and she follows breathless, sees Wilson and Clackton unruffled and calmly shouting, Wilson with his woahs and shooting whistles, the dogs circling the cattle. Away! Away! Clackton stumbling through the bog to encircle two cows. Hoot! Hoot! Hoot, would ye, ye bastards.

With unthinking feet she finds herself coming head-on upon three cattle, her arms outstretched, hears herself roaring at them. Eye to eye they meet and she sees into their eyes and what is held there, the basic fear of such animals, and she feels her mastery over them. How easy it would have been for the animals to trample you, she thinks, stamp your head into the bog. And yet you ran at them without fear. She waves her arms and soothes them, marshals them back to the group. She looks to see what it was spooked the cattle, some sound perhaps the rest of us didn't hear, or the sight of a bird perhaps, for cattle too have their superstitions.

Soundpost's cheeks are scoured with agitation. He stares pop-eyed at the cattle and pulls at his hair. It has taken twenty minutes to induce the animals into a group and now they must be left rest a good half hour to calm down, according to Clackton. In the maelstrom, Soundpost has lost his nibbed pen and his hat, wants everyone to know. He is blaming Clackton for this also, though how could it be his fault? she thinks. Clackton has enough to do leading the booley without keeping watch of what's in a man's pocket.

Colly says, I'm sick of his moaning—a buck eejit is what he is, knows nothing about cattle and if I find that pen let me tell you what I'll do with it.

Soundpost is combing the heather on hands and knees when Wilson picks up his hat and brings it to him. Soundpost stands and dusts his hat. I must offer an apology to you all, he says. The shame of language that came out of my mouth. But you should have led them over the river, Clackton, one by one. I don't know what you did down there. I knew I should have brought horses for this. And where is this rain you spoke of?

Wilson stands holding Soundpost in a squint. He leans across to her. Horses? What in the fuck's he on about?

Clackton nods at Soundpost. Quit your shouting unless you want to spook the animals again. Wilson, keep those dogs quiet. There are to be no whistles or calls.

A sky of old cloth and the sun stained upon it. After such spookery it is slow work keeping the cattle in file. With the dogs they walk wide patterns around the cattle that no longer walk as one mind. When a cow steps deep into a rut it takes Soundpost pulling on a rope and the other three to heave it out. Even Wilson has grown quiet. He is slicked with black bog water from boots to the hip.

Then Clackton shouts the booley to a halt, stands scratching at his neck. Soundpost stomping past her with loose arms. She walks forward with Wilson until they see what it is. The narrow road formed by cart track and footfall has come to a complete halt in the sedge. How strange, she thinks. The way a road for no reason goes no farther. She squints at the far-off but there is nothing but bogland, it seems, low dun hills and perhaps some distant green, it is hard to tell.

Soundpost half shouts at Clackton. I thought you knew where we were going.

Clackton says, this road we were on was supposed to meet the main road to Pettigo. I know it in my own head.

Where are we, then?

We're near to Pettigo, I guess.

How near?

I don't know. A few mile.

Mercy. Just keep going on, then, in the general direction.

The general direction of what?

Of where the road was supposed to be going.

But the road is not going anywhere, Mr Soundpost. It appears we were on the wrong road all along.

Mercy! Mercy!

I suppose we'll have to keep going over the bog the way we were.

Mother of all patience. That's what I said.

What you said is—

Mercy! Mercy! Just leave it.

There was supposed to be a booley hut in the valley outside Pettigo but there is no valley and no hope of that now. Soundpost muttering to himself about all this dawdling. She looks at the sky and sees how the day has been dragged to its darkness. The colours of the bog shading into alliance.

Clackton says, what would you think, Mr Soundpost, about sleeping here in the open? We'll take turns staying awake to watch over the animals.

She studies Soundpost's face. He mutters and stamps his foot. She wonders if a face can get any redder. The mule, a reader of thought, stamps at the ground and brays loudly.

Colly says, see how it starts with the whinny of a horse and then becomes the hee-haw of a donkey?

He begins to hee-haw back and in the same breath makes whinny noises, keeps on doing it until she puts her fist to her head and shouts, stop. Wilson gives her a strange look. Who are you talking to? he says.

Soundpost is still staring at Clackton. He says, let us have some sense and make towards those trees. He is pointing to a stand of distant firs that hold already the darkness. We're at the mercy of the cold and wind out here. The cattle will wander.

Wilson says, that's the cleverest thing anybody said all day.

Clackton turns and shakes his head. Those trees are three mile off by my reckoning. It will be pure dark before we get there. Anyhow, there's a rill nearby. Listen.

Hee-haw, Colly says.

In final light they make camp, each of them abraded to silence. Their shadows flung in off-shapes by the fluttering wind-smoked lamps. Look, Colly says. Those clouds are like the crumbling rib cage of some long-ago giant. But she cannot be bothered to look. Wilson is hatcheting at bog wood. Clackton's face flashing out of the dark as he works the firestriker. It is like a face seen in a dream, she thinks, a face of the dead being remembered. She wonders how it is in sleep you can see someone long forgotten. Sometimes she thinks this way about her father. How she never knew him to remember and yet in dreaming there are shadows you can reach. She finds herself staring in wonder at Clackton, the flashing of his face again, and if a man like this might have been her father.

The four of them are soon held in the gleam of small-fire. Soundpost seems agitated, stamps among his animals. They can hear him sighing to himself, over and over like some lamenting old woman, until Clackton mutters, would you listen to Deirdre of the Sorrows. Threesome laughter like that of conspirators but then her laughter is met with a strange feeling. How she wants to laugh at the silly sighing man and yet she wants to console him.

The air is soon thick with the burning of Clackton's mealcakes. Soundpost is poking at the fire. Wilson serenading the animals in the dark with some made-up song, a doleful air, she thinks. She wishes it would drown out the yammering of Colly. Watches Soundpost take off his hat and squint at the music as if his eyes could become his hearing. Mercy me, he says. He really knows how to strangle that melodeon.

Clackton tests a finger in the water pot then stands and rubs his knees. He nods in Wilson's direction.

He says, that fellow claims them cattle are trainable to music. Wants to turn us into some kind of traveling circus.

One of the collies lets out a yowl and they slide into laughter.

She says, it's not even music but the rumour of a bad song.

Colly says, tis the tune the old cow died of.

They fall into the quiet of eating and drinking and then each sits back in completion. The fire throwing myriad faces to the wind. She pulls a piece of flaming wood to her pipe.

Colly says, let me have a hold of Soundpost's blunderbuss. I want to see how it works.

Would you ever give my head some peace?

Go on and ask him, would you.

Wilson says, listen.

She can hear the far sound of church bells.

Clackton says, like I said, we're only a few mile from Pettigo. Who wants to take first watch?

She can feel Soundpost studying her though the beams of his eyes are dark. What's that you're asking? he says.

She bolds up her voice. Give us a look at your blunderbuss.

He says, mercy, mercy! That gun belongs to my brother.

Clackton says, let me guess. The eminent doctor of Newtownbutler.

Soundpost studies her a long moment and then reaches for the gun but Clackton leans over and stops him.

He says, that gun is loaded and won't be straying into the arms of some hobbledehoy. Don't want no stupid accidents. Don't want no fools falling over a gun.

In the flicker-light it is possible to see him smiling in the direction of Soundpost.

The weapon and its sudden weight are dropped in her lap. Soundpost seems pleased with himself. Clackton mutters something and resumes scratching himself.

Colly says, do you reckon I can take the gun apart—I'll bet I—

Soundpost takes the gun off her. Wilson groans into standing and rubs at his knees. He walks quietly to a cow and cradles the animal's head in his arm, rubs the cheek with his fingers. It is like magic what happens, she thinks, the way the head dips as if brought to an instant sleep. The cow sighs and lies down.

Soundpost stands to his feet. Mercy! Mercy! How did you do that?

Wilson stands half obscured and edged by firelight. When he speaks she hears darkness in his voice. He says, it is a trick that can't be taught to the likes of you.

She has taken first watch but wishes she hasn't. If the night had eyes what would it see? The outline of her sitting figure. A lamp put to dark. Her eyes like the blind staring into what cannot be seen. She thinks, if the night had ears could it hear the sounds of my heart? Her ears still sounding with Clackton's talk of bog bodies. The murdered, he had said. Those fallen into death, the drunkards and fools stumbled into bog ruts and never getting out, the pagans drowned in tarns, the young girls ritually killed by throat-cut and left out for the gods, the women stolen from their loved ones by bandits taken up here to be raped, the great warriors who fell forgotten, the chieftains assassinated, the children born with the wrong hand or a bad arm or born to the wrong woman or born too early without the blessing of God, or born with the wrong twin, the crippled and disabled stoned to death behind a bush, the lost and forgotten in the whole of history lying out there in that dark. These boglands are full of such dead, they are resting, waiting with their long brown fingers, their twisty fingernails that keep growing over the thousands of years, waiting to climb out.

Just Clackton's eyes she could see in the flicker-light. And then his mouth wide open — a rictus laugh as if he were not laughing at all but signalling some threat of violence, or as if he had become one with those slack-jawed long-dead. Wilson beside him bent with laughter.

Colly says, they were only winding you up — it is just jest, that's all, a story he was telling — if it was the Samhain it might be different, but you know the rules, no air demon is allowed out on an ordinary night like this.

The three of them are all stupid, she says. Even Soundpost. Proud and stupid like a silly hen the way he goes on. I'm glad he lost his pen. And I know there's nothing out here but this bog. There is only the cattle. Most of them aren't sleeping yet. It's the same dark as Blackmountain. Think of it, all those years of silence on the hill and we were never bothered then.

Colly says, but what if there were raiders coming to steal the cattle, isn't that what this protection is all about?

Nobody knows we're out here.

Then why are we keeping guard, Clackton lying with that rifle by his chest — we hardly went unseen up the backs of them hills, you could have heard the cattle bawling from miles off.

We're here to stop the cattle from wandering. That's all there is to it. Now give my head peace.

Later she thinks, perhaps he is right. The boglands are as vast as the sea in this dark. What was it the old man Charlie said? Be sure to see the sea and when you can't see it get off it. She imagines what cattle raiders might look like. Bodies footing quietly over the bog, a gang of men with faces hidden behind crepe. Just their eye whites peering out. They would travel with a lamp, surely. Even if it were a mile away, you would see them twinkling like stars. She stares again at the dark. Anyhow, she whispers. How would they ever find us in all this black?

I'll tell you how—just listen to all that shuffling and sighing of the cattle.

The lids of her eyes are like stones she is so tired. And yet it is a wonder the others can sleep, what with Clackton's scratching and snoring. You must stay alert. You must stay wide awake. You must be ready in case something should happen. She imagines the pooka in the shape of that Donkeyface Boyd fella roaming across the bog in the dark. His wicked laughter. Planning tricks to play on them. If it was the pooka coming they wouldn't need a lamp. The pooka would puff out the candle of moon just to confuse the hell out of us. She recalls again what Clackton was saying, those dead pagans sacrificed to the gods. Fights the mind's slide into sleep. Begins to imagine herself as some young woman and what it would be like being left out on the bog as an offering. Imagines herself bog-bodied—dead—the way you are not able to speak anymore or move any part of yourself, a tongue of trickle-water in your mouth, the earth's silence in the gone-place of your heart—the taste of turf, the taste of rain, the taste of snail, even, the taste of ten thousand days and nights and the sound of the rill in your hair keeping it washed—sleep-sliding-sleep—and then she is singing to the birds, the wagtails and the wheatears, the blackbirds and the crows—and then she hears it, a sound faint as thought itself, hears it louder—the sound of other voices, of women calling out—and she calls out a song to them that sounds like screaming and it is then that she hears the voice of the woman nearest to her, a woman calling her name—Grace, she sings, Grace—and the woman begins to tell her the story of a girl lost for seven years, seven years in the wilderness and seven years with the dead, where you will grow into an old woman and when you return nobody will know who you are—and she knows the voice of this woman, this woman who is asking her to make a promise—stay with me now for seven days and seven nights, stay with me like this, and I will reward you, I will save you from your seven years in hell's prison, where you will grow into an old woman, I will return you to Blackmountain as if no time had passed—and she is trying to answer, to tell the woman that she will, but the words go unspoken and cannot leave the cave of her mouth, and she screams mute over the earth's silence, over the mountains and bog fields, for nobody can hear for there is nobody to listen, and then the woman is behind her with a hand on her shoulder, the woman speaking in whisper, and she can hear her now, the hand shaking her shoulder and the voice speaking out—you awake there, young fella? Are you asleep on the job? And she sees a cat-headed woman. Sees a man with twelve fingers. Sees the pooka sitting down beside her breathing hard. It is Clackton and his odour of gin and sweat and oiled hair.

She blinks her eyes at him.

Course I'm awake. I'm just thinking is all.

After her watch she falls exhausted to sleep and then deeper still, beyond sleep into a cancellation of self so that what is of the night cannot enter. When she wakes dreamless in first light she is like wood unturned in the place of its falling. It is Wilson's boot stamps that stir her. She gruffs at him to fuck off. He kneels down and whispers. Something happened during the night. Soundpost is acting crazy. He's mad with suspicion. Says we're being followed.

She blinks at where the sun should be and sees the fire gone out. Clackton is talking to Soundpost while coughing into his fist. She stands up, bangs her arms off herself for warmth. Says, if something is wrong why weren't we woken?

She watches Soundpost counting his cattle.

Wilson says, I don't know nothing. Clackton told me when I woke up. Says he heard something strange during the night when it was his watch, he will not say what, though—he never explains nothin. But he cocked his rifle and soon as he did Soundpost was up beside him, oiling the backside of his breeches. Soundpost wanted to wake us all up and light the lamps but Clackton said if you are fearing for the security of your herd right now that is the last thing you should do. So they waited until the dawn like that and now the pair of them are exhausted and I asked Clackton what did he see when the sun came up and he said they saw nothing, that there was nothing at all to see but the pair of us asleep and that a few of the cattle had wandered off a small way but not very far and—

Soundpost is stomping in their direction. His face crinkled with rage and he is sucking hard on his teeth. Mercy! Mercy! he says. I just knew it. We've been robbed. There is an animal missing.

Wilson stands up and frowns and does a quick count with his finger. You've made a mistake, Mr Soundpost, he says. I count thirty-four cows and that is the number we had last night.

No, I tell you, it's not. There's one animal missing.

Colly says, what's up with these fools, can't they count a head of cows or what?

She says, I've counted thirty-three cows.

Wilson looks over at her. That's what I said.

No you didn't, she says.

Soundpost scratches furiously at his nose with his fist. Mercy! We started out with thirty-four cows. Look here. He shows them his notebook and she has to squint to read his compact handwriting. His finger taps the page. Thirty-four. See. I have it written down.

Perhaps there were raiders after all, Colly says. And they just snuck off the one animal.

She says, it is as if the bog opened its mouth and swallowed it.

They are all looking at Clackton but he is slow to speak. He stands very still watching the expanse of bog, his eyes red and heavy from lack of sleep. Finally, he says, there are bog holes big enough to swallow a man. Perhaps we should take a look around again.

Of a sudden Soundpost turns and points a finger in the face of

Clackton. The net worth of that animal, he says. It was your responsibility. You were the one got us lost. That is what I am paying you for. There will have to be deductions.

Clackton takes a step forward closer to Soundpost's face. He says, the net worth of that animal or the criminal price you paid for it?

Something crawls all over her skin. Like the tickle of an insect that shifts when you scratch. She thinks she might have what Clackton has, but knows it is dried-in dirt and sweat. You're a stinky wee bitch, Colly says. When was the last time you washed, you're starting to smell like the back end of a cow—if Mam were here she'd throw you in a river, you and all your dangleberries.

She knows this is true, but what is she supposed to do about it? She has watched Clackton and Soundpost strip out of their shirts to clean themselves with stream water because these are the class of people that wash. Soundpost smooth and shining to the gills until the splash sends him howling with pimples. Clackton standing there like some shape-shifter, half the creature he becomes in sleep. His shoulders hairy as a brush, his chest like a rug, his skin rashed red all over. A low hum as he douses his nape. A wet hand reaching down his trousers to wash his manplace with vigour. Neither of them seems to notice that she does not wash. Wilson does not wash either.

Just as well, she thinks. And thank goodness these clothes are hanging off her. The way the shirt hangs like a bunched sack. For there have been changes to her body these last few months that please and trouble her. The budding on her chest has gotten worse, or better, depending on what view you make of it. She would like to take off the shirt and examine herself but how can you do that? Instead she finds her hand wandering under her shirt as if the hand were another's. The way her hand roams now under her shirt morning till night. A strange tenderness like pain. Wilson has taken notice, laughs and says to the others, Tim's got the itch same as Clackton! How she pretends to scratch but really what she is doing is cupping the place where she is becoming woman. I am becoming like Mam, she thinks.

What in the hell are you doing? Colly says. You're supposed to be Tim, a boy called Tim—what kind of Tim goes around with big diddies?

How the world colours as they leave the bog. Ruptures of evergreen like signals of spring. Trees lording as if life were the only province. She looks at the creamy sky and sees a cloud like a torn dress. Clackton leads them to a narrow road that stretches the booley into an eel. It is then the rain falls. She curls her shoulders against it. This bastarding rain, Colly says. The way it trickles cold down your neck.

She watches Wilson walk in front alongside Clackton while she takes the rear with Soundpost. If you put weight to his resentment it would weigh the same as a cow, she thinks. Or if you were to put a price on it, his resentment would be twenty shillings. Sixty shillings if the times were better.

They pass a farmhouse where nothing stirs but flags of ivy slow-crawling a gable. And then a woman steps out of a byre, her face rain-squinted, the bright in her smile when she sees they are herders. She waves at them holding a hen to her chest. Two children heedless of the rain run to the gate and watch.

A bend in the road and she becomes aware of a feeling that gnaws her. It's not the rain but as if something is held in the rain. It is the feeling you get when you're being watched. A bally of mud cabins laid out in no particular fashion and yet the place seems lifeless—thin smoke from only half the cabins and a silence that is the absence of animals. Soundpost glaring at these cabins as if he suspects each one could hide his missing cow. She kicks a stone that caroms off the track, looks up to see the sudden emergence of people from their huts, the way they advance upon them with strange carriage. From a distance it seems each one is decrepit and yet she sees these people are all ages, their rag clothing upon them as if it were the wind that dressed them. The winnowing of these people comes as a shock. She knows people are hungry but has not yet seen any like this. Everybody is carrying something. The rising up of their voices into some tuneless air as the booley becomes encircled. They are enmeshed by sweet-talking voices and prayers. Everything is for sale, it seems — chairs and creepies, dressers, tables, bed ticks, straw, rag items of clothing, a mottled iron crucifix, two discoloured Brigid's crosses that could have been made twenty springs ago, a pair of bent spectacles, a torn Bible, a fiddle half strung, an old melodeon with the song torn out of it. Why aren't they selling any animals? Colly says.

The ghost weight of an old man pulling at her elbow. She shakes him off but the old man keeps up at a goat-clip beside her. She cannot bear to look at his shrivelled mouth. Three people around Soundpost charming and cajoling him, one touching his elbow. Sure aren't you a strong-looking fellow, Mr Booleyman, the fine head on you, look at this coat of mine, sir, would you not buy it? What a fine price I can put on it.

She sees what the man sells is hardly a coat and that he is wearing only a ribboned shirt that reveals the sunken cage of his chest. Soundpost is ignoring the man, shouts at the booley to keep onwards, shouts at Clackton as if this were his fault, which no doubt he believes, she thinks. Some woman takes firm hold of his elbow. Mr Booleyman, would you take a look at my son, a fine strong boy, so he is, and good with the cattle, would you take him with you, he'll work morning till night just for a handful of meal, knows cattle, so he does. And she sees the boy being talked about, a figure not fit to scare crows. The old man keeps at his goat-clip, the way he smiles with watery rotten eyes. She hates the sight of him for the revulsion he rises in her. She finds herself wishing he would die and is ashamed at the thought.

The old man's voice is tough and whispered. So you found Sircog. Nobody has found Sircog in the longest while. If I were you I'd get out as fast as those thriving legs can carry you because it is curst.

There's nothing to be had here but rocks and *cíb* grass and we'll end up eating that yet and some of them do. We lived off the cow's elder for a while but that's come to a stop. Look at my teeth. They're done in from sucking rocks. Nothing's grown since summer's end. So keep moving on unless you want to be damned like us rock eaters. May God give you long life. You'll give me a coin, won't you?

The old man's eyes continue to wolf. Their yellowing and the way they are orbed in the skull speak a clear reminder of death. His bone-hand to her wrist and what he does then with his thumb, how he trails with his thumbnail the underflesh of her wrist as if to startle her to his plight, to mark her with his existence. Her arm jerks back. She puts a hand into her pocket where she finds a mealcake half eaten. Here. The old man snaps it out of her hand and gobbles it like a dog. She looks across to see Wilson with some string of a fella, chatting as if they were old friends, handling first a melodeon and then a fiddle. Wilson trying to strike a deal for the fiddle with two crumbling mealcakes. He is wearing on his face the bent spectacles. Some woman in a gnawed old dress walks beside Soundpost leaning into his strength. She whispers, a farthing for a bit of relief?

It is then she sees the mule encircled by four others, three men and a woman, and she does not think but pushes quick through the cattle, Colly roaring at the top of his voice, fuck off, fuck off, the lot of ye! How they fall from the mule like shadows.

They are dreamwalkers who leave that village behind them. How those mask-faces linger like what haunts a dreaming mind. She looks to the land to see what is real. The trees solid-stood. A knit-stone wall that could take the weight of a bull. She does not know what she feels, this almost-fear. Thinks of the booley weaponed against thieves—the rifle, the blunderbuss, the cudgel. Wonders if they are weaponed against hunger. She looks to Soundpost with the blunderbuss unslung and realizes now she has separated from one world and is part of another. Soundpost mouthing on for all to listen. It were one of them stole my animal, I know it. And now that godless lot want the blessing of my Christian charity—

She cannot listen, joins Clackton up front. There is soothe in walking alongside him. In side view she sneaks a look at him, tries to imagine her father. He is the only man among them, she thinks. The way he walks within his own peace. You can learn from him, Colly. You can learn how a man is to behave in trouble. You can learn how to keep hold of your head. The way he never even reached for the rifle in warning yet Soundpost threatened so he—

Clackton suddenly sputters on his gin. She watches him cough into his sleeve.

Colly says, aye, yer right, I can learn how not to drink gin.

An ancient washerwoman stands on the road with a weasel in her hand still soft from the kill. When Clackton salutes her she scuttles off-road into hedgerow. Grace watches Clackton take another sup. She studies the town rising before them. A trace of cold light sketched on rooftops. The enfold of church bells and how after them the street empties into silence. Just one quick face peers out of a doorway to see upon the coming bustle and then disappears back in.

They halt the booley in the town upon a skewed triangle of streets. A broad-armed barrel roller stops to watch them. Wilson whoahing and whistling at the dogs. He stands with a teacherly air in his new spectacles. Clackton supping from his flask. He says, I can't believe they named a town after a skin condition. I must have Pettigo all over. He begins scratching himself. She looks at Clackton blankly, as does Wilson.

Soundpost has an errand to run—for a relative, he says. He alludes to legal documents. He smiles, she thinks, as if he were the father of importance. You would think, says Colly, the way he taps his nose that the secret is housed in that great honker of his.

She watches Wilson step through a shop door that tinkles a high bell. Down the street a two-horse gig pulls up with a wobble and two men get off and go in separate directions. Clackton is talking to some stranger and when next she looks they have walked off together. She eyes the jook of a lone magpie by the church tower. Knows she is transfixed by these ill-spoken birds yet wishes she wasn't. Such plumage when you see them up close — not black at all but jade and turquoise — and yet she cannot shake the feeling of ill omen. She watches the noisy flit of the bird. One for sorrow, she says, two for joy. She sighs with relief when another magpie joins it.

Colly says, how can it be that one bird can change luck — they do their own thing without any magical powers, they're not even aware of us — they are trapped in magpie land doing their own business.

Maybe they look at us and think we bring them bad luck.

I reckon what they say about magpies is to teach you that life is whimsy — one minute you are in sorrow and the next you are in luck and the wheel of life is always turning.

Another two magpies wing down upon the bell tower. That's two more, she says. You know what that means. Three for a girl, four for a —

Soundpost is suddenly beside her. Who are you talking to? he says. A large brown envelope is tucked in his oxter. He is giving her that look again, the frown that peers past her eyes as if to see into the place that holds the lie. He stamps his foot, reaches for his watch. And where now has that Mr Clackton got to? Give me patience, patience and peace.

Wilson has returned from the shop. Soundpost shouts at her. Go find Mr Clackton.

She walks past an old man bent dragging a gunnysack, passes a girl her own age leading a cart horse by the bridle. And then there is Clackton, in a laneway running his hand through his hair talking to some fellow, his back turned to her.

Colly says, what's he up to?

Soundpost grunts when she says she could not find Clackton.

Then Clackton is behind her as if he were there all along. He is looking over the mule, begins scratching his head.

Soundpost says, you are holding up the booley once again, Mr Clackton.

Clackton stands staring at the animal. Christ almighty, he says. Are yez stupid bastards or what?

Soundpost turns on his heel as if struck. All eyes follow Clackton's pointing finger to the fastening straps on the mule that have been severed. Clackton scratching at his head. He says, that fucking meal bag is gone. Which one of you were supposed to be watching it?

She feels for these cattle as they idle in the street. Their eyes skite with agitation and hunger. She rubs at the pregnant belly of a cow she calls Kira, who seems permanently vexed. Another called Ailbe keeps butting the cow before her. You can tell a lot about the mood of a cow just by watching its tail. When they are happy they let their tails hang down. When they are frightened or sore they tuck their tails between their legs.

She turns and watches the street where Soundpost marched off waving his arms in search of a new meal bag. His crimson cheeks no match for the colour that came out his mouth.

Colly says, that Soundpost had his tail tucked into a third leg—how long now is he gone?

She says, who knew he had such fine words?

Colly says, some of his curses have not yet reached Blackmountain—you ass-backwards bastards—hee!—I liked that one in particular.

What was the other?

I heard him say cockchafers.

I think he put syphilitic in front of it. What is syphilitic, do you think?

I asked Mam that once, she said it is something to do with Sisyphus.

It is later that she feels sorry for Soundpost. How he has vexed the group, reduced them to sneaky-eyed contact, whistles and herding calls. And yet he has fallen further into himself. She knows he is angry but also unsure and all over some stringy cow that's gone missing and a bag of meal.

Colly says, in all my days, I've never encountered a fellow so unfortunate.

Clackton behaves now as though Soundpost did not exist. Quietly he has assumed control of the group. Led them off-road onto some hill track without consultation. She would like to say, please, Mr Clackton, no more rock eaters or thieving townlands. Soundpost walking with the blunderbuss cradled, watching the new meal bag as if the pooka could secret it away. He stares at every *sioch* and furrow. Stares at Clackton and she wonders what he thinks, if it was Clackton sold the meal bag. She wonders, did he see those beggars in Sircog trying to cut the bag free with a knife?

As Wilson walks he has a go at his new fiddle. Has no idea how to tune it. When he strikes the horsehair it sounds like all the pain in the world gathered at once and man's inability to express it.

Finally Soundpost snaps. Mercy! Mercy! Mercy! Make the music stop.

It is evil that blooms out of a field or just the frightening shape of a boy. She cannot decide because what she sees makes her feel both sickened and fearful. How the boy stands on the verge like something whispered. Closer still and she can hardly look, for there is something so awful about him. Colly calls him a monkey but clearly he is not. It is not his tattered clothing Colly refers to, the stick shape that makes it seem something within the child is broken. Nor is it the hair thinning on his head that makes this boy of perhaps five appear like an old man in miniature. It is the fur on his face. The fur of a half animal. The fur of a cat. The fur of a mule. The fur of a boy who has had the gab taken out of him by the pooka. For sure it is the fur of hunger. The way he stands stock-still but for his hands that knead with worry. There is a roar and a wave from Clackton that bring the booley to a stop.

She says, Soundpost is going to pop his hat.

Colly says, he'll think this is a trick, that's what.

Clackton bends to the boy and the boy takes Clackton's sleeve and tries to pull him with urgent solemnity towards an off-road path. Clackton puts some question to the boy but gets no answer. She sees Wilson intently watching. Her eyes flit the tree gaps, shoot like sparrows through hedgerow. A mud cabin stood in its own winter at the eye's long reach. And then Soundpost is upon Clackton and the boy, his hands nervous with the blunderbuss. What in mercy's name are you at? he shouts. This could be a trap. Mercy! Mercy! Haven't you caused enough trouble as it is?

Clackton still upon his knee looks hard and long at the road and then at the child. He stands slowly and meets Soundpost with a look that seems to bore through him. Put away that gun, you fool, he says.

He walks to the new meal bag and unstraps it, drops it with a thump, scoops his cup into it, and hands it to the boy. Soundpost begins as if to protest but stops.

Clackton says, you've got five minutes, wee man, to show me what your trouble is and then we'll be on our way again.

They could be father and son upon that path to some distant observer, but she has seen the child's ill-nature.

She says to Colly, he could be a demon sent by the pooka to lead us wrong.

Colly says, mind that story about the she-wolf that stole the baby boy from the woman, carried the baby off in her mouth, and then gave suckle to him with her cubs—I'll bet that's what happened to this fellow.

Sight of such a boy stirs up thoughts she had earlier when they came through Sircog. How you are made to feel both despair and disgust. How you want to help and find you cannot. How you want to show kindness and yet feel loathing. That raggedy old man and scratch of his yellow fingernail. It is disgusting to be touched unless you decide to be the toucher. It is hard to help those who give you horror.

She watches Clackton grow smaller, his left hand upon the rifle strap. Soundpost holding his blunderbuss as if ready to use it. He eyes the air as if air itself could fold in concealment. He eyes the fields, where shadows could hold crouching shapes to a mind that wants to see it. The unsettling dart of a bird. The world reshaping itself into cunning and disorder. He turns and looks at the empty road behind them, studies the distance. Finally he says, you two. We're moving on without him. This is a trap, I know it.

He is trying to bold up a voice that sounds cracked and fluted as if Clackton's ghost were standing a boot to his throat. She glances at Wilson but he sends back a faceless look. He seems tense, different somehow. The spectacles are gone from his nose. He has put the cudgel on the ground and holds instead the satchel.

She steps towards Soundpost and it is then she becomes another, or perhaps it is that another becomes her. How she touches his wrist and says quietly, wait for him, Embury. There's nobody hiding to steal your cattle. That boy is just sick. You need Clackton to see the booley through.

In the moment she says it she realizes what she has done—fingers upon flesh and the clammy charge of his skin.

She has spoken and touched him as a woman.

The moment widens as if time could allow for her expanding horror. Soundpost snaps his wrist to his hip while she turns to hide her blush. She hears Colly's laugh, waits for Soundpost to make some charge at her. She thinks, how can this have just happened? You should have bound your chest down, just to be sure. Now you have given yourself away to him.

She hears the thumb-flick and click of Soundpost's pocket watch.

Five minutes, Soundpost says. Five minutes is all he's getting.

Colly says, you've just confused him is all—now he just thinks you're in alliance with Clackton.

They stand alert to all movement, watching the distance. The cattle bawling their blithe conversation. Soundpost fidgeting.

Colly wants to know how raiders might come, if they come upon you all at once or sneak off your cattle one by—

It is then she sees Clackton. He is an ant shape traversing hell's half acre until she can see him draw near, a slumbrous way about him and slightly bent, his rifle easy. The boy is not with him. When he meets the booley his eyes see only some private darkness.

Soundpost says, well, then? What is it?

Clackton, it seems, has been infected by the boy's soundlessness. He will not give an answer. He runs a shaking hand through his hair and restarts the booley with a grunt, foots forward with slack shoulders. She watches his hand reach into his coat and withdraw a bottle of gin.

Hee! says Colly. So that's what he was getting in Pettigo.

She watches Clackton soak his mouth and her mind fills with visions—that small cabin and what was in it. A portal to hell itself and all evil, Colly says. And Clackton meeting face-to-face with the devil.

She finds herself walking alongside him, knows he needs comfort. Watches the way he grips the bottle by the throat, the way he has suddenly drunk half it. She sneaks a sidewards look and sees the man is crying.

The warmth this spring evening is like the coming of summer, she thinks. The quartz in every stone wall glitters like gold struck by sun. She has been debating with Colly about the weight of a soul. If a cow's soul is heavier.

Not necessarily, says Colly. The human soul is more complex, full of sorrow and anger and guilt and all them other things that make people bitter, whereas the soul of a cow has no weight in it, eating grass all day just fills you with hot air—now, a horse, that is a different—

Of a sudden, Clackton sits down on the side of the road, then slumps forward. She turns and shouts for the booley to stop. Wilson roaring commands at the dogs.

She studies Clackton and thinks he is dead.

Colly says, that demon boy put a spell on him.

Soundpost takes one look, says, that man is drunk as a dead donkey. Mercy! What a fool. Throw him up on the pack animal.

Wilson grabs hold of Clackton's empty gin bottle and throws it high into a field so that for a moment it gathers the sun into itself. Then they lift Clackton and flop him pendulous over the back of the mule and the pack animal complains with a loud call.

Colly says, that Clackton has got the tunnies for sure.

Soundpost waggles his finger at the road, tells her to lead the booley until camp. Just follow the general direction, he says. Soon, she has forgotten the day's troubles. The downing sun throwing lanterns of gold and everything haloed in that light seems rapt in its own greatness. She is high and happy, begins to feel a new power over herself.

She thinks, I have been gifted the world. Leading this booley in such peace and freedom. She begins to count everything in the luck of sevens. Seven steps forward and back to one again. Sevenly clusters of rushes. A sextet of bunched ponies near the house of some rich man and how they open to reveal a seventh. The way they stand aloof, eyeing the travel and file of such lesser animals, and then they step forth nodding as if in approval, lean out over a tangle of rotten fencing that would sigh if it could sound for itself.

The track travels downwards to meet a higher road. Soundpost waves his hat to continue. She wishes the length of the moment. They meet a fellow leaning his weight into a pushcart who stops and salutes, shouts hello, taps the tin that hangs off the cart signing his name and occupation—Butler, Cutler. Any wares for sharpening? Then he stares at Clackton and points. Is he kilt or what?

Later, Wilson begins again at the two-string fiddle and what he finds is the song of an untuned instrument lamenting its player, or perhaps he is in tune with something else, the despair summoned deepest from the place of all hearts. Clackton begins to sing in some drunken drone-song softly rising but then he falls quiet.

She says to Colly, look at me now, earning wage and leading the animals. It is me who is in charge. Who could have expected it?

She imagines returning to Blackmountain triumphant. Waving money and buying enough food to last until the new crop. She tries to see their faces, the new wean called Cassie, but their faces slip like smoke into the blind of what holds them.

They camp on dry ground under trees near a river. Clackton groaning when they drop him on scutch grass. It is Soundpost who notices his smell. Mercy! Mercy! What has the man done to himself? The others lean in with their noses.

Hee! says Colly. He's gone and shit himself.

Wilson hunches against the breeze-cold slapping mealcakes together.

Colly says, riddle me this—what's white as goodness but black as sin, loves the water but won't get in?

She sneaks Clackton's soap from his pocket. Takes the pail and follows a path through woodland to where the river appears pooled and hidden. A conspiracy of gorse and fir trees for cover. She is quick out of her clothes, slides slow off the bank. Her teeth gritted as the water fangs at her ankles, gnaws at her hips. She dunks down, slides completely in. A vise-tight coldness that brings all thought to hush, the self to floating stillness. She washes herself slowly, imagines rose toes, porcelain skin. She wonders if it is the soul of the river she can hear and then beyond the river she hears the carry of some haunt-sound that surely is Wilson working ache from that fiddle.

She lifts herself whitely and shivering onto the bank, begins to examine herself. She squeezes at a breast not yet as big as Mam's, she thinks. Soon the booley will be done—another two nights of this, Soundpost has said. And then I can go buy good cloth to bind my breasts. She watches two rooks flutter and take rest on a tree as if to watch this spectacle and it is then she hears it—the snap-sound of weight upon twigs. Her hand flies to cover her chest and she crouches and reaches for her clothing. Her eyes in haste to the place of the sounding, her foot trying to find a leg into her breeches, and it is then she sees him—a bent shape scuttling through trees that is the shape of Soundpost. She closes her eyes, sees in her mind the river, the staring black head of the sheep.

This wait now for what is to happen but Soundpost utters not one word. Her insides trampled as if by wild animals let storm at such stupidity to reveal herself. She watches Soundpost without watching as he chews his mealcake. His face lambent by firelight and yet his eyes darkly withholding. She thinks, he is buttoned-up and smarting. He will think the others are in on it, that my being a girl is some conspiracy against him.

Wilson prattling on again about marking the cattle.

She thinks of the pain in her feet, how her boots chew at her skin.

Wilson says, they are neither marked nor branded. I cannot fathom it. There is a way it should be done that will not hurt the animal. You've got to touch the iron briefly to the hide and then wait a moment before you scald it again. It numbs the pain out. I can fix this up for you, Soundpost, in Newtownbutler. I'll go to the smith. Your initials or something more fancy? The name of your woman, perhaps?

She takes off her right boot and holds her foot to the fire, begins to nurse her clean toes.

A groaning Clackton brings his stink to the fire. He says, I'm frozen stiff.

Wilson says, it's the dried-in shit in your breeches that's stiff.

Then he leans over and points. Look at Tim with his wee girl's feet.

Her breath clumps like dry mealcake in her mouth. Soundpost quickly stands up, steps away into the darkness. She gruffs her voice down and sends it towards Wilson. What about your wee boy's cock?

Of a sudden, Wilson is unbuttoning his trousers. You mean this? He holds his appendage in his hand and begins to wag it but of a sudden Soundpost is upon him, spins him around, pushes him away from her.

Mercy! Mercy! Have you no decency or decorum? This place is not your private commode.

When Clackton speaks he sounds like his old self again. Like I said, he says, bunch of small-cocks.

You do not sleep, for how can you? You lie awake seeing the unfolding of what comes next, all outcomes imagined to their inevitable conclusions. The moment, perhaps, when Soundpost puts it to Clackton and Wilson. For he has to say something, does he not? If only to let them know he knows. What, then, when the others find out? The lies you have told Wilson, making him believe you are his second cousin or what have you. Those red hands turned to fists.

She lies awake listening with her ear cocked. Listening to the full scape of night noises. Breathing as absence and swell. It issues from the cattle, from the mouths of the men she has to figure on. Clackton asleep now, surely — those are his snores. Wilson is utterly quiet. She spends a long minute moving soundlessly into sit, another minute to standing, another reaching out her ears. Then she moves soft-foot, steps forward past Wilson and Clackton, sees the outline of Soundpost asleep under his hides. Closer and she can see he is flat on his back. A minute, it seems, getting down on her knees, time expanding as wide as the dark. Then she is upon him, her hand stealing slowly for her knife. In ember light she can see his eyes are open, that he is staring at her with terror. His eyes blink twice. She brings the knife to his throat, rests the blade to the apple, cups her mouth to his ear.

Listen up. Not one word to the others, you hear? Not one word or I will sink my blade into your daft heart. Blink once for yes.

She watches him blink. His apple bobs as though he were swallowing fear.

He whispers. What are you?

It is some unknown self who leans down and kisses his lips.

Have no fear of me, Embury. Now shush.

Two men like slow-flighted arrows come diagonal through a field. Clackton is leading the group again, his trousers river-washed and how he sat bottomless in good spirits watching them dry by the fire. Said aloud, there weren't cows in America until 1611, when they were first brought by an Irishman. Any of you know his name? He walks with his pockets hanging out to dry. Watches the men approach but does not seem bothered. Soundpost's walk stiffens and he raises the blunderbuss in his arms. The same pussed face that crawled like some sly animal from under his hides this morning. The strangers step through a gate and wait by the side of the track. Both the same height, labourers, by the look of them. Closer still and she sees they are lean elderly men, two brothers. Like two dying dogs, Colly says.

They walk alongside the booley. One says, we're the two finest men you've ever seen in this land with cattle. Been working 'em sixty year.

The other says, had to sell them all off. Any chance of some work? A bird never flew on one wing.

Soundpost points his gun at them and Clackton tells him to cool it.

The rest of the day in an icy sun Soundpost utters no word. She thinks, he is the most distressed man I have ever encountered.

When they rest up for water it is Clackton who notices. He says to Soundpost, keep your finger off that trigger. You'll take the head off someone.

When Soundpost does not respond Clackton reaches and points the gun down. Soundpost's eyes are black to him.

As she walks within the booley's encircling clamour there are times she hears it as music. Hoof thuds forming suddenly into a single beat. The mule's pack-weight that squeaks a march step. Sometimes she claps or hums the intuition of a wordless song. Sometimes she thinks Wilson hears it too, the way he starts scratching something on his two-string fiddle, seems to find the same rhythm, or swings the melodeon onto his shoulders, squeezes out some strange air. Colly joining in with more of his silly word games. Then he starts to sing.

Grace and Embury under a tree.

K. I. S. S. I. N. G.

First comes cattle. Then comes marriage—

Fuck up, would ye.

She thinks of Embury walking behind her, touches the lips that kissed him. The faintly remembered taste of what was on his lips like tea mixed with sweat or perhaps the taste of consternation.

The cold morning bites her awake. She sits up among the sleeping others and it is then she remembers. What happened during the night. Or didn't happen. It lies in the gulf of some dream and the real and she cannot decide the difference. She stares at the ground and wonders why dream and memory sometimes conspire so that you do not know the difference.

Waking in the middle of night to hear the presence of another beside her. Her own tub-thumping heart. Thinking of Soundpost with a knife to kill her. Knowing for sure it is him from the signature of his breathing. A quarter moon casting light like milk-water upon the flanks of the cattle, upon the hard earth, upon the body of

Soundpost naked from the waist with his breeches at his ankles. The sight of him in full arousal. Standing over her empty-handed as if awaiting some invitation. And how she lay there with one eye half open, her hand slowly taking hold of the knife. Lying with her eyes closed pretending to sleep and perhaps she was asleep, for when next she looked he was gone into dark as if she had dreamt him and who is ever to know in the middle of the night what is real and not real?

But still, she thinks, do not even look at him, and then she does and he sits there chewing his mealcake. He is chatting to Wilson, who is going on about some route they must take.

Clackton knuckling with two hands at the necks of both collies. Says to Wilson, what do you know of this country?

Wilson insisting on a particular route.

Then Soundpost swings around and stares at her with a smileless smile that sees into the all that is no longer hidden.

Soft-bump of cattle as she tokes on the pipe, the river-unison of their walking. They have entered a deep glen, the road narrowing onto yellowed scrub and a track worn through. Trees grab at the light on each side and she has forgotten her sore toes, tells Colly to stop annoying her. Some song he sings over and over.

A piss when I wake in the morning.
A piss before I bed.
I'll piss on your bloody finger.
I'll piss all over your—

Wilson walking fast up the side of the booley and there is something strange in his carriage and quickstep, the downwards lean of his head and his shoulders hunched as if this were the gait of another. She watches him come up behind Clackton, draw alongside him as if he is set to deliver some urgent message or point quietly to some problem with the animals. Colly starting to sing again, his voice mighty, Wilson for some water, Wilson at a well— there is an odd soft-sounding clop that seems to break upon the air and echo thinly towards the trees. She stands on tiptoe to see over the rippling cattle slowing to a stop, sees Wilson turning—Clackton, Colly says, where has Clackton gone to?—for where there were two men there is now only one and she sees a small plume of smoke rising. Wilson beginning to march back down the booley's flank with his head lowered—where is Clackton?—and she sees Wilson clearer now, sees in his left hand a blanket folded thick and smoke rising off it, sees him dump the blanket, sees him throwing to the ground the pistol and producing another from his pocket, cocks it as he walks, and what comes to her is the dark of knowledge that brings to light the world turned inverse, this dark of knowing that sends her into a run shouting Clackton's name, sees first through the spindled legs of cattle the skywards point of his boots, pushes a cow out of her way to get to him—the man flat to the earth and how she will not forget the eyes, the eyes not of a man but of a grappling child, staring with incomprehension into what cannot be fathomed, his hands painted with blood, his hands quaking and trying to shovel in what has unspooled from his body. She becomes pure motion in the same unthinking as what bends the grass and treetops, is bent in aid to him when Colly alerts her with a shout—Soundpost! He is going for Soundpost!—and she realizes she has been holding Clackton's innards in her hands, her own hands painted with his blood, trying to place the innards back into the man because his hands have stopped moving and his eyes have rolled to whiteness.

What she does is scream, a lung scream no boy could muster. She sends it shrill towards Soundpost in arrowhead. Can see through the scrum of loosening cattle the quick walk of Wilson towards Soundpost. She watches Soundpost bring up his blunderbuss. Wilson bringing up the pistol. A fat-bellied gunshot heard upon the sound of another and the cattle as if kicked begin to scatter in all directions. She is struck by a cow and falls to the ground and it is then that she sees them, shadows in the trees that become men stepping forward. Then she is up and running she does not know where, sees Wilson being struck by a cow, sees that Soundpost is alive and running for the trees, the young man's arms like the slackening of some half-strung marionette, his weapon abandoned, Clackton lying in stillness. Colly is shouting, get away to the trees! She sees three others at the far side of the glen and their carriage tells her they are weaponed. She turns and runs through the confusion of cattle and what pictures in her mind is the manner of one of them, a certain walk and the shape of a hat on his head.

The face of that Donkeyface Boyd fella.

She lies in the trembling of herself. All time thrown. It is Colly who had suggested it—to crawl under the rotting trunk of fir. Amid her screaming head, his was the voice of reason. It is a Colly she has not heard before. A Colly that sounded more grown-up. How he directed her to gouge with bloody hands a cranny to lie in. Suggested she blanket herself with leaf-rot. Just her eyes peering out like a frightened animal. Counting the breaths. Counting the bellows breaths to silence. Counting what moves on the air. The *clack clack clack* of some bird. The scurry and patter of some creature, Colly says. That's all it is. Just a creature. This *clack clack clacking*—

It's not them, he says. Listen to them shouts—that's them rounding up the cattle. That's what they came for.

She tries to listen and hears it is true, wonders if the cattle understand what has happened. If now they are horning true sorrow. She hears Wilson's dogs bark, some bird *clack clack clacking,* thinks of the dogs coming to find her—thinks of Clackton. Shuts her eyes to see his face watching her, his hair oiled with blood.

She says, that Boyd was the pooka all along, I knew it. He had put the evil eye on Wilson. It was a spell he was put under—

Colly says, keep quiet—that boy is nothing but evil, he was in on it all along.

Footfall nearby in the wood. An echoing cough and men talking. The hand that slides over her mouth is Colly's. Voices weave dimly through the trees and then nothing. She imagines Soundpost running for his life. Running out past the glen to what lies beyond. Realizes she has been waiting for the sound of gunshot to go off. The sound of Soundpost being—

Of a sudden she hears Wilson and then another talking. Cannot make out their words. She closes her eyes, thinks of the wood lice that scurry all over her. Insects bedding down between clothing and skin. How the unseen of them looms large in her mind like the shadow of something small held to a candle. The voices grow distant and fall away.

She wakes shivering and shook by dream. There was night and now daylight and Colly is whispering. They're long gone, he says.

She has spent most of the night crying in her sleep.

Get up, Colly says. Get up, they're definitely gone, so they are.

What if they left someone to watch for me?

They'd go after Soundpost, not you—why would they hang around here with the cattle?

She climbs like some wood-stiff creature birthed from the tree, her walk hobbled. She is covered in wood-dirt, shakes off what scuttles in her hair. She is sorrowed through. Steps slowly through the wood until she stands at the tree-edge watching the glen. There is nothing there now but a breeze upon the yellow sedge. She walks into the centre of the glen and with every step imagines being shot at. She sees hoofprints, Clackton's blood brown on the grass but no body.

She says, do you think they killed Soundpost?

Colly says, they were Donegal men, I'm sure of it—were probably following us and planned it all along, Wilson in on it—they'll take those cattle back with them or do a quick sell for money, would have gotten to us earlier, I reckon, if Clackton had not gotten us lost on the bog.

She stands squeezing her hands open and shut.

Colly says, the bunch of small-cocks.

A long day just walking. A slub of great anger building inside her. She finds seat hidden amid a snarl of tree shadow that twists outwards upon the ground in lightning shapes, the same shapes as those inward feelings that bolt their darkness through her. The sudden illumine and burn of memory. The face of poor dead Clackton emptied of himself. Soundpost fleeing. His legs and arms in some kind of star shape, running, running, and then she imagines him tripping over some tree root, turning around into the snort of a gun. Or just tiring out from being chased, giving up, turning around to plead with them. Mercy! Mercy! Take my money.

Colly says, he had a good chance.

She would boil their bones. She would eat their cadavers. She would gouge out their eyes with a knife nice and slow. Hex all of them with the evil eye if she had the powers. How does one become an air demon, Colly? That is, if they exist at all. I'd torment them all their lives before slowly killing them and stopping just before the end to torment them some more again.

Then she says, my head is done in. Tell me a story, Colly.

He says, do you remember that one about the legend of Bran—how Mam used to tell it, that he went sailing for hundreds of years through all sorts of wild weather, had all the salmon he could eat and plenty of seals, for they enjoyed clubbing the bastarding heads off them—it was quite the adventure and seemed to them they were only away for one year but then one day they reached land and one of them oared in and soon as he put foot on the sod his body turned to ashes.

Why always so grim, Colly? Can you not tell me a happy story?

Where would be the truth in it—isn't life just insult and woe?—sometimes you are better off facing up to misery and having a good laugh at it, there is no use pretending it doesn't exist—do you remember what happened to Ossian, how he had this great white horse and used to ride about thinking his adventure was only the length of three years but really it was three hundred years—hee!—the stupid fucker, found that out, so he did, when he went showing off, leaned over his horse trying to roll some great boulder, only to fall off his horse, turned there and then into an old man—but what I want to know is, if he never got down off that horse, how did he sleep, did he sleep sitting up on it or lying down holding on to the withers, and how did he do his business—you can imagine doing your number ones standing up on the horse but your number twos would no doubt cause the horse some bother, the horse almost certainly would object, buck you off, plain and simple—the very thought of it, how come nobody ever puts that into the story—I think if you are going to make up a legend it should at least be plausible—

Stop with it, Colly! Stop with it. My head is done in.

She sits for a long moment watching the wind harry the low branches. Then she says, I see what you mean, though. That's what I am. An Ossian or a Bran. If I go home to Blackmountain it will turn out that hundreds of years have passed. I'll go in the door and turn into an old woman and fall dead on my feet. Nobody will ever have heard of me.

III

The Wonder of Days

Her fingers root through mouldy straw for the oval-hard of an egg. Her ears hang by the door. Colly won't stop yammering. Did you ever think about the wonder of days? he says.

Shush, Colly. I think he can hear us.

Time—hee!—how it is arranged mechanically in such perfect fashion, how the hours number twenty-four and not a moment more of it, how there's not, like, twenty-five hours in a day, for example, unless you've got your head in a twist, isn't it a wonder, Grace, that no matter how many days go by the hours don't ever stretch past it?

Fuck up for just one minute.

She can hear the padding of a dog near the door. She has found an egg, puts her thumb over the sucky hole.

Imagine, Colly says, you can live your whole life and a day will never fall short of its hours, it would make your head fall off, how perfect the great minds have it worked out to the minute and the second, with the leap year and all, the celestial motions, the movements around the sun, that the hours keep perfect so that even when you wake from sleep it is always the right hour when you stir up, that's what I found when I had a loan of Nealy's watch that time, and yet if you ask me—

Shush up! I can hear that dog.

—dreaming is a tricky business because all dreams are timeless, aren't they, them learned men might have figured out time but they haven't yet figured out what kind of time happens in dreams, and memories also, you never hear people talking about that, do you—I don't think there's one kind of time at all, I think there's many, I'll bet that—

Colly!

What has come by the door is a hound large enough to wolf off her head. The inward dark of the barn keeps her hidden but she will be betrayed by her smell, she knows it. The hound enters and she backs away slowly until she touches the wall, waits for some gobbling woof. But all the dog does is judge her. It is the saddest of looks, as if the dog can say, I can see you in the dark, I know what you are up to, stealing eggs, but I can also see that things are not going so well for you right now and anyhow, you smell like a nice person.

She watches the dog with one sullen eye and sucks the last of the egg. How it is, she thinks, that some dogs can remind you of a person. She steps towards the dog and rubs its meaty head.

Colly says, that hound was only curious—do you think, Grace, that if the sun were to move backwards or forwards in position that it would change time, that the days would grow longer or shorter—that if something were to suddenly happen to the sun and it moved farther away that I would grow less, that I would be stuck at this height for longer?

She has walked deeper into the deep of the world, spent nameless days on these nameless roads that twist and turn with no ending. There is such weight in this sky, she thinks, clouds of ashes as if the heavens burnt out. In the west she can see far-off lakes that look like mealcakes if you see them in a certain manner, some great river slowing through them.

Colly says, that would be the river Shannon.

She says, and how would you know?

He says, because it is a fact.

She dreams her old self. Thinks, I am sliding out of my life, sliding into the life of another. And yet you must walk on because there will be something better and there is nothing but trouble waiting for you back home. She has dreamt of Boggs and Mam and that Donkeyface Boyd fella in angry colloquy. She dreams of Clackton. Sees him on the road, his little appearances, turning up in the faces of others. She has seen the back of Clackton in the shape of a stranger curling and uncurling his hands. Seen Clackton's slumping mouth in the wrinkled infant face of an elder. At night he haunts her with gibberish talk, sits her on his lap, runs blood hands through her hair.

Colly reckons them cattle-thieving bastards are long gone back to Donegal. She can see them walking the northwards roads with their hands dripping blood. But still, she says. We must go south. Keep pushing on, just in case.

In every ditch she sees shadows that might leap to kill, cuts at shadow-men in sleep with her knife.

Colly says, keep your eyes open for forage. But the cottier fields are cabbaged clean and every ditch is stripped of its nettles. Even the chickweed that Mam used to soothe the rashed botties of the youngers is being sold in handfuls. Women calling to strangers waving fistfuls of the herb. For your soup, they say. She counts the months that have passed since the failed harvest. Can see that the wintering has only deepened in spring. So many fields now along these roads lie unbroken by harrow. They are returning to an ancient wilderness, she thinks, as if nature were weeding the workingmen from her fields. Such men now walk the roads following the devil's footsteps. In their slump-walk you can see them coming slowly undone. How they look like they are losing both their inwardness and outwardness. Or those too weak to work sit about watching the road. How they always ask first for work before getting to what they really want. Have you the kindness of an offering? Can you spare a coin? She is growing indurate to what is held in the eye of such men. Men stood with that dead-staring of donkeys. Their faces eaten in.

How they watch you from the moment you rise from the road to the moment you disappear past them. You can tell a wild lot from the far-off of a walk. The rise of a foot. The slump of a shoulder. The hold of a head.

Who is and who isn't.

This year, every fool, it seems, is making Brigid's crosses, though the saint's day has passed. They sell them on the roads, some holding a single cross aloft, others hipped with baskets. They wave them at walkers, wave them at the drivers of gigs and coaches as if they expect them to stop, each hand movement unique to its waver and yet she reads each movement the same as every other — sees in it the gesturing of want or a person gone past want to a point that is longing narrowed down to the forgetting of all else. One fright-of-a-face young woman in a faded blue shawl steps alongside her, waves under her nose the musty smell of a cross. A younger on her arm with curled fists, just six months old, she guesses. The child's cheek pressed to her mother and drool-lipped, the outward face hot with bother. And yet the child seems oddly peaceful, more sunken than sleep. The woman's breath is rank, her voice tired. She says, it will bring you protection. Bring blessings upon your house. It will bring help to your people. How much will you offer for it?

The way this woman looks at her and for a moment she sees Mam in the look. She wants to speak as a girl plain and simple and yet she grunts at the woman to leave her alone. She looks at the basket as the woman walks away from her, sees that all the crosses are made not of rushes but of straw that should have been used to feed animals, and why didn't she sell the straw to somebody else who would need it?

Colly says, what protection could them crosses bring if they don't work for her neither, the state of her, she must have made them with her left hand.

The heat of shame she feels for the way she talked to that woman is like the heat of that child's cheek.

She sleeps a few nights in a broken-down church. The figures of five frightening faces carved in stone above the doorway. She dreams of hungering faces. Wind sounds coming out their mouths. Wakes to see the moon candling the stonework. Sometimes she lies thinking of what she has seen, the road now so full of trouble you can hardly look at it. She thinks, what is happening to the country? She has seen an entire family hilled together with their belongings on a passing cart, rooted together in silence like some old tree gone to wither. Or the sight of a man under a faltering sun dragging two youngers on a sack, the children sloped like sleepers. How Colly went on about the man's devil chin, that he was one of Satan's helpers taking the youngers off to drink their blood and eat them whole to the toenails. How she had to shout at Colly that the children were being taken for burial.

That same day she met a woman drawing water from a roadside well, the woman warning her to be careful. What she said — many's the time I lived on the road, took shelter along it, was given a bed of straw for the night. Took the hen's share of whatever was being offered. But not anymore. The doors are all closed. The customs are dying out because the people are frightened.

How she walked with the woman a little, caught the woman's hand sneaking into her satchel, pulled the knife on her. The woman giving her a defiant look then laughing high and strange at her. What she said — sure wasn't I only warming my hand?

Sometimes she wakes and hears whispering voices and cannot be sure if she has dreamt them or not. She has grown tired of waking with the knife in her hand, begins to imagine herself as a druid wielding magical powers, casting spells for safety. Colly making lists of the spells he has heard of.

What we need right now, he says, is some string, a candle, and a trinket—we can make a spell for bringing good fortune, only I canny remember the words to the spell, only what we need for it.

We've got string and a candle, she says, but where are we going to get a trinket at this hour?

What about the matchbox with your hair in it, do you still have it—didn't you wear it once?

What I could do with is a charm for beauty.

She hears Colly whispering some strange incantation.

She says, you're making it all up.

No I amn't, I can feel it shaking my arms, it's coming into power.

Colly's prattling is as long as the day. She watches the sky snapping shut. A great dog in the far-off growls but there will be no rain for a while yet. So into a town, a long street that busies into a diamond. Colly says, see these fellas, let me do all the talking.

She steps into a huddle of men and proffers an open palm among them. Says, I'll trade you this fresh-air mealcake for a pinch of tobacco, you would not believe how good it is—fresh as the morning's dew, go on, have a taste.

There are tough stares and a silence so long she wonders if trouble will come at the end of it. Then a man laughs and another shouts, I'll take a bite of your mealcake. He reaches for it and chews it laboriously, eyes the others and rubs his gut. Boysoboys, yez missed out. That was the tastiest treat I've had in a long while. The same man brings her pipe to life. Gives her a good pinch of tobacco. Says, what ways things, wee man? Welcome to Clones, County Monaghan.

She finds a wooden crate and drags it in front of the church and begins to holler at a half-empty street. I have a great new corrector for the hunger! It is called, ladies and gents, the fresh-air mealcake! It is quite the comforter. Would you like to try one? You, sir! Don't be wary, now, it is most moist and delicious! It is economical and not lumpen to the teeth! She watches the town give up some ghosts who gather around, faces that scowl judgement or gape without expression. Colly says, try that man there with the black lips and teeth. Hey, sir! Try one. Now give me a few pennies for it, it is so pure it will not rot your mouth like that baccy. The man stares with ill humour but another chuckles beside him and then others begin to laugh. One man begins to clap. That's right, he says. That's right. She says, I'll bet none of you has ever thought about the difference between time in the real world and time in your dreams, let me tell you—

Faces begin to frown and then the crowd breaks away leaving one woman standing, her face half hidden under a hooded cloak midnight in its colour. The woman eyes her up and down, steps forward with long fingers and tests with a squeeze the strength of Grace's shoulder, peers at her hair.

She says, you've not got nits, have you? I can't have some boy working for me if he's going to give nits to my dog. Let me hear you cough.

Then the woman says, and don't think I don't know you are a stranger in this town. I have no time for a blatherskite. Here, carry this and follow along.

She thinks, there are all sorts of reasons why a woman might pick a boy for work without knowing him. And who cares if it happens this way or that, all that matters is that the woman has flesh on her jowls and that she stands soft to the light not sharp like most others and that there will be some scrapings to feed on.

She whispers, Colly, that spell of yours is working a charm.

He says, if things go to cac you can always rob her.

The woman calls herself Mrs. Gregor. She walks with an ashy hand on her hip. She is stoopy and loud-breathing and sighs little complaints to nobody in particular and perhaps not even to herself. Colly reckons she is a rich miser, that she has a disease, that her cloak is so low her feet might not touch the ground, that she might be the pooka.

This walking going on now for at least an hour, the sun past its height staring down at a plate of hot food while the young hills in the far-off look like baking bread. They walk past a mill with its wheel stilled to the grabbing water and she feels a sudden thirst.

Colly says, did you see the big black spider on her cheek?

It looked like a mole.

It's a big black spider, I tell you, whispering to her instructions on how to eat us.

They begin up a hillock path that cuts through an idle pasture field and she can see between trees the off-white of a small farmhouse. Colly says, is that all it is? I was hoping for better. She hears herself sigh and hears the woman sigh also and perhaps this is the way of things, she thinks, that everything in life is disappointment and that even at this woman's advanced age you never get used it and you must be careful of having too many dreams.

The woman pushes open a crabby gate and the farmhouse stands grey and bereft in its own expression, the roof sunken and a cart wheel lying to the wall like some ruined drunkard missing half its limbs. An old dog taps its tail and rises with yawning slowness. Grace looks away in disgust, for the creature is lumpen with tumours. The woman turns and drops her hood and her face hangs bloodless like wax and perhaps a little younger than she has imagined and that thing on her cheek, Colly says, I'll bet her insides are full of spiders that come out at night.

The woman points for her to wait in the yard and she stands unsure what to do with herself, begins to play with her hands, watches the woman put a key to the door.

Colly whispers, I've changed my mind, I don't like the look of this place, let's turn around now before it's too—

But her nose is reaching towards the house, is reaching under the door, is reaching towards the smell of food.

In the creeping half-light she hurries water from the pump, hatchets wood into flitches. Now she stands sucking at a splinter. The woman watching, it seems, always from the window. Colly says, if you don't look at her you won't know she's looking. And yet she cannot help but turn around and look.

Everywhere on this farm is the absence of a man. Tools gathering dust and a pair of scuffed boots beneath the hollow arms of a man's coat hung by the latch door. A few trees have been axed on the hill and left coined in the yard and she wonders if it was the same man did the work and where he is now. She takes the splinter between her teeth and pulls it out, senses the woman behind her, reels around to that bloodless face.

Mrs. Gregor—Spiderwoman! Colly calls her—hands her nettle soap and points across the yard to the pump. Take off your clothes and wash, she says.

She can feel the watchy eyes upon her as she stands awkward at the pump, keeps her clothes on, begins to run the cold in bitter bursts. She holds her breath and douses, brings her head up to see Spiderwoman come abruptly behind her. She grabs Grace's wrist and takes the soap. Grace stands blinking water, can hear Spiderwoman scouring the soap into lather. She says, nothing I hate worse than nits. Work that pump, will you. The woman cat-grabs her neck and dunks her head under the water, pulls her back out, puts two hands to her head. Grace gasps then relaxes, for there is surprise in the touch, hands supple-soft that melt the skull like butter. Such soothe brings her eyes to swim and something comes undone. She feels that first feeling as old as herself. Through a dark she is a child again tubbed with her mother.

She is fed a quart of milk and stirabout with peelings and the smell is enough for heaven never mind the taste. She watches Spiderwoman boil hawkweed in a pot then strain it and leave it cool. This is for your cough, she says. She thinks, this Spiderwoman is some kind of herbalist, for there are jars of dried herbs and leafery on a shelf. She thinks of Colly's good-luck charm in that broken-stone church, thinks there might be something in it after all. For this food is better than scrapings. This food is the cat's comfort. This food is—

A man's low coughing can be heard behind a door. She turns in surprise, the coughing coming not from the bedroom she has seen Spiderwoman step into but a second room. She looks to Spiderwoman's face for an answer—a brother, a husband, a son, and why has he been hiding in the room all along?

Spiderwoman grabs Grace by the arm and pulls her towards her as if to shake such thought out of her head. Are those nits gone? she says. She produces a comb and begins to examine her. Why would you not undress and wash properly? A boy like you has nothing to be ashamed of. You are a bad boy but you are a good worker. Badness and goodness always mix.

So there is a man here after all, she thinks. She cannot help but sneak a look towards the door. Imagines someone scrawny and sick.

Colly whispers, I told you she was up to no good—she's keeping some old fellow locked up, lets her spiders feed on him at night.

She watches Spiderwoman light a tin lamp and follows the woman out into the yard the way that dogs do, upon the woman's heel awaiting some command to lift or move or haul, whatever you are asked, Spiderwoman walking towards the barn but of a sudden she stops and her arm comes up like some clock pulled askew. She whispers something that sounds like fright and she turns and grabs hold of Grace's wrist, begins to point down the darkening slope. Grace squints at the dusk, can just about see a man walking the far edge of a field as if he has been walking downhill from this house and then he is a shadow and then he is ditch and in the far-off she can make out a cluttering of mud cabins, three or four close together.

Spiderwoman begins to shake Grace's wrist as if it were Grace who was caught in some act of intrusion. She whispers, the first time I was nearly murdered it was by them below.

She turns and stares at Grace and her face has gathered into its expression the growing dark. Do you know what it is to wake in the night and think you are soon to be dead? To be tormented like that? To be living in fear on your own hill?

The way the woman begins to talk at her and Grace does not know where to look, for where can you look, she thinks, you do not want to look at the woman's big feet and you do not want to look at her head because Colly is whispering about her head being full of spiders, and you want to laugh even though the thought makes you squirm and anyhow how can you laugh if there are murderers about?

Them people, she hears Spiderwoman saying. They pass through my fields to taunt me, poach my wild rabbits, that Michaelín fellow, him and his half brother. I found him the other day standing right inside my yard. Right there where you are now. He said he was looking for his dog but his dog is this big. The blackthorn stick he carried with him. They bang the windows when I am asleep. They tap the door. They take from my supplies. They lift my vegetables and herbs. Two of my hens have gone missing. They are so clever about it. She turns and points to a far cabin on the low side of the hillock. Those others are gone now, them Conns, took away off wherever they went. They had better manners and kept to themselves but they had no religion so God's help was gone from their door.

She hands Grace the tin lamp and points towards the barn.

Take a sack from the shelf on the left as you go in and fill it with straw. You can sleep in the house beside the dog. He is the cat and you are the rat, that's what he will think. You are the rat drinking the cat's milk.

She stands at the door of the barn trapped in some aspic of thought, looks towards the sky's vanishing light. She thinks, how easy it would be to run away from the fact of this woman with her strange talk and that man locked up in that other room and that mole on her face that seems to have grown bigger these last few minutes, the little hairs wriggling into legs, the legs beginning to— she swings light into the barn as if expecting to see the face of some stranger, rests the lamp on a stool and rubs at her wrist, this feeling that the woman's hand has defiled her.

Colly fumes at her. Get out now, you silly bitch, that woman is nothing but trouble.

She sits on the stool and lights a snug pipe. Says, here, take a toke and be quiet. She sucks on the pipe and says, how long is it since we got fed like that? What price can there be to pay for it? A bit of silliness, that's all. That woman is just lonely, an ugly old saint being kind to us.

Colly says, I'll tell you what she is, she's Saint Hairy of Spider, that's why she's so strong and well fed—hee!—at night all the spiders climb out and run wild over the countryside sucking the blood of animals, sucking the blood of that man behind the door, so watch out while we're sleeping, mark my words, we'll stir up only to find ourselves a pair of shrivels with our blood sucked out.

She goes to the barn door and stares downhill. Through gloom the distant cabins push dark smoke into the almost-night and she takes a quick peek around the corner. There is Spiderwoman painted into dark, watching her from the window.

Her stomach tightens when she hears Spiderwoman bolt the door of her bedroom, the sound of a man's coughing coming from behind the other door. She tries to imagine who he is, some sick son or husband, or a person like you, Colly says, taken from the town and now held prisoner. She beds down by the dim fire listening to the dog eyeing her in the dark. How thoughts stir strangely together, thoughts of sleep beside that damned dog's damp smell, thoughts of strange men sneaking about and rattling the windows and threatening to kill and she imagines them watching her now through the window, thinks about what the woman has said and the way she said it, that perhaps what sounds is just loneliness.

She lies listening to the night's noises. That is the sound of the house settling and it is not the sound of men stealing by the house, the prowlers taking a hen, getting ready to tap the window in delight. She can see herself waking in the night's empty hours, creeping about the room and filling her satchel, stealing out the door. Takes hold of the knife just in case.

She wakes—blindness and the sound of a soft-pressed foot—does not know the room—BlackmountainRathmullanBooleyhut—the knife real in her hand. Another foot softing the hearthstone and she can hear the ride of a long breath. Not rats and not the half-dead dog smelling beside her and not murderers but Spiderwoman. The woman's breath giving presence to her figure stood in the room such a long while now, and she can feel the look of watching. Then the woman is moving, makes a soft *clink* sound, her breathing loud, the woman stepping into her room leaving the latch door open and why is it she doesn't use a candle?

Colly whispers, Saint Hairy of Spider, millions and millions of spiders wriggling around inside her.

She lies staring at the dark and what she can see is an image of herself rummaging blindly for food and then leaving out the door but the walls of the house are watchers also and amplify every sound. And then it occurs to her that this is probably what the woman was doing all along, taking the food she left out into her room.

Let's hope, she thinks, that is all the woman wants and not something else, not the company of a boy in her bed, for there are stories of such things. That way she keeps resting her hand on me.

Days are spent hewing and hauling wood, the ax swing burning holes in her fingers. Colly keeping watch over the storebox of winter vegetables and the cabbages still unpicked in her garden. Spiderwoman's watchy eyes creeping into thought so that Grace begins to think the woman knows her thinking, for she knows too the woman's thoughts, the gap in a stare that could fill a well with loneliness, that judging look that shouts, you are starting to smell like a tinker, why is it you will not undress to wash?

She fangs the ax too deep into the wood and cannot shake it out, wrestles with it and curses and kicks at it and a man's voice says, that's hardly going to loosen it. She looks up to see the face of some murderer, the hen stealer, stepping across the field towards her with a jaunty look. He stands by the gate and her body becomes wood and she looks to the ax useless as a weapon, looks behind her for the watching eyes of Spiderwoman.

The man greets her with a touch of his hat and she can see how his clothes are patched all over so that he is made up of not one suit but a hundred suits and of as many colours as there are suits and there is a smile in his eye she knows is not danger.

He says, where did you appear from? Would you like me to unfix that ax for you?

She thinks about letting the man come into the yard, thinks about what would happen if Spiderwoman saw such, waves at him to go away.

The man shrugs and begins down the fields and shouts over his shoulder, keep your legs wider than your shoulders.

Spiderwoman is waiting with the nettle soap, puts the bowl angrily onto the table. She says, take off your clothes and wash. Grace goes to the pump and begins to wash her face and hands, looks up to see Spiderwoman gliding across the yard in her cloak. She comes behind her. Take off your clothes, I said. Grace continues to wash but will not remove any clothing. The woman takes the soap and lathers it and puts her hands rough to Grace's hair. Her voice has cut in it. She says, just be warned, boy. Whatever you are planning, I sleep with a gun in my bed.

The food tonight is some awful slop, she thinks. A pig would not put his snout in it. She devours it and licks her teeth and wonders now if she should leave soon-as, get one last night of warm sleep and go.

This guilt feeling that comes upon her as if the woman has reached into her thoughts. Spiderwoman is sulking at her, sits silently in her chair pulling at her shiny fingers like rosary beads. How her eyes seem to have become smaller while that thing on her face has grown bigger. Without word Spiderwoman quits to her bedroom before dark and bolts the door and a moment later she opens the door again and huffs into the room for a jug of water, returns to her room.

Colly whispers, silly bitch forgot to bolt the door.

How Grace wants to tell her, it wasn't my fault, it was only a man I talked to not some murderer.

She would also like to tell her to go and fuck herself.

Colly says, she's just an auld grumpy bitch, it's the same sulk Mam used to get into, she will feel better in the morning.

She thinks, all I did was talk to the man for a moment.

She thinks, all the things I can do for her.

She half wakes woven with the voices of women familiar yet unknown to her, faces that become like dim memory sliding into all that is hidden. Yet Sarah's voice remains, and so she must go to her, rising from the dream through half dream, stepping through the murmured darkness, her feet soft upon the hearthstones lit with the dawn's roseate. The dog opens an eye to watch as she steps through the latch door into the other room, the room near dark and the room known and full of old faces, stepping now towards the high bed, pulling at the covers and climbing into it, putting an arm around her mother. Of a sudden the figure of Mam goes stiff and arms shoot out to fight the blankets. Some guttural sound escapes from a throat that opens into an animal noise as the figure flees the bed. What comes to Grace is an alert and awful knowledge, that she has climbed into Spiderwoman's bed. Slowly she climbs back out and steps towards Spiderwoman, who stands as if cornered by the wall, goes towards her with her hands out trying to cancel what has just happened, trying to explain with her hands what this is, that it is not herself but her sleeping self that has caused this trouble, searching the dark of her mind for an expression of truth but the truth is she does not know how this has happened, her mouth wood and then Spiderwoman finds her voice.

Defiler! she shouts. Defiler! Thief! Murderer! Help!

The dog starts up its heavy old woof like the awakening chime of a grandfather clock and it is then that she runs, jumps over the dog, jumps over her thoughts of the sick man in the room, grabs hold of her boots and satchel, turns the key and unlatches the door and flees outwards, can hear behind her the woman's screams and shouts, the cold stinging her ears as she runs out the gate and then she stops after a shout from Colly, turns around and runs back to the garden and pulls a winter cabbage. Leaves on the path behind her a bread-crumb trail of earth.

Her steadfast walk slows to a stroppy shamble. Her head lowered into tussling thoughts. She wants to sit down, kicks at a rotten fence until it crumples. Finds a rock to sit on. Gnaws a little on the raw cabbage.

She tells herself she has escaped the slavery of that woman. Tells herself what just happened did not happen, that it was all a dream. But Colly is wild with laughter. That was lively, wasn't it, the face on that woman!

She sits and stares into some deep horror, this void in herself—what winged up out of the dark and carried her along.

She says aloud, how could you think she was your mother?

Night riders! Colly says. That's who it was!

The who? she says.

The night riders. They come when you are asleep and trick you just like the pooka.

She sits wondering how it can be so that you can still be yourself and not be yourself at all in the same moment, tries to think of her earlier self walking into that room but that walker was another.

Clones is beset by something unknown that shapes a strange quiet. The doors are all closed and the beggars keep to the shadows. Colly yammering on about selling more fresh-air mealcakes in front of the church but then he stops. Two constables stand in front of a grain store and one of them is looking at her or looking past her and her legs thicken with sudden weight.

She thinks, what if Spiderwoman somehow got to the town before us? She imagines the woman standing with that spidered face pointing her out to a detective.

Colly shouting, holy fuck, muc, take a look at that!

She steps towards a tumbrel tipped sideways onto the street. Its horse lying broken-necked in the arms of its shadow. She is met with the feeling she has dreamt all this, her feet on the street, the constables' watching faces, this feeling of being caught, this feeling of the dead horse, and then the feeling passes. It is then she knows the policemen aren't watching for her but are watching the town because trouble has struck.

She steps behind the two officials and sees that the last look of the horse was at the suddened sky, sees somebody has butchered meat off the horse's hind. A constable turns and shouts something at her and she hunches away puzzling at the policeman's words, his strange accent.

Get last, yes kite. Get lost, you skite.

The town diamond is strewn with loose straw and masonry and almost as many official men and soldiers from the barracks. The people are beginning to stir up, Colly says. Some kind of gathering or protest has turned violent. She watches two children swing from wrought-iron railings. Sees the sky sit in a shop window with a jagged hole of broken glass as if the heavens could rupture.

A detective stands in a doorway talking to some elder and then he takes a look at her and steps towards her and she thinks of the cabbage in her satchel, wonders how Spiderwoman could have gotten word so quick, the man and his immense height then upon her but she is surprised by his voice. It is gentle like an old teacher.

He says, where are you coming from, young fella?

She has never stared fully into the face of a detective, sees behind the man's eyes the faceless absolute of power and how it can take you out of your life and send you away to Australia. Words form in her throat, words that might say, it was only the cabbage I took, I swear, I can go back and replant it. But out goes her hand and she offers the detective a fresh-air mealcake, plain enough, sir, but still a good chew on it. The detective's face as still as stone but his mouth betrays the wrinkle of a laugh. He says, if you know what's good for you, you'll get gone from this town.

The wind slings a bitter cold from the east. And what month is this? she thinks. The sky shaped like winter and yet it is supposed to be spring. She is done for now with slavery and madwomen and done with the towns, their watchy officials prowling about, looking at you as if you were the cause of all trouble. She will ghost the farmyards at night under the noses of dozing watchmen, pass the days asleep in barns.

It is such luck, she thinks, to find a laddered hayloft without a single soul asleep in it. It sits at the remote side of a farm half a day's walk from Clones. She does not count the days here, carries the smell of musty straw about her as she makes her nightly prowls. Stealing oats from horses, leftovers from the dog's bowl. Lying idle during the day having to listen to Colly. Riddle me this. Which is faster, hot or cold?

She wakes one night seized with knowledge of another. She has learned to listen, how to map the dark with shape-sounds. Knows this is a man, heavy-footed, nosing about, something being pulled at, imagines hands padding about in thick-coated blackness. The bustle of a man alone with himself, breathing heavy as he beds down. Her hand eases from the knife. She thinks, keep a total quiet, do not even breathe a sound. The stranger turning and then turning again and what follows is a serrated cough that has no end to it.

Finally she sits up. Would you mind, mister, stopping that cough of yours?

It is a frightened man that hinges up. How he comes to be out of that dark by match light. A thin fellow leaning forward, blinking in the flicker-soft, the whites of his eyes made yellow. Hup! he says. What are you trying to do, scare me out of my own shadow?

Be careful with that match or you'll burn the loft down.

He puts it out on his tongue. Are there others here or is it just you?

Colly says, have you got any baccy?

The man says, you don't have anything to eat, do you? Here, give me your pipe.

She reaches the pipe across and the man grabs hold of her wrist. You're not dangerous, are you? You're not going to bite?

He lets go the wrist and does not see how she holds the blade in line to his heart.

I can tell you're a grand fellow. Hup!

His name is Blister. She smokes with him in the dark, listens to his lips make a pop sound as he finishes each toke. Watches him with her ears as he beds down in the straw, the endless rustle of a man trying to get comfortable, his cough keeping her awake.

By daylight she sees he is ageless and has filed sharp edges to his teeth. His yellow eyes signing some private madness. His body tells a story of the road, she thinks, his face run with scars and his knuckles burst and how he likes to burn matches down to a black thumb and finger. He lifts his shirt to show her the bruising mapped on his body. He says, all they got was me matches, whereas I gifted one of them a mouth in the back of his head. Hup!

The main rule, Blister says, is get yourself the face of a dog. Carry a file with you and work your teeth down. Look at my teeth as an example. You want to look more frightening than anybody else. That way trouble will take a look at you and run off. Filing your teeth also gives you something to do at night when you have nothing else to be doing.

Another rule. Slow travel. No point rushing your way along the roads because the man who is in haste misses his own life. All them new people you see out on the road know nothing about travel. They go about the place with a blind look. Better to walk slow along the road and listen to the chatter of the trees and the birds and you might learn something. You'll also see opportunity when it is presented.

Another rule. Always wash in cold water. It has long been known that washing in cold water cures aches and pains. It also keeps you free of disease. But you must make sure it is clean water and not brown water from the bog because that stuff carries deposits in it that go under the skin and eat the brain. If I seem a bit strange in the head that's because I grew up in a place where there was only brown water.

Another rule, and speaking of impurities, stay away from iron, pig iron in particular. I don't know why that is. Don't go near it, sit on it, or touch it. It has transferrable impurities that cause agitations beneath the skin. And headaches. Many's the headache I got from leaning against an old fence.

Another rule. Be careful what wells you drink from. Sometimes there are animals with disease that have fallen into them. They lie there rotting themselves into the water causing pollutants so that what you are drinking is the disease that killed the animal. I know at least two people who died from the brain rot that was caused by plagued cattle. I would say take a good smell of the well first if you are able. Then examine the water.

Another rule. There aren't any rules. Hup! Things are getting worse now. The country is starving. The world is going to fuck. The old times are done for, do you know what I mean? We're going into the getting-worse part. That's what I think. But whatever God almighty in heaven wants He can have it, so long as He looks after old Blister.

At night she listens to him talking to himself, gibberish words, conversations with dead people. Then comes a night when some person—a man, she thinks—is heard trying to climb into the loft. She takes hold of the knife, wonders if Blister has invited some friend up to rob her. Blister creeping towards the loft door and then she hears a thump and a grunt and then shouts of abuse.

Blister whispers, I just kicked some cunt off the ladder.

She is certain she can hear in the far-off the crying of an infant. Or perhaps it was a cat, she thinks, you cannot sometimes tell the difference.

She thinks of the old travellers' tales she heard by the fire in Blackmountain, people passing the night in a stranger's house, always the offer of accommodation and comfort. People inviting the pooka in the guise of strangers into their house, such was their hospitality. How those days are gone or maybe it was all made up, and wouldn't it be nice to give shelter to everybody from the cold, but how can you be sure they aren't night crawlers who will rob you even if they have with them a child?

Blister sleeps by the door—just in case, he says, there might be more of them. Have you got a stick or something? You must guard where you sleep with your life. You let me in but you are a rare good one. If you let them in they will rob you and probably cut you. You must show them who's boss.

She wakes to the sound of Blister rustling through her satchel. Enough noise to wake the big house, never mind his cough. She waves the knife into his face and he backs away from her.

He says, so you had a knife all along. I'm just keeping you on your toes, young fella.

She watches him back away to the loft door, then he begins to move down the ladder. When he is just head and shoulders he stops with a smile and she thinks she might always remember his face, how his mouth is cut with furious teeth and yet how he cannot hide that look of loss in his eyes.

He shouts, keep warm, young fella! I can smell trouble in the weather. Tell them all Blister says hup!

Colly says, just wait and see, he'll come back tonight with others. And so she walks until she finds an outhouse on a narrow farm where the floor is dry and that will do and there are shadows enough by day to hide her. She can feel a knife-point turning in the weather, for each night now is colder than the one before, and who was it said this was spring?

She lies on an old rug mottled with mould, holds the blanket tight to her neck, pulls jute sacks on top of her. And still the cold walks in the door and climbs on top of her and reaches through the floor with its grabby hands. She lies awake thinking of the morning to come and ignores what creatures scurry over her.

Quiet as a mouse during the day, for the farm belongs to some rough man. When he steps into the outhouse she stands in the corner holding her breath. Watches him send away stranger after stranger from his door, spalpeens or whatever, asking for work or a bite to eat. Watches him sitting on a stool in the corner of the yard tending a harness, his fingers steady and patient but quick and rough with the necks of his children, pushing and pulling at them, shouting at them like dogs. How she would love to go to his door but you cannot ask anything from such a bruiser so she pockets loose parts of a plough to sell later in a town, plans to leave in the morning. When she wakes in the dawn Colly begins at her. Hurry up, muc, he says, I need a leak. She steps sleepy from the outhouse and does not hear until too late the footsteps that come behind her, meets unseen a fist that drums sudden the world to darkness.

* * *

When she comes to be again out of her own dark it is to the probing of a stick. She blinks into pain-light, closes her eyes, sees the burning of stars and the stars burning out and renewing like some fantastic vision if there wasn't so much pain behind it. Some younger, a wee girl, her face a frozen blue, is standing over her. She sees the sun is high and hidden behind cloud, knows half the day has swung past. The girl is poking her in the thigh with a twig, keeps saying some unintelligible thing. *You are going little please. You are going little please.* It sounds to her like some childish rhyme. The girl is wearing a gown made of horse flannel.

Pain slices at her head as she tries to sit up. Ugh, she thinks. I've been axed in half! I've been decapitated! She squints at the girl and then shouts at her, get away with you. Sees farther down the road the watching eyes of another child, a little boy. What's that you're saying, wee girl?

It is then she sees the farmhouse has disappeared. Gone as if it has fallen into the nothing she has just woken out of. This place different. Gone is the low hill that rose away from that narrow farm. Just flat tillage fields and not a single hill in the far-off and she cannot understand why she is covered in mud and leaves. There comes a lurching nausea as she tries to stand up, the world slantways to her vision.

She thinks, I've been boxed in the head! That brute of a thing carried me here. Colly? Colly! Where are you?

Colly says, my head is splintered.

What did they do to me? Were we carried here on a cart, do you think?

She touches her body as if afraid to find something broken. It is only her head that hurts.

Colly says, I think we were dragged through the ditches, dragged like an auld sack.

She can tell the little girl is afraid of her, watching this mud-boy trying to stand up on the road, leaning strangely, retching on an empty stomach. The child stepping quickly towards her and waving her stick like some occult wand, uttering the same unintelligible thing, the words sounding to Grace like some evil charm of strange undoing and surely that is what this is. The girl runs off but leaves her words hanging. As Grace wipes the twigs and leaves from her body she understands what the girl said.

You are growing little trees. You are growing little trees.

She stands and stares dazed and dumb at the road. When she begins to walk the thought strikes like a second fist. Where is my blanket, Colly? My satchel? Where have they gone to?

She runs back to where she found herself, searches the road and ditches.

He says, you must have left it in that outhouse.

She eyes the sky and the nameless fields but the world has come undone of direction. There is only the sun to follow. She puts her hands to her head. Her voice a whisper. It's gone, I don't have it, it's taken. She searches her mind for even a shadow of the man who struck her but there is only mystery, silence, darkness. She searches her pockets. She still has the knife but the plough parts she stole have been taken off her.

Tell me, Colly, what is real and not real? What is natural and unnatural?

Is that a new riddle?

She wants to be angry with herself for being so stupid. She wants to feel angry for being fooled all the time. She wants to roar out for what the cold will bring in the absence of a blanket. But what comes instead is laughter rich and thick and easy as breathing and Colly can't help but laugh with her. They walk along the road, roaring with laughter under a starling sky, the birds vibrating in their single shape with darkness and light.

She thinks, laughter itself is a riddle. The way it hurts your chest yet brings such pleasure. It leaves you as hollow as a drum and yet feeling full.

She watches the starlings take the form of a rain cloud and then scatter into giant raindrops, an augury of what soon comes — rain in downswings heavy enough to soak her. She hunches into her walk, moves like something sunken. Colly starts giggling again when she finds an evergreen to sit under.

This giddiness has to stop, Colly.

And then they are off again, giggles that soar into laughing whoops, fall to earth in a wheeze. She laughs because everything is so wrong. She laughs because she no longer knows what is real and what not real. If people are who they say they are. If anything that is said has meaning. If everything is a trick, the whole world just some made-up story. Perhaps this is what growing up is like. This is what they don't tell you. That the realness of the world is its lies and deceit. That the realness of the world is all you can't see, all you can't know. That the only good in life is your childhood, when everything is known for certain. She laughs so hard she no longer knows if she is laughing or crying, or if the two of them are really the same.

She understands it remotely before it travels as thought. First to eyelash, then to chin. Feels it wetly on a knuckle. From out of the forever the sleet-fall comes. She watches with horror as it descends in lazy fashion. Spring is clocking backwards, she thinks. You must keep going. You must grin and bear it. Don't grit your teeth or the cold will grip your muscles. Colly, sing me a song!

But Colly has gone quiet. She walks with a hand nursing the hurt in her head, watching the sleet become snow.

Finally, Colly says something but it is only a whisper.

She says, what did you say?

He says, I said, so this is what the end of the world looks like — I always wondered.

* * *

The open country is hasped under hulking clouds that harry snow upon it. A company of cabins off-road and she knocks at every door but only one door opens to a closed face. Take a good look at yourself, Colly says. You're covered in blood and muck. So quickly now has she been run through with cold. The road an immensity of quiet.

Into view comes a work yard that sits in crumpled silence. She sees slag heaps beginning to whiten, work huts that could provide shelter, perhaps a fire. She looks for signs of smoke. Of a sudden two black dogs zip towards her all snapping teeth and she is barked away from the fence. She spits at them, sees an old jute sack caught in the mesh, pulls at it with colding fingers and cauls it over her head.

She passes a whitening graveyard that slopes in solitude away from the road. She thinks, where there is death there must be people. She squints to read some of the tombstones as she passes. Fulton. Dykes. Platt. A man called Wilson Stringer. What kind of name is that? The year of his death 1762. Tries to travel her mind back such distance, a world so strange and old-fashioned, tries to imagine this Wilson Stringer, how he would have borne himself upon this road. Pictures a stranger in silly clothes that turns out to be Clackton. He doffs his cap and smiles with blood teeth. Get away, you, she says.

For some time now, she has had peace from Clackton. She thinks, what would Clackton do now if he were leading their little group?

She says to Colly, nobody walks the road in this weather but the dead, and even then, I haven't seen or heard a single ghoul.

He says, I wouldn't be so sure about that—what makes you think you could tell the difference?

Her teeth are beginning to click out a jig. She quickly pumps her fists.

Grace.

What?

Do you know something?

What?

This is no way to live.

There'll be someplace just around that far corner.

I just thought I'd tell you before we die of exposure, before we're found under the snow—here lie the remains of two thick-as-fucks, may they rest in their own stupidity.

Thanks for the reminder.

And do you know something else?

What?

This is no way to live.

She eyes a farmstead nestled into a whitening hill. Watches the snow laying quiet upon quiet, sees herself knocking at that door or sneaking into a hayloft until her thoughts are met with the report of a gun or the shadow of a fist and she finds herself walking onwards, for there is no room in such houses for the likes of you. This worry now that wriggles like a worm in your gut. Trust you to find the loneliest place in Ireland.

Grace.

What?

This is no way to live.

She comes upon the cabin and knows it is abandoned and even if it's not you are going to go in. The way it stands smokeless in the snowy air, holds its own silence. She had taken a turn off the road, followed a track hoping for a townland. Dreamt of some four-square of white-washed houses and the North Star glittering in the snow-bluing light and firelight winking in the windows, a voice calling out, come in and get yourself warmed. Instead she has found mazed country, everything taking the same erasure of white, the track and the hedgerow and the bramble thorning through it. Colly saying, you're on the wrong path, so then she took another. And then out of the white it came, the sight of a mud cabin in front of a wood watching over distant ploughland. The middle of nowhere, she thinks, and this is what bone-cold means and this cabin must do.

Colly says, go up and knock just in case.

Keep you quiet.

She clears her throat as she approaches the door, knuckles seven times for good luck.

In the wait for a sound the darkening trees issue silence. Something flits, she does not know what—dark, like what forms feeling before thought but not the thought thing.

She says, there's nobody in it.

Of a sudden Colly's voice tightens. Grace, I don't like it, I said I don't like it one bit, let's—

She thumbs the latch.

I want to go home to Mam and the others.

Would you ever quit with your fluster?

Hello? she calls. Doorlight maps the gloom into quiet, the mud walls and the thatch sooted and so turf-smoked that the reek of how many years' burning is marked into this place—like the echo of all fires and that echoing made stark by fire's absence—dampness, and how the room receives her with such astonishing loneliness, the door uneven on its hinges, and as one foot steps slowly inward she senses the emptiness of the hut, senses as if all the world were suddenly emptied of people and what that world would be like—the silence of nature, how greenery grows to take place-name back into itself, as if all knowing had never existed and the shadows cast were not the shadows of fire and lamplight but the dark of what the sun has abandoned—all this in a single moment of thought by the door, and much in that same instant her eyes alight upon half-forms in the dark—a single chair and a burnt-out fire, a Brigid's cross on a bare crockery shelf, a picture upset on a nail and cast into its own dark—hello?—and then, over all things, through all things, through the dust and the damp and the dark—Oh!—a stench that now comes to her as inhuman and brutal, dominating the room—Oh! Oh!—her mind stepping back before her body is able to, footing backwards out the door and her shadow shrinks into the light as if she is meant only for this life and this light and not the other darkness within, backwards into the clean cold air, sucking and sucking it down deeper, her mind reaching for an answer—Oh, Colly! Oh! Oh! Oh!—the smell, and a strange sweetness mixed up in the smell, a smell like nothing she has ever smelled before, as if sweetness can be at one with evil, and she knows upon smelling it she will never forget it, that it is a message of death, and she knows that what Colly is saying to her is wrong, that it is not the smell of a rotting animal, that it is—Oh! Oh! Oh!—for she knows now this smell of death is a person.

She stands squeezing her hands open and shut. Will not open her eyes.

Yes you are.

No I'm not, Colly.

But you must.

I can't. I won't. I will not.

You will.

Hmmph.

It's either that or sleep in the snow, I'm frozen, we'll die out here, it was your idea all along.

But you said you wanted to get away from this place.

No I didn't.

Colly is quiet a moment. Then he says, it's only a body.

What do you mean it's only a body?

It's a body under a blanket, there's nobody about, if it were a dead dog or a dead hedgehog or whatever, would you have any bother dragging it out, would the smell of it bother you then?

You're not making a single bit of sense.

Listen to me, now, they're both the same thing, it's logic, we learnt it at school.

She sighs. It is not logic. It's a person.

Colly is going on now about something else, but she doesn't want to listen. She shakes her head and begins away from the cabin.

The snow has saddened everything away, saddened away hope and goodness. Rags of snow thicken her lashes, burr cold to her face. She watches a lone farmhouse far in the glen that sits like something painted, can make out a window of light upon a room that is dry and warm and people eating but no welcome for me, no doubt. This creeping cold. My clothes growing damp to the skin. The fields without motion and how the bare trees could teach you resilience, holding still throughout, waiting for the season to right itself. But the trees don't get cold, she thinks, and me here like some scarecrow getting snowed on. Of a sudden she is met by a vision of herself living as Sarah. Mam before Boggs ruined her. An image of herself as woman, full-chested. Clean and happy with herself. A crackling fire all warm. Making do. Finding forage in the wood.

She does not know what it is but something moves as if to escape from inside her, some enormous frustration or sorrow.

She turns around, begins back towards the cabin.

It is Colly who sees it. That spade there beside that dunghill.

Later, she does not remember how she spaded the corpse onto the jute sack. Her eyes shut and watering to the smell, her coat knotted to her mouth. Leaving it down for a while then going back to it. What she hears is the hiss of the dragging sack as if the corpse were hissing at her. How weightless it is. Light like dragging a sack of sticks, that's all it is. Light like pulling one of the youngers along, the way you used to pull Bran along on the sack down the heather, racing down the hill. She enters the wood and her sight falls full upon the body and her stomach twists an empty retch. She casts her eyes in every other direction. Tries to tell herself that what is also isn't. And yet her mind holds a perfect picture—that what lies on the sack is a very old woman, dead as dead is, her body shrivelled to just a coating of skin, her rags falling away from jut-ribs. The face sideways and no hurt in it at all but enough of a face to haunt her.

How the mouth and teeth are green as if she died eating forage, her chin weirdly bearded.

She screams at Colly. Why won't you help me? Why are you being so useless?

Colly says, I can't — it's a witch, it is a dead witch you are moving — look at the hairy beard, I won't help you.

Pulling the sack towards the trees, veering away from the house. She thinks, a witch! Imagine the trouble that could come of it. Can a dead witch haunt you? Trying to speed along and get this thing done but the ground is knotted with roots that bump and then one of the bumps rolls the body face-forward off the sack.

Eooohhh!

She is afraid to look at it.

It's all your fault, Colly, she shouts. It's always your fault.

I will have nothing to do with a witch.

Having to spade the body back onto the sack again — Oh! Oh! — not even breathing now, for the smell she knows once inhaled will never leave her body, will corrupt her skin, will eat at her brain, eat her dreaming, this demon witch of an old woman that will live inside her —

Shut up! Shut up! Shut up!

The corpse prone on the sack as if asleep. Or just some dead old dog. It's Blackie you're dragging! That's it! That time Mam dragged him, do you remember? Up into the bog to bury him and then she came back down for the shovel and me hanging off your arm, and both of us pretending not to cry. That is what this is and I'm Mam and this is what grown-ups do and we can tidy the house and get it warm with fire and we will sleep the king and queen's slumber —

Twist and twist and twist of stomach until she bends and brings up mucus. Deeper into the wood now, wood-rot dusted with snow, twigs that crackle and click — Oh! Oh! — through the tops of the trees and how it looks as if the light of the world were coming undone into snow—Oh! Oh! Oh!—and then she can no longer do it, drops the sack down, staggers to the clearway. She falls to her knees heaving emptiness, rubs violently at her nose and her eyes with the back of her hand as if to undo seeing.

The stink. The stink. The stink. That witch's stink-rot has gotten its corruption inside her.

Colly says, leave it be, muc, it's in the trees, nobody will find it, nobody has to know but us.

Oh! Oh! Oh! Oh! Oh!

She thinks, this is a fine place, this is a fine place, this is a fine place, this is a fine place to live.

Colly says, open the window.

Whatever for?

To let the old woman's soul fly out, just in case it's trapped inside with us.

She has forgotten she is cold. The house stinks of death, she knows it, but what can you do? She thinks of Sarah airing Blackmountain, sending the youngers outside, the pair of them scrubbing till their hands grew stiff. She searches about. The place heaped with old rags and bottles that were of no use to anyone and she wonders if the old woman was mad. Beneath the smell of old woman and death there is also a smell of dog. She puts the old woman's bed tick and blanket to air by the door, leaves the door open to do its work. The last of evening's light reaching in carries a little snow like breath. She goes to the window. Would you look! Colly says. There are matches on the window shelf. The box is damp like everything else, for the roof drips its leaky snow-water and the walls have a sticky sweat. Three matches. That is all there is in the box.

She goes into another part of the wood and gathers sticks and wood dry enough to burn. Colly says, three matches! You'd better get the first one to light or we're done for.

The first match comes apart when she strikes it. She takes out another, holds it a minute, steadies her hand. She strikes the match-head but it crumbles. The box empty but one.

Colly says, fuckity-fuck them damp matches, you'll have to dry it out.

How will I dry it without fire?

Later, as she sits shivering in the chair, her knees to her chest for warmth, Colly says, mind what Mam used to say—if you are cold, go out and play on the track, it's better than nothing.

She leaps about. Works forgetfulness into it. Hurls her limbs about the small cabin. Unsleeves herself into rhythm and chant. A-huh-ya. A-huh-ya. A-huh-ya. Weeee! A-huh-ya. A-huh-ya. A-huh-ya. Weeee! I am the bringer of fire. I am the storm-wind. I am the crow who sits warm in his feathers. Colly clapping and chanting. She jump-scuffs her crown off the low ceiling. Cartwheels into a flop that wallops the wall. Falls over herself laughing. The woman's dead smell is everywhere around but at least now you are warm.

She sits at the doorstep letting the air do its work. Listens to the wild story of the night. This wait for tiredness. Wishing the smell out of the house. Wishing for nights of summer, when the sky is clear with stars to twinkle some suggestion of heat. In the glen below, the farmhouse winks each window to dark and the world closes around it. A short while later, Colly says, what in heaven is that? She maps the dark until she can see it, some strange orb of light traveling slowly. It has appeared, it seems, from the farmhouse but perhaps not. A yellowing mote that moves steady and in one direction like a cat's-eye caught by candle. She thinks, it is a walker's pace. Somebody out to check on animals in the snow. Then the light disappears.

Not a soul to be seen or heard, her mind a wandering stare through the night's dark. She is trying to unthink everything that has happened, all the trouble of the world reduced to black and stillness.

So this is what freedom is, she thinks. Freedom is when you are free to disappear off the earth without anybody knowing. Freedom is your soul in the emptiness of night. Freedom is this dark that is as great as what holds the stars and everything beneath it and yet how it seems to be nothing, has no beginning, no end, and no centre. Daylight tricks you into thinking what you see is the truth, lets you go through life thinking you know everything. But the truth is we are sleepwalkers. We walk through night that is chaos and dark and forever keeps its truth to itself.

The cat's-eye of light reappears and she watches it bobbling like hope towards the farmhouse below in the glen.

Colly says, he's a poisoner of horses—that's what he is.

It could well be a person up to no good.

Maybe it's not a person at all, maybe it's another witch and we're living in the valley of the witches.

Maybe it was the glowing eye of the pooka.

Maybe it is the work of a smuggler, or—hee!

What?

It's just somebody from that farmhouse gone to the outhouse for a dump.

To sleep now covered in rags that stink with the matchstick in her pocket. She closes her eyes and tries to name the night sounds, Mam's voice in her ear, for once you name the sound it no longer troubles you.

That is the breeze rattling the window. That is snow dripping through the thatch. That is— Colly, what is it?

Colly whispers, I'll bet you it's the witch.

She squeezes her eyes to listen better. Movement outside, the crunch of snow under hoof or foot. She hopes it is an animal.

I tell you, it's the witch!

So cold and yet she falls into a dreamless sleep that lasts until the old woman visits her. Shadow and then shape and then a voice scratched out of air, the sour breath as the woman leans over her—hey, wee girl, hey, wee girl, wake up—and she is aware of the voice first as her mother's, and then it is somebody else's—hey, wee girl, hey, wee girl, wake up—and she tries to wake herself, tries to shake and move her legs but they are still sleeping—wake up, legs!—or perhaps it is the witch lying on top of her, holding her down, and she refuses to open her eyes, wants to run blind out of the house, run into the morning sun and leave all this behind, and the witch's hand is taking her wrist and the witch is shaking her, saying something she cannot make out—do not look at her face!—but she opens her eyes slowly to see the wrinkled, wind-thin woman standing over her with that bearded smile and coins in the place of her eyes, whispers coming through her green and grinning mouth that sound like some raspy animal—do not listen!—the witch taking Grace by the throat and she cannot breathe and the witch is saying, this is a fine place, this is a fine place, but you must bury me first, you must bury me first—

She wakes shivering into the softening light.

Her coat is caught around her neck.

So it was a dog—a crazy circle of paw prints in the snow and everything white-carpeted and this supposed to be March, she says. She tries to still her chattering teeth, dreams of fire leaping from that single match, and if it doesn't, she will rain fire from the sky, scream fire from the trees.

She stops to listen—upon the air comes a distant grinding sound, perhaps the workings of a mill.

Colly says, if there's a mill nearby there's also a town, perhaps beyond that glen, could get ourselves some baccy and matches—my mouth is itching for tobacco.

She bundles old rags and builds sticks and wood around it. The match is brought lone from her pocket. She fingers it, says, it's dry now but I don't want to do it.

Colly says, this is how it's done.

The match flares and flames the tinder.

She says, it is a miracle.

He says, no, it is skill.

She ties twigs into a broom and cleans out the cabin. This is a fine place. This is a fine place. Now, Bran and Finbar, you sit down there. And sup on that nettle soup I made you. And don't move away from the fire. Bran, put that down! And Finbar, stop pulling at his hair. Finbar! Will you quit? Bran, put that down, I said.

Later, she says, what do you think of this place now, Colly? Do you think the smell is gone?

I'd say for the moment it's liveable.

She bundles firewood and finds a hatchet in the snow. Later, a dog comes to the door. It is the strangest-looking creature, half dog and half wolf by the looks of it. The dog watches her without soul in its eyes. She tries to coax the animal but it will not come, its ribby grey coat scuffed and balding. The dog with a funny sideways walk, wary, she thinks, as if it expects you to leap at it. It is then she sees healing upon the dog's neck a welt made by a knife.

What dreaming she wakes out of—a dream of a body and that she has caused its death, her mind shouting out, murderer!—for she has murdered the old woman and buried the body in the woods and yet for some reason she doesn't recall any of it until now in this dream, as if some child-self had done the work of killing and forgotten, a casual thought tucked away only to return in the dream as a sick-guilt feeling that haunts and devours her, as if a killing can be so easily forgotten—and now she knows where the body is buried because she can see it in the dream, and now she knows they are coming for her, Boggs-as-wolf hurtling in his anger-light and leading a mob, the roaring of their voices, their slash-hooks agleam in torchlight—and then she sees the rattling of a door, the door being kicked open, and she is in the arms of her mother—she does not know what she sees—sees men coming in, Clackton huge and staring at her dead-eyed, a man who is also her father, and they are all calling her name and they are calling the name of her father and she wants to tell them it was not her fault, that she does not remember, that her present self had no part in this, that it was something to do with her childhood, that it was her childhood self, and then she is running and running and running—

She opens the door. Dawnlight blankets blue the snow like muslin. The awaiting air rushes in honed and alert like an animal.

She thinks, that dream was not real. This is what's real, the here and now. She inhales and expels dream-guilt in a long hoarse breath. The barren air and the crunch of her boots as she goes to the wood with the hatchet. The snow sullied by dog prints and she can just about see the drag marks from the jute sack, faint now like the memory of what happened, she thinks, how memory layers on top of memory until horror becomes a half-remembered thing and not the horror itself, and perhaps you can pretend to yourself the horror didn't even happen, put it down to mind trickery.

You can do it. You can do it. And then you will be tormented no longer.

She stops to gag her mouth with her coat. A pair of robins plump with their own blood tick and whistle. She steps through the trees to the place of the body and what she sees is the dog resting its paws lordly like a lion upon the snow-powdered remains. The dog casts her a look of indifference, drops its head and continues eating. She gags and spins, turns and finds herself rushing at the dog with the hatchet high above her head, the dog ignoring her until she reaches it and boots it in the ribs. The dog yowls and flees into the woods.

She cannot look at what—

Cannot look at it.

That the dog would do this.

Colly says, that dog was getting its revenge, the woman tried to eat it, so she did, it is only natural for the dog to feed on her or the other creatures in the wood, for that's what they do, a dead person is all the same to them.

She hatchets the earth loose and then spades at it. It takes her all morning under a hidden sun while birds chitter around her. She can dig no farther than one foot down, this scrawl of rootwork like some ancient text, she thinks, and what might be written there, that there are ancient laws in every land of what is acceptable and not acceptable and you are trespassing now into some forbidden territory but what can you do, life has led you here.

Dragging without looking the jute sack into the trench.

Oh! Oh! Oh! Oh!

Her eyes closed as she kicks the earth over it.

Colly says, you'll need to put rocks on top to keep that dog and the others away.

Later, she returns and makes a cross with two sticks. Says to the old woman, you'll leave me in peace now, won't you?

Lonely the nights and days that follow and yet she wishes for nothing. The world forgotten, the days a simple pattern of living that hold a kind of truth. Long mornings spent in bed thinking about this dream of a life or sitting at the door talking with Colly, who complains for the want of baccy. Why won't you go into town? he says. She gathers wood and gleans herbs and takes water from a stream. Finds here and there some strange and bitter tuber she has no name for. Guesses it must be April, for the rains have come to pull colour from the earth that will bring forage to live on.

She has never let the fire go out. She has become good with a stone, brings down the occasional wood pigeon, climbs for magpie eggs, two for joy and one for sorrow. Makes tea with chickweed or hawkweed or dandelion roots. Sometimes eats a mushroom. Watches a trio of swans sound through the sky, their huge wingbeats wheezing sorrow.

She keeps to herself. That old woman's dog has not returned but there are other hounds that come along the track, sometimes a stranger too. She has seen families living in rough camp at the northern side of the woods, spalpeens, no doubt, and sometimes the trees echo with their talk and she hides and listens to them and sometimes she goes to their camp just to hear them, sits until the coming of night, their bodies winnowing into dark.

She dreams she is the dead woman, that she will live here now until her days are over and her younger self discovers her body, that this is her strange punishment. She cuts her hair and studies her face in the piece of looking glass and sees the deepening of her features, you look like some kind of boy-woman now. Holds the mirror to the sky. Sees it is almost summer.

She loosens her hearing like rope. That is a man's voice coming up the path and that is muffled laughter, a bird whooping in agreement, and then she hears a second man's voice. Without noise she hinges upright and lets go the hatchet, breaks into a run towards the woodland, crouches behind a holly bush. Shadows through thicket become the shapes of two men. A tall man dressed all over in black like a priest only he's not, she thinks, for he wears a layman's hat. The other man frowning, some kind of book or ledger under his arm. A heavy fist rattles the door. In the tree beside her a wood pigeon flutters and coos loudly as if awoken by the men and now it calls to them, look!

She eyes the bird with a shut-up look.

Colly whispers, that bird can be gotten with a stone, it's that close.

Shush up.

Let's kill it.

She thinks, my ears might fall off from listening. What will they see? The hatchet on the grass and the trickle-smoke through the hole in the roof. Perhaps they are rent collectors. A man's voice shouts out a questioning hello and his voice has a note of foreign in it. Of a sudden the stone flies up and she watches the bird fall through the tree in a horror of slowness. How it falls into a bush and begins to spasm and rattle. I got it! Colly says. The tall man steps by the side of the cabin. He shouts a loud hello.

She holds her breath, though Colly says, holding your breath is as useless in this instance as closing your eyes.

She watches the men go and yet continues to listen for them, watches the dark creep over the house, worries the fire will go out. Those men are gone for sure, Colly says. She reaches into the bush and takes the dead pigeon. Says to Colly, why are you always causing trouble? Do you think those men will come back?

Colly says, who knows what they will think when they see you living in that witch's house—they will think you killed her.

All night she is awake circling the thought. Just how will you explain it? They'll hang you in the town. That is what they will do.

Within the dream she is an ageless child trying to speak to Sarah, her mother present and yet not present, then into the dream comes the sound of the latch and she senses the shadow, how it steps into the room, the shadow leaning over her, the dread voice she has been waiting for, finds herself rising as if through water into the room's confusion and sees the tall man standing over her. Her mind shouts escape but his hand has taken grip of her elbow. The man says, now, now. We've only come to help you.

She blinks, wonders if he is going to kill her. The fully open door and the daylight reaching around the figure of another.

The knife, she thinks. Where did I leave the knife?

Big-man says, he's a bit thin but neat-looking. Born to the work, though. Needs a good scrub but don't they all.

She can see that Big-man's face in the half-light is lopsided, cankered by old illness, hears the bellows of a great chest, the other man by the door coughs into a handkerchief. Big-man pulling and prodding at her as if he were a doctor and perhaps he is, she thinks, and she eyes the sill where the knife sits. Big-man stands up and goes to the small window as if he has heard her thought. He wipes at the glass with his elbow.

Where are all the others, *gasúr? An bhfuil clann ar bith leat? Cá bhfuil do mhamaí agus daidí?*

Her tongue tangles in the sudden rush of thought. She hears herself think, if he was going to drag me out, he would have done so by now. The man begins nosing around the room and he picks up the pot and stares into it. What kind of bird is this? It looks like a—

She waits to be asked the question—what happened to the old woman? It will take two seconds at most to reach the knife.

Big-man turns towards the door. What's wrong with you, Mr Wallace? Are you afraid to step in?

She watches Mr Wallace wave his handkerchief. The saints and all their mercies, Dr Charles. That is a huge deal of a smell. It's like something—

Come on, now. It's hardly worse than what we met this morning.

She hears herself say, they're all gone out, master. Gleaning in the woods. Just the mam, sir, and the youngers. I'm minding the cabin.

She watches this Mr Wallace writing into his ledger. How many of you are there?

Five, sir.

What did you say your name was?

Tim Coyle, sir.

That is strange, I have another name on the list. It must be another cabin.

She hears herself giving to him the individual names of her family.

Big-man says, this man by the door is from the relief committee. Why aren't you out at the public works? You are of age, are you not? The best thing you can do for your family in these straitened times is to be out earning coin. It will see you right. Report there tomorrow—nine pence a day for a full man, but seven pence for you, isn't that right, Mr Wallace? Out past Cavan town near Felt. They are digging a road.

The other man peers in the door holding the handkerchief to his face, brings her to a suddening of anger.

She says, is there something wrong with the cabin, sir?

Big-man stares at her and then booms into laughter, turns to the man at the door. We'll get you into a cabin yet, Mr Wallace.

For two days she is smarting with Colly. On and on he prods, his voice a stick in the ribs. You are the most stubborn wee bitch I have ever encountered, a thick pig's neck on you, the backside of a mule has nothing on—

Oh shut up or I'll have you sent out of the cabin.

What's the word Mam used to say, *intractable*—hee!—that's what—

She shuts out his voice, thinks to herself, is that what I am? Intractable? How Colly's words twist with the same knife-tongue as her mother. Sarah always scolding at her—chiselling on and on, most of it pointless when all she was ever doing was being herself. This heavy yoke from her mother as if it were she who asked to be born. Mam's badgering growing worse each year like some tree twisting towards the hedgerow it is meant to protect. Why can't Colly see how unfair he is?

She will not speak another word to him, lies in the dark caressing her grief. Searches for the right word and finds it—unjustness, that's what all this is—feels it sitting on her chest, a different pain from the dullness of hunger.

Colly says, but you'll be able to buy meal with the money, you'll be able to buy bread.

She thinks, why should I go out and pretend to be a man again? Don't I have my freedom?

In the morning she stands upon the threshold of the door. Coldbite and the slow of night's unsleeving into twilight, what is unknown finding sureness, everything to the true of itself. She does her toilet in the wood, can hear Colly behind a bush. Imagine, he says, what it must be like to be a spirit or the pooka ghosting about, how strange it must be for them, you think you are hidden doing your business and they are sitting there watching—

Of a sudden, she has made up her mind. How this dawn paints a promise of other worlds. Cloud shapes in the far-off like reflections of gold. She hopes while she is gone nobody will steal the cabin.

She binds down her breasts with old rags.

Colly says, hee! I knew you'd give in.

She sets off up the path watching the sky, thinks of her mother telling the old stories of Mag Mell. Wonders what it must be like to live in a kingdom full of song and laughter and great eating and no dying whatsoever. The sky unfolding now like some great river yawning blue and extravagant. There is a great change coming in the weather, you can feel it. It is a sky to trick the heart to hope again.

So there is a town after all, she thinks. Cavan town is what Dr Charles called it. And just a few miles beyond the cabin.

Colly says, what were we at, you silly muc, staying so close to the wood when all this time we were short of baccy?

She asks some foul rag-boy for directions and the look he gives her up and down. Fuck off with your look, she tells him. The cabin path has led to a low road and then a high road and now this drowsy town, rags of rain-silver in the scars of the street and a reaching smell of bread. She watches a gentleman step down off his jarvey and offers to mind his horse but the man does not even look at her.

It might be spring but the wintering is here, all right, she thinks. There are people chinning their knees on the doorsteps and cadging at every corner. Two bony boy-beggars seem to follow her and she turns with a grin and waves her knife. What follows instead is the lingering bread smell. Such smell has the power of a ghost, she thinks. How it haunts the air and follows you about and even the commotion of a passing carriage does not disturb it. She sees her own spectre in the bakery window, peers at the stacked loaves and how the bread rolls are arranged like defiant fists. Watches a servant girl step out of the shop, a festoon of hair past her shoulders, the smell of a loaf hidden under a check cloth in her basket, the girl stepping past without even a look. Colly grunts some pig noise and the girl quickens her walk. What it would be like to rob her, she thinks, to follow her down some laneway and hit her over the head.

Colly says, it's a wonder this shop has not been broken into—I mean, I'm hardly here a minute and I've had the thought in my head three times—that smell of bread is an evil upon us, that bakey, crispy, buttery-licky smell has some power over you, don't you think—to do this to ordinary people is criminal.

The hidden road is revealed to her first with sounds of knocking. She hears it disperse into the sky, a thud-piercing sound that rises and becomes brittle. It sounds like distant gunshot or somebody smashing rocks. Do you hear it, Colly says, it sounds like the work of a giant—hee!—you remember the one who done in the head of a bullock with his fist, what's his name—

She cocks an ear and looks towards a stand of evergreens on her left. Cannot be sure where the banging comes from. No cabin-smoke to sign the sky with life. This lonely road rising into bogland and a kind of sadness when you stare at the length of the road. How southwards out of the town she has noticed that same deepening silence.

She looks to the sky now as if the hammering sound were issuing from it. Colly says, that's definitely the work of a giant, sitting there behind them trees splitting skulls, or maybe it's a hippogriff having his dinner, half horse and half griffin, except the griffin part is made up, for it is really a half eagle and half lion, that's what teacher said, which means it is quarter lion and quarter eagle and half griffin and half horse at the same time which means it is half-half—

She knuckles her head and winces. Says, that thud-clatter is coming from behind them trees. She has hardly pointed when two men step along a bosky path snorting pipe smoke.

Would you look at that, Colly says, a pair of hippogriffs just as I said it.

She walks through the trees and meets a vision of men cutting some kind of road into the half-bog. Walks past men breaking rocks with lump hammers and meets a long line of men trenching a road. There must be a hundred people here, she thinks. Most of them ragged, some of them like twists of bogwood gathering the wet and mud in their hollows. She looks to see if there are any women, sees one leaning into a barrow with an infant bundled to her back.

Some of the men are dressed loosely in flannel or sackcloth. In their long looks she sees donkey faces, horse faces, dog faces, not many human faces at all, most standing in an expression of abandonment, their laughter or their sorrow or their worry or their anger gone missing and you won't find it digging here. She can feel the air packed with stares, though when she looks no one is looking at her. She walks head-down towards a wooden hut, knows the two boss men from the heavy pure wool and cut of their waistcoats, a greyhound beside them yarding its tongue. She isn't sure which man to talk to. One of them is holding a glass of water to the sky.

—this water's brown, so it is, it tastes brown.

The man stops and turns to look at her. He says, what colour does this look like to you?

She says, some kind of brown colour, master.

The second man says, tis a trick of the light.

The first man says, you taste it, then. It tastes like— it tastes like brownness.

How can brownness have a taste?

It just does. Here, try it.

I'm not going to taste your piss water.

The second speaker slowly swivels his nourished grey head towards her and hangs his thumbs from his waistcoat. The first man puts the glass upon a card table. She can see a woman step out of a ditch carrying a pickax on her shoulder, her hair a swinging curtain.

She says, I was told to come here for the work.

The first man says, don't ask me, I'm only the pay clerk. You need to ask the gaffer.

Where can I find the gaffer?

The second man speaks. I am the gaffer. Who are you?

Tim Coyle, master.

With a sigh he pulls a sheet from his jacket pocket and unfolds it.

You're not on the list, he says.

I am so. They told me to come.

Who told you?

The committee man.

What committee man?

Mr Wallace.

You're too late to start the day.

I walked here since dark. I didn't know how many mile it was.

This site starts at eight and not a minute past it and any man not here for roll call can go home.

She gathers her rage as the gaffer turns his back, can hear the man muttering something about filth and the pay clerk laughing and her arm is moving before she can will it still and she takes hold of the glass of ditch water and she drinks it down with one eye watching the men. She wipes her mouth and says, were you laughing at me, sir?

The men stare at her without expression.

She walks away from the site cursing herself.

Colly says, that fucking water tasted brown.

Such a long walk back to the cabin. Her head ringing all night with the sound of their laughter but in the dawn she returns. The gaffer putting her to work at a wheelbarrow. Hunching into the weight of rocks. Her fingers strips of ribbons, her shoulders like screaming birds. A gaunt-faced rock breaker says, I suppose they'll let all types take the work now. Another rock breaker says, first the women and now children.

She finds a fresh tobacco pipe on the ground and quickly pockets it. Some old fellow pulls her by the arm and says, slow down there, youngster. Just count the hours and don't worry about the work. That man over there is watching out for the gaffer. He'll shout soon as he comes.

As the man talks, she eyes the others at work, sees their shovels half full, shoulders swinging like lazy clocks. A good many men just standing about.

That old fellow is right, she thinks. Half the men, when you really look at them, are too weak for the work. One man and the way he stands is the broken wing of a bird. She eyes the old fellow for clues of his life. He tamps his pipe with a finger and licks the top of it.

Colly says, ask him for a pinch, why don't you, go on.

I will not.

Ask him, ask him, ask him, ask—

She stares into a long blink for a moment. Says, won't you ever shut up? Opens her eyes to see the man looking at her, his face puzzled over his pipe. What's that? he says.

She looks about. What's what?

You just told me to shut up.

What I said was, won't you ever light up? She smiles, produces the pipe from her pocket. Could you share a pinch, mister?

Later, he says, the name's Darkey. And let me tell you, this bog road is nothing but folly. We're only digging it so they can give us work. He tells her the road site is called the Harrow. Says nobody knows where it will end. They haven't figured that bit out yet. And the gaffer here doesn't know what he's doing or where he comes from and he's never called work on a road, that's for sure, but he's happy enough taking his money from the Crown. Some say this road will go over the mountains and cross the channel into England and head onwards I suppose towards China, where it will meet with the Great Wall and then it will keep on going to hell because that is what roads do and because men were made for digging them and nothing else. And while you're at the doss, do enough to make yourself look busy but no more. Save up your energy, son, and give your pennies to the devil.

She thinks, this is easy enough work, rolling splinter-rock up and down in the barrow. She has learned to guard her strength, to dally with the barrow, stares back when anybody looks at her. The lazy hours thought out in portions of bread. She watches those who are not able for the work, how they are wintered out yet work beyond the last of their strength. She wonders why Darkey does not go up and tell them to slow down or not work at all. Keeps an eye on the few women who do the work same as the men. She watches the woman with the infant tied to her back and wants to talk with her but if you talk with her, she thinks, they'll think you're a woman. Then comes a moment when the woman walks past her and she hears herself saying, is the child much bother for you? The woman stares at her strangely and Colly laughs. Fucking eejit, he says, what kind of boy asks questions like that?

She hears the names of all the townlands these people are from. Some of them are a walk away as long as a day. Northwood. Drumryan. Stragelliff. Indigo. Shannow. Corrakane. A place called Kilnarvar if you can trip it off the tongue. She tells them she is from a place called Rush. A man says, which one? Each day Darkey refers to her as his little laughling, though she thinks he has not seen her laugh once. He pinches her cheek, gives her a pinch of his quarter plug. Points to the women workers. Says, them bitches should be home with their young ones not out here stealing a man's work. They should be home foraging dinner. Which one would you ride first?

The drop-weight clink of coinage. The queen's head in the palm of your hand. Now she can let the fire go out if she has to, for she has bought matches and hankers all day for the smell of the bread shop. That first full loaf she devours before she can get it home. Says to Colly, I need a drink of water, I'm after giving myself awful dry brains.

Colly says, what has no beginning and never ends, is there to stop hunger, and yet the more you do the hungrier you get?

Sleeping each night in the cabin like a dead person.

She looks up to see two men laughing at some fallen rock carrier. How one of them stands over him, his laugh all teeth. The air that smells of ancient earth smells suddenly of trouble, men turning to watch and others walking over. She watches the fallen man pick himself up and the laughing man says something to him and his hands threaten to become fists.

Colly says, I heard it—he called that man a *citóg*.

She cannot explain to herself what she feels when she sees the fallen man come to standing. His face. Some passing shadow of knowledge or recognition, for she feels she knows him but cannot explain it. He is young, hardly a man at all, she thinks, and yet he wears the mustache of an older fellow that horseshoes his mouth, how it is the look of a youngster trying to look older than he is. His neckerchief is vivid red. Then a chill passes through her. He has turned fully into her vision and she sees his right arm and how it sits shrivelled into some half arm as if caught at his birth, his hand having only two fingers graced in their ugliness to take the neck shape of a bird.

A man shouts, come on, Bart, don't stand for it.

She looks at the huge rock on the ground, wonders how this Bart fellow got it up on his back. His strange self-possession as he stares into the face of the man who felled him. He dusts himself with his good hand, sleeves the sweat off his mustache. For a long moment nothing passes on his face. Then he says, I'm only turning a coin but you want to see me kilt. I never done nothing to you.

She watches the way the other man's body seems to swell with the prospect of violence. He says, what are you going to do about it, you kitter-fisted cunt?

The air tightens all mouths to short breathing. Colly whispers, he is going to kill the cripple. She wonders why nobody shouts for the gaffer. It is then the cripple answers for himself. He is so fast she does not see that he holds a knife drawn from his right flank, a knife held in reverse so that it does not gather the sun but gathers the other man instead. He takes the man to the ground and the knife does quick work. Men begin laughing when he stands up. Someone says, good man, Bart. The other man slowly lifts himself like some hapless fool, his mouth agape and then he bends and picks up a piece of his ear off the ground. He pushes away through the crowd and a trio gathers around this cripple called Bart, hands clapping his back. And then the gaffer is among them, pulling on the brim of his hat, rubbing his hands together. Boysoboys, you might give me some notice next time so's I can put some money down.

All day she watches with odd fascination the comings and goings of the knife fighter. The way he walks with each rock balanced in the sockets of his back. The dangling useless hand. Darkey leaning in with his tickling laugh, shakes his head in wonder. That fellow John Bart, he says. They put upon him a bad spell at birth.

She wakes and thinks she might be dying. This pointing pain in her gut. It is not work pain, she knows, the kind that haunts your muscles, nor is it hunger. She thinks she might be poisoned. Thinks of some evil chomping her insides. She stands at the cabin window watching the dawn unravel, today's light like light echoed from some inferno, the last of all light and not the first of this day.

Colly, she says, I think I'm dying.

You silly bitch, didn't I tell you last night not to eat in one go all the bread.

Later, the barrow has become an extension of the pain that begins in her back and carries through her hips, shocks through her arms to become one with the load. She imagines her body falling to rot like this mush of bog earth all colours of brown. She thinks of what Darkey said once, that this ground used to be ancient forest, rotted down into peat. She stares at the earth and wonders how long it takes for a tree to die and then rot to become stringy brown turf, how many thousands of trees over how many thousands of years and of a sudden she can see the crooked trees at Blackmountain and what it might be like in thousands of years.

She says to Colly, I need to sit down. My hips are going to sunder.

She finds herself watching John Bart, has yet to see how he gets under a rock, such a curious thing, she thinks. Watches with a secret wish for someone else to trouble him just so she can see the quick of his knife. She watches him swinging a stone off his back, hinging upright to light a pipe, leaning back in laughter with another. Twice she has seen him go up to the foreman giving out about some problem.

Colly says, looks like he was born the wrong way out.

Who?

That horselicker John Bart, that one-armed—

I don't like that kind of talk.

I know why it is yer looking at him.

I'm not looking at him.

Yes you are but it's all right, there's no arm in it.

Shush or he'll cut you up. You saw what he can do with a knife.

I will admit he's very handy.

Stop.

Now you have me thinking, what's the definition of agony?

Listening to you all day.

John Bart hanging off a tree with an itch in his—

She thinks, John Bart. What is it about him? She knows she has been taking sneaky looks. Trying to puzzle him out. How it is that he carries himself like any other man, a man with two arms or almost, smoking all the time while carrying rocks. How he has been marked out as different by the bad birth of an arm and yet he drives pity out. The answer lies, she thinks, not in what you see but in what you feel. Perhaps what is known is the man's loneliness.

She is barrowing smash-rock through the slipslide of mud when she is seized with sudden pain. It comes from her hips, shoots through her with burning zest. She thinks, this is it, my body is done in. She drops the barrow, takes a look at the sky and sucks in a long breath. What she wants is to hang off such clouds and mix with the sky and be no more of it. To be carried by wind and fall like rain into unfeeling. She turns upon the roaring voice of Darkey. Hey, laughling! Wee boy! She sees him by the sitting rocks waving his pouch of tobacco.

Colly says, my lungs are starving for a smoke.

Darkey says, look at you, all frowned up.

Two others beside Darkey lean their pipes into flame. She does not know them, watches their eyes become blank as they take the first toke. Darkey eyes her, sups from a tin cup, puts it down, drips his fingers with tobacco. His fingers are oiled and dark-stained as if he has pulled himself to life from the bog having moulded each stubby finger out of the morass. He sucks a string of tobacco off a finger.

She lights up, takes a seat upon the rock.

One of the men says, there's others now swelling the numbers that aren't from about here, some women also. Tom Peter says some of them walked from as far as Collon to get here. That's twenty miles. Thinning out the work for the rest of us. Them women should fuck right—

She tokes her mind into quiet, the same and simple abeyance of toke and exhale as the others. The sounds of the site—the general thud-clutter, the hammering rock-men, the voices rising in echo and coming loose in the sky, the agitations of a tethered dog—all lose their stridency, soften out, unbecome on the air like smoke. When she is finished her smoke she stands and taps the pipe empty off the rock. It is then one of the men issues some strange curse. He stands up. Hey! he says. Hey! She turns and sees his puzzled look is upon her, how he goes to speak but his tongue hovers dumb in his mouth as if what he has begun to say cannot be said. She follows the man's pointed finger to the rock she has been sitting on. The rock seat is covered in blood.

She is aware of herself putting her hand to the seat of her breeches, watches the hand return red.

Their looks now upon her, Darkey beginning to stand up flap-mouthed and then his face packs down in confusion.

The horror now of what is. She can feel blood to her cheeks, blood to her ears, blood to the tips of her hair. Can feel blood in the down-below gushing out of her body, this blood that has been silently secreting itself. She knows she is going to die right now in front of these men. She stares at the rock and then dares the men with a savage look, shouts, what are you lot gorping at?

She watches herself walk as if watching from someplace in the sky. Watches the men watching her. What lies in their eyes, their mouths, their hearts. She steps out of sight behind the toolshed, dips her hand in the horse trough. Blood water skeins her fingers and even Colly has gone quiet. She thinks, for sure now I am dying. My insides are melting blood.

She strips horse flannel and dips it in water, puts it down her breeches. Picks up the barrow where she left it. She wants now to fold into herself, disappear completely from all eyes, to lie down in the trench and be covered in gravel. She is aware of Darkey staring at her, something in his look that frightens her. Can imagine their whispers gathering into laughter or anger or worse and that worse is something you do not want to think of. She looks to the sky and thinks, this will be the sky I'm to die under. She dares a look again but nobody is watching.

* * *

It is the longest walk home. She walks in terror that the bleeding will not stop. This bleeding that comes from her private self. She washes the rag and the butt of her trousers and a memory comes from the summer a year ago. Sarah with a rag of blood. Sarah asking if she has bled yet. Is this what she meant? And what if it isn't? What if it is some disease? What if it is the old witch's curse?

Colly has nothing to say on the matter, has started humming loudly to himself as if he doesn't want to listen. She hears herself shouting at him, what if I were to die here like that old woman and nobody finds me but for the dog? What then?

She moves through her mind all night long, searching down darkest paths for knowledge. The waking moment from sleep into dark and the relief she is not dead yet. She is aware of the night passing under her as if she were in deep water, its travel soundless like some tidal pull. In the early morning she hears rain burst upon the roof and drip inwards over everything, drenching her thoughts with blood. When she examines herself she finds the rag has more blood but is no worse than before. She washes the rag and takes a drink of water. Eyes her grey face in the shard of looking glass and thinks, don't you just hate the sight of yourself?

The days pass and she gathers her quiet. Is aware now of different kinds of looks. Not all the men, just some of them. She thinks, if the looking of a man could be measured, you would measure it in weight. The look that glances is light as a feather. But the look that sizes you up and down weighs a full pound. One long look she gets from a man adds up to three pounds' weight or more, she thinks.

She stands trying to heave the barrow up a hill of mud and then a man appears and takes the wheelbarrow and drives it on without word, leaves it down for her.

She stands unsure of herself, mutters something about the man being ridiculous. Wonders if the rules are changing but nobody has said. Catches Darkey watching her from the smoking rock but his face has no expression and she will not go over to him.

Colly says, who gives a box of fucks about that Darkey anyhow? You've got your own tobacco now.

Colly wants a go at the barrow. Go on, girl, gimme! She is thirsty and sore. The pain that pricked her hips all week has passed, become now the usual dull pain of work. She scratches her mouth with a dry tongue, watches a man dip a cup into the drinking barrel.

Gimme a go. Gimme a go. Gimme a go.

Fuck up.

Go on, girl, let me.

Colly harrumphs as he takes over, springs the wooden wheel of the empty barrow into the air off a rock. To mud again, rolling forward, the barrow veering around one fellow who stands folded into a hacking cough. They are not seen stepping out of the bustle. How they bring the day to quick when they block her. She sees that two of them are from the smoking rock that day with Darkey. The other is the man with the weight of looking in his eyes. She eyes the bit-rock and dust in the empty barrow, eyes the scrim of mud on her boots, a black toenail peering out. One of them snorts or perhaps it is the horse tethered to a post and half crazy the way it stares into the far-off. She gruffs her voice low. Get out of my way.

The man who speaks is the watcher. So, barrow boy. What do we call you now?

His mouth smirks but his eyes are dead looking at her.

The third man says, Anvil here has something to say to you.

Colly starts singing and she wishes he'd shut up. Three blind mice—hee!—three blind mice—

She says, Anvil? Did somebody bang you on the head that much?

Nothing moves in the eyes of this Anvil and then he purses his lips and wolf-whistles at her. She thinks of her cheeks, how the nature of a blush is that it sneaks up on you before you can do anything about it and you have never stopped one yet. She eyes the men with venom. Everybody at the Hollow is filthy, but these three disgust her with their loose teeth and mashy faces. They are hardly even men yet. She gruffs her voice again, says, get the fuck out of my way, tries to shunt the barrow, though the two hands of Anvil hold it firm. He nods his empty eyes towards the fir trees. Says, we were thinking, perhaps you might fancy a smoke with us. We've got plenty of tobacco. Come with us over to those trees after work—

Of a sudden some rock carrier bulls right through them and then she sees it is John Bart under a stone. Get off the fucking path, he says. The men move quick to allow him through, though Bart knocks into the shoulder of one of them and continues on. Anvil steps forward and takes hold of her shirt, brings his face towards her, goes to speak but what is formed by tongue and teeth does not pass his lips, his face to white as the sharp of her blade is pressed between his legs.

There is pleasure in the way he backs away from her all sneer and teeth. The two others staring mutely at the knife.

Colly is singing for the rest of the day.

See how they run—hee!
See how they run,
They all ran after the farmer's wife,
Who cut off their cocks with a carving knife—

Foot by foot this going-nowhere road deepens through the bog, gathering new workers into its expression of noise and mud and tree bones. The weather that comes to dress it, sun one moment and rain the next, though the morning wind is the worst, she thinks. How it strips you cold for the rest of the day and you can never get warm after it. There are more women now doing the same work as the men. They all come in disturbances of dress and body, many thin-skinned, their countenances whittled to rock. They take their children and leave them by the side of the site, though most of them do not play as children but sit white and silent. So many people now are hungered and bone-sore and half dressed. She wonders which ones have walked here since the middle of the night, twenty miles for a day's work and nine pence.

She hears talk that men are agitating against such strangers, against the women who are joining the work, against the gaffer watching over them, a rumour going about that he is going to drop their pay to afford the new workers. Each day she watches the pay clerk set up his payment table, the heavy way he walks as if his entire body complained of some disadvantage, about having to be here at all. He is only half here, she thinks. How he puts the money in your hand without looking at you.

Again and again she finds herself thinking about the contours of her body hidden under a man's clothing. What she has done to herself—strapped her chest down and ragged herself shut, just in case. Sees herself as some character in a story, one of Colly's great yarns, the one he told about Étaín—thrown about the world by others, turned first into water and then a worm and later a butterfly. She thinks, it's better to be a butterfly than a worm but what's the difference really when you can't be yourself? And that great wind sent to blow the butterfly over the sea for seven years and all that fluttering and flying and never alighting and did she not grow tired with herself?

This day now and just to be done with it, she thinks. Watching the day slip from its shell into dusk. How the last light of each day is lengthening and yet such a walk to the cabin, firewood to be found. She drops the barrow and widens into a yawn.

It is Colly who suggests it, to take some of the bog wood back in a sack. We can take turns carrying it, he says. It will burn better than anything we can find in the wood. The twists of wood are quickly sacked and slung over her shoulder. Most of the others have left in small groups. She watches the wind blowing through the rags of the remaining walkers, wonders how far each must travel, their vision locked towards some inner-seeing of home many will not reach till dark.

She says, tell me a riddle, Colly.

He says, how about this one—what's always the same weight yet keeps growing heavier?

She adjusts the sack on her shoulder. The road turns for another road and then another and Colly starts up.

A pat on Pat's hat,
A pat on his cat,
It's time hurrah for dinner.

The road is empty and her shoulder is smarting. She stops and rests the sack on the road, rubs at her fingers red and newly disfigured, rubs the pain out of her hand. She bends to lift the sack by the throat and it is then the men step out of her unnoticing. Two men far enough back to remain faceless, slow and silent and thick in the way they move, and yet one of them stops and then both step off the road. She thinks of the men who harassed her, watches the trees for hiding shapes. The empty road and how the trees bind the grey-soft and the coming night together as if to say nothing is the matter.

A pat on Pat's cat,
Who has come for Pat's rat,
It's time hurrah for dinner.

Cabins begin to thicken the road as she approaches the town. They smoke the air but there are few faces and no animals, not even a dog. A finger of wood prods at her shoulder and she turns to adjust it, sees the two distant men behind her on the road and how they stop also. A sudden light feeling swims her legs.

She thinks, it is always the simplest thing and not the most complicated, isn't that what Mam used to say? Those men are just walkers.

The west becomes a low sky-fire. The hedgerows are losing their colour. Gloom spreads over the fields. She wills herself to slow her walk but the two men do not catch up. She hurries onwards, a vision of faceless men footing like phantasms behind her.

Colly says, maybe what they want is the bog wood.

She thinks, I will knife off their dicks if they come near me.

Colly says, you'll lose them in the town, I bet.

She stops by the bakery shop and awaits their disquiet in the window, the world reflected into shadow like a dream of strange water, some shadow-man leaning drunk against a barrel and all such who walk past, a shadow-child who flits the street, shadow-horses dipping a trough, that shadow-gig that shakes the glass, her own shadow-face deeper and older and watching as the two men do not show themselves.

She counts a long minute and then another. The men have gone into a pub or a shop. She chides herself for being so stupid.

Pat's rat chased by Pat's cat,
Makes a run into Pat's hat.
Pat's cat has lost his dinner.

There are gleams of candlelight in a few of the cabin windows outside the town, though most are dark. She turns onto a low road, the sack as heavy as the falling darkness. She does not notice that Colly has stopped singing.

Grace.

What?

Them two are following us again.

She can feel them without looking, sees in her mind all the various turns from the road they did not take and now this one, this one road she happens to be on and still they are behind her. She turns and sees their two shapes clearer now. Oh! Oh! How everything in twilight seems cloaked in slowness but the men now are catching up.

She begins at a high walk, bending with the weight of the sack, hears herself panting.

Colly says, faster, faster.

She looks again and the men are closer. Oh! Oh!

Colly says, they want the firewood, that's what they're after.

She drops the sack like a bad thought upon the road, continues at her high pace. The men walk past the sack.

But oh! But oh!

Faster! Faster! Faster!

Now she knows it. That she cannot return home. That these men whoever they are want to know where she lives or worse. Her mind fighting the unwilled thought of what they might want. Soon it will be dark and that is the road splitting in two and one of them leads home, where you cannot go. She follows the unknown road. Wishes for all her life's luck to come at once. She studies a wood and thinks how it might hold her and how it might not. Walks past a farmhouse set back off the road, lamplight in all three of its lower windows and how she would like to knock but what if they take ill at the sight of you or refuse to answer and them two behind you at the gate like patient dogs.

Faster! Faster! Faster!

She is sticky with sweat and panting. She thinks of the sanctuary of trees, how it would make sense to just run for it and hide but perhaps the dark of the woods is not dark enough. How every bird now is calling down the darkness. Crows are rioting an oak. She takes a turn for another road and knows she is lost, turns to see the two men following at a high walk.

Oh! Oh! Oh! Oh!

Faster! Faster! Faster! Faster!

Close enough now to see the strength in their walk. Her ears alert to any change in their sound. Everywhere she sees places she might hide. The back of a stile. An old barn. The darkening hedgerow. Trees, trees, but none of them thick enough. She passes another farmhouse. She considers the sharpness of her knife. There is something ahead and it shapes into a stray dog and she thinks, if that is a black dog my luck is done for.

It is a wandering collie blazing white at the neck.

She hears a change in their movement, turns to see them coming at a slow run.

Oh! Oh! Oh! Oh! Oh!

She is wind over a gate, has no memory of touching it, skirts a hedgerow, turns to see the men climbing the gate. Now she is at a full run, meets another field, meets a dark road, knows she is lost.

Colly says, those men are nothing but demons, that is what they are, demon men on the road, like—

Shut up! Shut up! Shut up!

The world has fallen away to just these two men. She thinks, I will run all the high roads of Ireland, run the night into morning, run until your ankles snap and yet still you would stump onwards.

She stops to stifle her wheezing breath under a gauntlet of trees, hawthorns, she thinks, but it is too dark to tell and if you can't tell the trees then perhaps they can't see you. Watching the dark. Watching the laneway hold the dark. Then she sees their two shapes and she wonders now if Colly is right, that the two men are demons, for how else can they keep following you like this in the dark or perhaps they can hear your loud breathing. Running now into a field and then another, tearing her skin in a ditch, and she is terrified her legs will give in, terrified at the thought of these demon men and what they will do to her, and she notices now it is night and only night and what is mind-shadow is also world-shadow.

Now here. The where of it she does not know. The knife in her hand. Her lungs a flailing old coat. She thinks again of poor Étaín, how good it would be to be turned into a fly or a puddle of water or a butterfly that could fly over the trees. How you would trade seven years and all for it. At a moment's notice she will run, run, run. Then she bolds herself up. The dark is my friend as much as theirs. I will cut off their demon dicks and stick them in their ears. She watches the night, waiting.

She haunts the late morning with her look. The way she steps onto the Harrow, slow and slightly bent as if sluggard thought could be made physical. Her eyes almost lidded. The foreman away up the site but the others are watching her, this slump-shouldered thing mouthing words to herself. Someone says, Darkey said aye for you at roll call. She sees Darkey stalling his pickax to look at her, wonders perhaps if there is concern in his stare. She is clagged with mud, shakes whatnot from her hair, picks at a briar hitched to her back. Thinks about what she must look like. Something half born. A little ditch sleeper.

Some youngster all elbows has a firm grip of her barrow but she pulls him off it. The boy braves a hard eye at her but she tells him to go and fuck.

Colly says, you dull-brained bitch, you are nothing but a dim ditchdigger—what is it you are trying to achieve by coming back here—don't you get what just happened?

To get through this day under the weight of such tiredness. She would sleep if she could standing in her boots. The cold breeze reminds her she is still damp from the ditch she slept in. She closes her eyes for a moment's rest and still she can see them clearly, two forms like shadows lifted into life off the road. They could be any two men out of all the men working here and she is afraid to look at such faces for what she might meet, a recognition, the meeting of knowledge that is certain and what then? And how she would love to tell somebody what has happened, tell Darkey or the foreman or some other, but how can you say it? Because they didn't catch you and even if they did who would care?

She goes to the sitting rock out of sight of the foreman and puts the pipe in her hand and closes her eyes. She wakes from a drifting dark into rain-cold. Turns and meets the stare of John Bart. He is either looking at her or staring past her.

Colly says, I'm telling you, it must be him.

She thinks, do not look at his funny arm, but she does.

There are things you can do to keep secret the course home. This long toe-cutting walk with the breeze at your back. She routes through pastureland she has never walked through before and keeps tight to the ditches, jinks through sudden gaps and unpicks the bramble. She thinks of the violence held in the greenery of a ditch, how you swallow the dog to catch the cat and swallow the cat to catch the bird and swallow the bird to catch the spider and swallow the spider to catch the fly and everything eats everything else and the man wants to swallow the woman and the world calls it nature. Her hand of its own accord keeps touching her knife.

In woodland she moves in zags like some animal of strange bearing and instinct, waits and watches to see if she is being followed. She has avoided the town and can see it in the distance, thinks of yesterday's watching window, the assembly of faces passing in the glass and how you are blind to the who and the what of them, and that is the trouble, how you may see in a window's reflection what appears to be true and yet it is just shadow.

Twilight is touching the woods when she meets the bridle path near the cabin. She is spent and sore, wants to take off her boots and burn them. It is Colly who senses it—quick! he says. A tap soft to the cheek. A wet mark to the forehead. Hee! Running then towards the cabin, arms flung out, blinking against the downpour. She stands at the door when it happens, the awareness that blooms out of its own dark in the second before, the soft sucking sound of a foot rising from mud. It is an iron arm that nooses her neck, lifts her off her feet, a great weight pressed to the back of her and then she is dragged backwards and useless and kicking amid grunt and drink-smell and in her ears she can hear her own strangle—how the sky twists and heaves sidewards suddenly and out of it the evil sun that is the face of another. She is shout-trying, shout-trying, tastes her own blood, and there comes a second hand that cups her mouth and she wants to spit the filth-taste out. She is trying to breathe, squirming useless now against this physical power. In the midst of all this it occurs to her that she does not know the who of these men, these men dragging her towards the shade of the woodland. She finds herself pinned utterly, a rough hand at her mouth half covering her eyes, a face all teeth above her, another hand rough at her breeches. A button pops off and she knows now she is done for, that last night she used up all her life's luck. That everything now is folding into the one kind of dark, the light in her mind closing down to a nothing, thought burrowing deeper past thought, past any sense of herself, until it finds a gleam of something that could be called light or could be called strength and it might be Colly who does it—knees the man in the groin and a great wind comes out the man's mouth. He buckles and her legs come free enough to roll herself out from under him—Colly grasping to pluck the other man's eyes out and it is then—she does not know what happens. The hand gone from her mouth and she screams—Colly!—finds herself free, finds herself wriggling backwards from the sound of a fight, grunt sounds, the sound of someone hitting the ground—Colly!—and she is trying to crawl to the safety-dark of the wood—Colly! Colly!—crawling and crawling until she hears the sound of another behind her and she quickly turns to see a man coming upon her, sees an arm held shrivelled to a chest, sees the other arm loose with a knife, sees the tough eyes of John Bart coming upon her—Colly! Colly! Colly!—sees behind John Bart where a man dark with his own blood is slowly moving away down the path. The shape of another lying on his back.

The hand of John Bart putting the knife into a scabbard.

The good hand of John Bart lifting her up.

Her ears are full of thunder-blood. Blood of the dead man not ten paces away, one leg funnied beneath the other and his arm spun out as if waving farewell. She watches the trickle-red from a knife-cut to the throat. John Bart walking silently in circles, his head lowered as if trying to see past a puzzle and she watches and a thought occurs he cannot hide his youth even with that mustache. This moment and how it seems to hold suspended and then it falls out of time altogether, as if time has to gain something back, some equilibrium from the sudden of what happened—John Bart, worrisome, walking in circles and her own breath stunned in the throat and how time can be like this forever.

Colly is breathless. He says, I had him kneed in the balls, that one on the ground—hee!—that's all was needed, and that other, I had his eye near pulled out, we could have run off, we didn't need the help of that Bart fellow, who does he think he is, some kind of hero?—now we are in all kinds of trouble with a dead man and whatnot.

She thinks, that is a man dead on the ground, for sure. Stares at this Bart fellow, for he is a man is he not and what thoughts are in his head also? She sits on a rock and tastes blood where cheek flesh was gouged out. She eyes the dead man, straightens when she sees the still hand rising to the throat. The dead man is trying to sit up. What she sees in his eyes when he meets her look is not the look of an attacker but the terror of a man staring into his own end. The stumbling mouth of the man. Otter. Otter.

Colly says, he wants water but tell him to go and fuck.

She does not know why but feels hatred for John Bart. She goes into the cabin and twines her breeches safe to her waist with a knot. Can see in the glen below the windowed amber of the farmhouse and how good it would be to have a life like theirs and not her own where such things continue to happen. She brings water to the lips of the injured man. John Bart watching her from the tree stump he sits on, the woodland darkening now like great wings about his shoulders. Then he goes to the man and drags him by the collar, sits him to the stump.

Colly says, we will have to kill him now, we have no choice but to be murderers.

Bart says, you must come with me now. I know this man and I know the other I cut. They're rough dogs, travel with a rough crowd. They will come back here or seek me out.

She eyes the cabin and thinks of the fire gone out and thinks of the bed and thinks of the wildflowers she's picked to make the place look brighter, the mouse-ear that is a single green orchid, thinks of the dead woman she had to drag out. Thinks about Bart, for he is a man and men are nothing but trouble and how are you to know what is in his head, he could be planning something also. She scowls at him. Says, I didn't ask for you to kill anybody on my account.

He looks at her with astonishment. Of a sudden she knows what he is and what he is not. He turns without word and starts for the path without her. She stares at the path and stares at the dying man, another body left lying about and you'll be the one who has to take care of it and maybe you'd be safer with this knife fighter.

Wait! she shouts. She goes into the cabin and bundles her blanket and belongings. When she steps out of the house the dead man has gone.

She says, what did you do with him?

He says, I did nothing with him.

So where is he gone?

He got up and ran off.

I thought he was dying.

Obviously not.

Colly says, I'm not going nowhere without some tobacco.

Bart walks down the bridle path and grunts for her to follow. After a minute, she suddens to a stop. Stands eyeing an alder freshly axed and lying off the path, its wood the colour of blood.

John Bart turns with a snappy look. He says, what now?

She says, we'll not go down this path. We'll go through the wood. That alder there is a bad omen.

He turns without word and continues down the path.

Colly says, I'm in a right mind to burst him.

IV

Ride the Wolf's Mouth

It is like the worst of black weather, she thinks. Having to follow behind this *citóg*. This ridiculous rush of a walk. I'm just some cat's paw to him, being made to tramp through this wood having your eyes twigged out, he'd ask you to put your own hand in the fire.

Colly says, I'm still in a right mind to burst him.

The tangle of a ditch and they emerge to find a road quit of starlight. The night thrown open into its full dark.

She thinks, John Bart, you have killed all the stars tonight. She stares at Bart but he has coalesced into the dark like a trick. Hedgerows huddle along the road and mutter the breeze like watchers. Bart announced by the shrill clack of his hobs on the road's rough stone, his breathing heavy as utterance. She wants for him to stop. She would like not to follow. She would like to be able to go back to where she has been suddened out of, the cabin she called home. Colly whispering, he is some customer, all right, I'm sick of this marching—tell me, why would they be coming after us, they would be coming after *him,* that kittery cunt—hee!—he is the one who cut them with the knife.

She mouths soundless abuse at Bart, would love to sneak up and box him where it hurts. The way he steps unrelenting through the dark, a power different now from any power she can muster. How he seems to be made only of will and of necessity like some force that will take no account.

Rain suddens heavy and tuneful, makes all the earth sing a blind song of itself. Soon she is sodden but still Bart walks on. Bull of a brain! A john mule's bollocks! His shoes sound off the stones their infernal *click-click*. She shouts for him to stop but only his boots answer, *click-click, click-click.*

She comes alongside him and tugs his sleeve, says, we're getting soaked.

He says, fuck the rain.

She says, what is the point in getting so wet?

He says, it's only the wet, the wet never hurt no one.

Her hands become fists and she fights the want to strike him, turns without word and steps off the road towards a grouping of trees wrapped in night shroud. John Bart's *click-click* fading until it folds into an all-dark that widens vastly and without seam. She stares and feels the panic come quick in the pure blind of all this. Imagines them—who?—and yet she can see them—out there in the dark—marauders of some kind, air demons coming down from on high. She stares at the dark and wills loose the gripping thought, says aloud, only wee boys are afraid of the dark.

Colly says, who are you calling wee?

Then he says, tell me, what was the point of all that carry-on, that marching and getting soaked—even the birds are asleep.

Hardly has Colly spoken when a quarter moon appears, spills slow milk on a figure stepping towards them—*click-click, click-click,* Bart then hunkering down beside her with his smell of rain-sweat and rain-tobacco and all that energy that is his decidedness and yet—she feels some class of victory over him. For a long while they each keep quiet and she wonders if he is asleep, if perhaps she should sneak off into the dark, thinks about the cabin and gasps the loss of four pennies she has left hidden in a matchbox.

Bart sighs and says, what now?

She does not answer, thinks, to hell with him and to hell with this.

In silence they watch the rain speak itself out.

* * *

Everything that is wet shines with ghost light and everything that is itself becomes also what it could be. She marshals hate to power her through this weariness until her hate becomes a memory dulled and dim beyond feeling. She becomes the cloudy moon winking into her own dark, stepping forward into a walking dream of those two men who attacked her — not the face of the man who was trying to climb up on her but the full fact of him, the man's weight as his fullest expression, how he was not man in that moment but animal, bore the strength of a mad dog, and she thinks about his intent and how want can mix so cruelly with hurt, sees him stumbling down the bridle path with his left hand held to his throat, the blood smile John Bart gave him like a brand-new mouth, hears the mouth begin to chatter — didn't we get what we deserved, dead man? Attacking that girl like that? Now give me a toke of that pipe in your pocket. Dead man reaching into his pocket and putting the pipe into his throat-mouth, the man wheezing as the throat tokes in satisfaction —

John Bart is shaking her by the arm. He says, nearly there.

She answers, nearly where?

She wakes into cold and gloom and shawls her arms about herself. From a dream she carries the feeling that the last few years of her life were not lived — that in this moment of waking she is fully her younger self. Then dimly it comes — the knowledge she has awoken from a memory of the past that isn't and she lies suspended in this slipway between dream and the new day that quickens its truth upon her. A barn of some kind. Daylight writing the rafters with letters of light. She does not remember having entered. She can only remember the road and this *citóg* now with his soft-snoring beside her, watching him sleep like some sort of cat creature curled in delight with himself. And then she sees how he nurses in sleep his bad arm to his chest.

Colly whispers, go now, would you?

She picks up her bundle and begins towards the double doors of the barn but Bart's snoring stops as if somebody has put a hand to his mouth. She holds her breath, can hear him rustling upwards onto his wrist. She has stopped by the door and blithely picks straw off her jacket as if it were the most natural thing in the world to be standing here by this door and who would be thinking of running off at this hour when we have spent the full night trying to reach whatever this place is?

Bart says, what you think you're going back to is not the same as what you've got coming if you go back there.

She looks at him and says, whatever does that mean?

He has a weird sit, she thinks. It is just like Colly's — the way he crosses his legs under him and leans back on his sit-bone. Her legs have always been too long for her body and so she prefers to sit down rather than squat. She sees the legs of an old milking stool poking out of the straw and grabs it, wipes the dust off the seat. The stool complains when she sits then breaks beneath her, throws her backwards knees over head. She stares at the rafters and thinks, my arse-bone has been hit by a hammer. She is waiting for Bart to laugh at her but he does not. His dark eyes stare at her instead. She scours him with a look, opens her mouth as if to shout away his judgement but he motions a shushing finger to his lips — reddening, she is reddening all over. She feels — she wants — she picks up the stool and hurls it off the ground. Shouts, shush up yourself!

Bart gets up wordless, sighs like a young man who wakes to find himself in the body of some old man weary to the task of living his last days, goes to the door and takes a long look out. He returns and sits his strange squat, continues to observe her. She meets the full of his look and sees it is nothing but coldness. She thinks, it is the look on a stoneloach you'd pull from a river, the look on the face of a cat toying with a mouse. This fellow so satisfied with himself. He is so — she cannot think of it. Eyes him back with as much ill will as she can muster. She thinks, what—he must be no more than eighteen years old and already so Mr Conceited Breeches in his manner, going about with his full man's mustache, he must have fallen under the farrier, had that horseshoe shod to his face. She studies his stubbled cheeks and the red neckerchief and some sort of beaded string on his wrist. Those eyes again. They are eyes that permit no watcher to see into them but see through you instead.

Colly whispers, I'll bet he doesn't know a single fact, all he knows is that knife and there's no way he can do a headstand against the wall with that one arm, go on and ask him.

She eyes for the peep of his scabbard. He eyes her bundle.

She says, I was better off by myself.

He says, your attitude astonishes me. Have you a hole in your head?

What is it you have got that I haven't?

His face tightens. What do you mean by that?

She does not know herself.

He says, I've got my wits about me, which is more than I can say for you, acting the blithe fool around dangerous people and pulling me into your trouble.

She says, you can take your wits away off with you. I was doing just fine. She nods to his knife but quickly wishes she hadn't, for it looks like she has nodded to his bad arm. Quickly she says, that knife of yours is nothing but trouble.

All movement holds in his face and then his eyes drill past her eyes, past bone into the place that holds her weakness and guilt.

He says, well so, let us see what you've got.

She grabs hold of her belongings.

Colly says, don't show him nothin.

She says, why would I show you any—

He moves so fast she cannot respond, the bundle grabbed off her and then he opens it onto the floor. A blanket holding rags and a pipe. A ball of string rolls loose and the useless shard of looking glass as it falls brings light to itself. The knife Sarah gave her. Bart picks up the blade and laughs and she shivers as he runs it harmless across the palm of his bad hand.

He snorts, ties everything back together and throws it at her.

Well, he says. That's that settled, then.

What's what settled?

That. You have nothing, not even a knife.

This pounding walk southwards all day and she is growing to hate the back of him, dawdles to make him wait, and how when he waits his face darkens. They argue over which direction to walk. They argue when she wants to stop by a well—he would argue over the time of day, she thinks, argue the colour of the sun, the wetness of rain, the colour of a dog's look.

Colly says, why are you always letting him win, him with his stupid twig arm, half man, half tree, he's only an auld willow, which if you ask me is the stupidest of trees—what is the use of it, it's not even a tree but a shrub, who was it put him in charge of our journey?

She walks with her arms folded better to bosom her anger. Says over and over, he's not in charge, never mind him, he's only just a so-and-so.

Everywhere she sees the betiming of summer—a con man's trick, she thinks, for it seems as if the world can only know glory though perhaps that is the case, perhaps everything can be fixed. And yet stamping through one frail village after another she sees how each is held in the same quiet, a calm without chatter or the clamour of animals, for the fowl and pigs are long gone and whatever dogs you might see are rawboned and silent. They do not bark, Bart says, because they are losing their voices. He speaks as if he has heard the thought in her head and she wants to say, who asked you? They pass one dog that throws them a hoarse look that says, not so long ago I would have been up and at you with my bark, the loudest in this village of all the dogs, but now I am too tired, I do not even chase cats, not that there are any, it is such a long while since I have eaten, please throw me a morsel of food if you have some.

The big houses along the road do not trouble a look but the mud huts and stone houses are all eyes that watch and wonder at these passing strangers. She thinks, they are eyes that empty your pockets and pinch the flesh on your hips.

They walk through a village built entirely on a hill and there is a farrier at work who turns to look at them and says something and spits at the road. She does not know why Bart grows tense, his good hand hovering near his knife. She comes alongside him and whispers, what did he say to you? He does not answer and she looks over her shoulder but the road is clear and when she asks him again, without looking he says, it's nothing, we have a follower. She turns and sees the hoarse-talking dog is following along, poking the air with its bones.

She begins to see it is the poorest who act the strangest towards them. If she were alone on these roads she would be bothered by beggars at every corner, joint eaters, Colly calls them, people who would break your shoulder leaning over you to tear at your food. Always the same type of fellow with the hand held out. One or two that look like Auld Benny, the man whose lungs rattled and collapsed. And yet for now, even the beggars leave them alone. What she sees are people muttering at Bart as they walk past. Some begin to incant aloud and bless themselves. One fellow steps into the rough and turns as if looking for something lost from his pocket. She knows they look at Bart's arm as a curse. She thinks, he must have been getting this all his life. Tries to imagine a childhood full of such and what that must be like. She has known the kind of these others who treat Bart with such contempt. She thinks, well worshippers, Mam would call them, the sort who worship made-up saints. They are people who think if you are born with a missing instrument, you will bring evil upon them. She knows what they think, all right. That if they meet Bart first thing in the morning they will think themselves unlucky the rest of the day. That if he looks at anything with fixity they will see doom in the glance. And heaven help them if he so much as looks at a child. That child's arm will wither, or worse, his head grow afflicted and he will die of it.

John Bart walking through all this like a horse perfectly blinkered.

Or a horse too proud to look.

She builds up the courage to ask him. So anyway, she says, what happened to that arm of yours?

He is silent much too long and she thinks he is offended, thinks, what did you go and ask him that for, you don't need to know. People will see the way we are walking together and think we are courting. I will say I am his sister.

Then Bart says, my mother told me I shared the womb with a wolf. The wolf grew starved and chewed at my arm. Then I was born and the wolf ran out and now it roams the countryside and I've been chasing it all over Ireland ever since. That's why I became a wanderer. Of a sudden, he laughs and she has not heard his laugh before, how it is open to the world and infectious. Can you believe I believed that muck for years? he says. How is anyone supposed to know what happened to it? Didn't it happen before I was born?

Of a sudden he stops and props a boot upon a fence, ties his bootlaces with thumb and forefinger.

Colly says, how in the fuck—that is some trick, do you think he can teach it?

She thinks, whatever you can say about him, people are leaving us in peace on the road. If people see him as a curse then he must be some sort of protection.

Her foot is plagued by an itch but Bart will not stop. Without word she stops and twigs at the itch, hears Bart cursing. The road passes through a village and she thinks, there is no wintering here. Good houses painted a bold colour. One or two yards echoing with pigs.

Dogs in full throat—three of them barking not at these strangers but at ghosts, wind stirrings, nothing in particular. Then Bart stops and signals for her to wait beside a tethered donkey staring into patience.

Colly says, you again, wonkey!

She turns towards Bart, says, don't be telling me what to do, what are we stopping here for?

But Bart has already stepped through a latch door and shut it behind him. She gapes at the shut door, anger tightening her teeth. She sees it is a shop.

Colly says, that ballock-handed bastard hasn't got a penny on him.

She bends to wiggle a finger down her boot.

She is being eyed by two goosey women by a doorway who fold their arms as they watch her. Pair of beef eaters, Colly says. What is expressed in their look makes her aware of her body and she tries to stand in a different shape, straightens up as if Sarah were chiselling, stop slouching like that, straighten your back, people will think we're spalpeens.

Rags of children idle in silence by a bridge at the village limit. She shows them the tongue of each empty pocket. So the wintering is here, she thinks. It is just not allowed to enter the village.

Colly says, tell me, muc, let's say I have a rooster and you have a donkey and your donkey eats my rooster, what is it you would have?

What?

You'd have one foot of cock up your ass. Hee!

The donkey stands impassive. She reaches to tickle its ear fur.

Colly says, why is it donkeys don't laugh, or animals, for that matter—I knew a fella who says his dog laughed all the time like a hyena but I was not convinced of it, I'll bet if you were to cut that animal open you would find something missing, some kind of humour box in the brain, my particular theory of laughter is that—

She says, how do you know animals don't laugh? He could be laughing at you on the inside, you would never know. You are not attuned to their thinking.

I wouldn't want to be tuned to their thinking, or his thinking either, that one-horse-handed bastard John Bart, I tell you, I don't like him one bit, he thinks he's smarter than everyone else, he doesn't listen, you'd find more humour in a stone, he snores way too much, he speaks with a stupid west-of-Ireland accent, and he lacks a pair of fighter's fists, he—

She puts her fingers in her ears but still she can hear him.

—and have you seen the size of that thumbnail on his sick hand, it's like something off an animal.

Would you ever give my head a rest.

Do you think he will teach me the knife?

The shop door swings open and Bart emerges all quick-step. He drops into her arms a pan and a pound bag of oats and pulls her by the sleeve.

Quick, he says, put them in your bundle.

She says, quit pulling at me.

Then she says, how did you get all this?

He says, all I had to do was touch it.

A sudden ill-feeling as she marches past the children. She decides not to look because if you look at them you will have to do something for them, share some of what you have.

Colly says, look!

She turns and sees some oldster coming at a hobbling half run while carrying some sort of firearm.

She prods Bart's back. Do you think that man there is after us?

There is peace to be had bellied by firelight. She is heavy with eating, licks porridge from her teeth watching the fire tongue at the night. How two worlds touch where she lies, the cold upon the breeze and the heat of the fire and wouldn't it be nice to be warm all the time though you can't have one without the other. Bart is whittling a stick and then he laughs. That bog road, he says. Nine pennies a day—what could a man do with that? Put a few nails to your boots, perhaps. Like why would you be bothered?

Why did you do it so?

I fell into it by accident—took a walk up to that part of the country just to see it. I didn't intend staying long.

Where did you say you're from, then?

She stares at him when he does not answer and thinks, so what anyhow. Better the dark and she closes her eyes and slides into a near sleep that conjures strange and looming faces but she comes alert again when John Bart takes a sudden leap out of his sit.

Right, he says. He motions with his hand. Up with you.

She turns her head, moves sullen onto her elbow.

He is standing over her with the knife, his body silhouetted to the fire so that he is made different now, she thinks, some twist-shape of John Bart, his face near masked and his eyes pooled into withholding so that he has become John Bart black-souled, twinned out of dark into madness or worse. She studies the way he holds the knife, climbs up slowly, wary, takes one step back from him. He holds out the knife. Take it, he says. Her reach is slow but then she grabs it and pulls it quick to herself. He seems to be smiling, it is hard to tell.

Look at it, he says. See? Come closer to the light. It must be a knife like this one—fixed, with a double edge. Do you see the difference? That one you have is no use but for peeling things. We'll have to get you one in the next town.

He takes the knife back off her, blades it at the dark. Says, you must have the knife always within reach. See here where I put it. You never know you'll need it until the moment you do. You'll want to lead with the hand not carrying the knife, it gives you range and confuses them, though that technique won't work for me.

She wants to slide back into that easy near sleep but again he presses the knife into her hand.

He says, another thing — you must be able to hold the knife with a sweaty or a cold hand. He takes her by the wrist. Have a go.

She says, don't be a nuisance, I'm no good at it.

He says, it's easy to learn.

He shows her first how to stand, how to protect herself, how to read the eye of another, to watch the stance of an opponent. He shows her how to step sidewards and parry an attack. She says, I cannot imagine doing any of this with a real person.

See, he says. You can direct the other knife back towards its owner.

He shows her how to thrust when the person has been brought open.

She says, I don't want to do that to anyone, not never.

He says, you may not have a choice in it.

Colly says, cut him in the ball sack, take his head for a trophy!

She stands eyeing Bart's dark and uncertain shape.

Colly says, if he were any good he'd be able to throw that knife right into the heart of the other person.

She says, how can you fight well with one hand?

She wishes she had not said it.

Bart starts to laugh and his good strong teeth are showing and she thinks, how can a man like this have teeth like that when everybody else's teeth are rotting?

He says, with a knife, everyone is equal.

Colly says, knives are so old-fashioned. I want a firearm.

Bart says, if another person comes at you with a knife you will always get cut. But you can use this knowledge as strength.

He rolls up a cuff with his teeth and shows her his wrist. In the flicker-light she sees his wrist run with scars. She gasps, brings a hand to his skin, and at the touch withdraws it. Bart does not seem to notice, continues talking, but she does not listen, watches him instead. Wonders at what kind of life he has led, how he has been brought to here, this moment with her, moving now pure as spirit in front of the fire, like a dancer, shadow and knife.

* * *

They hear it first before it comes upon them. The earth drummed by hooves. A great bellow disembodied of its driver. Then they see it coming over the hill, a closed coach of some kind drawn by a team of galloping horses. She steps into the ditch and watches it come, counts six horses, turns and sees Bart standing on the road. He spits and says, typical. She studies the advancing coach and studies Bart and looks at the coach again, how each horse is becoming visible, their ankles socked whitely and the coachman in black with his mouth at full roar and his hand cutting *X*s with the lash. Then she sees there is a second man in the off-seat leaning out as if to see better the who of this fellow standing on the road.

She shouts, get out of the way!

Bart does not move. He shouts, they think they own the place. Expect us to climb the hedgerow.

She knows the horses will not be brought to a stop, shouts again at Bart but he stands defiant. How this hoof-thunder and their bawling beast-mouths like despair drum her heart. She can see now the horses' musculature ripple in the chill sun like light flecks on rolling river water, begins to imagine worse than what is — sees in her mind that what is advancing is hell opened onto the world, the driver some devil and his demon in the off-seat, pounding towards them as if from a breach in the spirit realm — that what is advancing upon John Bart is the full incarnation of evil. The devil and his henchman shouting and Bart not budging an inch and she wants to close her eyes to this thing that will happen, the killing of Bart, but in the very instant the horses are upon him, Bart steps lightly off the road, and in that same moment the man in the off-seat hangs off the carriage and kicks Bart in the head.

Torn air pulls after the carriage and dust coils the road.

She sees Bart lying dead in the thicket.

She sees Bart slowly moving.

Then he is sitting up like a man after sleep. She runs to him shouting, are you dead? John Bart squints at her with one eye open, holds his hand to his head.

What is wrong with you? she says. Why didn't you get off the road? Why are you so stupid?

He stares at her with eyes that sudden her to think of some black pebble you might pull from a river glazed in its slip-coat of water, its mystery of origin held within, and then his eyes leap at her with anger.

He says, I am not stupid in the least. Don't you see what is going on around you? The have-it-alls and well-to-doers who don't give a fuck what is happening to the ordinary people. You saw that village yesterday and how prosperous it was, untouched by this curse. The arrogance of that driver. This is the way of things now. It could be the end of the world for the likes of us, but to the likes of them, they aren't bothered. Do you know what I think? Those who are starving on the roads still believe deliverance is going to come. But who is going to deliver them? Not God and not the Crown and not anybody in this country. The people are living off hope. Hope is the lie they want you to believe in. It is hope that carries you along. Keeps you in your place. Keeps you down. Let me tell you something. I do not hope. I do not hope for anything in the least because to hope is to depend upon others. And so I will make my own luck. I believe there are no rules anymore. We are truly on our own in all this. If they have left us to fend for ourselves then we will do just that. We should meet it standing up. I believe that if I want that goddamn carriage to slow down or get off the road I can make it happen. I really believe this. Either I win or they win. There can be no other. I will make it happen, for how else am I supposed to live? What is happening now is no different from the end of the world, the only difference is that the rich can continue to live without affliction. The gods have abandoned us, that's how I figure it. It is time to be your own god.

* * *

We must look like some pair of raggle-taggles, she thinks. Crows circling the field for the worm. Bart on the road with his sleeve rolled up, daring people to look. And the way she is growing out now, in every direction, she thinks. She has stopped tying her chest down with cloth. Keeps her boy's cap in her pocket. Likes to run her hand through her hair.

Womaning, Colly calls it. You are womaning all over. You are turning into Mam. You are daring him to look.

She finds herself staring at Bart. Tells herself she is trying to understand him. How he has eyes that listen. Eyes that stare into the deepest part. She feels the loosening of things she has willed down and forgotten. Hears words that come unbidden from her own never, words that tell a tale of her life. When she says her name aloud to him, Bart smiles. He says, in my head I had taken to calling you Girly but Grace is better.

She whispers her name to herself. Grace. The sound of your own name is like stepping into some old-known river. Now you can be yourself again.

She asks him to tell her his story but he shrugs and doesn't answer.

Later, he says, I came from a fishing family but I was quite useless to them. He laughs and then his face falls and he goes quiet. One time I awoke to see my brother burning to death in a blanket. He fell asleep drunk beside the fire. What could I do with one hand?

The roads are lit with wildflower and the world to bright. Cowslips wittering the ditches. The dandelions spoken in their best yellow lean over each other like brothers. An orchid one time, white as you like. Now and again, despite Bart's hand, there are people who want to walk with them. An old drover half deaf, his hands wagging in the empty air as if to express the loss of his cattle. A woman in a man's woollen cap who tells them she has walked nineteen miles since sunrise, walking with her arms folded, leaning into the thought of how she will ask a cousin for assistance. She thinks, it is easy to tell your story to strangers because no one on these roads judges another.

There is a certain look from Bart and they make their excuses and leave such walkers, find turnoffs they aren't taking, return to some farmhouse they have their eye on and wait for night. They knife open padlocks, trick open latch doors, flat-foot through sculleries, whisper to awakening dogs. Bart says, you take just enough but no more unless you get into one of the far bigger houses, then you take what you like.

They walk the roads supping ketchup from a bottle and she can feel some sort of gathering power, the world widened for summer and how it throws open the evening sky. She wonders if they are part of this beauty, part now of nature's natural return to power. She finds herself looking strangely at Bart. How often it seems he has tricked open the latch door of her mind. The way their minds seem to meet in the middle. The way he says the exact same thing she is thinking at the same time.

That house is empty.

or

The face on that one!

or

That was some dog.

She says to him, when I was younger I used to lie awake thinking about time, the length of it, the idea of God, lie awake thinking of what it might mean to live forever and ever, of what that might be like, trying to live for all eternity in heaven but my mind would fall inwards at such thought and I would get into a panic.

Bart says, I thought I was the only one who did that. When I was nine or ten I used to lie awake all night trying to imagine the idea of endless time in heaven without day or night or the need or want for anything, no need for sleep or food or heat or another's comfort and yet it seems to me that everything in life is related to these things otherwise there would be nothing to live for, and so I came to the conclusion that it was fucking pointless to live like that and decided I wouldn't like to try.

They enter an abandoned cottier's house and she is struck by the feeling she has been here before. How the world keeps making strange places feel familiar — the sight of hills at a certain angle of light or the shape of a tree she could never before have seen and yet it is like she knows the tree from memory or the memory of a dream. And now this room and how it echoes with the feeling of being known to her. She watches Bart touch the wall with his hand. He says, I feel like I was here once before. She startles him with her look.

She says, do you think someday when we were younger we just dreamed all this, forgot it until now?

Upon the morning road some black-dressed fellow is trying to catch up with them. Then she sees it is a priest, how he walks leaning into hurry. He calls out for them to stop. When he meets them he is sweating, wipes at his brow, pleads with them to follow. He says, the men who were hired did not show up. It is a sad matter.

She notices now he does not know what to do with his hands and that his voice, lush and deep, does not go with his figure.

Colly whispers, I'll bet he's one of them fake priests wandering the roads, men dressed in cassocks asking for alms, taking their cassocks off at night and climbing into bed with widows and daughters, praising God and all the saints while trying to pierce their insides, and how can you know this man is telling the truth, that this isn't some scheme he's up to?

Bart offers the priest his hand without discussion. She bends to pluck a dandelion and blows the seeds at his back.

Colly says, what did you wish for?

She says, I wished for that other hand to wither.

Throwing hate now at Bart, who chats to this priest as if he has always known him. They are talking about the trouble. She hears the priest say, the tree that is leaden with its own fruit breaks its bough come winter. It is greatness that leads to the ruin of itself. That is what they will find out.

She wonders who he is talking about, priests do nothing but spout easy wisdom.

They are taken to a house of three coffins. There are two men in white shirts and waistcoats, three women and a boy. A woman says in a low voice, she's dead now, God be with her in heaven.

Grace tries not to look at these people with their woes, the boy casting her a malevolent look as she gets under a coffin, an ash box full with the body of some weightless child, the sound of a woman gasping as the coffin is lifted. She studies their house for something to steal.

There is a forever to this walk, she thinks. Colly going on and on, says, coffin work is other people's bother, why did you say yes to it? She says, I didn't say yes, I never even opened my mouth. Never has she felt so embarrassed, carrying the coffin of some child you have never known and everyone looking at you. Her eyes eat at the ground, eat at the trees, eat at the sky as if asking to be lifted away out of here. She thinks, how far away is this churchyard? Why didn't Bart ask? And what are we doing carrying the coffins of strangers? Every time she looks she finds the boy staring. She tries to imagine the life of the child she is carrying, to imagine the child doing different things but each picture in her mind is a version of herself, or it is Bran or Finbar running out the door to fall on the ground and sit crying or she can see them pulling the ginger cat's tail before the ginger ran off because that is what cats do if you torment them like that and you were warned but you didn't listen. She wonders if the boy who hates her with his looks will always remember this child she is carrying, but what will happen when the boy grows old and dies, who will remember the child then? Of a sudden she sees how memory works, that all memory eventually falls into a great forgetting that will include herself and everyone at Blackmountain and everyone on earth and the thought alone is enough to make your head burst.

Song-smoke. A room darkening to firelight. They have come back to the house and she stands silent by the wall watching the way they are gathered, hating the songs that seem to dream sadly out their mouths, hating the talk of their dead. A man saying, their road has ended, it is God's will. The boy burning his eyes at her. She thinks, why is it Bart does not notice? Colly whispering, come on, let's go. She tries giving Bart the full look of trouble but he seems to be enjoying himself. She slides along the wall towards the door, comes up against a pair of heavy black tongs, slips her coat over them, slips outside into the gloaming and away down the path, away from that bastard—

Bart shouts for her to wait up.

Colly says, grab him by the balls with those tongs, see how he likes it.

She turns and sees him produce a kettle out of his coat. He starts swinging it by the bool.

We're some pair, he says. You'd almost think we'd planned it.

The leaves are trembling gently. The leaves are letting go their light. How the leaves release their light whispering grief to the dark and tomorrow the same of it. They pass over a bridge that echoes the life-rush of water. Water turning the stones. Water giving way to water in endless follow. Walking now a narrow road through a glen with old trees, larch and alders, she thinks. Such trees soon to be coffins. She tries not to see herself being laid in such a box but when you tell yourself not to look at something your mind does not listen and does what it wants.

Bart going on about that priest again but she doesn't want to hear.

Colly is spitting. Why's he always deciding things for us, that spuddy-hander—hee!—I would have said no to the priest, said, go and fuck off, holy father, we were grand before they both came along, we knew what we were at.

She thinks about what the look of that boy did to her, how his look wormed hate inside her, and now it sits wriggling under her skin and all she was doing was helping. And now she is carrying these stupid tongs as if anybody in the next town or some tinker on the road would even buy them.

Colly says, clatter him over the head with them, show him who's boss.

Bart is still going on. He says, did you hear that priest, he was some sort of intellectual. Told me about the grief of Achilles. Said that he was overcome with grief for his friend Patry, Patro—whatever his name was, Pat, and that Pat's mother, or was it Achilles's mother, came along and gave him some elaborate gold buckle that had everything beautiful on the earth engraved on it and that made him happy for a while, made him forget his grief, imagine—

She wants for him to shut up with his talk of death and buckles. She wants for— she shouts, would you ever shut up with it? All this stupid talk. What would you know about Achilles and that Pat fellow? All that talk the other day and you got your answer for it—a kick in the head. It's made you daft, so it has. It was you made us go and carry those coffins. You never asked me. I never felt so stupid in my whole life. And here I am crying and carrying these stupid tongs and I don't know why I have them.

She has not noticed she is crying until she has said it. Takes pleasure in watching his face crumple, the sinking of his brows and his mouth. How he falls into silence. For a moment he looks as if he wants to say something but cannot quite figure it, his mouth hanging open and then closing beneath that ridiculous horseshoe mustache. His walk seems to thicken. In the far-off there is something approaching, some slow horse and cart.

When Bart speaks, it sounds to her as if he doesn't know whether to be soft with her or defiant. He says, what I said the other day is— what I said is that there's no point sitting around hoping for things to get better. You must make them better yourself.

Like what? she says. Like what? Like this? She steps into the centre of the road and sits down and folds her arms, puts the tongs across her lap. Stares at the oncoming cart. Bart stops and stares at her.

C'mon, he says. Get up off the road, will you.

He tries to pull her up by the elbow.

Colly says, stay where you are, show him who's stronger.

She says, touch me again and I'll tong the balls off you.

She eyes what comes and sees the cart is a gig. Wishes it would hurry. So slowly, slowly does it come she wonders if she should bother with this protest, wonders what she is really doing, this cart will come and clatter you on the head.

Bart humps against the hedgerow watching.

He says, that thing is so slow we'll be here all night.

She can see the outline of a single horse and two people on the gig. A side lantern swinging uncertain against the dusk.

Bart says, quit your stupid game and get off the road.

She says, fuck up. I'm only doing what you tell me.

Slowly she stands up and eyes the coming gig so intently it is as if the world has narrowed to a tunnelling dark and she sends into it her will, decides she will prove him wrong, or right, whatever, wishes the vehicle to a stop. The gig seems to slow and yet continues to bear upon her and she thinks it is not slowing down but speeding up, hears a warning shout that is not John Bart's, the rattle and hoof-fall and the screaming in her head and there comes another shout but then the gig slows and comes to a shuddering stop. She cannot move her body, though her breath has already run for the ditch. Colly shouting, you did it, you mad bitch!

She finds herself staring into the faces of some elderly couple in the getup of townfolk. They are sitting very still upon their fear. The leaden way the man moves his arm across the woman's bosom as if to protect her and then he stands up and he is watching the trees both sides of the glen and he is watching John Bart's shape in the ditch and then he shouts, please, whatever you do, don't harm us, I'll give you what you want.

It is then that she sees herself, a person half dark standing centre of the road with these tongs in her arms like— they are the length of a firearm and I see one thing and you see another and what the man sees is a gun.

The man lobs a heavy stone with his arm and she watches it rise and strike the road with a chinking thud that is not the sound of a stone, the shadow of Bart fleet from the ditch to grab it.

Her breath is squashed. She is spiked all over with soreness. Running and running while still holding the tongs. They slow to a wheezing walk and watch the night close around them in strangeness. They do not know for sure where they are. She thinks, how luck like that can fall from the sky, or perhaps not, perhaps you made your own luck, perhaps Bart was right. They step through darkling trees and she can feel Bart watching her strangely as if trying to puzzle her out. Then he laughs hugely.

He says, you are some woman, do you know that? Some woman. He shakes his head as if he cannot understand her.

She looks at him strangely. Nobody has ever called her a woman before.

He says, the pirate queen of Connacht, that's who you are. Grace O'Malley—ha! Now, isn't that a coincidence. That's what we'll call you from now on. To have the nerve to do something like that with a pair of tongs. My God.

She doesn't know where to look, so she sits on a rock and looks at the sky instead.

He says, hold out your hands. He pours the coins into her butterflied palms and then they count out their fortune — three pounds and ten shillings and twopence.

She says, do you think it's enough?

He throws away the kettle, says, ha! Enough for what? The high life? You are some woman.

Then his voice quietens. He says, we need to be watchful. That was a big thing we did back there. They are going to come looking for us now. That will bring them out, all right.

Her breathing is ragged and there is weariness reaching for every limb. She wonders for how much longer she can run like this, can see herself running through the night and the tiredness eating in and the horsemen catching up because bodies get tired, that is what bodies do if you do not rest them and you are scuppered if you haven't a horse for such matters. She looks up to see the dusk's last light and the weight of night on top of it.

She says, what do you think will happen the day the world ends?

Bart's brow puzzles. What kind of question is that? The world is not going to end. It will just keep on going. But if it was to end at some time in the future, it would look just like this. There will be clouds there marching westwards carrying rain and somewhere else it will be raining already and somebody will be getting wet and cursing about it. The same as it ever was.

She tells herself, the pirate queen of Connacht.

She knows now they are ancient and young and will never die.

The dreaming world is shaking free its shadows when they reach Athlone town. Her eyes tug with sleep. She thinks her feet are broken, has walked the night tense for the sound of their coming—a vision of grouped torchlight in the far-off. Just a bit farther, Bart kept saying. Yet here they are now, her heels scorched, into the town without bother. She tells Bart she wants a room and a bed, wonders what it would be like to stay in a boardinghouse.

Bart says, we would just make ourselves known to them.

She says, then tell me, what is the point of all that money?

Colly says, do you think we can get a room to ourselves?

She watches the dawnlight creep the doorways and lanes and courtyards. It shows the rough sleepers for who they are, slumps of thought made physical. And yet the streets carry a better sort of person, early-rising men in fine capes and overcoats going to the day's business and women in fine-cut cloaks just the right size. She watches the early risers for watchy eyes. A wide enough street with signage for everything. A man dragging onto the road a sign that announces the best in parasols.

They walk to where the town seems to end and they meet a great bridge. Bart says, this is the Shannon and that is a notion of hell right there. He is pointing to a great army barracks on the bank of the river. Nearby women are tramping linen at the waterside, the water passing by bruised and silent. A man walks past them wearing a coat with a sleeve torn off.

Colly says, perhaps this is what people are doing now, they are pawning one sleeve at a time—soon there will be people walking about naked but for one leg of their breeches or just a single sleeve—speaking of which, that cack-handed Bart, don't you think a witness would remember how he looked?

Shush up, she says.

Bart looks at her. Are you starting up again with your complaining?

I didn't say anything.

You were muttering at me just now.

I was not. I was just talking about taking my boots off.

She imagines her feet like bruised fruit, dipping them in warm water, washing gently until you bring out the skin's bright pink—to have the feet of a girl again.

Never before has she been on a staircase or entered a house such as this. Dawnlight like someone's long foot on the first two steps, the landlady haunting upwards with a candle. She walks behind Bart, Colly gasping. This house is a ten-roomer at least, he says. The house and the staircase seem to lean sideways as they travel upwards and she hears a man hoarse behind a door whispering some conspiracy while the wood mutters agreement. Upwards, upwards with falling-off thoughts until she grabs hold of Bart's coattail, Colly whispering, you're his little limpet, stuck to the rocks of his arse, and she lets go and holds on to the crooked wall instead. A strange man stepping down past them hauls after him the vapours of drink and the staircase and walls begin to narrow and lean farther sidewards until she is convinced the entire house will topple over under the weight of their walking or the staircase will collapse under them and she will fall all the way down into damnation. And who is the landlady faintly candled but Mammon holding the keys to hell.

Two beds crammed tight under a slanty ceiling. Bart says, Christ, is there a window at least? She catches the landlady staring at Bart's arm. He says, send up a basin and hot water and hurry up with it. Bart then to sleep like a man dead and she lets her feet out of her boots and washes them in the candlelight, slowly at first, sadly, for she hasn't washed her feet with soap in such a long time. The reality of her feet. How they have been unshaped by boot, corned and thickened, the heels like stumpy rocks. The flesh not pink or even white but blue and sometimes black and she climbs into bed saddened, finds the wrinkled coarse sheet still warm with the heat of somebody else, the same vapours off the blanket as that man they passed on the stairs. How the ceiling presses down upon you.

She says to Colly, the house is going to topple over while we're asleep and then we will be dead.

Colly says, if it happens in your sleep you might not notice.

She has worried herself awake despite the bed's comfort. She thinks, Bart with his one arm, Bart picking up the purse. Colly is right. He will be easy to finger. She tries to think of sleep and pretends she is asleep in Blackmountain, realizes she can no longer be sure of her mother's face.

She whispers, Colly, are you awake?

I'm fast asleep.

Colly, I can't remember anything of Blackmountain.

Ugh.

Tell me something to remember.

Like what.

Whatever.

Do you remember the wiggly hole you could put your finger in?

What?

The peephole in the door.

And now she can see it, kneeling to the hole with a squinting look, the world blurred outside. The faint smell of old resin. The echoing of a voice that is the voice-shape of Mam held but not seen and why can't you think of her face clearly when you think of her?

Do you mind the way we used to crow-squawk the door—hee!—opening and closing it over and over, driving Mam demented, leave that door closed, she'd shout, shut it, would you!

Now she is standing by the door looking out upon what she always saw, the forever of those hills and that ancient traveller of light walking upon them making different each day.

From blackest sleep she is poked awake by Bart, can hardly open her eyelids.

Colly says, if he does that again I'll put my fist through his head.

Bart says, some person, a drunkard, I think, came into the room while we slept. He didn't take anything. It's a good thing I sleep with the money.

She thinks she can remember half waking to somebody coming into the room, some silent figure that stood by the door as if awaiting permission to step into her dream, the door being closed again, moving through sleep to see who it was and then too tired to care. She wonders now if Bart had not said anything would she have even remembered, moves to the side of the bed and wiggles a finger through a finger-hole in the blanket that might also be the wiggly hole in the fir door of home. Tries to match this Bart beside her with the Bart from her dream, another Bart who stood with two fine hands and how he turned before the wolf and put his hand into its mouth.

The real Bart turns around and whispers, put on your boots. What kind of person barefoots when they can afford lodging?

She says, and you with your robbery-arm hanging out.

They are shape-shifters that step out of the store and into the parade of the town. The afternoon sweet with light and her feet light in these new booties fit for a lady and everything so pleasing and how could you stop looking at them, a pair of calfskin side-laced boots so strange she is unsure how to walk in them, their leathery-upwards smell, the glide and press of the cut.

She thinks, a fish cannot become a bird, or can it? Maybe it can.

Colly says, perhaps if you'd stop looking for yourself in the windows you wouldn't walk like a hen.

She thinks, you should be watching for watchers, and yet she knows that no one is looking, that Bart was wrong, first saying no to the buying of new clothing, then saying we will only attract attention. Now he looks so pleased with himself wrapped in a thick-knit charcoal cape that hides his hand so well. He seems to walk straighter but then he turns as if nettled by some thought and snaps a comment about the way she is walking, drawing attention, he says, and she answers with a flutter of her new ivy-green cloak.

She watches the well-dressed ladies and wants to be noticed, for you too are now a woman among them. That cloak is nothing compared to my cloak, my cloak is newer than yours. She thinks, the carriage of these people. If the world is ending most of these fancy Nancys don't seem too bothered about it. And yet the streets are haunted by faces made long to the bone, sunken eyes that reach for you. They pass by the coach stop and it is crowded with beggars waiting to harry passengers from the next coach.

She cannot decide which is better, to be hungry in the countryside or to be hungry in a town. Who would want to live in a town? she thinks. When she was young she imagined the strangeness of big towns but she sees now each town is the same as any other. The same high buildings and how the spaces between buildings echo the same sounds, always the same bridge with the same layabouts and louts watching everything that passes, eyeing you over and under. Streets that brattle with beggars and boot-boys and criminals and always someone shouting at a mule or a horse and how animals stare silently back at you. The gentry wear perfume and no wonder, she thinks, for people dump their toilet under their noses and though the river blows freshening air it is nothing like the air that comes down off Blackmountain, heaven-scented and devout in its duty to clear out the house.

She stares into the face of a meaty man leaning over a stall of gizzards and chicken heads and is astonished by his prices.

Bart says, we will eat at the lodgings tonight and not on the street, where children will be hanging off you.

She says, oh will we, now?

Bart wants to play billiards and is halfway up the stairwell but she stands at the door and will not go in.

Colly says, would you look at that scrab-arm, who wants to play billiards against the likes of him?

She turns and Bart comes back down after her, his face deepening with rage, his eyes with their popped-out look.

He says, what's wrong with you now?

She does not want to tell of this new fear of going up staircases, that in the dream she had the staircase collapsed and then the building fell on top of her and she was awake in her own dream even though she was dead. She wraps her cloak about herself and puts her back to him, begins to dance from one foot to the other, jumps in the air and spins around, opens out the cloak in some final dramatic flourish.

Bart's stare is long and cold and his eyes do not blink.

Then he says, you're some woman.

They have bought enough tobacco to smoke hurt into their lungs. Two nights in a bed and she can feel her bones thickening in gluttonous sleep. Tries not to think of the dirt on her lady booties, because nothing lasts forever, not even new shoes. They are walking through Market Place when Bart takes hold of her wrist and points. He says, I know that fellow.

He hurries her along, his face with a questioning look. Then he lets her go and marches onwards, his nose become that of a pointer hound to the breeze. She follows as he pushes through people, watches him rise on his toes to see better, turning down a narrow street and then another and she sees the man they are following turn into a lane that takes the world to quiet, sees him climb into some temporary erection of wood that is a shelter thrown together. Her hand has gone to her knife. There are rough sorts slumped here under this wood and a gnawed dog has lost its growl. She hears Bart shouting, is that you, McNutt? Sees a pair of large boots stirring and then a big man climbing slowly out. He stands to his full height and the man is all boots and he is a head taller than Bart. His mouth falls open and then he puts his hands into fists and steps towards Bart, grabs him by the lapels, and goes for a head-butt, and she is running now with the knife and it is then she sees Bart smiling, the tall man pushing Bart away in mock fight. He holds out a right handshake and leans back and laughs, offers his left hand instead. Bart takes it, pulls him into a hug.

The man called McNutt says, John Bart. How in the fuck?

Bart says, I saw you just now on the street, knew the head on you a mile off.

McNutt says, you clop-armed cunt, you.

She knows McNutt is in winter, watches his face as the three of them sit at the landlady's table. He has the look of one who sucks on his tongue, she thinks. His cheekbones held high at the angle of want and not beauty. His eyes are too close together. His boots too big under the table. His hair is falling out from all that chatter. She watches his eyes lick at a piggin as it is filled with goat's milk, his eyes grabbing at the landlady's backside, as if to eat her haughty flesh. When he reaches for the milk she sees the arm of a man in slow perish. He is a man rescued from hell, she thinks. And yet, the on and on and on of his talking as if he has endless strength. The constant hoopla and performance. The little jinks he makes with his elbows. Since he has arrived she has not gotten a word in.

McNutt says, I was in Galway for a while killing stray dogs, a nuisance to the streets, let me tell you. They told me I was only to use one bullet per dog but how is a man supposed to take a clean shot every time one of those hounds sees you coming and smells its own death? I'm sure it's true that dogs are more noble when they decide to die by themselves, take themselves off to a field or whatever. But they are noisy as fuck when shot in the leg and trying to make a run for it. Did you know that dogs scream just the same as humans when they know they are going to die? Most times you'd have to finish them off with the club—

Colly says, will the man ever shut up?

She catches herself looking at McNutt's hands.

—that job ended when I threatened to put a bullet through the forehead of a certain fellow so I came down here to the belly button of Ireland. That's what I call it. Did you ever hear that one before? Got here on the side of a car chatting to this crooked fellow who says he was going all the way to Cork but spent the entire time eyeing my pockets and I told him there was good reason why Cork was at the arse of Ireland and then I got the watch from his pocket because I figured if he was going to make an attempt to rob me he might as well rob his own watch. Got work as a packer at a warehouse out the road from here and then that ended and got work as a gater—

Colly says, shut the fuck up, McNutt!

—figured a way to let some boys in now and again, if you know what I mean, but then that ended when— well, I'll tell you later. I had work lined up for next week when you found me but I won't bother with that now, seeing as we're all laughing the three laughs of the leprechaun.

She watches McNutt drain the cup. He moves his huge boots under the table, taking up all the room. He says, this is some party, do you know what I read in the newspaper, that it takes six goats to make the milk of one cow, but all things being equal, the milk of the goat is as good as the other, in other words goat's milk goes underrated in certain parts of—

She can hear two women—whores! McNutt says—talking about money on the staircase and she wonders at the who of them, hears the door open and some coachman enters without word. The way he looks at them without looking. McNutt goes quiet as the man takes a chair by the fireside and she watches him light a pipe, watches him unfold a newspaper without taking his eyes off them. McNutt begins chatting in a low voice with Bart. It is the talk of old brothers, each buckling into laughter. She stares at McNutt but he pays her no attention, knifes Bart with a look. A pair of low dogs, she thinks.

Colly whispers, I don't trust him one bit, he watches everything with his fingers—how can you trust a man whose eyes are so close together?

She thinks, it is a kindness that we are doing to him. This hardman with his broken fists. A jester with a falling mouth. You'd think he would be grateful.

Colly whispers. Riddle me this, what gives a good stab and has only one arm? I'll give you a clue, you can use it on the fire.

McNutt says, anyhow, I stopped me from going on.

They watch the landlady saw bread and put it on the table, three hands reaching for it. She eats bread and wants to stroke her lace booties. The smell of meat cuttings cooking over the fire is the greatest of all smells until she turns and sees the coachman is watching her and what lies in his look, how the smell disappears and she lowers the new boot she has been admiring with her fingers. Something in the coachman's physicality that suggests a comfort with violence, a man whose arms can take a full team of horses. The way he is twirling his knuckle hair as if he were Boggs, and this meat smell suddens her to the table at Blackmountain, the orbed white starving eyes of the youngers pleading at her and the landlady's voice is Sarah's and she dizzies to standing and closes her eyes, finds the door, finds her way up the staircase, Bart shouting some question after her but he does not follow.

Wake up, the voice says. It is the voice of her father and she feels herself being gathered into his power, the smell of him uniquely, that ancient smell, old as the world is and brought to her from so long ago, and he is shadow and he is voice and he is the deepest hum—

Wake up, I said. She opens her eyes to a kingdom of dark men. Bart is poking at her, leaning over her with his warm breath, McNutt is to the wall beside a guttering candle that throws him about the room in frightening long shapes. He is picking at his nails, ignoring her.

She sits up, punches Bart's hand away from her. What?

Bart says, we have to leave. Now, up with it.

She cannot blink the dark from her eyes. She lies back down because it's the middle of the night and that is what you do when you are in a warm bed, you sleep and let that be the end of it.

Bart pulls her into sitting.

Colly says, do that again and I will break that good hand.

Bart says, that lodger in the dining room tonight. McNutt has seen him before. He's a detective from the barracks. We are under suspicion.

She looks to McNutt, who nods solemnly at Bart. I've seen him on the street before. He took an interest in her, all right.

They are but shadows that slip the bolts of the door and close it with a click. Silently onto the street, their breaths bold before them and feathered in the moon-blue cold where the river sends up sound of itself. The streets are empty but for some hacksaw-coughing fool who might be asleep in a doorway and in another street there sounds the echoed roar of a drunk, his voice ringing like bad iron hammered by night, like a warning shout from someone else's dream, she thinks, while the sound of the river is the sound of whatever you want it to be, the scolding whispers of the dead. She sees the drunkard begin to sit up and McNutt goes to him and swings a kick that flattens the man into his shadow. Bart pulling him by the coat. Enough's enough, McNutt. McNutt stepping back with his hands in the air as if to say, I hardly touched him. Then he says, a paid scout for the barracks, no doubt. Something about McNutt's carriage that tells her this danger he speaks of does not belong here but is carried and made by him, and what if this is all some tidy plan to get in on our scheme?

Of a sudden McNutt turns upon her as if he has heard the very thought.

He says, tell me, pirate queen, what are you taking those tongs for?

Colly says, tell him to fuck off, these tongs are a holy relic.

They walk two nights under the muffled stars making for the mountains. The dark as tight as a fist. She speaks to the moon like an old friend, watches it come and go in silence. In the black of nowhere they hide from the road and watch a passing procession of shadows, ten people, she thinks, perhaps more, and two pack animals. Not a sound between these walkers and how it seems as if their silence is holy and she thinks of Christ and his disciples walking some ancient road, watches these people pass by with their mystery hidden and at one with the colours of night.

McNutt keeps complaining about the dark, about the want of candles and brown paper. He says, I want to kill somebody but this is nothing but treacherous.

Bart says, you'll get used to it.

Colly is deepening into sulk, for he can hardly get a word in.

Sometimes she thinks she can hear laughter in the curling tongue of the wind. They walk until the sun knifes open the horizon and wait for evening again.

By day these boreens and townlands are busy enough. They watch from their hiding places the passing beggars, the people carting belongings, the children tailing elders along the road. But by night when you walk these roads the villages are sudden silences, stacks of huts that rise soundless against the dark and even their dogs are quiet. Having to tell McNutt to shut up as they foot through them. If he is not complaining then it is a hundred songs a night and always with the stories. Did you hear the one about the man who sold tin to the devil? Did you hear the one about the evil eye on the washer-woman? Did you hear the one about the king and the crow? Did you know that if you can hear a crow talking you will be both a king and a wise fellow? Do you know how the wheel of luck turns?

Colly wants to know all sorts of impossible things. The place of the soul—where it is kept. Do you think it resides in the organs or could it be inside the body but not of the body, or could there be some kind of box for it in the brain, like the place where humour is kept, it makes sense that it would take the shape of the body because it would be easier to travel with, but if that is the case, what happens when you lose an arm, like John Bart, for instance, does his soul have a bandy arm also?

She thinks about her own soul, all that has been put in it, wonders how a soul can be of the same essence when you are changing a little bit every day, when you are no longer the same person, because you are not the same person at the end of the year as you were at the start of it, and sometimes you change during the day, depending on certain events. And if that is the case, and you die at one age rather than another, would your soul not be completely different? That is a mystery for the sages.

She picks fuchsia flowers from bushes spidery in the dawn, sucks the faint taste of honey. The Slieve Bloom Mountains rising before them. How they hold to the sky like some great wave from the sea.

The mountains greet them with mist. It seeps and clings, hangs mystery over everything. The rising track humped with sedge disappears up the hillside. A crow shouts some message about the loss of its body and the trees wait like marauders. The world-sound so still but for the boom and echo of McNutt. Did you hear the one about the old crow that slept in the eagle's nest? Twas the coldest of nights and the crow was fed up with the constant chill. So he takes to a nest that is not his own, finds a fledgling in it, and what does he do but take the fledgling off and murder it, buries it under a rock. Then he goes back to the nest and waits for the eagle to arrive, and when it does, it thinks the crow is its fledgling, sits on it, and keeps it warm all night. That's the type of cleverness I like.

It is Colly who sees the figure first. He says, there's a man sleeping in that ditch. Legs and boots prop out of a bush as if man could root with a tree. And yet how the eyes know before they can take full measure that the man is dead. The feet at the unusual angle of dying. An odd stillness while everything else in the ditch trembles in the life of the wind. Don't look, she warns Colly, but how can you help it? The strange fact that is a dead body. What it is and what it isn't. She sees the dead man's hand open as if to express in death the full measure of his want, the hand reaching for something to eat, or perhaps it was because he was dying alone in this ditch that he was reaching into memory, reaching for the hand of a woman he loved or for the hand of his mother, for they say all men call for their mothers upon death.

Colly says, do you think that when the birds ate his eyes, his soul escaped out his eye sockets?

They stand over the body and McNutt gives it a kick and she shouts, stop that, you brute pig.

McNutt says, I'm just making sure he's dead.

Bart says, toss him a coin instead.

McNutt says, I have no coins to give him.

She takes out the purse and counts what's left, puts a penny into the dead man's hand. Watches McNutt lag behind as they walk onwards, sees him bend to the dead man, take the coin back off him.

He says, I'll give it back to him in hell.

They have waited and watched this lordly house and the steepened valley behind it. The comings and goings of a fashionable carriage. Watching evening take the house to dark. She catches Bart's eye and they share a look that is strength. They are creep-foot towards the house. Music reaching from a bright-lit room and then McNutt's fierce knocking brings the tune of the fox hunters' jig to a stop. Voices tangle then untangle and she can hear a man and then a woman and it must be a servant-woman's voice worrying through the great door. Who goes there? McNutt's physique seems to change and he holds his hand oddly aloft in the air as if finding the true pitch of a song. Then he speaks in the voice of a gentleman. She cannot believe it, it is like a voice you would hear in a town.

He says, I am sorry to trouble you but I am a member of the gentry. My carriage took an accident farther up the hill. I require some assistance urgently, if you please. My coachman needs a doctor. If needs be I have letters of introduction. I am Philip Fulton of the Fultons of Ballinasloe. The grain exporters, you know.

She watches Bart snicker into his fist, looks at McNutt in wonder, cannot understand how a brute can magic such words out. They hear whispers and a woman's voice saying, let him in, let him in, and a servant-man's voice she guesses arguing back and she smiles at the dark when she hears the bolt being pulled and then the great wind of McNutt gales through the door, brings the man down with his fist, marches into the house with a shout.

Cock-a-doodle-doo.

She sees through her teeth, feels it surge as she enters, this anger that has risen fanged and fearless, wide as a wolf's mouth. McNutt now is widened, a warrior who marshals the housekeeper and the fallen man, who might be a butler, into a room down the hall. Bart like wind passing beside her and she sees them both in the hallway's great mirror, how their eyes shine whitely out of mud-painted faces, her hair braided with twigs, you look like some creature that crawled from a ditch.

Bart takes a lamp out of the hand of the servant-woman and steps quietly up the staircase. She follows McNutt into a parlour room full of screams and shouts, two women standing guard over a young boy and there is the homeowner, Mr Moneybags or whatever you want to call him, his bursting red face, and McNutt drops him to the floor with his fist, the man getting onto his hands and knees and crawling to his family the way a baby would and McNutt chasing after him, kicking him in the seat of his pants. The man trailing piss along the carpet. In the commotion of knocking they must have laid their musical instruments upon the floor and with a splintering kick McNutt sends a fiddle to the wall.

He shouts, now, cunty, where is your gold hid?

He leans into the face of Mr Moneybags, who sits to the wall reddened and cowered and squeezing impotent fists. McNutt waves his knife alive in front of the man's face, says, did you just fucking piss yourself? In front of your own family? I would not be sorry to kill you.

She leaves the room and finds the pantry deep with food-smell. She inhales it for a moment, takes a sack and bags a five-pound weight of meal, bags a loaf of bread, slides a slimy tongue off a plate into her bag, takes it back out and wraps it in a cloth and bags it again. She grabs a side of wrapped meat. Caterwauling and havoc reach then from the parlour and she runs with the knife, enters to see McNutt has lifted the boy by the ruck of the shirt with his teeth.

Bart then into the room with two fowling pieces hung off his shoulder and a horse pistol stuffed into the band of his breeches. He nestles with his bad arm a powder horn and shot bag. One of the women begins to shout. Why are you doing this? Do you not know who we are? I am on the committee that has been trying to bring relief to the area. I have been writing to Dublin and London. We have been collecting subscriptions. We have been doing what we can. Why would you endeavour to rob us?

McNutt says, shush with your gob music.

He kicks a chair to a wall and climbs up and begins to wrestle with a plaque of stag antlers, frees them with a backwards fall. He comes to standing holding them to his chest, bends and puts them to his head and begins to circle the room and howl. No part of her now belongs to thinking. Her hands are upon the brass candlesticks and they are upon some books and they are upon crystal glasses and she denudes a table of its linen and then they are running for the exit and their bodies are a high song and she sees McNutt fighting the antlers through the door. The same wind that brought them into the house carries them out and they go glittering into that dark riding the wolf's mouth.

The path is treacherous and their walk hushed, Bart leading the group with a papered candle. The moon has sucked the clouds into whirlpool and her feet are constant shouts, her arms near done in, for the weight of their haul is making them grow longer. What she sees in the lucent trees are the faces of men, can hear in the chattering leaves the planning of hounds and horses, riders with arrowed looks, forces being ranged against her ready to follow into the mountains. She thinks, we will have to be like the wind and then they won't find us.

Of a sudden McNutt begins to wheeze a low laugh. He is still carrying the antlers. Then his laugh explodes into a fierce dog's holler. He tries to speak, did you see— I'd love to— just to hit that cunty a dinger again— just to see the piss on his pants.

Colly says, it was a prize left hook, muc, a boxer's best.

She finds herself giggling along with him, for in laughter there is relief. Bart turning to shush them. In the glow of his papered candle he does not look like himself but some stranger, and perhaps that is so, she thinks, perhaps now we are all different. The path steepens and then Bart has them walking across some slippy sheep track. She tries to banish the thought of how one wrong step could send them falling into the downwards dark of the valleys that would surely lead to hell. Her eyes leaping about for something to hold on to and then she sees it—the ruins of a cottage roofless to the stars. She points it out to Bart and he says, it will surely do.

McNutt says, you are a great see'er of things in the dark, Bart. How did you find such a good view?

They make a fire and roast the meat to scalding on a stick, wet their lips with fat. McNutt makes a show of drinking from an empty goblet, begins making toasts, to the high kings of Ireland, to the chieftains and their fighting men, to God in heaven and all the saints who were kind enough to present us with this feast and let us not forget Philip Fulton and all the Fultons of Ballinasloe, who were kind enough to lend us their name, the bunch of cunts.

Even in this dim light she can see Bart staring at her, can feel the weight of his look that is admiration and perhaps also a look of longing but she does not want to think about it. When he has turned she sneaks a look, his face clear in the moonlight that beams through the roof and it is then she sees him different—his whiskers made brilliant and his skin a ghostly silver like some etching in a book, like some great fighter, she thinks, from the olden tales stepped onto this very hillside. She cannot explain this feeling that beats inside her, thinks it might be a feeling of power and freedom, wants to holler aloud to the mountaintops.

She says, nothing in the world is right or not right, there is only this.

McNutt turns upon her with a confused look. What was that?

But now she is up and yelling at the dark. Burn it all, she shouts. Burn everything. Their eyes are moon-caught staring at her and then McNutt is all leap as if finally he has understood. He puts the antlers to his head, hunkers into a low-hipped dance, fashions some unearthly animal sound from his lips as he shuffles around the fire. She takes the linen she stole and billows it upon the blaze, begins to throw onto the fire everything she has taken—hears Bart shout, everything but the candlesticks—a picture frame with a painting of a tree and a child's wooden toy with wheels and two books that sit for a moment resilient to the flames until they too catch fire.

Theirs is a song sounded from the top of heaven and it rolls down the silent mountain to the fools asleep in their beds, and then Bart stands up as if in sudden anger and he leaps to life and they dance it all out, the moon watching behind the peep-hands of trees, dancing the dance that is the laughter of forgetting, the laughter that shakes the pain out, the laughter that makes you a god.

Long days pass listening to McNutt yarning wool with his mouth. Stories of courage and war, slaughter in the four provinces, his dog days in Galway, some old mad nun who followed him about taking her clothes off. What finally brings him to a stop is an encounter that makes him whiten—two shapes sighted nearby in the mist. How they seem not to walk but hover, pass like bundled smoke. Then there are three of them and her heart warns with drums, for who knows what they are, constabulary or soldiers or perhaps they are just people out for a walk, but there is Bart readying the pistol and she is holding the fowling piece and wonders how she will aim it, McNutt not touching his weapon but sitting down like a man brought sick.

When the figures have passed Bart turns upon McNutt. He says, why didn't you ready your gun?

McNutt whispers, this place has the haunting, I know it.

She hears her words flung from her mouth. Who knew you were so superstitious? That is nothing but fool's talk. Those men might be out looking for us.

The quip is tongued before it has been thought to belief. Bart turns to look at her and she cannot read what the look says. She thinks, sometimes the devil waits on the road and walks with you and other times the devil waits inside your head and gives you thoughts to speak.

McNutt leaning back with his arms long on his lap and his big boots splayed out as if nothing were the matter. Then he smirks at her. Run along now, pirate queen, and take the good hand of your lover.

Bart says, it might be time to leave.

They summit the mountains watching the drab evening light for movement. Nothing but bogland and rocks and a wind that moans of ancient loneliness. A wagtail nearby with its whistling suck. Colly starts with a song.

Wee Willie wagtail hopping on a rock,
Mammy says your pretty tail is like a goblin's—

Colly!

They follow a path downwards through bogland that rises then into woodland and meets a clear view of the lowlands. The south a patchwork of green as if all the great fields of Ireland were quilted together, she thinks.

Bart says, that there is very different country. Those are the richest farmers in Ireland.

McNutt says, I've seen a better class of farming among peasants in other districts but anyhow I see what you are saying.

In a lonely ravine they meet a rough cabin. Its walls more mud than stone and it is roofed with tree cuttings that release the thin smoke of a low fire. They hide and watch the movements of a young hermit strung with a hungry look, how he sits on a rock for a long time just blessing himself. McNutt says, his sort will not be missed.

They wait until night and creep upon the cabin. McNutt pricked red from wrestling with a holly bush, calls it a hoor, drags it as quiet as he can, which is not quiet at all, she thinks. Bart's face stern with concentration. They take their different positions around the cabin and she stands holding her breath, wonders if the hermit is asleep or not, begins softly, makes the sound of a mad cat that could also be the sound of the pooka. Colly begins barking. McNutt joins in, rattling the bush with a donkey's braying that would shake a house. Bart begins neighing like a horse. They haunt their strange rustling animal music into the hut until she sees the wooden door burst open and the hermit flee down the mountain dark.

The hermit has lit a good fire and stacked the room with wood.

McNutt has to lie down such is the cramping laughter.

Bart says, he'll think the pooka have come for him. We'll be able to stay here for a while.

Colly begins to woof and they all laugh and McNutt puts a hand to his belly and begs for them to stop.

Candlesticks bring light to eating faces, McNutt all fingers and teeth and she thinks, he is not a donkey at all but a mad dog. They drink bucket water in their goblets and McNutt gives toast to the hermit's health, this fine hut, the wood he stacked for us, and let us hope the man tells the story for the rest of his life about how he was once haunted by the devil.

Later that night, the mountain wind rises and sends the fire-smoke back into the cabin. It enters her eyes, her throat, seeps into her thoughts until she steps outside to breathe in the cold night air, eyes the dark with her arms wrapped to her chest. This wind that carries the same sound as Blackmountain.

Dog days pass under summer's mountainous skies. Such clouds, she thinks, weight the day on top of itself. There is no hurry to anything, neither the gentled heat, nor light, nor time, the days so slowly gathering.

McNutt says, hungry July must be at an end.

This is what Mam always called it, she thinks, that endless month after the old crop ran out and then the wait for August's harvest. This year the wait is thirteen months long. Soon the crop will come and everything will be right again.

She watches the way McNutt handles the meal, pulling his big fist out of the sack. Go easy, she says. He does not look at her. Instead he sits growing into strength. There is a restlessness now in this cramped hut. Bart digging into wood with his knife and Colly chattering about this and that and some other. She wonders if the occasional foragers she has heard nearby have heard McNutt, the way he talks night and day, sitting with his back to the wall, his boots hogging the fire. Shut the fuck up, McNutt, Colly says, but McNutt is a river without a low day. She throws private looks at Bart that say, how can you put up with him? Or perhaps the look says, how are we to get rid of him? But Bart does not answer, sits staring into his own thoughts, chipping at some piece of wood.

The empty meal bag sits like a crumpled mouth. Colly won't shut up either with his ideas—contraptions to be built, giant holes in the ground. He says, we should gather wild dogs and unleash them. She knuckles her eyes, wishes he would stop. McNutt says, what do the newspapers say of such matters? How is it the others get caught in the assizes?

She takes cautious walks down the mountainside. Just to get away from the hut, McNutt's big feet nearly as big as his mouth. In the lowlands it seems all eyes are wishing the autumn to come quick. Even the dogs sit watching the fields, thumping the earth impatiently with their tails. The waving green that brightens the day, glitters a million eyes in the rain, gathers the ripening moon at night. All thought reaching around what fattens beneath, what cannot be rushed or harvested just yet.

There have been nights when they heard the sky echo with gunshot. Now she sees the gaters in the fields put there to scare the hungry like crows. How the crops whisper among themselves about those who dare crawl in the scrawn-light of the moon with hands eager to pull the unripe lumpers. She kicks her anger on a loose stone. Can picture the rich farmers gobbling at food with their ruddy red cheeks. Thinks, in times like this, you must be both eel and wolf.

She watches McNutt lean into firelight, straighten a ruck in his breeches. When he leans back there is just the song of his voice. He says, one time, Bart, I was in Kilroghter. Went drinking with this fellow I knew by the name of Horsebox. He got into a fistfight with some fellow his own height and strength and came back later with a blackthorn stick and came up behind the man who was sitting at a bench and broke his head in like butter. The man never the same again. The next time I seen Horsebox I says to him, what in the hell did you do that for? And Horsebox answers only one thing and this is what he says. He says, that fucker rode my sister. Now, the thing is, Horsebox never had a sister.

She cannot think, feels her mind closing in with all this chatter, Colly trying to get a word in and she shouts at him to shut up.

McNutt quits sucking on his teeth and leans forward, holds his eyes on her. He says, what are you?

She looks at him and sees the eyes not of McNutt but of someone dreamed in this dark hut with only the yellow of his fire-caught teeth, such teeth that have emptied their meal bag.

She says, why can't you be quiet? I'm trying to think.

She lights her pipe and speaks. If you meet head-on a power that is greater than you, you will be devoured. But power is useless when met by what is formless—like rain, weaving itself in and out.

There is a listening look on the face of Bart.

McNutt leans forward, opening and closing his hands. He says, no one can ever understand what the fuck it is you are on about.

It must begin in willow light like this, the everything-falling of dusk. She watches the sun throw last light on a hillock and squints at the far-off. How they have watched this high road through the blue hour of yesterday. This gloomy corner of road far from any settlement. The world shut out by sycamores great and tumoured with rookeries. Now Bart is hunkered sentry by a hawthorn at the road's turn. McNutt is in the trees. Nothing has passed by but an hour or so.

Colly says, do you think, this time, McGob can keep shut?

She thinks, and what about you? You've been rattling on since birth.

Of a sudden, Bart signals with a whistle. Through a bush she watches two figures dally into view—foot passengers, Colly says—the build of two men rounding the corner and she can see their tatty suits, can hear the echoing crows in the trees, can feel the sky's silence, and for a moment she feels she has seen all this before. The men blow pipe smoke but do not talk. The larger of the men holds a carry-case.

She says, a draper and his assistant.

Colly says, a tinsmith and a tyke, a sailor and his cabin boy.

To know that you are the watcher and the watched know not.

Her ears are tuned to the far-off for wheels and horses. These two men are not what they are waiting for. When the men have passed their pipe smoke still lingers.

Colly says, oh, for the comfort of that—go on, light up, give me the blast of a smoke—

He starts wheedling and cajoling, sings in a high-pitched voice that is the voice of a crone.

The bee loves the flowers, the small birds the bowers,
Fair meadows look gay when the sunlight they see,
But ah, more sincerely, my heart prizes dearly the bloom of
thy pipe,
My sweet smoked tobaccy—

A short, sharp whistling signal from Bart and everything is thrown alive. She squints, feels dizzy, sees a light blurred and solitary. Could be anything, she thinks. A stranger with a lantern on foot. A fairy light, even, though she has never seen such a thing. Sound and sight gathering in the near-dark into the single eye of some darkened animal—clawing at the earth towards us, she thinks, waiting to gobble us up. Then the far-off light blinks through trees and is gone, though the night continues to gather its sound, releasing it, rolling it forward until in her mind it becomes all things. Then she is movement, her arms weighted down, and there is McNutt standing centre of the road with the torches placed and then he has one lit and then another, the road taking on the colour of fire. And then McNutt turns and though his face is lit it is dark with mud and on his back sit the antlers roped and the weight of them, she does not understand how he is able to carry them, the light shaping him so that he looks like some animal from the past—one of them three-headed things, Colly whispers, one of them creatures that—

Stop! she says. Settle your breath. She leans into the sound and then the light of a lamp becomes visible at the corner giving shape to a closed coach of some kind. The driver standing up and then sitting down in the single motion of alarm. He shouts at the horses brought to fright by the fire, the animals snouting upwards as if to see a path above the flames where they might alight for the sky and beyond it. And then the coach suddens to a stop and the jangle of harness music rings the air and the horses snort their fear or derision. McNutt says aloud, not a fucking bother. She feels dizzy, shaky, sick. Another moment, another moment, and they stand their ground watching the shaft horse shake its head as if letting loose all its thoughts, letting the light gather upon their pointed weapons.

She climbs the footrest and grabs the handle and shouts but the handle does not budge. A muffled man's voice says from inside, that door is broken, you'll have to step around. She stands still a moment and thinks, they might just have locked it, climbs back down and goes around the back. Scarce light and still she can see the harnesses are worn, the horses pinched, the coach in want of paint like some disheartened old cockerel called to account without feathers. The door opens from the inside and she orders whoever it is to come out. She can see the coachman leaning dangerously to one side, a growling look aimed at Bart, who stands pointing the pistol at the coachman's head.

She thinks, we should have waited, let this one ride past.

Blunderpuss! Colly shouts. Keep the gun up.

She shouts, I said get out.

She looks about for McNutt, who is supposed to be beside her. The sagging weight of her gun and she moves into wide stance, sees from the open door a man step wary onto the footrest, slowly, slowly stepping down onto the road, his hand reaching to help a woman step down, the man closing the door behind them. She notices the narrowness of the woman's ankles. Colly shouts, where is McNutt? She takes a quick look over her shoulder. He is supposed to be here pointing his gun while she searches their belongings, and then she sees that McNutt has climbed upon the roof of the carriage, sees how he has become something demonic, winged of skeleton, ready to fly death upon them. Now she is judge over this couple and she sees the moment as if she were watching it through the eyes of another, her stick-of-a-self holding the rifle, the woman with half a small foot slid out of her slipper, the man rooted in military boots. He squints one eye as if he were seeing himself through the metal sight of her weapon, then he juts his jaw upwards and shouts at the coachman. I can't believe eight pence was paid for this ride.

She finds herself watching the woman, how her meekness pulls every part of her body tight together. Neither rich nor poor, these people. Neither nothing, Colly says, this is not what we were after, they'll have nothing to give us. She hears herself shouting at them again to give over their belongings. The man does not blink but stares at her instead, stares at the fowling gun, then he takes a step towards her, says softly, look at you, you are not even holding it right, a pair of girl's hands on you. A shadow slips from the woman's shoulders. It is her blanket. Grace feels her heart drop through her hips. She wonders if he is an expert, can tell she has not fired a gun before. The man taking another step forward and she thinks, he must be over six feet tall. Then the man says very quietly, you're only some stupid little bitch, aren't you? She shakes her weapon up and down and shouts, stay where you are, I said. Hears Bart shouting at the coachman to keep still.

The woman surprises with her voice. She says, we have a pound of tobacco and a bag of feathers that we kept to sell. It's in the coach if you want it but we have nothing in the way of money or belongings. A great wolf howl comes from the sky and she looks up to see McNutt bellowing on the top of the coach. A strange sound escapes from the woman's mouth. It is then it happens, the man cat-quick is upon Grace—Colly roaring out, shoot him! shoot him!—Bart roaring at McNutt to fire, her mind trying to shout against this man's strength, how he has shaken the gun out of her grasp and what comes in the midst of all this is an awareness that she would like to disappear, for the night to close in, that this man is right about her, you are only some stupid little bitch—flash-smoke and then she is on the ground and it is dark and then it is half bright and her ears are ringing and she sees McNutt flying on skeletal wings out of the night sky.

The moment has opened wider than the dark. There is the sound of a woman running up the road. There is the sound of a man drinking his own blood. She finds herself following the woman into the dark but does not know why she is following. The woman no longer a meager thing but something animal and hell-bent in its running, Colly shouting, let her go, let her go, but she wants to stop this woman, to say something to her, though she does not know what, to convey some thought half formed, that this is not what she wanted at all, that this has become what it was not. The thud and ring of gunshot behind her and of a sudden the woman falls to the ground, McNutt panting like some bone-winged dog as he pounds past her.

McNutt says, I'm not doing it, you do it. Bart says, there's no way I'm doing it. Grace, you do it. They stand eyeing the carriage and a horse snickers as if to say, look what you've done now. Inside the closed coach is the sound of a ghoul, a wailing that would wake the world's dead. She cannot move, her heart has stopped, her flesh and blood bone-rigid. She watches as Bart steps onto the footrest and how the carriage leans towards his weight as if to whisper its secret, but no whispers are needed, she thinks, for you know what is in it. She remembers the dead man closing the same carriage door and stepping down when he was alive only a moment ago and now he is dead and you did it. Bart pausing, his hand before the door. She thinks, there is always a time before and a time afterwards and there must be some line that separates the two and this is that line.

Bart opens the door and climbs into the carriage, emerges slowly carrying in his good arm an infant bundled, screaming, orphaned. And her stomach twists a tightening knot and she colours the ground with sick. McNutt wrestling the horns off his back and then he throws them into the ditch. Fuck, he shouts. Why didn't she take the baby outside with her? We would have seen it then.

She is bent and heaving again, can hear McNutt saying, they only killed themselves, that's what it was, they were told what to do and didn't do it.

She turns upon McNutt. It was you who did it—you were told what to do but you had to climb up on the coach like some thick-as-fuck showing off. It was you that killed them.

She turns and goes to Bart and takes the infant off him, shushes it to her face, climbs into the carriage and pulls the door closed.

Hush, now, baby, hush.

Bart shouts, what are you doing?

She refuses to answer.

The carriage enclosure smells of sweat and tobacco smoke. She holds the baby to her chest. Can hear Bart stepping towards the door. He stands a moment in silence. She thinks, he is thinking of something good to say but there is nothing he can say that can change any of this, the road can only go one way and not another.

When Bart speaks his voice is softly smothered by wood. He says, I missed the coachman with the shot. He will come back with the constabulary, perhaps within an hour or two. The baby will be found and looked after. It will be got.

She holds the infant tighter to her chest and its cries are the same cries as were Bran's and Finbar's, this crying that is becoming louder, that is filling up the coach, filling up her ears, filling the sky, a song asking to be heard by the dead and even the dead would not refuse an answer.

Bart says, think upon this for a moment. How can you look after it? How can you give it what it wants and needs? Leave the baby here and it will be found. I promise you. It will be safe and better off for it.

Colly whispering, riddle me this, you silly bitch, what is both dead and alive at the same time?

She turns her back from the door when it opens, steps down off the coach with empty arms and closes the door without looking.

Bart's voice is very quiet.

Come. If they find you here they will hang you.

What is summer but the nagging of flies, midges in their swirl-clouds, horseflies and their sneaky bites, McNutt's wagging mouth. Three weeks of July she counts hushed in this hut. Their great gale broken. Their food run out. They are watching the hills and tracks. They are watching each other. They have waited for the hounds to come — the constabulary, the troopers on horseback with their huntsman's grins, the horses straining to breaking, their eyes popping out. McNutt has said, they're hardly going to be creeping up. You'll hear the sound of the hunt long before it comes. And she wondered why he laughed at this. What she sees now when McNutt laughs is the face of death, McNutt winging down, all eyes and teeth. Bart teaching her how to listen to the night. There's no point jumping at the sound of every fox pawing about. You must lie still for a while and listen. Map all the different sounds with your mind. Then when you hear a new sound you can relate it to all the other sounds. That way you can rest up. You'll know trouble when you hear it. An old soldier taught me that.

She lies very still listening to the night.

That is a bird upon a bush.

That is an animal rustling about.

That is a baby crying.

There are times when even Colly knows to mind his own business. She leaves him in the hut with the others, McNutt snoring with his boots spread out, Bart in sleep curled like a sickle. She follows the rain-soft shepherd's path until she meets the rushing stream. It is here under the almost-sun that she watches the water run with this blood come upon her, washes the rag clean. She watches the water wash the stones, the water wash the mind, the water wash away time until the world is clean and light. It is then she turns and startles at the sight of another, some woman upstream bent in a cloak, tasting the water with her hand. The woman comes away from the stream with her face hidden under a hood. Too late to hide in a bush, she thinks. Too late to run down the track. She stares at the water as if by staring at it the woman will not see her. When she turns around again the hooded woman is beside her.

The woman says, this water is so lovely. I had forgotten what it was like to taste water.

She hears her own voice awkward in her mouth. How can you forget what it is like to taste water?

One eventually forgets everything, isn't that so?

There is a note in the woman's voice that disturbs her. She turns to look. Sunlight upon the woman's white hand rising to lower the hood and then Grace's mouth goes dry. She is talking to the dead woman from the coach.

The dead woman says, what is wrong with you? You would think you had seen a ghost.

Are you trying to be funny or what?

I don't know what you are talking about.

The dead woman looks at the rag. She says, I see I have disturbed you in a private matter. It is the woman's time you are having.

I cannot get the bleeding to stop.

There is no need to be upset or afraid of it. Every woman has it.

She finds herself studying the woman's unslippered feet, the grass curling with affection around her porcelain toes. They are a real woman's feet, not like her own pig's trotters, and such lovely ankles for a dead woman.

She says, who are you?

My name is Mary Bresher, but you can call me Hilly.

What are you doing here? It is not the Samhain just yet. You cannot roam about just as you please.

What a strange thing to say to someone. I can come and go as I like. I wanted a taste of water. Why shouldn't I have some?

Grace is silent for a while. Mary Bresher sighs and pulls up her hood. She says, I must be off now.

She turns to go and stops. Says, they took my baby from me while I slept. Have you seen it?

Her body moves involuntary along the shepherd path, kicks at loosened scree, her mind meeting images unbidden of woman and man and child and blood mingled into a family of death and this is what happens, she thinks, you get what you ask for. It is one thing for the living to track you down to your hillside hideout but the dead always know where you live.

Later, Colly says, listen, muc, you must have been dreaming, I've never heard of a person being haunted on an individual basis, and anyhow I've decided now that what I am is a rationalist, so I don't believe in ghosts anymore, this is what the schoolmaster used to call thinking people, the ones who figured out mathematics and time and all that lark, rationalists, I think the word comes from the Greeks when you would turn up for a feast only to be handed out small pieces of lotus food and you were skeptical about the size of it.

She finds Bart and McNutt sitting to the side of the hut, their legs splayed out in an apron of sunlight. McNutt's face long with a puss. All this sitting about does his head in, she knows, his hands agitating for something to do. McNutt sits picking the muck between his toes and rolling it in his fingers. He is talking to Bart about the clipping of dog ears and it is hard to tell if Bart is listening or not. He sits with his head hanging downwards, idling his knife at wood. She gathers them with her shadow and McNutt looks up, holds her with a long stare that is a new and different type of looking.

He says, her holy grace has returned. Here, yank me up.

She ignores his outstretched hand, sits down beside Bart.

McNutt puts his boots on and steps into the hut.

This new way McNutt has of looking at her. She thinks, for sure, there has been a softening in his look. How the eye alone can communicate longing. She pulls the shard of looking glass from her pocket and wipes it with her gown. She widens her right eye and stares at it in the mirror.

Bart says, what's wrong with you?

Nothing's wrong.

You act like there's something wrong with you.

She looks to the door and whispers. We need to get rid of him. He's nothing but trouble. You've seen what he is like — he is stupid, dangerous. He is not right in the skull. He did not do what was agreed upon. That man. That woman. He got those people killed.

She catches sight of herself in the mirror. Her hair has summered, reaches past her ears curling into woman.

Colly says, you are the spit of Mam.

No I amn't.

Bart says, you are being hard on him. McNutt is the way he is. That is what makes him McNutt. He cannot be any other person.

She cuts a look at him, says, your beard is getting too long for your face, it's time you cut it.

McNutt steps out of the hut with a hurt look on his face. He says, and what about my beard? Do you not think it is getting long also?

She watches him root a stone from the ground with the tip of his boot and hurl it down the hillside. For a moment it is a bird flying for the sun and then it hurtles the fall of the damned.

This morning she is a forager, roams the crags barefoot under a sun half hidden that could be the tip of a pale finger. Her stomach cramped and the hillside damp from last night's rain and an hour's roaming without luck. Anything at all, she thinks, to get out of that hut. Like twins with their brown eyes pretending not to look at you.

There is nothing now in that hut but dead air. McNutt has sucked all the good air out. Even the sound of his breathing would madden you.

Look! Colly says. Her shoulders become taut when she sees the starry white of pignut growing beneath a low blackthorn.

She says, I hate them things, Colly. Do you think it is an ill omen? What was it Mam always called them? The increaser of dark secrets.

Colly says, I heard the bitter berries of a blackthorn can make a woman pregnant.

She crawls beneath the tree and with her knife roots out two pebbly tubers. Then she slides back out but slips on the wet grass, falls into the mouth of the tree. The bite comes quick into the fleshy heel of her hand.

She shouts, fucking auld git!

Colly says, you'll be poisoned to death, them blackthorns are lethal.

She would like to cudgel the tree with its own wood.

Colly says, you'll be dead before you know it.

She can feel the thorn under the skin but cannot get it out. Finds Bart alone in the hut and presents to him her hand. He holds the palm aloft and squints, rests it like a saddler on his lap.

He says, there are three ways we can go about this. I could make up a poultice to draw it out but that would take a day or two. If we had a bottle we could drop some matches into it and draw the thorn out. That would be the quickest for sure.

Her shoulder jerks at the sight of his knife. Her elbow begins to wriggle.

Bart says, hold still, will you. If it is a blackthorn, you'll want it out now.

His eyes narrow as he brings up the knife and she snaps back her hand when the blade touches her skin.

Ach! she shouts. You are going to slice my hand off.

Hold still, will you.

She bites her lip, watches him score the flesh until the tip of the blackthorn peeps out. She likes how he has gentled the knife. Then he takes her hand to his mouth and kisses it — no, he is sucking the flesh to suck the blackthorn out, but still her face reddens.

Colly says, I hope he doesn't expect you to suck him back.

Bart spits the thorn on the ground and he is still holding her hand when both look up to see McNutt watching from the doorway. He spits at the ground between his feet. Says, you should have said so, cunty.

She snaps back her hand from Bart, says, I got stabbed by a blackthorn. Look.

The way McNutt looks at Bart but does not look at her. He pulls at the strings that make a smile on his mouth. Says, so you had a little prick in you?

He has stepped a foot farther in the door and she cannot see his eyes. Then he roars, Jesusfuck, and she can see the true dark of his mouth. He stamps out of the hut, begins to roar at the hillside. They watch him grab a rock and hurl it off another. He is not McNutt now but some other, a great rock smasher, an angry god, his arms pitchforking in different directions of violence. Christ, Colly says, the top of his head is going to blow off. And then he is breathless, comes to a stop, does not look at them. He turns and begins downhill.

Bart opens his mouth to shout but no words come out.

Finally, she says, what's got into him?

She watches the dusk draw dead souls from trees and rocks. A soul being loosened from a whin is shaped like a shout. Or some wild woman's hair, Colly says, it's like the hair of your dead woman — hee! — that'll be the look of her, all right. A hand touches her shoulder and it is not Mary Bresher but Bart handing her the last of the pipe. She sends a ring-fort of smoke towards the lowlands.

Thinks, such a lovely quiet without McNutt. Who cares if he doesn't come back.

She would like to tell Bart she is haunted, but how can you explain such a thing? He would not believe a word. He would say, show me this ghost you are talking about.

She says, do you believe in ghosts?

He says, I think that some people see ghosts because they need for ghosts to exist. We do not like to believe that things must end. That's what I think anyhow.

Colly says, fuck this ghost business going around stalking people—hee!—when I die I want my soul to become part of a machine like a big cog or rivet.

The air becomes humid, burrs the skin and sticks to sleep. She finds Bart outside watching the dawn with the same frowning attention he uses to read a newspaper. He says, this close weather is troubling. She thinks, perhaps McNutt will return or perhaps he won't, who cares about him anyhow.

Another humid day and night and in first light she awakes to see McNutt standing over them. He stands greaved with mud and clung with thorns like a man who has crawled through the worst of a ditch. There is hurry in his voice. He says, you've got to get up, the pair of you. Come now.

His eyes are blood and he looks like his more dangerous self. And yet, she thinks, he seems to stare past them into some faraway thought.

It is then she sees he is wearing brand-new boots.

She says, where did you get them things?

He says, you must come down off the mountain. It happened in a single night. It happened again. It happened.

They brazen onto the hill road like locals. You could be anyone at all, she thinks, people wandering the county in search of work or food and certainly not some band of murderers. She studies McNutt's new boots as he walks, wonders if his feet have shrunk to fit them. It is then the smell meets them on the road. She wants to think it is the smell of some dead animal lying in a ditch or the smell of bilge-water. But then they see the smell made visible. They should be green. They should be lush and tall. But what should be no longer is. In every field and lazybed the lumper stalks have become slippy with rot, the crops become scrawny old legs withering to their last moment. The same thing she saw last year.

She sees people frantic and plunging spades and not a word said between them and by the side of a narrow plot she sees a white-bearded man pinching his face as if trying to awaken his eyes. A younger man stands over a shovel and weeps into his fist. She sees a young crippled woman propped on the back of a cart staring at a handful of black lumpers. She searches every face she meets, their asking eyes avid for signs from every other that this is not true, that this is not happening, because sometimes you wake and find you are still dreaming and you can go back to sleep and wake up properly later on and everything is all right again.

Bart's face is white. He says, I must sit down.

She watches the sky and she watches the earth, sees that what is future-held is not held at all, that they have stepped through the world as dreamers. Her mind holding what isn't and what is, the one supposed to be the other and now it is the other that is, begins to see that what carries over these fields has come as easy as breeze, drifting upon all things and through all things, this death wind haunting towards them.

McNutt is pointing an accusatory finger at nobody in particular. He says, I'll tell you what people are saying. That this is God's scourge upon us. That God sent down this to punish the people for their sins. Because people do not pray enough. They do not praise the saints. They do not put their hand in their pocket for the priest's collection. But I'll tell you what this is. The people got it wrong, so they did. God sent this down because people are cunts, pure and simple. That's all there is to it.

Bart stares at the ground shaking his head. He says, that is utter nonsense. I have read plenty about this in the papers. It has to do with the warm air coming in from the Continent. There are men who say it is a scientific matter.

McNutt leans back smiling. And who was it sent the warm air from over the Continent?

The country is facing a second year without a crop, she thinks. It is as if some secret door has opened to let in all the forces of the otherworld. The year will drift to winter and what then?

Bart says, let me tell you what is going to happen. Soon there won't be a living animal left on this land. The cost of a hundredweight of oats is already at a pound and it will climb higher. The merchants will hold on to what they've got. It will be a pound and a half, two pound before the year's out. The prices will go up and up so that the rich can protect themselves and that is always the way of it. The Crown will have to do something. They'll have no other choice now.

McNutt says, I don't plan on hanging about watching all that happen. While you two were playing at Diarmuid and Gráinne, I went about my own business. Maybe I'll let you in on it.

He stands up and shakes his boots and taps his nose with knowledge.

The moon tonight is mountainous, comes around the world to prise the dark. After the rain everything glistens for this night sun. The path has come loose with wet and her feet are glad when they meet the road. Southwards, downwards, the road winding towards the lowlands and the smell of field-rot rising to meet them. She thinks of what McNutt has said, imagines a divine hand dispersing vapours, such a mean way of thinking if that is so, and this is how they said the plague was spread all them years before. The fields no longer whisper their gossip but send instead their silent rot-smell to haunt alongside you. Smells like mouldy eggs, Colly says. You must hold your nose like this and breathe through your mouth and then the smell won't enter you.

Another suddening of rain and they wait it out under tree-cover within sight of a village. In all lands across all time, she thinks, the dog is guardian of the night, but so far this night they have met not one dog bark. The dogs are no longer kings of this country.

She watches McNutt lean his gun to the tree, his face reversed in mud. There will be no odd business this time, he has promised, hand on heart. And yet so far this night he has not shut up.

McNutt says, let me tell you about a fellow I once knew called Salter. He was some fellow, all right. Used to stop in at Bracken's place. Not right in the head at all. Always leaning on the right elbow with his hand circled around his drink staring quizzically at everything. He was famous for telling anyone who would listen that he was off to America. And then finally he went. With great fanfare. They held a wake for him and everything. He puts a sack of mucky spuds in a rowboat and sets off on his own one morning. His mother had knit him a pair of fingerless gloves for the rowing. So he rows out past the pier and rows and rows for three days until the tiredness overcomes him. Now, the thing is, he is not a natural westerner. Not a seaman at all. And his strength begins to sap. He discovers that while he can wash the spuds in the seawater and get them to a nice shine, he cannot eat them, for eating them raw give you the cramps. So he eats them anyway and soon his stomach is in bits. It is then that he curls up in the boat and begins to drift. The rain soaks into him. The wind hurls him about the place. The sun scalds him red all over, even the tips of his fingers. The cold turns him blue all the way down to his toes. Then he finds himself watching the sky on a night just like this, drifting, watching the same stars as ever there were thinking to himself that this will be the last night he'll ever see them. He prays to God and gives thanks for giving him such a good life even though his life was mostly difficult. He lies there looking at the sky waiting for a long death. And then comes the dawn in all its glory and what does he see but a shoreline in the distance like a miracle. He cannot believe his luck. He begins rowing like a madman, for he realizes he has drifted all the way to America and all this on the strength of three raw potatoes and the stomach cramps. He rows himself with all the energy of the devil and his galley of dark lieutenants roaring at all the burning slaves of hell. Gets himself ashore and drags the boat up onto a little beach and hauls the sack of spuds over his shoulder and sets off to make his fortune. He goes up to the first person he sees, some old man staring at this wild sea-creature coming before him sunburnt and blue. He says, my name is Salter and I've just rowed here all the way from Ireland. And the old man looks him up and down with the sure look of one squinty eye and he says, arrah, would you ever fuck off with yerself.

They break a noisy path through corn. Colly says, rich men plant corn while fools plant potatoes. Shush up, she says. Shush up yourself, he says. At the end of the field a stile unfolds shapely like a man with warning arms. Soon they can see the solid dark of the farmhouse. It is wide and two-storied with outhouses and cottages behind it. A field between them and a yard much too long and a plantation of trees to the right. In the old days, Bart whispers, you'd light a fire at the door of the house and watch them climb out the windows. That's the way them Whiteboys did it. But they took delight in it.

It will be a simple enough matter, she thinks. We will move like the dark, weightless like shadow. We will move certain through the house. She pictures herself in a parlour room, gutting a chair with her knife, scattering the room with horsehair. An image of people asleep on plumped pillows. She will take all their tea and sugar and a two-pound weight of whatever you're having yourself, fat sir.

Colly says, let the rats drink the cat's milk. It is a war now, isn't it?

She watches Bart darkening his face with mud, rubbing mud through his hair until she does not know him.

She whispers, which door is it?

McNutt points.

Which one.

That one.

I can't see it.

McNutt spits. Bastarding stupids. Haven't I been in and out already?

He puts his hand in a pocket and produces a key. Let us go dine with them.

McNutt will go first to the house and watch for any gaters. He is a dark bird that flits along the hedgerow and then he zags into the open field making towards the yard. She wonders again at the mind of McNutt, how he seems to become alive in fright, how everything in his life is edged with laughter. She tries to follow how he moves, can just about make him out, and then, as if the night has swallowed him, he is gone. They wait and watch the night's stillness. How the night releases its bruised colours, the grass to blue, the slinking purple of chimney smoke.

Colly says, something's wrong, I know it.

Bart whispers, hurry the fuck up, McNutt.

They are waiting too long now and still McNutt does not come.

Then Bart says, come on, let's go.

They creep along the field's edges, their eyes wide to the dark. Closer now towards the field's centre, closer to the yard, closer to— it is then they can hear it, a strange sound like an animal sound only it isn't. Bart reaching for her arm and he takes hold and squeezes. His voice is strangely flat. Wait.

They hold still, send forth their ears to listen and she listens until she can hear past her heart, can hear the low moaning of a man.

Slowly, slowly, pausing to listen, slowly onwards again. How it seems in this moment as if the hedgerow has closed in and the house has edged closer, as if the house itself were some hulking animal creeping towards them waiting to pounce. She knows it now—the moaning belongs to McNutt, wonders if he has fallen and twisted his ankle, banged his head off a rock, wonders why she can't see him. And then they are upon the place of his moaning and still she can't see it and then Bart grabs her arm and pulls her back. The ground has opened before them. They are standing at the edge of a great hole in the earth. Bart leaning down. McNutt! Where are you hiding? What happened?

McNutt answers with a broken whisper. I am— all right. The bastards— seen us— coming.

Bart says, where is your gun?

McNutt says, I cannot—

She stares into the hole but cannot see anything, Bart curls his body to hide the strike of three matches, drops a butterfly of light into the hole. In the moment of its fall she can see the hole is a dug trap, can see the roof of grass and sticks made to cover it, can see McNutt lying at the bottom in a funny twist. And then she turns and sees them, shapes at first and two lanterns being lit that pull shadows into what they always were, men who were waiting, and now she understands what has happened, that the earth has reached for McNutt because these gaters have dug a nice trap.

Bart is quickly pulling the pistol and he is trying to shoot it, fuck, he shouts, shakes the gun as if trying to shake some sense into it, the weapon dumb in his hand and he drops it to McNutt, here, you shoot it. He grabs her wrist, yanks the wiring loose in her arm. She becomes her legs, becomes the trees they are fleeing for, sees herself as if from the trees running towards them, as if her mind has gone there in one leap, Bart horsing a knackered wheeze beside her. They reach the trees and she sees the trees are not safe at all but better than being out in the open and she looks again to see the men have not followed. What has followed instead is the spirit of McNutt's fear, the shouting of a man abandoned directly to his fate, the shouting of the last man on earth. The tracery of the moon shapes men standing weaponed around the pit, bludgeons, slash-hooks, two men climbing down into it.

They wait until no more McNutt's awful shouts. No more the men upon him. No more the moon. Just the dawn grey and bloodless. She thinks, the men are gone to their beds and why not? Like happy hunters with their job done and who would return to look? They creep towards McNutt and can see clearly the hole, a great pit dug deep enough to capture a man and not climb back out, the ground of the pit planted with stakes, the figure of McNutt lying broken, half his clothes beaten off him, his boots at a funny angle and his head turned as if to stare into some final thought. A sudden sorrowing noise from Bart and then his face slips and he drops onto his knees and grabs a fistful of earth and drops it over McNutt's body. She watches the soil fall like rain like black tears like soil simply for a dead man and it is then that she wants to kill them, wants to go to the big house and bring death upon them, set fire to the house—that would please her the most. Or shoot them in their bellies as they lie in their beds, Colly says, make fly their bed feathers with blood, we've still got one gun left, we could take back the two guns those gaters took out of the hole.

Her ears still ring with the roaring of McNutt, his voice like the peals from the blacksmith's hammer, blow after blow until the iron dulled and lost its voice. She can see it like a picture, Mr Big Farmer Man nightgowned, kneeling under his cross, his wobbling jowls as he blesses himself while his gaters lie in wait like wolves for McNutt to return with his key.

She says, let us avenge him, but Bart does not answer.

She hears him swallow a sob. She keeps watch over her shoulder almost wishing the men to come.

* * *

They quit the mountain—this place is cursed, she thinks. The blackthorn with its true poison has done its work. Bart says, they'd be bound to find us up there sooner or later.

Her eyes plead for sleep as they secret themselves out of these lowlands. They rest in a copse of stunted oak where the light is ribbed and the trees smother the world to quiet but for the eversound of a stream. She sits slumbrous against a tree and is followed to dream by shadow-men swinging billhooks and clubs, not six of them but endless men who hold the dark to their faces and she sees wolves that step from the shadows of trees and wolves that come pawing out of the earth and they are the shadows that make the violence complete.

In the dawnlight that is dreamlight she awakes and there is Bart in the curl of sleep. She rises and walks downstream, takes her comfort behind a whin bush, washes her face in the water. Looks up to see Mary Bresher stepping away through the underwood.

Grace shouts, wait!

Mary Bresher stops and turns with an uncertain look that widens into relief. She says, oh, it is you, I was wondering who was calling.

Where were you going?

I was just out for a bit of fresh air. The air is so clean here.

I expected I would see you again.

The world is small like that, isn't it? I'm always running into people I know and in the strangest of places too.

Mary Bresher lowers her hood and seems to wonder at the sky. She points towards a rock and says, do you mind if I sit down? She gathers her cloak and sits and Grace studies the woman, wonders how it can be so that the woman's feet are sticky with mud and that the forest floor makes noise under her weight. And those wrinkles worrying the corner of her mouth cannot belong to a dead person.

She says, are you in some kind of limbo?

Mary Bresher laughs a little girl's laugh. There you go again with your odd questions. I'll admit I haven't met anybody in a long while now. You are the first person I've talked to. I miss my husband. I cannot find him. Shall I tell you how I met him?

Grace reaches and frees a burr stuck to the pleat of Mary Bresher's cloak.

Mary Bresher says, what is wrong with you? Such a long face.

She says, I don't know what's what anymore.

Whatever do you mean?

I used to think I knew everything about the world but now I feel like some blind person stumbling through it. Tell me this, do you think that everybody in the world is born fixed into their position?

I don't know about that. It is certainly the case that everybody takes the same position in death.

It seems to me that a fish cannot become a bird and that the bird will attack the fish if it tries to fly. Perhaps that is the natural order of things. But why must that be so? I just saw men belonging to a rich farmer beat to death a poor man with clubs. They dug a trap to catch him like an animal, or like a fish if you think about it—pulled him like a fish from a pool. Poked his eyes out with their beaks. Things have gotten worse now. I think it would take some kind of magical effort for the fish to leave the water—

Snap-foot and movement and here is Bart stepping towards her and when she looks Mary Bresher is gone. Bart hunkers beside her, his face a mixture of mud and rough beard.

He says, I thought I heard voices. Are you chatting again to yourself?

She stands wishing at a field of horses. Knows where Bart's thoughts lie. They are back in that hole with McNutt, the same thought trying to undo what has been fixed in time's forever and still the mind wishes it. Her own thoughts trying to hold on to some moment of McNutt. His wagging mouth and you trying to get shut of it and look at you now. Later they sit in the corner of a field under high shrub watching a fire burn out, not a word spoken between them.

Finally she says, do you think he was just unlucky? Do you think he made his own luck?

Bart disturbs the cooling ashes with a stick. He says, do you remember when we first stayed on the mountain, that night when one of the rocks cracked like pistol shot and you and me nearly shat ourselves while McNutt sat there shaking with laughter. He put the rock on the fire to give us a fright but the noise when it exploded told anybody that could have been listening where we were that night. He couldn't do anything without a show. That was McNutt. But you've got to admire him. He refused to live off hope.

V

Winter

The devil has dallied these westward roads, doffed his cap in every townland. She watches the always-is of the clouds, tries to fashion from their shapes animals but cannot. Sees instead the shapes of children coat-tailing ragged elders wandering weary and in want of light.

Colly says, do you think Bart is getting sad with himself?

She thinks this might be true. There is a lengthening now to Bart's look. It is as if he does not see the road but can see ahead to the days that will soon unlearn for winter. Before you know, it will be the Samhain, the world to dark and what then? How the word *winter* makes you think of Blackmountain, its blue-cold colours, the sleet call of the wind. Those nights when storm would harry the house as if some great force had come to shake them off the hill. This feeling now as if some great wind is coming, something shapeless and unimaginable, something greater than the world that travels hidden between light.

In one small town they are met by two well-dressed women who shake a can before them asking for money for the building of a new church. The beggary come forward to wheedle and cajole when they see the quality of their cloaks.

Better to fox the dark than become one of them, she thinks. They shadow the greater farmhouses, test the ground with sticks for traps, watch for gaters, hush at well-fed dogs. They tap the downspouts of the better farmhouses for the sound of hidden money, search for potato pits and smash open larder locks. The most you'll find is a bag of flour lonely on a shelf. A wrinkled carrot left for a horse. A heel of bread. An admonitory clock ticks her off as she scoops into her palm bread crumbs from a table. One time they find hidden treasure—a box of seed potatoes growing arms and legs and stashed underground for the growing season. They roast the seedlings over a fire and Colly says, when you think of it, that is an entire field of future potatoes we've just eaten.

They pass through Nenagh town in the dusk and watch a field lit in circling torch-fire. A traveling show of some kind setting itself up amidst caravans and horses. She is astonished to see the silhouette of a man on stilts like some strange and slow insect wading the dark.

She thinks, these last few days on the road have been full of odd sights. What about that rich man's bullock standing on a rock as if he were afraid of the very field he stood in? And that horse standing with its face to a tree as if renouncing sight of the world? And what about that idiot of a man who walked past with a smile on his face and blood sicked on his shirt? These are auguries, all right. Every flour cart on the road has been accompanied by soldiers. And in these great vales of Tipperary, the farming estates are sometimes as big as a town. They meet villages where the gardens are tended, the houses fashioned and slated. The great fields of corn giving to the world their colour. How they crane their necks towards the flashing scythes. And yet there are the townlands you must go through with shut eyes, where grass grows over the doorways, where the fields learn colour only from the sun. The have-it-alls and the have-nothings, Bart says. I give it a year before the country splits apart.

She thinks, it is the sight of the children in such townlands that cause the most grief. She has seen children with fever, children thin from long illness, but never has she seen children such as this. Some of these children are losing their voices. Little boys without their shouts. Little boys with hairy faces. Little girls becoming crones.

Children being rushed through life to wear the death masks of the Samhain.

Bart says, I don't think the country will celebrate the turning of the season this year except in them big farmsteads. Think of the feasts they will be preparing. The fieldwork done. The larder full of riches. The baking of cakes and biscuits and the jellies and ham and tongue. We used to be told in whispers to stay close to the bonfire, for there are demons in the dark coming to get you. But the demons do not have to ride the dark anymore. This year they do not even wait for the Samhain.

Everything in life has a secret signal, she thinks. Like colour, for instance. What is colour but some sort of expression as to the nature of a thing? She thinks about this, wonders if she is right. What is the green of a tree but some kind of announcement? It doesn't speak and yet it shouts—I am a tree, here I am. Or the jimsonweed in the ditches white-sounding to the bees with trumpets of silence. There are other things too that secretly speak. She thinks about Bart. How he is trying to express what cannot be said, or if it can be said, he doesn't want to say it. This new thing he does as he walks, stepping a little too close to her, his left hand touching off her right hand. It is only a brush, made to seem like an accident, yet she feels it strong as a thump. She does not know what to do with herself, agitates a sudden hand through her hair or pulls at an eyelash, begins to prattlebox like some old biddy. And sometimes she wakes warm in the solitary cold of dawn and there is Bart in sleep—or perhaps not in sleep—with his body spooned into her and his good arm around her shoulder giving her his warmth. How she tenses, lies holding her breath, and then Bart turns away in sleep or perhaps not in sleep.

Colly says, riddle me this—what's got two legs by day and three legs by night?

The way Bart wakes and jumps into his body shortly after, his face as if nothing has happened.

* * *

They shelter by the damp abutment of a bridge a day's walk from Limerick city. Bart says, it's rare enough you'll find the underside of a bridge empty like this. They build a fire and she watches Bart produce a newspaper he has found and laughs at the sight of him. She thinks she might be giddy from hunger. This trick he has for holding and folding, resting the paper on his knee and turning it with his hand. She leans across and pokes at the paper to annoy him. Bart pretends to ignore her. Then he says, says here the costs of provisions have tripled—

She leans forward and pokes the paper again.

Bart says, will you listen. An article here says they are flying a balloon over parts of Dublin with people in it, the entire thing full of gas.

Colly says, I doubt that's possible, let me have a look.

Bart stands up in fury when the paper is grabbed off him.

Give it back, he says.

Hold off a minute.

Give it here, I said.

Colly says, you know, I always knew people would figure out a way to fly in the future but I always assumed they would do it with birds, lash people to the backs of condors or some other giant bird with rope, something secure anyhow—now, that would be something, being lashed to a bird, being able to fly over people you hate and shit on their houses.

Bart stamps off towards the river and she watches him go to where the grass has run wild. The way he steps easy out of his clothes. His white and shiverless back as he sits down in the low water and begins to douse himself.

Colly says, take your eyes off him, you dirty wee bitch.

She looks up and sees some woman stepping along the river path, sighs, for she knows who it is from the wringing of her hands. Mary

Bresher gives off a surprised look. She says, I was just thinking about you and here you are. Do you mind if I sit down?

She watches Mary Bresher gather the pleats of her cloak as she sits down beside her. Her lovely blue feet are filthy from walking. Through the long grass she can see the shape of Bart stepping out of the water, bold as brass and she pretends not to look but Mary Bresher is looking also.

She says, ah, the sight of a man. It makes me miss my husband something terrible. By any chance have you seen my child?

They have lucked themselves a lift towards Limerick. A cooper's cart with a canvas covering and the man black-faced as hell looking for a chat. Colly says, this fellow has the look of the devil, all right — he'll have our souls shut in a barrel. She whispers, shush up, and Bart casts her a vexed look. The cooper lifts her up by the wrist and it is then she sees his right hand has just two fingers and she thinks of Bart and she thinks how in some strange way this man could be his father.

Rock-away, rock-away, the cooper shouts, and the horses nod and whinny and she folds her arms and tries not to listen to Bart and the cooper's chatter. Her eyes close and Colly is muttering, pair of cripples, hardly a good hand between them, and then the world is borne by dark and it is not the cooper but McNutt who says, do you know how to drive this, and Bart says, I was hoping you would ask, and he takes hold of the reins and the horses strain and pull the cart into gallop until they take no heed of Bart's shouts and then she sees the road edging towards a great precipice and she screams at Bart and she screams as they go over it, wakes into the comfort of slowness, rainfall and its curtaining shush, the eaves of the canvas dripping their wet. Colly says, this cooper fellow's a right barrel of laughs — do you think he will float if we pour water into that hole of his mouth?

It is then she sees it, takes hold of Bart's hand and squeezes. Bart tries to slide his hand back into her hand but she has pulled it loose. She is pointing off-road. Look. The cooper blinks and begins to slow the horses.

Christ wept, he says.

The tree is a great spread oak and leaning against it is a cart wheel and tied to its spokes is the body of a youth. The arms and legs thin as sticks but loose in the rope that tied them. She cannot speak, can only think of the awfulness of such an act, who would tie a dead boy to a cart wheel like that?

Bart says, what's that sign say around his neck?

The cooper stalls the horses and they lean forward to read the words and she turns away, watches the wind scuttle across the road a fallen leaf that is a sparrow or perhaps the soul of a dead person while the sign speaks its solitary word.

Thief.

Into the city by night's silent hours, when the streets give no account of themselves. They are footsore and hungry and she aches for sleep and yet there is wonder — the shape of a city, Colly says, some of the buildings as tall as giants, everything so grand and quiet. Bart says, the fox will find his feast in the city. Even at night when everybody sleeps, she thinks, a great town gives off a feeling of possibility, it is not unreasonable to think things will be better.

They come through the old city into Newtown, Bart calls it, and Colly says look, they have brought the moon down to the streets. Gaslight upon the endless shuttered shops. Gaslight stretching down an endless street wide as Paris, one would think. Gaslight throwing bright upon the great high houses. Bart says the constables here are rough and we'd best be careful. Echoing steps that could be a policeman or just some ragman's shadow but certainly not a ghost, she thinks, because ghosts don't live in the cities and even if they did, ghosts don't hide anymore but walk about in the open.

Bart knows his way over a short bridge that leads into Englishtown. Everything becomes untold in dark but for a church's tolling that tells the hour of two. Colly says, Christ, this place smells of shit-rot. The buildings here are as high almost as Newtown but they are run-down and slanting. The narrow streets grip the dark. Even the spirit shops are shut for the night. And yet there are children. They web nakedly out of the shadows as if they have been waiting for these strangers, hoping to escort them to a room. Such children are the rats of the city, she thinks. They pull at their hands and their sleeves, plead and cajole — mister, mister — *cailín gleoite* — and Colly shouts at one of them to fuck off when a hand threatens to pull Grace's cape loose. Bart stops and puts his hand up, says hold on a minute, and she is startled by a boy who stands apart from the others blue-skinned and pimpled, naked from the waist up. A simple pleading look that eats at her heart. She nods at him and they begin to follow, the other children catcalling. They are whispered at. A drunkard shouts his face to a wall. Some groaning she can hear through a glassless window might well be the sound of dying.

The streets seem to labyrinth and then the boy turns into an alley so blind she is seized with the fear that they have been led into a trap where they will be murdered for their cloaks. She halts and grabs hold of Bart's sleeve but Bart is already shouting whoah to the boy as if he were a horse, the boy continuing to walk on as if he has not heard. They stand at the edge of the alley's dark until the boy reappears. Bart says, we go no farther. He waves his hand and points another direction and the boy signals that everything is all right, his hand gesturing to come along, come along, and then he leads them along another route, Colly saying, keep a watch out, I don't like this one bit. They go down slippy steps and one hand goes to a wall and the other hand to her knife, watching this boy light a guttering candle and then he puts his hand out for a coin. In the flicker-light she can see the sunken pallor of his face and yet there is an unmistakable boy-light in his eyes and it seems to her as if this moment were not happening now but is a moment that has happened in the long-ago.

Bart says, I am here for work so can pay you coin tomorrow. How the boy wavers with his eyes and then leads them into the house which smells of wet-cold and mildew and worse and try not to think of it, she thinks, downwards into a cellar cramped with sleeping people and perhaps the dead and that is what you smelled, and she sees their sprawling figures in the candlelight and the walls are wet and she thinks she can smell sickness, can hear it in someone's cough, and they find a space and Bart rests against her and too soon he is asleep.

Colly whispering, what new hell is this?

She knows when she wakes she has been trying to wake all night. Colly says, I have been sleeping inside out and backwards. A creeping numb-cold from hands to feet and Bart is looking shivery. A look on his face suggests he has not slept one bit. He is nicking at his boot with his knife. Colly reckons there might be three or four families living in this single room, twenty-four people is my count, and there must be six or seven rooms in this house, go figure. The walls shake with coughing. Tears stream down the peeling plaster. Grace stands quickly and goes to the door. We need to go, she shouts. Up the soot-dark steps shining from rainfall that eats through her cloak as it falls. How the buildings that stoop upon the narrow passage make her think of old men steadfast in illness against dying. And here is the boy stepping out of a doorway as if he has been waiting, his hand out for money.

She says, we'll have coin for you tomorrow.

The boy steps boldly in front of her and waves his hand again. Bart slaps the hand away and the boy stares at him with a look of willed courage.

Bart says, did you not hear what we said?

Of a sudden, another boy appears alongside him. He says, Deaf Tom don't hear you.

Colly says, then why didn't he say so?

She tries to see into his eyes as if to see into his unhearing, to see her own lips moving as if talk were to his eyes the simple fact of chewing, sees instead his eyes wrought with fear and hate. She pulls Bart by the sleeve and they turn and go up the street, can still feel upon her back the eyes of the boy.

Bart speaks aloud. We'll not return there tonight.

Every gobdaw in Ireland, she thinks, has come to Limerick. The streets are full of sleeve pullers, rogues and ruffians, tinkers, beggars, and pedlars. By the bridge into Newtown they huddle and shout, hold up ragged garments and bedding and what have you. She thinks, they'd sell their own limbs if they could find a buyer. You do not look at their faces. You do not search for what you do not want to see, the people who wear bluing skin instead of clothing, each bone that pokes in accusation.

Bart says, there's nothing worth stealing in Englishtown that isn't being sold here.

Colly whispers, I'll bet there's secret trade in mice and rats.

Straggling behind Bart street after street as he makes inquiries after friends he says he knew a year or two ago. The doors and gateways shutting before him and everybody he knows is gone. Jim Slaw, he says. And Mick the Hammer. Where in the fuck? They were always here.

The sky and the streets and the faces they meet have become the same washy colour. She follows behind Bart listening to the city, darning through sound her ear's stitching needle, the yelling and chatter and clatter and catcalls while some distant metal heart clamours near the docks. Matching the sounds to what she sees. The sluggish rattle of a passing cart. A hoarse man trying to find more voice as he pleads with two sailors at his stall. A group of children on kindling legs cajoling some official. The silence of the beggary. There are rumours of fever on certain streets near the river. There are rumours of a gang of vicious children robbing people in the backstreets of

Irishtown and for a moment she can see their faces, starving boys forced to become violent men.

They spend their last few pence on stale bread rolls. They are told where to find soup given out by some religious society or relief committee, nobody knows or cares. They join the queue and idle the hours listening to the chatter, it's as if they are trying to kill you with waiting, did you notice how every day they are handing out one drop less, dinner missed the belly and went elsewhere. Then the door to the kitchen closes and they turn away with the others and grumble.

Colly says, that fellow over there.

She takes a good look at this man he is talking about, he must be Bart's age and yet he moves with the ague of an oldster. He looks like a stick dressed by the wind, won't even last the night.

When they get back to their lodgings, Deaf Tom holds up four fingers to remind them how many days' payment is due.

She watches winter taking the city. It has come early this year. How it scavenges the light, sends despair to walk the streets. Or lie alongside the strung-out shapes that occupy each laneway, court, and stairwell. Each day the city seems to deepen its beggary, deepen the numbers who come from the country to gather on the quayside awaiting passage. They depart on the ships that Bart says are taking all the food out of Ireland and if this is true, she thinks, she wonders how anybody can allow it.

She wonders how a city can hold so many and yet how it can also hold so much wet. The rain hangs from the eaves and pools every corner, creeps into your feet, gnaws through your cloak, eats into your brain until you can think of nothing else. They stand under shop awnings until they are shouted at and she sees that a good many shops have their shutters down and Bart says a lot of the ordinary tradesmen now are done out of business.

Yet Newtown is another city. She has never seen people who look so continually pleased with themselves. Cockerel men in fine cloth standing outside great stone buildings talking about serious matters. Women fashioned in exotic hats and ribbons and colours walking under parasols. How the rain with its wanty fingers cannot touch them though the filthy streets dirty their booties.

She stands with Bart outside a coffeehouse reaching her eyes through the signed window, has never smelled anything like it. The men inside reading newspapers, supping and chatting. Quidnuncs, Bart says. Nothing worse than men acting like women. She doesn't know what he means but does not ask him, must be some word he's read in the newspaper. Watching such men in the coffeehouse and watching such men on the street and she thinks that these people have been born clean, born into a higher position, while all the rest of us on earth were born into a lower position and such a thing is all down to who you are and where you come from and the luck of the draw and there is nothing you can do about it but take it back off them, because a fish cannot become a bird but there is nothing to stop a fish from wearing the bird's feathers.

They return to the kitchen each day and sometimes you don't get in and sometimes you do. She watches the splashy ladle dumping its watery soup, feeling both glad and hateful. A heel of bread. A room full of vile smells and sucking noises and a man who growls while collecting the bowls. Better to be out, she thinks, where you can creep the quays, watch the backyards of the high houses, the backyards of shops and stores. They walk the streets and send out their eyes but the city has too many eyes to meet them, the length of each street that swallows your strength and gives nothing in return for it. Everything is bolted and never has she seen so many watchmen and policemen and you do their thinking for them and step about in guilt for the thoughts of what you want to steal from them. Bart whispering that they must be careful, twice today they have been watched and followed by youths who belong to the Ryan gang, he says, you know them by the way they tie their neckerchiefs, they take only horses and money but perhaps that has all changed now. Them two fellows were figuring us out. And she begins to see them everywhere, each neckerchief a signal or perhaps not, who is to know who is what in the tumult of the city.

Today Deaf Tom came with some darkening man who stood stoat-eyed and said, you owe this boy payment for seven days. The warning he gave them. Now it is two o'clock. She stands under an archway with Bart watching the not-sky and how it has come down to meet this not-river and churn it into sea. It is as if the Shannon has been swelling all night into something eyeless and calmly malignant and now it lies in waiting. But for what? she thinks. For all the things you do not want to think of. This wind reaching into every mouth.

Colly says, you would wonder why God didn't make us something else, of all the options available to Him—wouldn't it be so much better to be a lion licking your hot balls in Africa or an elephant in India, or even an eagle winging over Wicklow would be better than this—who wants to be an Irishman born into wet—and do you know something else, I haven't seen a single rat in days and you know what that means.

Ugh.

Grace.

What?

Do you know something?

What?

This is no way to live.

Fuck off, then.

Bart says, what was that?

She turns and stares at Bart pitting the knife into the heel of his useless hand. The flesh full of red marks. Her rage flies into shout and she feels like another person listening to herself. We have run out of luck. We should have had our pick of the riches of this city but instead we are penniless and getting worse with it. Why did we come here at all? This is your fault. It was you who said it. We would have been better off in the country.

Bart backwards against the wall as if her words were fists and then his eyes go strange, fuse into a look wrought by the cold and rain and what stirs in a soul hungry for nourish and what stirs in all souls in such a city and she sees what is held in his eye and knows it is fear.

He says, it might be time to put my cloak in hock.

She roars, hock your cloak and the cold will finish you off in a week.

Colly says, fucking spud-hander.

She has dreamt of a sudden laneway walled high and dark and a gang of children coming upon them not children at all but wolves set to devour their hearts. Just when it seems the deaf boy is going to run out of fingers, Bart finds them new lodgings. She eyes the tumble-down building and follows Bart through a crawl space into a near-pitch room. The wet from a broken window flies through the dark upon bodies asleep or bodies in agony or perhaps they are dead, she thinks, and really, does it matter, at least we won't have to pay for it.

A long night of cold and Colly prattling on about souls. She thinks it must be something to do with this morbid city, all this winter-wet. Listening to the city's dead-cart going by earlier on with a gloomy voice calling for bodies. Colly wanting to know if the soul has a memory box—like, when you die, where do your memories go—if the soul doesn't have a memory box, how can you remember your life when you die—and tell me this, that time when Roger Doherty got his head smashed by the horse's hoof and he went stupid as a mule, where did his mind go then—hee!—you see, that is the proof—I think there has to be a memory box of some kind in the head that stores all your life and his memory box got broken from the kick—but the thing is, if that is so, does that mean his soul will change as well and that he'll go off to heaven stupid as a mule?

She realizes Bart is not beside her because here he is stepping into the room. In the half-light she sees his cheeks freshly razored and that horseshoe freshly shod to his face. His eyes have new poke in them. He pulls her by the wrist. There's a commotion in the town, he says. Get up.

How Bart powers up the street like some groomed horse agleam and full of himself. She has not the energy for this march-walking. Colly says, let that horselicker go his own way. She folds her arms and scowls at his back, smiles when some fathead coachman lets out a deforming roar when Bart steps in front of him. Now they are standing before a crowd gathered by the gates of some grain house. Bart grabs her elbow. Over here, he says. The gates are warded by some twenty soldiers who stand impassive to the women and children sent to the front of the crowd, the women heckling and shouting at the soldiers, their men behind them laughing. She feels herself pulled forwards, inwards, inwards, holding on to the sleeve of Bart, and now she has forgotten her hunger and is woven with the crowd. A ringleader on a box is waving his arms and shouting and somebody roars out, let there be vengeance, and Colly shouts, cut the throats of those horselickers! A solemn man turns around and nods to her. She sees these are not the destitute of the city, not the ravenous scarecrows, the ragmen withered to sticks, the sick and crippled. They are dressed instead in the clothes of the city's working people, the tradesmen, the craft workers, the shop workers. Glory be to the poor man! End the distress! Let the grain out! Cut the throats of those horselickers! Bart pulls at her sleeve and nods her towards the sight of a man with a different look from the others, a detective, no doubt. Bart shouts in her ear, let's step back a bit. And anyway, she thinks, this is not the plan, standing here, shouting out for who knows what.

The crowd pulses to its own strange rhythm, pulls them leftwards until somebody shouts whoah and the surge settles down. They push to the rear of the crowd and she looks up and sees faces leaning from the windows of the factory buildings above them, thinks about how time has fallen away from the city, everything in the world stopped to just this, the silence between shouts, the whispered rumours being spread that they're going to open the gates, that they're saying come back tomorrow. Then some commotion behind them and she turns and sees some fool of a deliveryman is shouting and waving for his wagon to be let through and then some fellow with a grin is climbing the back of the wagon and he becomes a solemn Christ aloft with his arms held out, roars to the crowd, glory be to the poor man! He is met with a cheer and in the same moment there is a gunshot and the crowd unthinks into panic. She runs with Bart towards the wagon and there are others pulling at its contents and they take hold of a crate and she can see men unhitching the horses as if to steal them and there are men rocking the wagon and then Bart says, give it here, Bart the great rock carrier who gets the crate up on his back and moves away under it.

The sky behind them a shawl of whistles and roaring and then further gunshot. The sudden emptiness of a lane where Bart slides the crate off his back. That might be someone slumped in a corner or it might not, she thinks. She looks over her shoulder as Bart knifes at the box.

Colly says, I hope to fuck it's tobacco.

She says, we can hawk whatever it is. She is trying to work out how many warm dinners a guinea would buy.

Bart pulling loose straw from the box and his hand emerges gripping a dark bottle. It's some kind of spirit, he says. It is then the air changes around them and she knows them as wolves that peel from the shadows and of a sudden they are swarmed, somebody taking rough hold of her arms from behind her and she spits and kicks, tries to shout to Bart, can see Bart reaching for his knife but somebody has hold of him. In silence the wolves grab at the bottles and then they are gone and she finds herself staring at the ground bereft and there is Bart holding a hurt head and at least you are not hurt also, she thinks. It is then that she sees it, a single bottle that has rolled free and she runs for it, puts it under her cloak.

We can sell it, she says.

See? Bart says. We have made our own luck.

They walk through the city pulling at the sleeves of men outside the spirit shops offering sale of the bottle. She cannot understand why nobody will buy it. Colly says, they think you want to sell them piss in a bottle. One stringy fellow uncorks the bottle and takes a suspicious sniff. I don't know what that is, he says, but I'll give you this much for it. Bart stares at the open hand and says, fuck off with yourself. Two boys begin following and she thinks they might be something to do with the Ryan gang though Bart says they have not the look for it. Colly says, they've been sent by that Deaf Tom, I know it. In Englishtown a drunkard with red cheeks makes a grab for the bottle and Bart cowers him with the knife. Come on, Bart says, let's try Newtown again.

Their ghost-selves in the window have stopped to watch the occupants of an eating shop, the certain angle of shoulders hunched over tables, hands forking and cutting, wiping, fisting for a cough, curling to bring mugs to mouths, talking through half-chewed food, a huge fire roaring at the room. The shape of a woman leaning back laughing. Their blood is red with nourishment, she thinks, while my own blood is trickling over the rocks of my bones, and though you can learn to ignore hunger, not to give it a single thought, hunger is always thinking of you.

Of a sudden she is inside the eating shop and stands before a table near the door, her hand held out, the air sauced with smell and heat and she hears herself saying, just a morsel, your honour, just a little piece. An aproned man hurries towards her and roughs her out the door. Get your hands off me, mister. There is nothing in Bart's look and yet how she hates the sight of him when he helps her up off the street. She grabs the bottle out of his armpit and uncorks it and puts it to her mouth and drinks. Bart grabs the bottle off her and his mouth opens to shout but by now the drink is sliding its blade down her throat.

Bart shouts, what kind of fool are you? We can't sell it if you drink it. And anyhow, what fool drinks on an empty stomach?

Colly says, fuck him telling us what to do.

This coughing-hot strangeness and her stomach is shouting. Everything tingles and burns.

Bart holds her with a maddened look. Then he puts the bottle to his lips and drinks. What in the fuck? he says. I think this might be rum.

Colly says, go on, give me a drink.

She thinks, this is way better than baccy.

Bart grabs the bottle off her and takes a longer sup.

She feels the rush of some great and sudden giddiness, wants to laugh at the world, wants to laugh at Bart's face, this sad way he has of looking at her. She says, aren't we some trio of filthy magpies. She pokes out her elbows and lets roll a magpie's rattle that dilates into cackling laughter. Bart narrows her with a look and then takes another sup from the bottle. What trio? he says. There's only the two of us.

She watches some man dawdle a moment to watch their commotion and shouts at him to fuck off, mister nosy-face. She says to Bart, did you ever consider card tricks? Her laugh is riotous. Colly has started to sing and she hasn't a notion where he has gotten his strange rhyme from.

Diddley-aye-de-don,
Wee John went to bed with his breeches on.
Diddley-aye-de-doff,
Wasn't it big Mary in the bed took 'em off.

What in the hell is up with you? Bart says. He makes a grab for the bottle and wrestles it off her. She watches him eyeing her without blinking as he takes another long drink. She leans against the wall and studies Bart and thinks, I am sick of all this, sick of the rain and sick of the city and I am sick of his stupid face.

She shouts out, I want to go home.

Bart's face reddens and he roars out, what is wrong with you? You are always in a strop.

I mean what I say. I am sick of all this. I am going to go home tomorrow and there's nothing you can do about it.

How are you going to go home tomorrow, the condition you are in?

I don't care what you think. I am done with all this.

She is aware of the shapes of men and women gathering with laughing mouths to watch.

Bart says, keep your voice down. Listen, I will take you home.

It's no longer any of your business.

Yes it is.

No it's not.

Listen. I want to go north anyhow, go back to Galway. There's more luck to be had there. I know some people. He leans forward and whispers. Why don't we try and get some money here first. Then take a car northwards.

Would you listen to yourself. We are here since forever and have nothing to show for it except wet-cold and hunger and today you nearly got us dead. I am sick of it. I am sick of the sight of you. Get away from me with your stupid arm. Get away from me, I said.

She turns towards some stranger and points at Bart. Tell him to leave me alone.

Calm down, Grace.

The man steps forward and says to Bart, this young woman says to leave off, maybe you should leave her.

Bart pulls his knife and waves it. How about I chat with you instead?

She steps between the man and the knife and shouts into Bart's face.

I don't love you.

The way of Bart now and how she will never forget, so very still and something awful happening to his eyes as if a soul in a body could collapse, the way his mouth puckers a wordless hole and then behind him some stranger laughs. Of a sudden Bart pulls her forward into a kiss and she meets the strange taste of his mouth and a voice from her innermost shouts until she pushes Bart and strikes his jaw with her fist.

She shouts, I told you to fuck off.

She tries to shake the hurt out of her hand.

Encircling laughter fills up her ears and Bart useless before her.

Her body and her shadow coming apart as she takes flight down the street.

She sidles into the reeking chat-laughter of men outside the taverns, Colly letting loose one of his bawdy songs or a good yarn learned from McNutt, watches them laugh with her. Lets the smiling men buy her drink. Watching all the while for Bart, who follows like some stray dog, his face grown long and silent watching from the shadows. She points him out to other men, watches their mouths wag with laughter. She thinks, it is good this power you can have over another, like a hand closing over a fist. Later, when she turns to laugh at him, he is gone.

Into the night and how the world becomes strangeness, everything inwarding to thought. She is sad-happy. She thinks she is the best-ever of herself. Colly roaring his head off, then singing a song along with two strange men and she does not know where they have come from. She is amazed at her own voice. Men whisper and walk with her and ask where are you from, who are you now, would you like me to walk with you? She humours some of them and waves the knife at others and then she is walking the docks and who is that but Mary Bresher warming her hands over a barrel fire.

Grace says, I thought you had given up following me.

Mary Bresher says, I am not following you—who would follow you, the show you are making of yourself.

You sound like my mother.

Your mother would not know you.

I'll tell you what. Go away and fuck yourself. I am sick of your little hauntings.

Colly roaring for some tobacco and here is that fellow from earlier offering her a light and she walks with him, hears her own words as if another were speaking them, finds herself in a doorway with this same fellow and he offers her a bottle and she takes it and he is trying to kiss at her neck and she finds his hand between her legs and does not mind it. Time folding light into dark and of a sudden she is staring at her vomit all over the man's feet and he is roaring at her and she is coming at him with the knife and he is gone, what is the city and what is the night, and you must lie down here, lie down in this corner, so colding, so colding.

This murmuring city and then her eyelids open. Oh! Oh! She sees two low slum buildings and the sky between them blowing cold upon cold. Her mouth is turf and her head spaded. This everything-hurts-all-over. Oh! Oh! Oh! She is shocked to see blue fingers, pulls her fingers into fists and tightens her shivering arms about herself. Colly says, hey, muc, are you awake? She cannot listen, this dry-brains head and this pain beyond terrible. Are you listening, muc, I'm trying to tell you. It is then she realizes she has no cloak. She comes upright with a sudden alertness, leans crookedly against the doorway and tries to see about her feet. Colly!

Two street cleaners with a swaying pushcart go past her heaving a smell of human waste. The eyes of one ask if she is all right and her eyes study him as if he were the taker of her cloak but he is just some street cleaner, some old simpleton washed in dirt. She turns and stares at this doorway she slept in, this doorway that put her out of her own feeling, this doorway that stole her cloak. The city is cold and the sky is a barren country. She wants to punch the screaming gulls. Thinks, what have you done to yourself, your feet covered in vomity drink and everything stinks of piss.

She does not see the city as she walks but stares into the puzzle of herself, searches her mind for a story of the night but there is nothing but dark. How hunger has come ravenous and this eating cold and she begins to see the night as if in fragments from a dream.

Bart!

He has not returned to their room. She bends to a woman slumped by the edge of an unlit fireplace and asks if he has been seen. The woman lets out a long breath as if it were the last of her ghost. Outside and she washes her face with icy water from a tap and a boy tries to charge her until Colly runs him off.

Listen, muc, he says, forget that citty-armed cunt altogether, we are better off without his bad luck.

And yet she walks the city until footsore. This strange feeling that has come upon her. Seeing his boxy shoulders and march-step in every man who is another. And so what if you have become a sleeve puller like everybody else, things are different now and that's the way of it but things can also get better and so they will. She cadges tobacco from an old sailor with tarry fingers and fishy women tattooed on his arms. His watery wrinkled eyes surmise her head to toe. He asks if he can walk with her but Colly tells him to fuck off. She dulls the hunger with smoke, watches some fellow falling under the kicks of two constables and being dragged to standing and she wishes he were Bart because at least then you would have found him.

Day into night and night into day and she thinks she has walked every road in the city, the factory smoke becoming one with the morning's mist that creeps in over the river and how can you see who is Bart now and who isn't? She thinks, this is what life is, a great unseeing, the people who took your cloak gone into mist and the people you care about gone into mist and yet you go about living as if you could see everything.

She is struck by a feeling that Bart has taken the north road to Galway without her. This hunger worse now and she pulls at the sleeves of fine-looking men asking for a coin and Colly is rattling her ear with strange talk—bada bada, he says, let's go into that bread shop and rob it, bada bada, let's rob that young fella selling rats on a string.

How hunger wolfs through the body after so much walking. You must do what you can and who cares if they hang you. She climbs through the back window of a house in Newtown brazen as the day, comes face-to-face with a child in a high chair, Colly making faces at the baby as she whispers the milky bread out of his hand, hears footfall in the hall, climbs back out again. A breathless dash towards the high wall. Colly shouting, you stupid bitch, you should have grabbed something to sell.

She thinks, you should have grabbed a cloak.

She offers to hold horses for money. Does not count the hours in the room but lies turning through cold and the sound of coughing, listens to the heavy steps of some old man fumbling through the crawl space and along the wall, looks up and sees it is Bart. Even in this half-light she can see he has been undone, his face bloodied, his feet barefoot, and his body without cloak or waistcoat, his knife and scabbard missing. A knife-fight cut into his arm, cut into his shirt stained with blood. He does not look at her but drops like a rag at the wall opposite, curls himself in silence. She goes to him—Oh! Oh!—and he is shivering and she puts her arms around his shoulders.

Oh! Oh! Oh! Oh!

So out of this cursed city. The rain and the outlands whispering together some old talk that is the story of the world, both everything and nothing. Now they are road walkers the same as every other. Walking with a wanty hand held out. She watches how the winter light traps upon all things a film of wet that gives the earth a barren lustre. All that is greenworld passing to its dying colour.

They stand in a ditch to let a mudded mail coach come shuddering past them, Bart holding on to her elbow.

She knows this business of walking northwards is a gamble. Every rood of countryside is picked clean. The pipe in her pocket a gawping mouth and yet Colly keeps going on about a smoke.

Tappy-tap-tap, tappy-tap-tap, listen up, muc, we should at least put smoke in our bellies to tamp down the hunger.

There are others on the road but why would you look at them, she thinks. They hardly look at you and anyhow haven't you enough to keep you busy. There is Bart, for instance. He walks with rags tied to his feet and hardly speaks and when he does his voice is a scratch above whisper. He walks like a man who has given up, she thinks, like a man fondling some downwarding thought. His eyes have become like Sarah's, like that of the unseeing ox. Or perhaps he is just thinking himself forward step by step, his teeth set, his eyes staring into the far-off as if to unthink himself into will. Yet he cannot keep up.

Colly says, I think he is starting to tremble—that is what the cold will do, it eats into you until it has you all over and then you get the sickness.

Every so often she must stop and wait while Colly shoos at Bart as if he were cattle—hup! hup!

Bart will not meet her eye.

She whispers to Colly, it is as if he has left some part of himself in the city.

Colly says, he might have forgotten his shadow—look at the road, the shadow he throws is that of a small dog.

She wants to know what happened to Bart in Limerick but every time she asks he waves his hand as if it were some small bother. She asks him again and again, was it the deaf boy and his friend? One of the street gangs?

Twice today he has said that nothing is the matter. He whispers about people in Galway who will help them. Some fellow who owes him a favour. Says, Galway is only a horse-leap away. We will go there and get fed and rested and then I will take you to your people in Donegal.

They have tunelled through dark into this town called Ennis. Scavengers on the streets like stunned crows. The town watched over by buildings that might be flour mills. She thinks she will always remember the look of the fever hospital, the fright-shapes in the dark by the gates waiting to get in. Bart stops and leans out of breath against a wall. They find a place to sleep on the edge of town, some old forge, she thinks, though it might have been a baker's once. There are other rough sleepers who speak in coughs. It is the longest night she can remember. The wind now trying to fashion some tuneless song and Bart's breathing is not wrong but it is not right either. She tries to hold him and keep him warm but he won't let her, twists like a younger in her arms, his body inwarding towards sickness, she thinks. She lies listening for signs of fever. Bart turning away. She stirs from a dreamy thought, how she can see herself walking the road northwards without the leaning weight of Bart. Then she thinks, but you would hear in every lone step the sound of his coughing.

Today the wind smells of winter and raggy old women. Colly says, that crock-arm kept robbing my heat all night. She wanders the streets of Ennis town and sees how every space has a hand hanging out. There are people here who beg the beggars. Two beggars size upon her when she takes a corner and seeks charity. She finds a rusted tin on a rubbish heap and does a handstand against a shuttered shop, puts the tin out. The sky becomes the street's filth and the ground becomes sky-puddle. Colly singing some song and she thinks of the strangeness of the world when seen from upside down, if only for a moment the world could be like this, perfectly reversed, how their money would fall from their pockets and their baskets would toss out their food and their jewellery would leap from their windows and you could walk the streets and pick what you like and you would be nobody's fool.

Twice today Bart has stopped and refused to walk onwards. His head hangs with exhaustion. This road ever-long and every townland in shush. The ditches whispering for some morsel of food or for a swallow of water. She thinks, there is a gap widening between the luckless and the lucked. Heaven for sure is coming down to meet the earth.

It is the lucked who prise open the road's silence. Carriages thunder the road as if nothing were the matter. People passing by on their way to the city or for ship's passage, some of them dressed in their best clothes as if traveling to mass or a fair. Their belongings heaped and roped down. She wants to shout, the city is a trick—you think you can hide on its streets and escape this wintering but the city will eat you up. At least in the country the wintering sits on the road plain as daylight and you know where you are at. She stands with her hand held out watching such passing faces for some sign of witness but each is as blinkered as a horse.

Here and there in so casual a manner they come upon a body. Death harrows the silence and speaks as loudly as it wants. Every dead person wants to tell you the same thing, she thinks, that you think what has happened to me will not happen to you—

Bart is walking with his head down and does not seem to notice.

Colly says, the souls of the dead must be in great turmoil, for when you think about it, all a body wants is a shovel and some earth and some peace and quiet but they have been denied all that, have been left out for the birds and the badgers and whatever else as if they were wild animals, and when you think about it, the only thing that separates us from the animals is that we look after our dead and bury them, so it is understandable the dead would be annoyed—what is the world coming to when we let them parade about the place, it is the end of the world for sure.

They stand in the yard of an abandoned farmhouse that shapes its gloom over a barren garden, a feeling of emptiness like presence. She wonders why an elm has had its bark stripped to head height and sees another just like it. Colly says, this was a house of tree eaters, I told you this was going on. For a moment she can imagine them, strange creatures with long arms like that drawing one time passed around in school that showed a monkey-man wearing a stovepipe hat and a jacket and breeches that was supposed to be an Irishman talking to some Englishman, long teeth for nibbling.

She says to Bart, wait there a moment, points her knife and steps slowly into the house.

Wah! Colly says, that smell—this place stinks of bird cac.

Greasy daylight through the window and spatters of bird shit all over the walls and floor. The house two-roomed, emptied out but for the remnants of rough sleepers and some bird clicking by the rafter. There are splinters of smashed-up furniture and jags of broken delft in a corner as if somebody threw the crockery to the wall. Some fool has rolled into the house a log much too big to fit into the hearth and now it sits as a black-charred seat. Colly whispers, that's a wood pigeon that's got inside, I'll bet you I can get it with a stone. The bird hurls itself off every wall and window before fleeing out the door into the wider world, where she watches it dissolve into the all as if it were only a thought of food and that is what you deserve for getting your hopes up. Bart stepping slowly into the house. He sits down on the log, an old man staring into the memory of fire.

Nothing useful can be found in the empty outhouse or yard, not even a fire-striker. Just throwings of wood which she puts beside their unlit fire. The strange emptiness of an abandoned house as if people do leave something behind them, not a memory of themselves, she thinks, but a feeling for somebody else of who they might have been and that feeling meeting no answer.

Colly says, their wheel of luck turned all the way to bad, all right.

She stands at the door and stares at the everlow of cloud, can see houses in the far-off. Her voice brightens. She says, when we get rested I'll go and ask at nearby houses for a match or an ember, then we'll be laughing the three laughs of the leprechaun.

Bart stares unseeing at the empty hearth. Without the cloak he has become his bones. He is wheezing through a sucky mouth. She wraps her arms against the cold and sits beside him, wonders who it was tried to eat the bark, the people who owned the house or the wanderers who stayed here after, you'd want to be some kind of fool to eat a tree, let us hope things will not get as bad as that.

She says, I wonder what happened to them, if they became ditch-sleepers or maybe we passed them on the road or maybe—

Colly says, I'm freezing, maybe we can summon the devil and ask him to get this fire lighted.

Fuck up.

Bart looks at her.

Colly says, go out at midnight and you'll meet him on the road, he's bound to be waiting for you—can you imagine it?—hey, sir, Satan or whatever they call you, where are you—I'm here waiting, what do you want?—I want some wishes—right so, I'll grant you three things, what are they?—right, Satan, I want you to get me a great big fire lit and some timber and some nails to go along with it for building and some pig iron and bags of straw and plenty of hens and a milk cow and a field of lumpers and a loom and eight pounds of wool and a sheep and another brown cow while I'm at it and you can throw in a lake full of salmon and as for my second wish—

They lie in a corner and Bart is instantly asleep despite the cold. She spoons into him, rests an uncertain arm on his shoulder. She notices now a second exhaustion that creeps beneath the usual tiredness, a feeling in her legs and arms and chest that frightens her. Bart begins to shake with great coughing and then he goes silent.

She whispers, are you awake?

Bart says, no.

She says, do you think they ate the tree bark or maybe they boiled it? Is there nourish in bark?

Bart moves his shoulder as if trying to get away from her. Then he whispers. Did you not notice?

She says, notice what?

The air.

What of it.

The change in it.

So.

I saw it last night. There was a halo around the moon. You know what that means. There will be a change for worse in the weather.

Inside the dream, Colly is roaring—stir up! stir up! She feels herself loosening from the dream's entwine—Colly roaring, open your eyes! She awakes and can feel the dread thing before it is thought. Opens her eyes and meets the sudden knowledge of worse, the room heightened with white light, her breath riding before her into the room. A strange and deeper cold. Bart is awake and sitting with his knees to his chin clicking his teeth. His hair and shoulders are covered in bird cac and she wonders if it happened yesterday or during the night, looks to the rafter for sign of life. Bart points to the window and Colly says, you need to look. She says, stop telling me what to do. She gets up and goes to the door, opens it slowly to see what she already knows. Light upon light. The slack-fall of snow upon snow. The world deforming to white as if beauty can be done to the thing undone.

It is Colly who says, will you listen up?

She says, shut up, you.

Bart whispers, shut up yourself.

I'm not talking to you.

Look at the way he is.

He's fine, so he is. He's just freezing.

You must be seeing past him, or under him, or a ghost or something but you are not looking at him.

I'm looking at him right now.

He is getting the fever, so he is, same as the others on the roads.

No he's not.

Yes he is, you silly bitch.

Bart says, I'm not getting the fever.

Yes you goddamn are.

The trees stand in luminous shock. The snow makes guesswork of the road. Colly says, it is an early snow but even still you should have been ready for it. Bart stooping after her like a corpse. He is growling at the snow and growling at her, calls her a heifer, something mindless, finally he goes silent.

She thinks, he is like an old man for sure.

Colly says, you should have left him back where he was, he's nothing but a hindrance.

Colly sings every song he knows while she counts a marching beat. She knocks her blue knuckles on the door of every house and cabin, it does not matter now about pride or what kind of person you think you are, she thinks. She visits big farmhouses where the weather vanes keep the same frozen silence as the hinges of every door. She knows the hasty rasp of a bolt. The flutter of a curtain. She thinks, two people to your door like this looking the way Bart looks can bring only trouble. Every ear listening for the sound of coughing, for sickness tramps through the snow and leaves footprints and when it knocks at your door it wants to come in, lean over the fire, take a sup of your soup, lie down on the straw, spread itself out, and bring everybody else into its company.

Those who open their doors do so just-about and stand fright-faced and starving. They shake their heads when they see Bart round-shouldered with his razor cough, his face a funny colour.

An eyeball in the crack of a door says, you can come in to the fire but that other fellow will have to stay out.

Later she thinks, if only Colly hadn't spat at him and got it good in the door, he might have given us matches.

They meet a townland where sickness has been tramping about, all right, gone into three different cabins and brought down the fist of God. Each cabin with its walls and roof stoved in as if God finally had enough of their coughing. She knows what this is, that you do not go into a fevered house and tend to the sick or bring out the bodies, but you must close in the walls and the roof on top of them when you think they are dead.

Colly is watching all the time for birds, anything to throw a stone at. The sky silent as grief. Her feet numb and she has to listen to her stomach with its shouty mouth, stops where a fox has tracked ghostly across the road and imagines her hand burrowing into the warmth of its den, pulling it out and strangling it.

We have come too far, she says. It is time to get back to the cottage.

Colly says, the pair of you moping like sad mules.

He starts singing the same line of a song over and over and she starts to sing along, thinks, the more you sing the less frightened you are and isn't that always the case, perhaps we should be singing every moment of our lives and singing into our graves.

My arse has crossed an ocean,
And still no breezes blow,
And I would it had the motion,
Of but an ebb and flow.

Shut your eyes, she tells Colly. They walk past a young woman delirious in a ditch, the woman smiling as the snow gives last drink to her lips. The snow gowning her white for the slowest of country burials. The woman becoming part of the all, she thinks, that is the sky and the earth locked together in white and forgetting. You do not look but keep walking onwards. This feeling she has. It is not that she tells herself she is different. She knows she is different from all these others on the road, that what she sees around her will not happen to her also. That she will make better choices. So why would you look at them, they have made their choices and you made yours, they aren't even people, just sitters and starers with their cramp-hands held out like the grabby hands of the dead. They want what you want and would take it out of your hand or even kill you for it so why would you even give them a sympathetic look?

She does not know why they sit around the unlit fire. She thinks it might be the echo of a habit that is as old as people-kind but never have people been without fire so what is going on? She wants to laugh but there is nothing to laugh at. You do not think about the cold and you try to sleep but how can you sleep when your bones shout as loud as this? How you feel every minute of the dragging dark, cannot decide which is worse, the way hunger gnaws your body or the way cold gnaws on what's left.

She says over and over, the snow will lift, it will lift, so it will. Perhaps in the morning or the morning after. Then we can get you on to Galway.

No more does Bart answer.

Colly says, I told you we should have left him here, we would have got on far better without him.

Walking the however-long of another morning. The trees that drape their icy beggar-hands. A screaming oak on the slump of a hill and beneath it in a field she sees five digging men. They have turned a mound of snow and earth. The slow and heavy sway of a dead-cart moving towards them. The men spade at the ground and they gale their breaths into the frozen air, the ground like pitted teeth to their effort. And no wonder, she thinks. For why would the earth want to become a dead-house? You'd be stuck having to listen to the chatter of the dead complaining all the time about being lumped in together.

Colly says, is that what I think it is over there?

I told you not to look.

You do not look but keep walking onwards.

The beauty of snow is that it allows no smell.

The white road becomes a slippy hill that judges in silence two men struggling like drunkards. They are trying to get their donkey and tumbrel over the hillock. An old man shouting and then he stops and bends as if into thought. She falls like snowfall into the work, puts her back into the push, not an ounce of strength and the look they give her tells her they know it. A son with the same frowning look as his father. The cart unheeding their gruntwork but then it groans deep and moves with a squawk like some old bird shown free of its cage.

The old man stops the mule on the top of the hill. She holds out her hand but the son stares and shakes his head. She sees how these men are not well fed but they are not wintered like most others. She pulls her knife and waves it.

Would you look at that, the son says. Are you an idiot or what?

Colly whispers, don't back down one inch.

She stands facing them, watches the father step with heavy feet around the back of the cart. He puts a hand up, says, Patrick, leave it. I said leave it, now. He reaches into the corner of the cart and pulls towards him a sack, lifts out five pieces of turf, holds them out to her. He says, the Lord is thy keeper.

She wants to shout at the old man, fuck God's luck when you can make your own.

Colly says, fuck them hoors only giving us five pieces of turf.

She puts the knife between her teeth and takes the turf, grunts her voice down.

Gimme matches.

The cornered cold is creeping back into the room. She studies the shrunken fire and throws upon it damp wood.

Colly says, people say God is everywhere at once, but so is the devil and everybody knows the devil is fire and so God is the devil and that's the case proven.

She stares at the fire and remembers how it rushed to life and perhaps Colly is right, perhaps fire doesn't die because fire is both God and the devil, always waiting behind the air in some other chamber of existence, waiting to rush in and turn everything black with its hunger.

She thinks Bart's mind has grown slippy in fever. How he refused to lie beside the fire and she had to drag him over. The bitter things he has said. His little whispers. I dreamt you were dead and I liked it. I dreamt we were all dead. I dreamt the world died and everything was better for it.

She says, you cannot be dead and also dream the world at the same time.

He whispers, I can dream what I like. Every man is alone in his own mind. All this is an illusion. I close my eyes and it is gone. None of it exists.

She asks him what he means but he does not answer.

Later, he whispers, even a dog gets a noble death, takes itself quietly to a field.

She rests wet sticks upon the fire, anything to keep it lit but the embers test a weak tongue and haven't the hunger.

What days pass and it is a dream the last time she has eaten. The snow carried silent upon a howling wind that cuts downwards in blizzard. Everything to nothing, she thinks. Nothing to be had, nothing upon nothing.

You must try to eat some snow, Colly says, imagine it as otherness.

She thinks, how hunger slow-crawls then leaps like a cat. It claws at your thoughts, curls its shape into your sleep, and stirs restless. After a while hunger and cold become the same dullness, you cannot tell them apart. They slow the mind and soften the worry about the changes taking place inside her. The slump of her thoughts. This tingling weakness all over her body.

She realizes now the secret of this place. Why the others left. That there is some power here contained in the earth that rises up and has an effect on the brain, makes you sleepy, the trees whispering their madness to you and it is not you who will eat the trees but the trees who will feed on the dust of your bones.

Stir up! Stir up! Colly says.

She rests her hand over Bart's mouth a little too long. His breathing as weak as thought. She wanders heavy-footed in the snow. The empty sky and the empty fields and Colly wants to know where all the airdogs have gotten to. He says, if there's one thing in this country you can rely on, it's the crows. He has stones ready for throwing but the sky is shut of them. She uses all her strength to climb to a tree's rookery, shakes snow off the branches, peers for eggs in every abandoned nest.

Colly wants to know if Bart is going to die soon. Brittle light in the room but enough to see how his limbs have swollen. He has been lying in a curling shape for such a long while.

There are times now when she looks at Bart and does not care what happens to him.

The downwards sky into moon-dark and still she keeps walking. Everything floats in this snow-blue light. She knows now she has been here before, how the road winds around a slumpy hill with a screaming oak and the dead in a field beside it. In the dark she can hear the diggers still at work. They never stop, she thinks. They work night and day and still the bodies keep coming. She finds herself walking towards them, you just never know, one of them might help you. It is then it occurs to her these diggers are doing their spadework at night, no sound of carts or people talking. She coughs and the digging stops. She hears whispers, sees something ghost towards her, how a man's face comes to be out of that moon-dark, a man made only of bones as if he has borrowed his body from what hides in the earth, clothed it with huge eyes, an animal noise coming from his throat as he scares her off with a threatening gesture of his shovel.

She hobbles away as fast as she can.

Colly says, whatever a man finds to eat is his own business, a man has got to live at all costs—who are we to judge?

She tests her hand over Bart's mouth for breathing. Thinks he is trying to whisper something. Just his voice, a whisper without a body. Whatever he is saying, she cannot hear it.

Then Colly says, what is it you are eating, give me some.

She tries to hide it.

Tree-eating bitch, Colly says.

She wonders when the world fell away from her thoughts. If there is a sky now it is as wide as a whisker, weatherless, unwatched. Her thoughts slump before her in silence. Her sight has narrowed down to stillness. Sometimes she wonders what has happened to the cold, when it left her bones. She thinks Bart might be dead now and even if he's not he can only be a hindrance. She no longer tests for his breath, though sometimes she thinks she can still hear him.

She dreams she stands under a tree in snow and at the foot of it are dead crows, the birds fallen in hunger, no meat on their bones and horror at the dead in their eyes. She cannot understand why she does not collect them in her satchel. Then she knows it is not a dream or perhaps it is, and anyhow who can tell this dreaming from real, there is no such thing as real anymore. Bart beside her and he is trying to say something so she tries to listen. When I was young my grandfather used to tell us that old people always knew the exact hour of their death. Can you tell me what time it is? She knows that Bart in the truth of the dream is beautiful. She tries to see him but he has gone somewhere else and a voice says, a bird in the hand is worth fuck-all, and it might be Colly but who knows. She dreams of strength, knows there is still hope because hope does not leave until you are dead. Hope is the dog waiting at your door. She hears some mysterious woman knocking and she knows it is Mary Bresher come to tell her to get out on the road. Get out on the road! Get out on the road! Colly roaring at her. Stir up! Stir up! Stir up! Stir up! You stupid bitch.

She digs for strength and finds it in the hiding place. Tells herself, truly, everything is all right. You are only tired, tired so. You are not as bad yet as the others. Daylight to blind the eyes and the world to slush. Her mind quietening to the path of her footsteps. She decides she wants to sit down just for a little while and does so and then the day passes by and she becomes aware of horse noise then shadow and a man's voice says, why are you lying in the middle of the road?

Then the voice says, you aren't fevered, are you?

She shakes her head.

Sit up, then.

She turns and sees a head without a body climbing down off a cart. Hands under her oxters hauling her up. The headless voice says, you're just like an auld sack. Then he says, would this help you? She realizes now she is holding a piece of food. Old man hands filling her satchel with flitchings and some turf. It is old man Charlie, she thinks, rowed all this way in his boat on the snow across the fields of

Ireland, and she wants to tell him it is time he rowed her back to Blackmountain, that a promise must be kept.

The old man says, that's all I have to share with you now. I'm keeping some for the others. Some use having all the turf in the world when you cannot eat it, though some do I'm told. I'm holding out, holding out and you should hold out too because this spell of weather is nearly over and then we'll all be laughing. I'll have to eat poor donkey here but I'll get five penny from the skin dealer and I'll be *ar mhuin na muice.* If you know of anyone else who needs fuel, tell them to find me on the road. Keep the heart strong, for death is closing a lot of mouths. Here are some matches.

She nibbles the soft and it is apple and what taste, fights the sick feeling it gives her. Later she sees a woman tottering on the road. You must hide the apple from her, you must hide the apple also from that man lying in that ditch because if they see it they will take it off you. You must eat all this apple before Bart smells a look.

Colly's endless chatter is getting louder and louder. She wonders where he gets his strength from. Listen up, muc, it's time you let me be in charge for a while.

She takes the flitchings and turf out of her satchel and shows them to Bart. Look what I found, she says. There is no answer. She sparks the fire to life and watches it devour the flitchings and devour the turf and it is only when the fire has reached its brightest does she notice Bart is not lying where he was. That Bart has gotten himself up. She wonders how a man so sick could lift himself up like that. And then she knows. He has smelled the apple. He has gotten himself up to look for it. A sudden panic then at the thought of Bart finding her last bit of food until she remembers she has already eaten the apple. She calls Bart's name but he does not answer. She stands up, studies each wall as if the very walls could pull such a trick, cannot figure it, for days he has been too sick to move and now suddenly he is better, he was probably hiding food the entire time, strong enough now to get up and walk. She goes to the door and calls for him but does not hear her own voice. She reaches for a greater shout but her voice is faint and is its own answer. Moving through dizziness and it is then that she finds what look like two tracks in the slush, two odd tracks like the stagger of a scarecrow that stepped into life and for sure they are his, and she follows and then she stops for she has not the energy to follow, how the footsteps disappear like dog tracks on the road.

VI

Crow

Hee! Stir up! Stir up! Stir up, you little horselicker, look!

Nothing all night but Colly's titter and chatter, he has caught the delirium, she thinks. She turns from his tumult towards the wall, eyes closing into this sleepy-sleep and she can hear herself hack-coughing, hack-coughing and then easing into dark again. In this eyes-closed-now the black is comfort, all thought shut out, Mam a shadow waiting in a dream.

Stir up! Stir up, I said!

It is Colly now who is discomfort, Colly who is endless din, all night singing some song about the cock going to Rome, the cock going to Rome and now this new business, she would like to stir up if only to give him a clout, yank out some of his hair. A sneaky thought that says it might be best if he were—no you cannot think it, and anyhow it is a faraway thought, like shouting to somebody from the bottom of a hill and then they are gone and the thought slips to dark again.

Stir up, you stupid bitch—the tree has brought dinner.

She shuts her eyes and imagines Colly with a mouthful of bark.

It is Colly who must rise. It is Colly who must go to the window to look. It is Colly who mutters, this is no way to live.

It is Colly who starts laughing as if he were giving answer to somebody else's joke. The little fucker, he says. She thinks she can hear Colly kick something. Where's my cap? he shouts. When was the last time I had my cap? I'm going outside to trap this bastard. And fuck the cold.

He is pointing out the window to the elm that stands stripped of its bark and upon it the shape of a crow. Even through the smudged glass he can see the gloss has gone from its feathers. It is a mighty airdog, all right, huge and probably old-as. How the wind has fed on its meat, left just sinew and bone, the bird nothing but stare and beak. He whispers at the glass, you're the first airdog around here in a long while. He can taste the chew of crunch-bone, imagines sucking the bird's scant juices. The airdog seems to be staring back at him, caw-woofs as if daring him out.

He whispers to Grace but she doesn't budge. He urges the latch to unbed without noise, that's it, movement without rush, parting the cold air with a hunter's body. How the world glitters as if the air were dreaming itself, for the winter now has run to melt-pools like eyes to watch this crow under a winging blue sky. He sees the bird's black crown is ruffled with the same haircut Grace wore for a while. He ropes the bird to the tree with his sight, the crow upon a low branch spined with lastly snow. With a thought he kills the crow and can taste it with his eyes. Some old battler, he thinks, that has flown the ancient brawl that is bird against life and life against life and every airdog has its day but this will be your last. Hee!

The crow flicks its feathers as if shrugging away some idle thought or perhaps, he thinks, it is wishing the worm out of the wintered earth if there are any worms left. So riddle me this, Joe Crow, what eats and gets eaten, isn't that the way it always is?

The bird jinks its head leftwards then flicks and shivers its wings for flight.

Hold still, Joe Crow.

He sucks with his fingers a stone from the slush and slowly, slower, unhinges for the throw.

Fucker!

The throw goes wide over the tree as if the crow were protected by some spell and perhaps that is so, he thinks, for isn't it said that the elm provides a home for the pooka? Neither tree nor bird pays attention to his shouting, his aping of the crow with arm-wings, nor does the crow seem to notice the second stone that flies overhead, begins instead to nibble its feet, the bird half mad with hunger and cold by the looks of it.

Of a sudden the crow takes skywards and traces a vanishing circle, then inks a slow and wavering line.

Running now across some field in song-whisper.

Stick of a crow,
Prick of a crow,
You'll be pie tonight, don't you know.

The crow alights upon another elm and he throws another stone but the tree swallows it with a rattle of twigs and a gawping mouth as if asking for more. The airdog takes off with a great laughing caw-woof. He tries to hurt the tree with a kick. Follows the bird's flight on foot, watches it alight on a field post with its hands priestly behind its back as if to study him better, this Colly creature on two tottering legs, strange roars bursting from his mouth, one wingless arm aloft with another stone.

From a distance of thirty paces they eye each other and it occurs to Colly that the bird is not eyeing him at all, that he does not in fact exist in the world of this bird, that he might as well be hill or road, thinks of all the bird traps he has built and wonders how he has missed it, that it was the world that was the bird trap all along and how you didn't think to know.

Perhaps it is the dreaming light but the bird seems to rise without wing-flap as if lifted by string. He watches it wink into the high cage of blue, disappear into the far-off.

He runs with his face to the sky. He bats through prickling hedgerow, this everything-wet of last snow. He is thinking of eggs, hoping this airdog will lead him to a nest. Imagines striking the crow thoroughly with a stone—bing!—watching it drop from the sky. The way this crow disappears and reappears as it pleases. He thinks, this airdog for sure knows it is being followed so it might not be an airdog at all but the pooka, leading you to some secret place, a cave or chamber that holds all the world's riches. Of a sudden he trips on some witchy root and lands on his hands in the slush. He picks himself up and continues at a dripping run, I'll get you for this, pooka-bird. Running now towards white hills in the far-off and a goat path that takes him through some townland and only one or two villagers about and not one laugh out of them. Watching the flight of the bird describe some pattern or code, shaping each letter of an answer if only he could figure it.

The day's finish within sight but not this gone-again crow. Not one horse-cart or person on these roads now, the land changing shape, the fields and hills barrening to rock as if everything green were eaten.

Joe Crow,
Joe Crow,
I will yank you from the sky, don't you know.

He tells himself he has moved past tiredness into new strength, wanders watching the sky and the trees for flickers of life, though the evening light plays its tricks, for sometimes you see Joe Crow where there is nothing at all. He cannot stop shouting at the gone-again crow, notices he is not shouting but crying, tells himself he is not crying but laughing.

Fuck you, Joe Crow,
Fuck you, Joe Crow,
The day's not over yet, don't you know.

He will find this bird again. Wishes he had a slingshot, for this bird is some Goliath, don't you think, you would think it was the other way around but it is the crow that owns the sky while your heels are nailed to this rock. Of a sudden he hears it, sees it atop a lone hawthorn caw-woofing some curse. Now he knows that this bird has been waiting for him all along, the bird not bird at all but omen and how can you throw stones at an omen when it has come to tell you something? Fuck you, Joe Crow, the wintering is in and my belly is shrivelled and this is the last of my strength.

Joe Crow,
Joe Crow,
Thought it could survive the snow.
But Joe Crow,
Joe Crow,
Did not count on Colly below.

He knows it is dangerous running the dusk. Unseen things reach out to grab you, the branches of trees like wanty hands pulling at you. There is an oak shaped like some shouty old fellow and a nice seat beneath. He sits and watches his burning feet, the shadows puzzling around the tree into a single piece. Drifting into sleep and waking again to eye the dark and he thinks about the shape-shifting that birds can get up to. Perhaps if you fix your mind you can shape-shift also and why not? He thinks about being a hawk, wheeling sharply to dive upon Joe Crow, taking the bird in your claws, feeling the cold air's rush. It is lonely business this chatting to yourself, talking to a crow that does not listen. In the tree overhead there is sudden wing-flap and he knows the crow is waiting for him. Wait until morning, he says, wait until I can get some strength up. He needs to piss and slowly stands up and goes against the tree, cannot figure why the piss goes all over his legs, it's a bit too dark to see what you are doing anyhow.

* * *

He juts out of sleep with the sudden thought that he is chasing a curse, that he should leave the crow alone and return to the house. He dreams of fire and dreams of Grace keeping him warm, wakes briefly to watch the night's waters receding to light, closes his eyes and dreams he is Grace.

Dawnlight bloods his eyes with warmth. In this half-hollow of sleep he hears the crow shout, wake up, wake up. *Caw-woof! Caw-woof!* He looks up and sees the crow in flickery through the tree. *Caw-woof! Caw-woof!* He unroots a stone and hides it in his hand, steps out in front of the crow and asks, hey, Joe Crow, do you think good and evil exist?

The crow for a moment seems surprised, moves to another branch as if to consider the question from another vantage.

Colly says, I always thought the world was a simple matter, that God was good and the devil was evil, but I'm just not sure anymore, all the things I have witnessed, all the things you must do to survive, you cannot be considered evil if you are just trying to keep yourself alive.

The crow says, who is it told you the truth of things? It wasn't the world that spoke—

Colly sends a stone through the mouth of the tree and—bing!—the bird awfuls a flutter like some old screecher dropping her shawl that is a flutter of dropped feathers. He watches the bird sally awkwardly from tree to tree as if dying and he unroots another stone and gets right up to the bird, goes to throw, but the crow shoots airborne again. Now he knows this bird is not bird at all but the spirit of a dead person, wonders if it is someone he knows, can hear the crow caw-woofing again. Thinks, perhaps it is the devil himself having his fill of laughter.

The crow leads him up some hill and he shouts at the bird as he climbs up it, each step chewing at his ankles, his teeth chattering some message.

Joe Crow,
Joe Crow,
Is trying to kill you, don't you know?

He reaches the top of the hill but there is no crow, only the company of a ruined old tree and he asks the tree which way did the crow go but the tree points in every direction.

This land of rock has returned to fields that spring with wet and he is shivering after walking so far in the wet-cold, cannot talk so much. His body a thousand aches of tiredness. He sits by a stone wall watching thought slump past him like a beggar. He begins to walk and must climb a fence and the world throws itself upside down and he is lying on his back staring at the sky, feels as if he is still falling, a trick of the hunger, and perhaps in some way it is the world that is falling and how could you be sure it is not? And the silence of everything now is the song of the earth, which is the song of great laughter kept to itself. Upwards and walking— solid ground of road and house shape and two well-fed dogs tense watching as if they want to eat— no I'll eat them gobble them down and walk and sit here awhile and so this is what it is to be wintered and it isn't as bad as you would have thought because your belly has gone away off on some journey and your mind wanders and everything falls away to peace and stillness and feelings in your skin aren't feelings anymore and the cold is nothing and the earth will not wake from this winter so who cares. Into a trickle-water ditch where time creeps by on hand and foot, slowly through the puddles like an old man coughing gusts of wind, and he dreams Grace's dreams and wonders why when he wakes, a day and a night pass by within the one shadow and he is still in this ditch, says to himself, do you know something, what, this is no way to live, stir up, stir up, I said, so out onto the road, clop sounds, foot sounds, the sound of your own hand held out like the dropping of huge weight. How to get— how to get back to— just to go— this road is bigger and familiar and might be the road home— hee! Hello donkey hello man hello woman don't you walk away from me now— why is it dark when it wasn't only a moment ago? Rainlicker! That's it— I am not thirsty at all I can drink all the water I want— sitting down then getting up then sitting down again so this is what it is— others stepping past you slumpy auld ditch, hand out, hand out, my hand is speaking why don't you listen, listen to my hand! Strange yowls as if people were suddenly animals whatinthe— lick the grass, why don't you— notastegrass— walk some more you never know— trying-to-walking— just sitting, the same thing really— sound of— striking ears— the sound of digging in yes that field shovelwork man laughing somebody's laugh ringing the air pure as struck stone now that you think about it— can think— dream here awhile— that's another dead-cart gone past and see what is on it— you will be on it soon no I will not yes you will— and do you know why those men are digging they are digging at meat that grows in the ground— you are not dead yet— yes you are— no you are not— soon unless you do something you must— hee! Tell no one— tell no one who is to know, wait until night like those others you saw in the dark and now it is dark and crawl so yes I will— not crawling walking crawling careful careful in case somebody sees— hee!— shovel hands—hee!—shovelling hands— who is that laughing sounds like Grace— Grace is dead— no she is not she is waiting in the house— it is a dog, a dog laughing— the dog is here for the meat also— how to bring this meat to Grace— it is not meat— it is meat— meat does not grow in the ground— is meat— isn't— who will know anyhow— you won't even know if you don't think about it— dark and nobody is watching— to live is to die and to die is to live who said that— what silliness. Digging fingers meet the meat that lies under cloth— rip cloth— meat on the bone is meat in your hand will taste of mud and dead will it not and so what— the body won't know what it's eating, the body won't care— nobody will know—

nobody— nobody— nobody— nobody— nobody— and the taste of smell— gagsmell— whoah! Sicky feeling all over just the smell of it and— who is that— dog again— dog digger digging at the ground where did that other dog come from— more dogs also and dog growl— dogs want this meat for themselves don't care about you— gagsmell— that was a rat are the rats not all eaten— don't sick all over yourself the smell— there it is now bring to mouth— chew it off the bone will you— it is meat is it not? Why won't it chew off strong to the bone even in death is that not a hand at the end of it— it is a hand— all the things it is and is not— and putting the taste into your mouth— sicky sicky gag-rot— just chew— tell yourself— tell yourself I said— taste chew— taste chew you want to live do you not— tell yourself— tell yourself I said— it is cow— yes it is cow— it is bull— yes it is bull— what else is it— it is sheep— yes it is sheep— it is hen— yes more taste— it is pig— yes it is pig— it is goat it is hare it is rabbit it is dog— no bother eating dog— it is cat it is bird it is cateatingbird— it is crow— it is that bastarding crow— it is rook it is magpie it is finch it is feathers it is the poacher's grouse it is peacock you cannot eat peacock yes you can it is robin it is tit it is haha it is swallow haha— riddle me this how can you swallow a swallow— it is martin— martin who?— it is gull it is duck it is goose it is quail it is pigeon it is turkey it is dog again it is dogfish what I meant is catfish but dogfish will do— it is cod it is carp it is herring it is whalefish it is dolphin it is squid it is eel it is trout it is salmon without knowledge it is sea monster it is lobster it is shrimpfish it is mussel it is oyster it is seasnail it is perriwinkle it is whelk it is pony it is donkey it is mule it is jenny it is guinea pig it is rat it is mouse it is shrew it is doormouse it is river rat it is camel it is lion it is monkey it is tiger it is elk it is— I can't think of— wait now, don't taste just eat— it is deer it is fawn it is grass it is leaves it is butter it is bread it is lumper it is stirabout it is porridge it is oats it is griffin it is dragon it is ratmouse it is seal it is otter it is stoat it is that other thing it is badger it is bat it is squirrel it is worm it is snail it is slug it is all the birds in Ireland that's all of them in one— it is hedgehog it is the hoghedge it is the catbadger it is the finchotter it is the goosefish it is— don't think— it is it is it is—

Fuck off dog— sick on yourself— sick on yourself sick rot taste. Fuck off dog—

Roadcrawler— walking on hands like a younger—

Sleepy-sleep—

Slowwaking— morning sort of—

Lie— lie here— in the lying of the lie— not lying to yourself ha ah—

Sleep-lie— lie-sleep— sleep-lie— sleep

Listen you— hey you sir— listen up listen you— quit pulling on me— leave me lie here— listen listen listen listen listen— why can't I hear me— why can't you hear me— where voice— listen listen listen listen mister mister mister mister don't lift me— leave me here— don't lift don't lift— not into this cart listen listen listen listen listen listen listen these are dead— why won't you listen— I'm not— movingcart— lift yourself off try try try, movetry— can't move— come on try again— isn't this what you wished for— all the meat in the world— try try try try try— sleepy-sleep is easier sleepy-lie is it not then this goes away— close your eyes now—

pulling man wake up—

get off get off me— get off—

listen listen listen listen listen why won't you listen—

why won't my words sound—

listenmister listenmister listenmister listenmister listenmister listenmister

listen— list— liss— liss—

Don't put—

I'm not one—

Not—

Of them—

Don't— daghhgh—

Wriggle show them you can wriggle—

show them— show them— daghhgh—

sleepy-sleep— sleepy— listen—

listen up muc you can do this—

you can sleep—

trywriggle— trywriggle— try try try try try try— look at me— listen trywriggle—

Look at me! Look look look look—

gwahhhuh

no matter now no matter—

no—

no matter—

VII

Light

She knows this angel from dreaming and tries to smile at the hovering face, the angel's voice a sweetened milk that brings her back to Sarah. The voice says, quiet now, daughter.

She thinks, so this is dead.

She is made to sup soup from a porcelain cup. A hand floats a muslin cloth that brings soothe to her face. It is only a cloth and yet she is made physical by it. This feels like your body, she thinks, are you sure you are dead? Later the same hands help her into a feeble sit. Her eyes trying to gather the room. Mauve light outside and just the throw-light of a lamp that flutters gold upon the wall a tremble-throat finch and she wonders where such a thought comes from. She feels like a child again in another's bed-dress. The whoever-she-is of this woman beside her who says, quiet now, daughter, reaches the heel of a hand to take the weight off her face. Sliding into sleep, where she grabs at slippy thoughts, the likeness of this angel to her mother.

She knows the angels are watching her sleep, awakes to see five women gathered in day-bright around the bed, five faces not the faces of angels but simple women dressed in black gowns, the who of them she cannot figure. Their watching narrows the room. She closes her eyes but they do not disappear.

A voice says, rejoice, daughter, you are alive.

She opens her eyes. The speaker has lips that move but the eyes are without expression. Another woman steps softly forward and hands her a looking glass and she knows these hands, meets the woman's kindly eyes and takes the mirror and brings it to her face to see who she is, because you never know all the things that can happen, it might be that you went to sleep and woke up as somebody else, there are stories of such things happening. Her breathing fogs the looking glass and she thinks, this is my breathing, this is my breath, and she wipes the glass to reveal the face and the eyes that are not her eyes, not her face, she thinks, but the ghost of a face on a body that is dead.

She drops the looking glass onto the bed and the kindly-eyed woman reaches quickly for it. The sullen woman scolds. Let her look, let her behold the face of her own miracle.

The kindly-eyed woman says, what is your name, daughter?

She stares at each face. Like stones arranged the way each face is different and similar, their hair cut short but for the woman with the looking glass, who wears her long hair tight in a bun. She thinks she would like to tell them her name. She would like to tell them from where she comes. She reaches for the thought but cannot form words. She senses the words but they cannot be spoken. It is then that she knows her tongue has been struck dumb and no word ever again will sound out of her. A third voice says, rest easy, daughter. Another voice says, you will speak in your own time. The sullen woman steps around the bed and takes the looking glass from the kindly-eyed woman. She says, take a look at yourself, daughter. He said that a sign would come. That a sign would show the true meaning of His words. You are that sign. You are the miracle promised to us. Father has brought you back from the dead.

By night and by day a bare alder raps at the window as if asking to be let in, to whisper its thoughts perhaps about the where and the what of all this. She thinks, a day, a week, a month in this hidey-hole, what does it matter being among such folk and their strange talk?

Just nod at whatever they tell you. The soup is regular. Not once have you been cold. Far better here than being out on the road. She leans out of bed and sees her boots near the door. Better just in case to have them.

She watches the days deepen in length and colour and feels such strength growing inside her, everywhere except her throat. Unthinking herself into the same silence as the house, though in the early mornings and evenings she can hear the walls carrying voices in prayer. Sometimes she imagines their voices gathered to judge her, all the sins you have done and the guilt you feel about the things that have happened and why is it you are alive but others are dead? Sometimes she thinks they are the voices of such dead, that no matter how much you try and forget, a dead person is tied around you like weight. For isn't it true that every dead person has something to tell you?

Perhaps it is best you do not speak, she thinks. Then you cannot answer them.

Evening has sent the shadow of a tree tangling through the room. The door is unlocked and a woman enters. She is the kindly one by shape and footfall come to bring light. Grace pretends to sleep though in secret she watches the kindly one take the lamp and unscrew the reservoir, pour oil from a tin, screw the wick back on. The kindly one then strikes a match and utters a curse, drops the flaming match and sucks on her finger. She turns to Grace. Forgive me, daughter, she says. The devil hides his forked tongue in fire to remind us he is always present.

Grace stares at the lamp as it bouts smoke.

The woman says, you woke screaming again in the night. You had to be comforted. I had to come into the house and lie on the floor here beside you. It sounded like you had met your second death.

How the woman's words reach in and astonish her.

I must be dead so, she thinks. And this must be purgatory. That's why the door is kept locked.

She tries to remember the night before, but it seems to her the nights are black as if a hidden hand had poured all dream from sleep. It is then that it comes to her, a thought from the deep that grasps something unspeakable, not dream at all but shadow-shape, not something dreamed but something that has happened, something she has done, how it rises and like a snake comes hither. Backwards she flinches in the bed and the woman takes her hand, says, calm now, daughter.

She shouts at the woman to stay away from her, that it is death in the room not the devil, but no sound leaves her mouth.

Later this woman tells her, you shall know me as Mary Eeshal, it is where I come from. There is kindness in the way she fixes the blanket. Her face and hands a perfect paleness, she thinks, her skin almost without blemish. And though there is dirt under her fingernails they are the soft hands that come from good stock. She wishes Mary Eeshal would never leave, wonders where that other woman has gotten to, the sullen one with a face that speaks no forgiveness. Mary Eeshal seems just a few years older than she is and yet she is sister and mother. She wants to ask her where she is, if she is in some kind of convent or prison or if indeed this is purgatory, who knows the things that can happen to you.

Mary Eeshal says, Father is coming to see you tomorrow. He had to go to Dublin soon after you came. He is the one who brought you.

She blinks at the woman. She wants to ask, who is coming to see me? The priest? The doctor?

Mary Eeshal says, he is coming to see his miracle. He says that word has spread.

As she speaks her eyes glisten. She holds Grace's hands to her chest. She says, Father said he would produce for us a sign that would speak of his true knowledge of God. And that is what he did. We were traveling to a townland just south of here when Father called for the jarvey to stop. He climbed down and began walking towards— her voice catches as if caught on a hook. She takes a deep breath. It was a burial field, she says. Father began towards it and it was then the light came upon him and we all saw it, the light from the sky like a pillar and Father went past the sextons who were taking the bodies one by one off the dead-cart and all of them stopped to watch Father step into the pit, one sinner sexton telling him to get out, that the pit was full of people who died of the fever, and it was then that Father went on his knees and found you amid the dead, and he said the Lord's power had reached you because you showed him the sign, and he read that sign and took you in his hand and it was then that you were risen.

She hears footsteps and whispering women. A key asks the door open and the women enter barefoot. She watches the sullen one stand to the wall with the key in her hand, the other women fanning around the bed, Mary Eeshal and three others with severe faces while a man enters behind them and sits on her bed. It is his voice that says, wipe her brow, Mary Collan. She sees he is no priest and no doctor. He wears a white shirt open at the neck. His black beard running to grey. She has never seen eyes like this, for they are eyes that speak his thoughts into her. These are the eyes of the man who has saved you, she thinks. The sullen woman—Mary Collan—steps forward, her hand reluctant and rough with the cloth. She thinks, they must think you've had the sickness. That is why nobody but Mary Eeshal has ever touched you.

This man called Father. She feels him now not as man but as presence, the way his eyes hold you so that you see only his eyes and no other part of him.

Father says, they say you do not speak but I bet the devil speaks in your dreams, does he not?

He smiles as if her startle were her answer.

He stares into her eyes until she can see only his eyes and it is her eyes that speak not her mouth.

Her eyes ask him, who are you? Why have you rescued me?

His eyes say, from now on you will be with me, you will serve here and do whatever is asked of you and be among these women and that will be your peace, better than being out on the roads.

Her eyes say, is this a house of God?

His eyes say, yes, this is a house of God. He speaks out my eyes and He can hear everything you think so be careful.

He reaches forward and touches her throat, says aloud, you can speak, speak to me, daughter.

She feels a great blubbing in her throat, goes to speak, watches the others lean forward but no words come out.

Her eyes say, I try to speak all the time but the words will not come. The words remain hidden and maybe it's because if you say one thing it will lead to another thing and how could you explain it? The things that have happened? There are things in this world that cannot be met by words. I have done things I cannot speak of. I have—

Father says aloud, you were judged in your first life and you were cast down and then you were saved from your first life when you raised your hand to God.

He stands and bellows his hands open and shut as if pumping air to his thoughts. He turns to the others, who begin to murmur and nod.

He says, I've seen a lot on my travels. I've walked the ends of this island and farther afield and I've even been to Europe and I've seen the tulip eaters in the Dutch lands and I've seen the frog eaters in the French lands, though I have never been to China, for one does not need to go to China to see people eating dogs and cats. Sustenance—never has there been a more important question in a time such as this. What you put into your body. There is clean sustenance, fresh, natural, pure sustenance, and then there is the other kind that is the filth that gets eaten with the eyes, the mouth, the ears. The food of impurity and indecency that makes a body corrupted. Take a look around. What do the people put into their bodies? Take a look at the cattle boys standing idle and the spade men. The stone suckers you see on every road. They feed on sin. Their children eat sin. Their children sleep with their mouths open and Satan's worm creeps into their throats and slides all the way down. Satan's worm feeds on their sin and feeds its sin into them so that sin feeds on sin in a cycle of evil. This is the true nature of the world.

The worm makes the body hunger for ever more sin. Everywhere one looks you see drunkenness, lassitude, dissolution. The wretched feeding the worm. Is it any wonder that every craftsman and labourer across the land is out of work, for they have gambled away their livelihoods without true sight of God. But God has spoken. God has shown them the true meaning of hunger. God said this land would be smitten and it was. It was His blight that struck. And God said that famine would follow and it did. And God said that plague would follow famine and it did. God is starving the worm out of the earth. And now, all of a sudden, the country has been struck by religion. The churches are filling with sinners who've never seen the door of a church. Sinners looking for respite from God's wrath. Sinners looking to purge their sin. Where were you all before? Mary Collan, what were you but the spoiled daughter of a rich farmer? All of you have come to this mission in search of contrition. But what will one find when one is not truly repentant? It is written that there will be a final massacre to put an end to this world. Will you be ready and repentant? God's armies will come down off every mountain in Ireland. They will march down off Croagh Patrick and Errigal and Carrauntoohil, Cnoc na Péiste and Lugnaquilla. Godlight will travel through all things and there will be no more want or need or pain or hunger. Godlight will stand upon every field in Ireland and the bodily waters of every man, woman, and child on this island will be clean as if drawn from a spring.

It is then that Father turns and stares at her. How each word has entered her body and made her tremble. For everything has to have a reason, she thinks, and this is the reason for the wintering, is it not?

His eyes say, do you see now how I am going to save you?

She thinks, the black of your soul and the light in this room. She begins to nod her head.

He says aloud, you are the sign He has promised. You are a sign of His mercy. The power of life that has been given back to you is the power of God. You have been risen. Now you are a daughter among us, the sign of His miracle, the sign of His Grace.

She hears her name spoken and startles, cannot understand how he knows her name. She tries to push past the silence in her throat but cannot. This power he has over her, this power that pulls her towards him with his forgiving words and promise of a better life and no more pain and suffering, and perhaps you can learn to live with these people.

Father dips an aspergillum into a chalice of water then shakes it upon her. Water upon the bed, water upon her hands and face and forehead, and she thinks, this is what is meant by Christ's tears.

Everyone in the room speaking her name.

His Grace. His Grace. His Grace.

He leaves his eyes inside the room. She tries to close her eyes but still his eyes watch over her. She dizzies out of bed and stares at her bare feet and tries to unthink his eyes. These feet washed clean by Mary Eeshal, these feet thickened to the feet of some old crone. She watches the door as if she expects it to open, can hear the walls carry their voices in unison prayer like some wake for the dead, she thinks, his voice carrying over them and through them, and she steps towards the door and it is then her unseeing foot kicks the bedpan rattling towards the wall. She stands snared, waiting for the voices downstairs to stop and hurry towards the room but instead they carry on, and it is then she is struck by the feeling he can see her like this, can see her trying for the door, can see into her mind and hear every thought, knows everything she has ever done. That he is watching her now climbing back into bed.

* * *

Why does he not come? she thinks. He said he would come but he has not. She craves his eyes, dreams he has come into her room at night, stood beside the bed in silence watching her sleep, thinks she has awakened to this but cannot be sure, for who knows what is dream and what is real anymore? Perhaps it is a test, he is testing me to see if I am worthy.

She aches to test her tongue with new words, his words inside her that speak the truth of things. Now she knows that her first life is over. That it was Father who brought you back into this second life to stand in His light, it must be true that he is at one with God and perhaps it is true that you were dead even though you cannot remember having died or the days before it, cannot remember what death is like, perhaps you cannot know it.

She begins to feel the opening of joy like light.

Soon she will be ready and yet he does not come.

Why does he not come? He said he would.

The door has been left unlocked and now Mary Eeshal seems to whisper through it or perhaps it is the murmur of her clothing. Mary Eeshal begins dressing her, a full black gown pulled to her feet just like the others. Grace stares at her own body, testament to so strange a life. Mary Eeshal takes her elbow, guides her out the threshold of the door she has not passed since she entered, her foot hovering over the plunging first step. They descend the staircase towards the light of an open doorway and she counts three clocks and notices how every one has been stilled. The day outside ranged with cold blue light. He will be here waiting, she thinks. Instead four women watch her step towards them. They stand in a field beside canvas tents, the grass lit with spring-flower, Mary Collan and three others. She turns and sees she has stepped out of a large farmhouse, a wide yard and outhouses behind it, a strange stooped man and a woman watching from the gable side of the house. She looks again for Father.

Mary Collan points to her hair. She says, you have taken the baptismal water. Now you must do like us and cut your hair.

Grace stares at the grey cold skin of the woman's face and the grey cold eyes, cannot look at what is put before her. A knife. She stares at her feet and can feel inwards the rising of some black resistance. Hears herself think, no, not this again.

Mary Collan grabs Grace's wrist and tries to put the knife into her hand but her hand has grown slippy and will not take the knife. Her eyes growing wet and her body trembling and it is then Mary Eeshal steps forward and bats the knife away.

She says, it does not have to be so, Mary Collan.

Mary Collan stares at Mary Eeshal. She says, for you he made an exception but not for her, not for the rest of us.

Mary Eeshal says, it was you, not Father, whom the others followed.

Grace becomes aware of Mary Eeshal stepping behind her. It is then that she wraps her hands about her own head, lets go again, for the touch of Mary Eeshal's fingers is like breath through the long of her hair, her hair being combed and balled into a bun.

It is then that she sees him, the silhouette of Father on his knees, watching or not watching from the dark of a tent.

She worries about where she will sit, sends her eyes ahead of her body. This daily meal of soup and bread in the farmhouse's kitchen, riches off the farmer's land, and how today for the first time she will join them. She cannot take her eyes off Father, though he has not looked at her yet. Three saucered candles table-centre reach their yellow towards each face taking seat without word or fuss because goodness is as goodness does, she thinks. They rest their hands upon the table waiting to be served and she watches their scrubbed pale faces, stares into their thoughts for what they do and do not, how to sit, perhaps, or how to hold your person, how to hold your hands, Mary Eeshal and Mary Collan on either side of Father, you hold your hands this way and not that. The other women like women undone, she thinks, their plain pious faces like boys' faces quiet in thought, and who wants to look like that, better off with long hair.

And that is the farm owner, Robert Boyce, sitting with his eyes closed and his hands clasped muttering some prayer, he is stoopy even in sit. And that is his wife, Anne Boyce, with a servant-woman by the oven, each as meek as the other, Anne Boyce knifing at that bread smell, serving it up, and she surveys their faces and tries not to think what she thinks about them, that they are not people at all but effigies of wax, such a strange thought, she thinks, begins to admire her hands to make silent her thoughts because Father might be listening in, puts them prayerfully before her on the table, the whiteness that is scrubbed skin, her shining fingernails. She feels the weight of Mary Collan's eyes, looks up to see Anne Boyce bringing a basket of bread to the table and all eyes rest on Father, who raises his hands so as to begin prayer and later she will think, who is it that is in each one of us, who is it that is there when you cease to be yourself, when you act without the thought of action, perhaps it is Satan's worm inside you, perhaps it is another self, for suddenly she has leaped across the table and grabbed at the bread as if it were the very last of all bread.

She lies awake in the long of each night dreaming this second life. Mouth-feeling in silence the new name Father has given her. Mary Ezekiel. For you are reborn and your old name is gone. Mary Ezekiel. When she repeats her new name to herself she hears his voice and it is God's voice also, although she wonders what God would really sound like. She thinks of thunder or great rocks being hewn and she thinks of silence. Your tongue cleaves to the roof of your mouth because I made it so. You have been struck dumb so as not to speak of the world's deafness. She wonders what Father means by this, wonders if God will loosen her tongue when the world starts to listen and when might this be so? She lies awake imagining the world coming undone as he has spoken it, sees the mountains open, sees the vast armies of the great and the good coming together in war against Satan. She understands now that everything in her life until now has been evil, for how can you explain so much blight and hunger and plague as anything but reckoning? His words have entered her mind as rivers of blood surging from some high mountain of God, and now she dreams it, an angered rush that takes every man and animal soundless towards the sea, where in blood they meet the salted water that is both washing and forgetting.

Father has begun to look at her in a different manner. She knows the nature of the look and tells herself what is isn't, that one type of looking can be confused for another and perhaps he can hear you right now, is reaching in to remind you of the worm turning in sin. Father's eyes upon her during their daily meal in the farmhouse kitchen. Father's eyes upon her in the cockerel dark as he calls the morning prayer, his eyes reaching for her eyes as his mouth reminds the others that the dead have been risen and walk here among us.

His always-asking eyes, saying, why is it, Mary Ezekiel, I have not confessed you yet and yet I have confessed all newcomers?

Her eyes cannot answer.

Is it that you are telling us you are without sin, that you stand in your own Godlight unlike the rest of us? Or is it that your sins remain hidden, that you are a wolf in sheep's clothing?

She looks away from him.

She thinks, he has not yet confessed you because he knows the truth, the sins you have done, all the evil you have committed. You cannot speak it. That is why your tongue is stricken. And if you do not speak, how can it be true confession? And yet, and yet, she thinks. This ache inside her that is a wish for confession, for she would like to be among those asked by Father to his tent at night. Perhaps, she thinks, it is some form of penance, something to do with the amount of sin you accrue each day as the worm turns inside you.

Perhaps he thinks it is Mary Eeshal who has the most sin inside her, for more nights than most it is she who goes to him.

Time has folded these clockless days into the one. She thinks, where have the months gone? The rhythm of a new life—prayers at dawn and dusk, the ablutions of the body, repasts in the kitchen. Ducking the strange stares of the men Father has brought to build the new wooden cabins. These daily walks with their baskets of alms, bread baked in the house and how the smell off it would bring down all the birds. Asking for nothing in return but for the forgiveness of God. They have been shouted at and called pietists by strangers and chased off farm paths that Father says belong to God and the common man. They have stepped into mud huts and cabins no doctor would dare enter and not one of them has caught the fever because Father says the blessing of God is a protection.

She has seen the sleeping dead in the strangest of places, a woman awkward upon town steps, some father and his child propped against a shop door as if waiting for it to open. She has seen her own face in the faces of others and has given thanks to God, to Father, and to the mission. The world is in its last moments for sure, and yet, she thinks. How sometimes it seems that nature breathes a different breath, for amid these end days the earth has bestowed another spring and then a summer green with hope. And she has overheard Robert Boyce talk about matters in the newspaper, how the fields across Ireland have been returned to health and profit. That the potato stores are full this autumn. That the wintering has been brought to a stop. She thinks about this, how Father said there would be more teeth pulled by God's hand but it seems that nature has defied God and given bounty instead. And now it is October and soon the Samhain and there are turnips hanging again even from some of the godless houses. Mary Collan says the only reason the fields did not rot this year is that their soil is already too rich with blood.

* * *

This rock where she likes to sit in private. She knows they think she comes here to pray but instead she comes to sin, to smoke a pipe she has found and keeps hidden knowing Father has forbidden it. She sits with her knees to her chest and pulls tobacco from her pocket. Tamps it and brings it to light. A look towards the trees watching for the gaze of Father.

She dragons smoke out her nose. This rock, she thinks, is a giant's head jutting the field. There must be a great body buried beneath it, his nose overgrown with moss, an ear lopped off. Perhaps it was lost in some ferocious battle when he was captured in some forgotten century, tied down with rope, buried standing up to his neck, his face sun-baked slowly to rock. Left among an eternity of belling sheep. Watching the shadows of the field for what they might reveal, for sometimes shadows are not what they are but take the forms of what travels unseen, the dark matter of this world that lives in stealth and shapes your future and sometimes they are just what they are, the shadows of clouds, the shadows of tree branches, the shadow of someone coming along the track—it is Mary Warren, the newcomer. Ample Mary Warren, who never knew no trouble, it seems, big-shouldered beneath her shorn hair. Her black gown stretched and struggling to contain her. How her body ripples with all that worry within her. Grace quick-licks her finger to tamp out her pipe.

Breathless Mary Warren says, I dreamt last night of a crow with two black beaks. It was this field here beside the rock where you're sitting. I've come to ask you, Mary Ezekiel, have you seen such a thing? Perhaps you have?

She plucks the lie out of Mary Warren's piglet face. Something mournful and anguished in her expression.

Mary Warren says, so it is an omen. What do you think it means? Do you think it means the war is coming?

Her voice drops and she looks over her shoulder to where the mission sits obscured by trees.

Mary Warren says, Mary Trellick told Father last week she saw a picture fall from the wall in the house just as she was looking at it. But I was there and it didn't happen. Father said it meant death was coming. Do you think he knew she wasn't truth-telling?

Of late, Father has become obsessed with talk of omens, makes them tell of what they have seen. She is growing to hate the hushed voices after evening prayer that issue such lies. Signals in nature that speak of end times. A bird boldly pecking at a window. A dog that howls at an empty field. A green flame in fire. Father has tied Mary Warren to a tree for two wet days to make her see better, because you, Mary Warren, are blind to the signals, and if you don't learn to see perhaps you will meet the deceiver himself come to tempt you, ask you to leave our mission.

So now she dreams omens instead.

Grace slides off the rock and they stroll hand in hand towards the mission, their arms swinging a lazy pendulum to the open time of the sky.

Mary Warren says, I hope tonight it is I and not Mary Eeshal who gets the call to marry my soul to God.

Of a sudden she lets go the hand of Mary Warren and walks away from her. Watches the gossiping ivy along the wall by the lane, how it leans towards her as if to listen to her thoughts of Father and his always-watching eyes that are also the eyes of hunger. This mystery of why he will not confess her after almost a year. It is because you do not speak, she thinks, because if you speak you will have to lie and he knows what lies hidden in your heart.

She abrades her face with cold water until she numbs the signals of hurt. Now Father has said one must wash twice daily. How can you be ready to meet God if your body is corrupted, clung with filth, God will turn his nose from you. The body should be kept spotless, odourless, the skin smooth, the dirt scrubbed out from under the fingernails, the dirt washed from between the toes, the crevices between the legs kept watered, because better to be clean when you meet God than to be the sinful woman who washes God's feet with her tears.

She stands with her hair loose and washed to a squeak. Movement behind her and she will not turn to meet the look of Mary Collan, who spurns her still for her long hair, would see her into heaven with that loathsome look, Mary Collan, who has grown fat of late, who cut the hair of newcomer Mary Bunny to bleeding last week. But it is Mary Warren who pulls her by the elbow and stands as usual in her splayfoot and addled expression. She says, quick, the priest is coming up the road.

She turns and sees Robert Boyce goatlike upon the roof cleaning the gutters and how he becomes very still at sight of the priest, his stoop curving down the ladder. The women huddle and cluck but Grace steps past them bold towards the house and stands in the front yard watching the priest's dark shape, the man spit-faced, fuming into his walk as if marching to face some slaughtering wind, marching through the yard without looking at her and then through the front door without so much as a knock. She ties up her hair and sees Mary Eeshal step into the house.

She knows the priest has come again to remonstrate with the Boyces. Knows what the priest has heard, how in Gort last week Father spoke of a priest who had eaten a child. Twice now she has watched the same priest come to the house, has listened at the window and imagined the shape of the man darkening through the room, gathering them in with his anger, the man's glistening teeth as he shouts, this giving over your house and field and good name to a man who is nothing but a fraud and a sinner, a defamer, the great lies out his mouth, there is only one true church. You'll not build a new town here, not a church or a school or a community house, without my say-so.

She watches the priest go back down the road flapping like some blackbird. Watches Robert Boyce stoop out of the house with his prayerful face as if nothing were the matter. Anne Boyce walking backwards through the farmyard fanning grain for the hens, a woman who lives in the shadow of the man, staring into some great loneliness of thought. She has heard whisper that their two boys left for America, that a daughter got the sickness and died soon after, wonders if it is the same priest who administered to her. And there is Father stepping out of the dark behind her eye, stepping towards Robert Boyce and taking his elbow, can hear his thoughts before they pass his mouth, the churches and how they will soon fall, the Satanists in nearby Shanaglish, where the priest drove the first mission out. How the priests and all their money are nothing but the price of sin.

Faint light from a flickering candle paints their faces out of dark. How they kneel and squeeze their eyes as if the closing of your eyes weren't enough, she thinks, you must squeeze for the hurt that squeezes the worm out. Their hands templed to heaven while the great oven ticks its reminder of hellish warmth. She opens an eye and spies Mary Warren rubbing at a knee and then their eyes meet and share a glance that speaks the same thought, Mary Warren gesturing to where Mary Collan should be but isn't.

She thinks, three days now since Mary Collan left the wooden cabins and has not been seen at all. It is tipped on every tongue, where she is and what she is doing. She has heard it said that Mary Collan is on a mission for Father. That she is doing penance for all those secret dinners she has been eating. Though harelipped Mary Trellick says she saw her staring out the upstairs window of the farmhouse. Mary Collan, no doubt in the same room you first woke in, eating herself to fat. Woe to wash that woman's face if you are asked.

The best days begin with a wounded sky, she thinks. The clouds soaked with His blood. She curses the heavy arc of the pump until two pails become seeing eyes of water. In her ears the screams from sleep and she knows what the dead think of her, the dead who by day will not be conjured, this heart full of sin, how you cannot expect to let the beast into your life without becoming a beast yourself. She picks up both pails and carries them across the yard and along the gable side of the house. The mission below in the sloping field seems in this early light to hold darkness and silence to itself as if it were a place of menace. Soon there will be a candle in the window and the women will rise and wash. The pails whisper of careless spillage and it is strange, she thinks, to hear the cart horses in the front yard early out before prayer and then she sees the particular shape of Robert Boyce's horseman, Henry Good, walking towards the jarvey, which sits coupled to two horses. How the light always strikes Henry Good strangely as if to allow him something private of himself, climbing up onto the jarvey to sit hunched and waiting in the driving seat as if dreaming a painted chariot to war.

Not a sound from both pails as she rests them down, sliding her body to the wall. Reaching her eyes around the corner. The blood in the sky is running to water and the shadows in flight are coming alive out of the house and she knows them as Mary Eeshal and Mary Collan while the shape beside them is Father. They stop before the jarvey and Mary Collan stands with her hands upon her belly and how it is you can suddenly know the things that must remain hidden, and how this coach now will take Mary Collan down the road and into another life. Mary Collan begins to climb onto the jarvey but Mary Eeshal abruptly pulls her back and slaps her on the cheek, says, not before Father, Mary Collan's mouth opening and closing until her sob is the only word said, a strange animal sound calling the dawn and Father is shushing her, helping her up into the jarvey, Mary Eeshal looking at them with folded arms, Henry Good raising the whip and clucking the horses forward. The face of Mary Collan shaped into grief.

Three days of rain from a shivery sky and today the market square of Gort is deserted. The jarveys and coaches like dogs sat quiet to listen. Last week she counted twenty-seven townfolk gathered but today there are six, an unlucky number not counting the children, we need one person more. She thinks, who wants to stand about in this weather but the usual half-clads and draggles. She pities a young woman with her children dressed in mud, it seems. Most do not listen but eat with their eyes at the baskets of bread that will be handed out after Father's sermon. A lame boy has dragged himself on a sack and sits under Father, watches the way Father opens and closes his hands as he speaks as if making pliant some obscure knowledge, the boy nodding as Father sends tongue into every word to transform each one into something shining and terrible. Never has she heard Father speak with such spirit. Lately, she thinks, he has not been himself, snapping through prayer and cutting short his sermons and never a word said about Mary Collan. And the who that did it to her she cannot figure, there are different men about the farm and does it even matter, it was Mary Collan who invited the sin. Today Father stands broad to the street, lets the sickle wind curve the rain around him.

She watches the approach of a man who will be the lucky seventh, sees he is dressed much too well. Sees trouble in the step. The sun in his silk cravat and flashing cuffs as he folds his arms and cocks his head to listen. The way he smiles when Father shouts, the devil is riding into town on a bull! She tries to alert Father with her eyes but Father is fuming about the farmers of Ireland, how they have armed themselves against you, how they have kept their grain for the speculators, how they have taken animals off you in false payment—

He pauses for breath and the stranger seizes upon the moment. Nonsense, he says.

Father pretends not to hear but every head turns to look at this fellow. His matter-of-fact face and that mouth opening again to utter the same word, nonsense, sliding the word as if into Father's mouth, where it snags his tongue. An immense quiet has spread now. A strange catlike sound comes from the throat of Mary Eeshal.

She has heard the priests threatening away parishioners, words being shouted, pietists and such. But never has anybody stood up like so to Father.

She watches Father burn his eyes at the man as if eyesight alone could wish a man his death. Then he makes as if to laugh, says, what have we here but the very bull rider before us. Didn't I say the devil had come into town?

The man says, I am no devil but a doctor, John Allender, and I am well known here. There is only one of me but let me suggest there is one of you in every town, tying your flaxen beard to the face of Christ, speaking with false lips of miracles and such.

Somebody titters and she thinks it might have been the lame boy and she would drag him by his useless legs and hurt his arms for good. Then she sees his face is pained and staring at Father, who raises a finger towards the face of this man called John Allender.

Father says, now we know what we are dealing with. The devil's emissary stands here among us brazen in his false glory. Do not give what is holy to this dog. This bull rider who cares only for the lies of his profession, the priests who lie in simony and tend only to their rich masters, the shopkeepers who steal from your pockets, the merchants who collude with the speculators to drive the prices up and keep you in living death, the officials with their nods and their winks who allow such things to—

Of a sudden he lunges towards Grace, pulls her by the wrist in front of the crowd. Let me ask you this, what priest do you know of who has risen the dead? This young woman here was risen from her grave. God spoke and said he would send sign of His word, that He would send a miracle. We found her in her grave out in Kilcorkan and the sextons there were witness. Behold, I tell you. This is the face of a miracle. A living example of God's grace.

The man called Dr John Allender says, who says she was dead?

Mary Eeshal begins to shout at him. I say she was dead, I saw it. We all saw it. That is God's truth. Who are you to question?

The man called Dr John Allender says, did anybody confirm the death? There have been many fevered giving the likeness of the dead. Was the looking glass put to her lips?

The look on Father's face would turn a living man to dust. He turns and stares at Grace as if willing her to speak the truth of this gospel, but how can you speak when no words will come out, she thinks, and anyhow, what is there to say when you cannot remember a single thing, when you weren't even there at all, perhaps you were dead and perhaps you weren't dead, perhaps you were sleeping, who am I to say and how could I say it? And perhaps this Dr John Allender is right after all.

It is then that Father pushes through the crowd and comes upon an old harassed mule. He raises his fist and strikes two hard blows upon the animal's head and the mule despairs an old wind sound, drops to one knee before Father as if penitent. How he turns then lit by fury, begins to shout at the crowd, every one of you here is a mule, you take the blow, blow after blow, you stand blinking before your own corruption. May God strike every one of you down. His hand to blood and Mary Warren kissing it and there is only the sound of the wind whetting itself off every stone in the town, the windows already darkened and the rain carrying the smell of despair and the smell of basketed bread into every nose and mouth.

The dream comes in spate off God's high mountain, takes her in its river of blood, the blood quickly gathering from her feet to her waist and then it is rising, tightening around her chest, becomes a red mouth that reaches past her neck and carries her downwards until she drinks the blood water, rises to breathe but goes under again, tells herself this is drowning—dead rats in the water and strange animals swimming and they are animals she has not seen in any life, black-bodied with gleaming mouths and she can see the hand faintly of somebody under the water, the hand taking hold of her leg, the hand pulling her downwards into the blood, and she can see the face and it belongs to Colly, who now looks like Bart, and she can see others helpless and adrift and silent, and then she finds herself on rocks covered in blood and tries to waken, sees the man called Dr John Allender shaking his head, sees he is the old man Charlie and he tries to speak and she knows what he wants to say, that he will row her back across the estuary but first you must return—

She is awake. The room swims its black into her eyes. She can hear the low snuffling of Mary Warren crying on her mat. She lies still and tries to hear the dream, thinks she might have been screaming in her sleep. The blood-water taste still dreaming itself in her mouth. She thinks, dreams are not real but what she dreamt was so real she feels wet all over, tries to sit up and it is then she becomes aware of it, the wetness between her legs. Tests and is shocked by what she knows is the return of her blood, this womanly curse, cannot remember how long it has been, a long year at least.

She stares into the squeezed-shut of her eyes and understands it is a silence she seeks. Not all this, what is shaped by words, belief and anger, but something deeper and unsaid, a single truth that silence comprehends and cannot be spoken. Her thoughts come into the Boyces' prayer room. She has heard her name being said. She thinks, do not open your eyes, do not open— opens her eyes to see Mary Eeshal fixed in scowl at her, every other eye upon her too but for Mary Warren searching her knee for an itch. The eyes of Father like weight.

His eyes say, why is it you do not answer me, Mary Ezekiel, were you asleep?

Her eyes say, I was trying to listen.

He raises his hand as if to take something from her, the gift of her soul, the gift of her dumb mouth, this hand with the knuckles bruising around a pair of beads.

He says aloud, bring it up so that everyone can witness.

She does not know what he means, thinks she has been collared, that he wants her pipe and tobacco. Some fool you are, she thinks, you should have kept the pipe hidden and not in your pocket. She casts a look for some snitch face, stares at the metal tub hanging on the dresser and wishes it would fall with a bang to cover her own disgrace, this room today full of others, strangers in fine cloth who have come and asked to touch her, a man and a woman with soft unworked hands and money for the mission that Father will put into Robert Boyce's hand.

Father says, give it to me, this sign of your blood.

She feels the deepening puzzle, feels the smallness of the room and every eye upon her. Mary Eeshal's whisper is spit. Give him the rag.

She tries to turn her back to the room but how can you turn your back when you are surrounded by eyes, reaches for the rag wet between her legs and takes it towards him hoping to die, to disappear into whiteness. Father holding the bloody rag aloft before the others, a bead of blood gathering to drip. He says, the devil took form yesterday, came to denounce our miracle as shadow and deception. He spreads fear and doubt. But today we have our answer, the living blood of Christ, for this blood of Christ flows again in this woman whose blood went still in her grave. Christ has given his blood to you so that you can be woman again, so that you can be unclean again, so that you can purge the stain.

Today the talk is of a neighbouring townland where a lamb was born with two heads. Or so they say. Mary Rachel and Mary Child whispering of omens like conspirators. It sounds to her like superstition, something she might have heard said in Blackmountain. Last week there was talk of a man struck by lightning in nearby Grange. Ball lightning in a field that followed the man as he ran from it, Mary Eeshal said. God killed him in his own field, God's vengeance upon a great sinner.

Feet press the grass behind her as she walks towards the mission.

She turns because she knows it is Henry Good, come to sneak her some tobacco and ask for a kiss but not out in this open, where everyone will see. Twice now she has let him, though his mouth is too wet. She turns and meets instead the presence of Father. Her arms fold across her chest as if to guard the sinning thought. For a moment Father does not speak, then he says, peace be with you, walk with me a little.

Now she knows he knows her thoughts, every thought a sin. She wants to say, let me tell you of my guilt, the weight of my sin, wishes she could yearn for penance like newcomer Mary Rachel, whose hands were tied to her ankles so that she could not move from her knees all night in whipping rain.

His eyes smile at her. He takes hold of her elbow and says aloud, come to my room tonight and you can receive the spirit.

She walks rapt in happiness, Godlight in every thought and step. A confession will come and then true grace. She thinks of her sorrow, all the sins of a life and how they link together, one sin to another until the weight of its chain drags you down to the punishment of hell. Sleep will not come tonight but tomorrow there will be peace. She goes to her rock and sits with her knees to her chest burrowing pipe smoke, watches evening stoop to gather the last light. Of a sudden she grows restless. There is the shape of Mary Eeshal walking with Father. Considerate Mary Eeshal escorting Father with the lamp and what are they whispering together? No doubt, Mary Eeshal asking Father to confess her. How it is that woman brings the poisoned thought into every moment of goodness.

The others do not go to his room till past midnight. From a distant church she hears the clock strike eleven. Wait now, daughter. The room an awakened silence, every ear tuned to the steps of her feet as she rises and goes outside towards Father's cabin. Her hand a night orchid upon the latch of his door. Inwards then expecting candlelight but what she meets is his shadow upright in a chair lit by the nightblue window.

He says, wait till later, daughter, then come.

She returns to her room and hears judgement in the silence. They will think he refused to confess you. Watching this long hour of night. Watching the black of the room and what lies beneath it, the same dark always, she thinks. If black is sin and light is blessing then light and dark should never mix and yet they do, the dawn and dusk are not separate things but take the light and the dark equally. She can hear Mary Warren zizzing words to heaven in her sleep, dreaming up nonsense to talk of tomorrow, a pig with a wolf's head or a bat flying overhead with no wings. Sweet Mary Warren, witless and lying.

Mary Eeshal creeping towards his room— it is only a thought but do not wait another half hour, she thinks. Her hands feeling their way through the sinning dark until she finds his door and opens it. The room simple in night purple that illumines the room from a pocket window and wraps his sitting shape. She yearns for his eyes to free her of these dreams that howl at night. To free her speech, for she wants now to speak, not of what has been or what she has seen, but of simple things, this world now as it is.

His voice reaches towards her in whisper.

Kneel down there, daughter.

Then he says, we have been waiting such a long time for this.

Then he says, take off your clothes, daughter.

His words strike her like some unanswerable question. She watches now what awakens in his silence, his shape as it stands and moves towards her, his black shape not Godlight at all but an unspeakable dark and she cannot breathe, cannot move, the hand reaching to touch her shoulder some old man's hand the serpent's touch or a brand of fire, his hand softly to her shoulder and yet she recoils as if struck.

He steps back, whispers, easy now, daughter.

All time that is past and hereafter is brought to a stop in this room, the gap between them a strange emptiness in which nothing manifests and everything manifests and it is God's voice a roaring lion and it is the great silence of nature, the gap between heaven and earth. A long moment and she thinks he is measuring her every thought.

He says again, take off your clothes, daughter.

She can sense his reaching breath as he creeps again towards her, bread and milk and some sour smell. Can feel his eyes without needing to see and then he stops and moves towards the window. He reaches for the lamp and lights it, turns around and strikes her with his eyes. They are a long time looking at each other. She wants to get up off her knees but cannot, watches the lines webbing his eyes and wonders if he has met with sudden age, his hair and beard more grey than ever, his back so slightly bent.

He says, why won't you do what I tell you?

Her eyes say, what has my body got to do with my confession? I never heard of such a thing.

He says, you are an ignorant child, nothing but a wretch, a worm, vermin dug from a ditch, a miscreant and a sinner — tell me, what do you know of God's will?

Her eyes say, I know that I am alive again but that might have nothing to do with God's will.

He says, you are alive because of me, I gave you that power — if I had not come for you, you would be in hell right now dying a daily death. If it wasn't for me you would be in that grave with the sexton spading earth over you, into your mouth, into your ears, trapped under the weight of the earth with your sin —

He stops speaking.

Her eyes say, so what does God want with my body when He had it already?

He says, you behave as though you know the will of God, but you do not know His will, you can only know God through those who speak for Him.

Her eyes say, I know there is what God wants and there is what man wants but they are different. Why should God want what man wants? Why does God behave like a man all the time with his various afflictions?

He is silent a moment. Then he says, I know the devil visits you when you sleep—this is why you wake up each night screaming.

Her eyes say, what you want from me is sin.

Finally, he lifts his eyes off her. He says, you have come here for confession but will not give it. He begins slowly to lie down on his mat, waves his hand for her to leave. What she hears is the sighing of an old man. Sees herself kneeling on the floor wondering if she has sinned, wondering why she feels so ashamed, if she is one step further from grace or not. Of a sudden he sits up and stares at her, reaches for the lamp and blows it out. His voice aloud in the dark.

Get out.

The sound of hard rain hurtling through the dark is a cold hand that grips her. As it was in the beginning is now and ever shall be world without end. Thought falling out of prayer until she can hear only rainfall. She rests her forehead against her hands. How the rain carries the sound of eternity within it, carries the sound and shapes of other places, the mountains and the hills and the bogland where you come from, the sounds of other voices, the looks that others put upon the rain in other places and how the rain carries their looks, puts them down here. She opens her eyes and stares at the pitch window, the rain hidden, she thinks, our own lives hidden and everything falling.

It is then she sees him. Bart's ghost in the rain.

She watches Mary Warren carry herself plodfoot through the yard, how she moves through the world oblivious to the eyes that strike her. Now Mary Warren is coming towards her cradling an orphan lamb as though it were a child, suckling it from a bottle, her huge hands expertly gentle. She has heard how Mary Warren wept through the night when the lamb's mother died. Mary Warren begins pulling softly on the lamb's pink-white ears and the lamb's black-button eyes close in delight. She stands watching Mary Warren and sudden knowledge strikes her. That Mary Warren once had a child.

Mary Warren says, Anne Boyce says them people over in Knockshane were selling smashed-up coffins for firewood. Going around door to door asking. Anne Boyce says they came here and that she met a sexton who says they left bones all over the place the way a dog does. That somebody left a spaded skull lying in a field. Somebody's head—imagine.

Grace has stopped listening, for Father's face intrudes all thought. The way he lit his eyes upon her during first prayer, an accusatory, rancorous look. He will do the same at late prayer and supper. How a man can look at you two ways in public. How he has made her aware now of her own movements, the way she walks, the way she sits, the way every thought speaks in her head. She stares at the field and sees the head of Father severed on a platter and a grey crow eating at his eyes.

The grey crow says, lies, lies.

Of a sudden Mary Warren stops gabbing and reaches a hand towards Grace. Her mouth shapes a warning word but does not say it, their eyes now watching as Father and Mary Eeshal come upon them without smile, Mary Eeshal with her arms folded, Mary Eeshal, who clicks her tongue as she walks past Grace as if to announce the sins that remain unconfessed.

It is difficult to tell the hour as she goes to his room, his door smoothing open into an enclosed dark and his waiting shape another type of darkness.

She thinks, what is the point in you returning, you know what this is.

She thinks, all the sins within you, how can you live without confession?

She kneels before him and squeezes her eyes against the already-dark as if closing your eyes can squeeze shut your hearing, for if you hear him now you must follow his will or choose not to follow his will and then you will be out on the road, a rat in a ditch, no better than before.

He says, you have made me wait. Then he says, take off your clothes, daughter. His breath dogging slowly towards her, the sound of his movement following upon the dog's breath, and she thinks she can feel within such movement a violence coiled and ready to be made physical, a fist or a kick to the head. She tenses for the blow and dares not open her eyes but what happens is silence and then yellow-soft illumines her eyelids and she opens her eyes to see he has lit the lamp, spread a gloss of light about his body like last light over old and weary hills.

He looks at her a long time. He says, I fear you brought the devil in with you last night. I fear he is here among us, spreading lies, mistruths, suspicion. It is the devil who has gotten your tongue. It is the devil who will walk with you when I send you out on the road. You should think about that. Your soul in hell.

Her eyes say, how is it a man can have power over your soul but you have control over your own body, a woman should be able to pray to God all day long without having to be His wife.

She thinks, what if you have gotten it wrong about God and Father, all the things you have done, that Father is holy after all and all the people around him, it is you who will be damned.

She searches Father's face for the trace of an answer, watches his hairy ears, the beaten face, the eyes that drink in her skin, the hands that could beat her.

It is then he shouts. Get out.

The next day brings an ugly half-dark like winter. She passes the day on the rock hiding in plain sight. She does not care now who sees her smoking. Never has she felt further from God, further from the life she wants to live. She studies the sky's broken light and sees a gap of great distance between earth and heaven. Toking her pipe, exhaling blue smoke that shapes the sky with her guilt. She thinks, only one pinch of tobacco left but Henry Good will live up to his handle.

Father today is stepping about the mission with irritant blood, how his sleepless eyes roamed covetous upon her that morning. How he brought the hum of prayer to a stop and stared at her. How he said, we have someone among us who refuses confession. How he turned then upon her before the others. You will seek full confession. This is the last time I will ask you.

Mary Bunny, who has winnowed to a stick, is refusing to eat. Mary Bunny each day with her little significations, the way she sips just a thimbleful of soup, eats only a crust of bread as if God's wintering these past few years were not enough hurt for her, that you must choose to starve yourself as well in the absence of another's confession. Mary Trellick telling anyone who will listen about her visions of an end brought by rolling fire.

She thinks, how can you say no to him, all that he has done for you, your life here at the mission, the food you have been given, and aren't the women here holy in all that they do? Why is it they have no trouble doing what is asked of them? Wasn't it you who was corrupted until now by the devil?

Henry Good finds her in the field and she makes the signal for tobacco and he obliges. He says, we had a headback birth this morning. The third lamb lost this year, we're cursed with bad luck.

She thinks about this. Would like to know what happens to a soul denied of its birth and why does it happen? What kind of God changes His mind like that, allowing the soul to grow into a body and then at the last moment to deny it? Does it roam hurting for the loss of some unspeakable part like a twin who loses a brother?

Henry Good tells her that Father is in trouble because money he said would come has not come, that he has heard Robert Boyce complain of this, that there are things to pay for and land does not come for nothing and this is why Father is in foul humour.

The rock and the field and the sky meet in dusk and she stares at her colding feet, lifts her head to the sound of a scream and shouting at the mission but does not move, wills that something awful has struck then quickly unwills the thought. She thinks, it is probably about you. She watches the trees and thinks about those who say they can see something but cannot and why this might be. Thinks about how the wind never reveals itself. How it comes upon the rookeries like a thief, rattles them and makes trouble for the birds, who shout their warnings at this nothing-to-see.

She returns to the mission before prayer, meets Mary Child alone in the field, the woman's face wet with tears, some of the other women huddled by their cabin. Mary Child grabs at Grace's wrist. She says, you missed all the trouble. Mary Eeshal has been storming about the place all day, took the sleeping mats off all the sisters and threw them out. She tried to take the lamb off Mary Warren, told her she had no business keeping pets at the mission. But Mary Warren refused to give it, went purple in the face, something strange coming over her. Then Mary Eeshal pulled the lamb out of her hands and Mary Warren turned upon her and beat her with her fists. Robert Boyce came running and struck Mary Warren and now she has run off. Nobody can find the lamb.

She thinks, these are the things that happen when Father will not hear their confession and he will not hear their confession because you have denied him yours. It is just like you to ruin everything, you silly wee bitch.

Mary Eeshal comes to evening prayer with a knife in her hand and her hair shorn, sits down with a bruised face and bloodied scalp, stares at Grace, her eyes holy with hate, her eyes saying, it is you who is destroying Father.

Father has not left his cabin, is refusing to answer their knocks. They say he is fasting. Mary Eeshal leading their prayers, though Grace will not look at her. She stares at the plum shadows where Mary Warren used to kneel, thinks of their little glances, wonders what will happen to her, the woman walking the roads on her own, a simple woman; how the hunger might come back and what then and the same thing will happen to you.

After supper, Mary Eeshal begins to pour water from a pitcher and then stops, begins to cry into her wrist.

She watches a bridal moon haze the clouds and tells herself, whatsoever things are, they are also not. As she walks she thinks, perhaps this purpling midnight colour is the truest, for it gives enough light to see your feet in the dark but little else, everything else hidden, whatsoever things are, they are also not. She rises and steps through the dark watching her feet faint like mice pairing towards his door. She closes his door and the mice pair together. She watches him quench the lamp, his eyes upon her now and how he says the same words and how this time she slides out of her gown, covers her hands over her breasts, stares at the mice, their noses pointing at one another. Whatsoever things are, they are also not. Of a sudden Father moves and he is naked and he is clothed in the second skin of shadow and he is traveling towards her and her eyes adjust to the mass of his body filling her sight and she sees how his eyes are lit, his buttermilk breath reaching like hands to take her as woman and her body begins to will something different, a feeling that says no, not this, whatsoever things are, they are also not, but her hands speak and push him away. He utters a snort that is derision or anger or helplessness and he hunkers silently a moment and then begins towards her again, slowly, the wolf of God slowly for the lamb, his body dark purple, his mouth a sack, whatsoever things are, they are also not, and her hands become will again and begin to push against his resisting body, the pure will of his body a dream of creeping sin, and she pushes back and he moves away again. Now he is kneeling, coming towards her on his hands and knees and she can see his face and his eyes begging and then his mouth opens and he says aloud, I have heard you and felt you like none of the others, have felt the way you watch me, the way you reach into me, see into my sin. The others are nothing. Only through flesh can we absolve the sins of each other. His body moving towards her again and she pushes him away again and his laugh is sudden and strange, the laughter of a madman, she thinks. He bows his head and when he speaks his voice is wretched, a piteous child's voice. Do I make myself odious to you? Is that it? That I am too much the knower of sin for your grace? Tell me what it is you want and I will do whatever you ask. His body coming towards her again and she repels him with two hands, watches as he begins to crawl about the room growling like a dog and then he shouts, yes I have sinned, yes I am a sinner, I sin and I sin and I sin. Why is it you are the only one here who sees into my soul? Who refuses me? What dream did you come from? Do you talk with Him? That's what it is. You talk with Him and He hears your words. Father lowers his head to her feet and says, I will wash your feet, Mother, and she begins to feel the lick of his thistle tongue, pushes him away with a foot. He becomes a black shape hurling himself through the room with a ferocious dog's bark and she knows now the others will come, how the others will kneel by the door and listen to him as he barks out the loss of his mind, how he hisses and spits. Yes, I am dog, he shouts. I admit the dog. He comes to me and takes my spirit and I take his shape wanting the flesh of woman. And the dog knows that he who joins with the harlot is one in body with her. The two shall be made the one flesh. Father's barking becomes louder and she can hear noise behind the door and the sound of sobbing and she is trying to find her gown but cannot find it, Father barking loud enough now to wake them at the farmhouse, to wake them in Gort, and it is then she finds her dress on the floor and heaves her body naked from the room.

Dr John Allender permits her into his study, offers a horsehair chair by the fire. His voice grim and quiet and she points to her mouth and shakes her head and tries to say with her eyes, for now I can't speak, but soon I will, I hope, it took me a whole day to find you. He nods and calls for tea brought a moment later by some oldster who might be his father, the younger man become older man with no time in between. She stares at the doctor's gilt library of books, at the broad and implacable heat of the fire, the watercolours on the wall of some softened unmoving Ireland. She motions with her hand for something to write on. Later he leans an elbow upon the mantelpiece and reads what she has written.

> I saw you on the Street that Time. You struck me Doctor as a Truthful Man. I could not leave them. I did not know how. His Words had the Power over me. I could not think for myself. I fear they might come after me. Will you help?

She is aware when he speaks how he has a way of looking at her without looking at her. He says, their sort would blame God for anything. They would blame God for the very weather that hammers this land, the rain and wind and the worst of winter light that darkens the country all year. For what is light but the natural agent of God so therefore God is found wanting in Ireland.

She is not sure if the mockery in his smile is aimed at her. He leaves the room and calls to the old man, and she thinks, run away out the door. The man returns with a dark cape and a pair of women's boots. She tries to refuse them but he shakes his head and says, they are old and unused and will not be missed. It is not the tropics out there.

It is only when she is upon the brightening road does she notice the doctor has put coin in her pocket.

VIII

Blackmountain

These lonely roads where the movement of walking counts its own beat. Three-four-five-six, hands-shoulders-arms-feet. A pageant sky calls her northwards and remakes the day by the hour. She is glad for the cape. Now the raggy sky is peace but what gathers against the sun will soon war with rain.

So many people are gone, she thinks. The barefooters who walked the country roads in their droves have vanished. It is as if the earth has swallowed them. The silence broken only by a car or coach that scuttles the quiet with its commotion of horses. The low roads leading her through townlands where peat smoke may signal an occupier or two, a misty face witnessed through glass, or some oldster who hobbles out to see who she is, eyes that say I am too old to die and too tired to leave. And then there are the townlands you must hurry through, where the mud huts and cottages huddle together in unvoiced grief. The babel of chat and children and animals gone utterly as if some wind had carried them off.

She steps through each town with folded arms and a busy look, just in case anyone would bother you. The signs says Athenry, Moylough, Carrick-on-Shannon. She meets no trouble but for some wanty child pulling at her sleeve or an idle sitter pulling at her with a look. In one town after another now there are people selling buttermilk and lumpers, their baskets abundant with winter greens, their children wheelbarrowing each other in mud. She looks to the lanes and doorways and asks not to remember what gathered there, how every corner was hung with brittle looks that implored you for a penny or a cup of meal. Now the wind blows through such empty places.

The nights are wound so tightly with dark, she thinks. This silence that utters strangeness. But at least, she thinks, you can take your pick of an empty house. She likes to sleep in the smaller houses where there is a door still hung and the wind cannot send in its malicious thoughts. And still, what dreams. One night she dreams a sickly smell like mildewed corn, wakes and something tells her it is the smell of the graves. She rises and begins pushing the road through the dawn, will not look at the shrouds of dark that lie over the fields.

Off and on she is met by people who walk with her. A young man making a three-day walk in two days to get to Drumshanbo to meet his newborn son, an hour or two I'll get to spend, he says, and then I must be off. An old woman who has been walking the roads for well nigh a year in search of her son. They share their food with her, a potato with silken butter, a taste of buttermilk. They speak of simple things, an ache in the heels or a pair of boots that need mending, but they do not question her silence, for a woman in black must be a pilgrim of some kind or she must be in mourning and who isn't these days, she thinks, the whole country to grief and even the crows that gather plentiful in the fields must remember their absent brethren. How they cloak the trees like angry priests, cawing at her just like Father.

She sleeps under a winding sycamore and wakes to see women tramping linen by a lakeside, can feel herself among them as if she were at the mission, the comfort of talk, the comfort of women. Sometimes she sees the spit-mouth of Father rising without words from the road. The weather soon to turn winter cold and yet lightness now in every northwards step. The far-off hills gathering as they always do, rooted and restful old men wrinkled with light. My legs are as strong as tongs, she thinks. My feet a pair of muck-raking mules. Two-three-four-five, how strange it is to be alive.

* * *

In woodland farther north she meets a gang of vagrant children. They stand savage and soiled with wild hair but it is their eyes she notices, eyes that meet you like the sorry look of a dog. Not an elder to be seen among them. They live in rough huts assembled from cuttings of fir and she shares with them her bread and sleeps with them a night, watches the stumble of a young child never taught to walk properly. A boy keeps asking her questions. Do you think Fionn MacCumhaill is hiding in the mountains? Do you think he is waiting to return and rescue Ireland? The question-putter keeps pulling her by the arm as she goes to leave. He says, I had a home once but nobody awoke from their sleeping.

A great hand of rain is flung from the east. She counts the days behind her, guesses the days ahead, tries to see each bead as it falls as if you could watch so many lives.

Riddle me this, what goes up as the rain falls down?

She finds good luck on the road, a horseshoe lying in mud by a ditch. Is surprised nobody has found it. She bends and of a sudden sees into the ditch as if some horror were lying there though it is nothing but the ghost of thought, she thinks, a trick of the light, grabs the horseshoe and walks onwards. But still, she thinks. She watches the ditches with suspicion, that was then and this is now, the dead have lifted themselves out of the ditches and have gone to wherever they go.

A jarvey jangles the road behind her and comes to a stop just ahead of her. She is glad for the offer of a lift. A man with wrinkles folded into his forehead and tobacco teeth and a way of leaning without falling.

He says, will I lift you up?

He studies her in quick leftwards looks when she does not answer his questions. He says, you some sort of prayer woman? He recites an old poem in Irish and then he tells her the title is his favourite of all titles, that in English it means an isle made of glass. Then he tells her his three favourite places in the world, a bridge in the townland of Rath, where he grew up and used to sneak out a trout, the sight of the seaboard he saw one time on the coast of Sligo, a particular way the light was upon it as if I had painted it with my own mind, and the face of his wife dead now two years, and how glad I am for sleep because that is the only place I can find her.

The man takes another road and she can still hear his voice. How it rings with hope for the days ahead. The feeling then she will not remember him as he was, the make-merry of his voice, that the road he has taken onwards will become nothing in her mind but mist. She touches the horseshoe and repeats the names of her brothers like prayer. Closes her eyes and sends thought like flight. To ride the sky now a returning starling.

She stares at the twilight trickery and knows she needs sleep. The road leaning down to a bally of five or six stone cottages. A sudden crooked feeling when she sees elms with their bark stripped. A smokeless sky.

The evening shadows loiter as she passes among the cottages. She would like to call out, for you cannot be sure who is ever about and isn't it better to meet a stranger, a squatter, or even a thief or a drunkard than to be alone in an empty bally like this. She sees the wind has carried wet into some of the houses. The odd sight of fodder beet growing unpicked in a dead garden.

Walk onwards, she thinks, out of this townland, there will be someplace to sleep a few mile beyond. But the dark has come on so quick and her feet are complaining and she would like to sit. And look, that last house is still hung with a door.

She knocks just in case and then steps into the house, lies down on the empty floor by the wall and blankets her cape.

Morning will wash away the dark.

It is only this, an empty house.

* * *

It is only sleep and then it isn't. Who's there? she thinks. She has heard voices. There was a man calling out—footsteps at the door that could be wind or an animal or worse. Somebody trying to get in. She is trying to stir up, to sit on her fear like hands to be sat on. She does not know if she needs to wake or if she has already woken. Her tongue a drunkard that will not test the silence. She thinks, damn you, stir up! And then she does or perhaps she is awake, for it is so dark it is hard to tell this space from dreaming, lies waiting for them to reveal themselves, a feeling that there are people hiding in the walls, her ear a reluctant listener, and then she sees them, shadows finding form in rough circle around the fire, all of them with their backs to her, sees the shape of a woman rubbing mud into her hair and she is rubbing mud into the hair of her children, rubbing mud into their faces, another two men rubbing their heads with mud and then one of the men leans across and puts his head into the fire— the empty dark of the room as she wakes, the room freshened with icy air coming in through an unlatched door, the wind bringing inwards the smell of mud and drizzle.

Quickly onto the road wishing for the sun. The sparrows unseen chitter the world awake and then brightness touches her body. She takes a lift as far as Belleek from some journeyman who has a way of looking at her without looking at her. He whistles at his own thoughts and quietly slides in his seat until he is touching her. She asks to be let off on the edge of the town. He says, I'll be going back this way in three or four days if you should be on the road. She takes another lift as far as Ballybofey with an old cart man who mutters unheard-ofs at his mule. She cannot stop looking at the way his veins run like black spiders. They stop at a well to water his horse and in the bare field beside it there are seven rough crosses. The man watching the way she washes her hair, the way she washes her feet, his eyes resting questions upon her she cannot answer. She would like to say, I am returning home. I am from Blackmountain. It is in the far-off farther north, the very top of Donegal. She would like to say, you think you make your own choices in life but we are nothing but blind wanderers, moving from moment to moment, our blindness forever new to us. And to fully understand what this means is to accept something that is an outrage to most people. There are only the facts of where you are right now and when you try to look back the facts become dream. The rest is just talk for the horses.

She follows until a line of sky becomes lough and she knows it as the Swilly. Meets an echo of her younger self passing by. The sea in the distance opening a doorway. Familiar faces turning in half-light and sounds of speech and the way that each body moves uniquely in memory, each memory rising in its own kinked light that is seen briefly but not held, each memory breaking like surf one wave over the other leaving a wash of emptiness.

The reached sky lies past Buncrana. And how they rise round-shouldered from the earth to greet her, like old brothers waiting one behind the other, these hills called home. She sees how they sit under the always-is of sky as if watchers to a time in which three hundred years might pass in a moment. She thinks, this is how long you have been walking. An ancient woman gathering dust on her feet and if someone were to touch you now you would crumble like the ashy coal that holds its old shape. She sends her mind in flight over the hills and bogland, watches it alight upon the mountain road. Is arrested from thought by a gent riding a horse so black it gleams an undercolour of silver. The man touches his cap and wishes her a good morning. She is surprised when he smiles at her. That man was gentry for sure, she thinks.

How the road winds through bogland she has always known. A slab of lake and a lonely tree. This place unchanged and as old as it ever was, almost treeless and only the clouds that drift their shadows have changed. She meets the mountain road and walks until she reaches the pass and then she sees it, Blackmountain, the far-off shapes of two houses, and her feet grow light and her spirit is light as she walks onwards. This feeling now of what it would be like to be met by them, to watch them come out of the house, this feeling that she is no longer herself and yet you are yourself, for you cannot be another. Another feeling that grows with each step, how it tries to speak but she will not let it, how it wants to shout but she gags it at the mouth for you must, you must, you must.

A little voice comes to meet her and says, but where is the smoke? But where is the door? The voice is her own and it is the voice of who she once was. Closer and then she cannot walk farther. She sees there is no door only a doorway of stone that stands mute to an empty house. What rides through her body robs it of breath, gives the heart sudden weight. She steps into the house, sees how the damp and the moss have made their home, that animals have lived here, a few wandering ewes, no doubt. She looks to the hearth and sees it is a long time without fire. Stands very still as if awaiting some answer or clue as to what happened, if Mam made them depart in a hurry, or something worse than that, but the walls speak only of emptiness and the house seems so very small, much smaller than she has remembered it. She thinks, you must go outside and look for their graves. She circles the house over and over but the land has nothing to say. The hillside asleep under its barren brown coat. The trickle-water ditch that cuts through it. The sound of the wind calling its children.

She does not know how long she has been standing here ill to the wind, trying to summon their voices. A strange thought nagging her. That it is you who are dead. That it is your spirit that has returned hundreds of years later, that they went on living to the ends of their lives, that Mam lived to a great old age and the boys became men and had wives and many children. She takes a long inhale of cold breath and sees the ghost of her mother bundling her skirt and setting off up the hill. She knows now that this house cannot be slept in. The things you might hear.

She knows when she stands at his door that the old man's eyes disbelieve sight of her. But then his hands rise huge to take hold of her wrists and he shakes them like hammers. She watches him mouth for words but no words come out. Finally, he says, I thought you were— heavens. I thought you were—

He puts a fir chair near the fire and asks her to sit. She tries to hide the knowledge that came upon her the moment she saw him. The answer that fell from his eyes. She can see now how the Banger's thickness has gone, how his hands are too great for him. His hair gone to metal. And his eyes that watered when he saw her have continued like so, for they are the eyes of a man grown old. Her sight travels the meager room and she wonders how long the forge fire next door has gone out, what kind of day it was. What he said when it happened, if he sat down and stared at his hands. He looks at her now as if he does not know what to ask her, this man who was once a friend of her mother, a far-off cousin.

Finally he says, so you've been up Blackmountain?

He holds her with a strange look when she does not answer.

He says, where have your words gone?

She cannot answer.

He says, you had quite the tongue on you always.

His look has not left her but then something that looks like fear alights the surface of his eyes and before she can name it he is upon her, grabs her with the same old strength, pulls open her mouth with his fingers. When he lets her go, he says, sorry for that but I needed to make sure your tongue was not cut or that you weren't the pooka come to get me. God knows I've been waiting. I heard there is a woman out in Glen who lost her words also. She'd seen enough.

* * *

He cannot look at her eyes because her eyes are full of questions. Then he rises from his chair and rubs his great hands. He says, I do not know— I do not know what happened to them. It went very bad in some places. Went very bad around here, all right. Though mostly it never touched this house, thank God. The things I seen you cannot ask me. All I can tell you is that house was empty when the worst of it were over. That was the worst winter I can ever remember. I never saw the sight of it in my life. It brought distress like no other. A good many departed from around here. They took to the roads or went for the boat and many entered the churchyard down below and the fields are full up with them. I never went up that hill during it, though maybe I should have but there was such misery and you had to mind what you had because in a wink it would be gone. I never saw them come down this way, that's God's truth. Thank God it never touched this house.

A shaky hand runs through his hair. He spits at the fire.

He says, you'll see one or two big houses gone up around here as if nothing happened. There was a few got their makings out of it. There is always a few who bide their time until things get to their worst and then they buy up what is going for cheap. A lot of fine stock was bought by the grabbers for gutter prices. People cleaned out for almost nothing in return. That Columbo McLaughlin. I don't know if you remember him. Spent his time with the purse in one hand licking the tips of his counting fingers. Fattened his household rightly, so he did. And a good lot of houses lying empty now. This forge hasn't seen smoke in two year. As the cat's still got your tongue I will inquire after your people but I doubt much will come of it because I would have heard word by now. And I should have asked as there is blood between us. She was a good woman, your mother. It was— it was a time of terrible disorder.

He turns to look at her and his eyes brighten. You are very different from what I remember of you. God took you off a wee girl and sent you back a beautiful woman.

* * *

She wakes to a voice that is her own whisper. Rises to see the shape of the Banger breathing the sea's breath in his chair. She wraps the cape about her shoulders, opens the latch door, sees how the throw-light falls in peace upon the lapped hands of the Banger, his legs sprawled and his feet turned inwards, his mouth open as if agog to some dream. The animal rush of cold air and she puts behind her the road that twists uphill to Blackmountain, walks towards a sea of ashes that sends upwards a rusted knife of wind. A sudden pair of watching red eyes in a field that belong to a bull.

Too many places now hold memory against her. It is, she thinks, as if memory were hidden not in thought but deep within the physical arrangement of things. How the cornering road gives up sudden movement that is the dancing of ghosts she tries to outwit by staring somewhere else. She passes her own ghost walking with her mother. Some unremembered conversation and a feeling of long and endless summer, a future of infinite space. And in the breakwater she sees some lost day under a forgotten sun. She closes her eyes and is her own ghost diving into the water down to where the worldsound holds still and there is only heartbeat and the shape of her brother lissome in the water and perhaps you can now accept what is.

The road takes her around headland that winds the sea around its many fingers, the sea taking the headland in its breath, an endless coarse breathing, this sea-wind that blows from the gulf of who-knows-where and what it whispers, that I have been here since the beginning of time and will whisper these rocks to dust. Children appear from a bally of houses and begin to shout and walk alongside her. A man stands at a door with two pails and shouts some comment at the children. A brazen girl no more than seven pulling at her gown. Who are you supposed to be? What are you doing? The girl follows alongside Grace in exaggerated march-step then falls behind with a hurt face when Grace does not answer.

She finds the house she seeks under a gathering rain-sky that stoops to pale the tone of the hills. The freestone cottage is low off the road and kept guard by high holly and blackthorn and hounds that loll and woof. She can see streaking through hedgerow the russet hair of some younger. A trio of hounds snapping towards her and she puts out her hand and commands them to shush.

She faces the door. The wrong woman answers. They eye each other up and down and the woman says, who are you?

She thinks, for goodness' sake, speak, would you.

But she cannot speak and then a grunting voice from inside says, who is that? And then it is him, Boggs, filling the doorway, blinking at her, looking without knowing. And how small he is, she thinks. In her memory he is a haystack, had arms that gathered everything about him. Now she meets him eye to eye and takes the measure of a fool. Sees the way his dull eyes read her full body. How his scant horseshoe of hair and beard have lost their red colour. She reaches her eyes into the house, reaches her ears for sound of them, tells herself, but you already know the answer.

His stupiding eyes say, I don't know who you are.

Then he steps out and pulls the door closed, wheels her gently by the elbow and begins walking. Come along, he says.

He bends and puts his fist into a sack and rains feed for the hens.

He says, is he ill or something? Tell your father I am wild sorry about the trouble and that I will soon get it fixed. That villain from Inch did not deliver as promised and has left me to look like a fool. It is sore toil to maintain oneself in living these days and my eyes are at me as you can see and most things now are becoming dull to my sight. But listen, I don't want to be troublesome. You have your own trouble to attend to and let us all go merrily to heaven.

The way he smiles at her then and she looks at him strangely and when he turns she studies the back of his head for the mark of the wound she put there. She turns and sees a redheaded girl following them like one of Boggs's dogs. Of a sudden Boggs turns and says, get inside, you. She watches the girl retreat to the back step, where she continues to watch, and she thinks, some part of you will forever be this girl watching Boggs walk about his backyard unless you ask him, and she looks at Boggs without rage, can feel the words rise within her, these words she must speak, for if you do not speak them they can never be said and she wants to say, what did you do with them? Tell me where they are, for she was beholden to you. She would have done nothing without you.

She tries to will the words but the words collapse under their weight.

The rain stippling her face and Boggs is watching the sky and he blinks slowly and says, is your gig at the top of the road? That rain. I could lend you a jute sack for your head.

This hammer rock where she sits summoning her grief. The ghost wind that whispers guilt but does not answer. Watching memories leave the rocks. Watching what moves amid the shadows of the empty house. How the ash trees in the wind twist sudden images. She wants to shout at the trees, at the silent rocks, at this road that does not speak, but what can you say that will ever be answered? She meets a strange calm that says perhaps they are and perhaps they are not, and if they are not you might still find them. She remembers a story told by Sarah when she was young about this very rock, that a devil wings down and takes seat on it every night while you sleep, writes down every detail of your life. The book of fate, she called it. The things you would read in there, she thinks, if you could read the rocks.

She reads again the script the Banger gave her with his address. You will write and see if I hear anything and that there is the priest's address. Just in case I don't answer, for it will mean the pooka have come for me.

His laughter and a look as heavy as his hands stay with her.

His voice that says, once you get the wandering into your blood it is hard to shake it out. So and anyhow. We are a funny country, are we not? In all this time we never yet learned to look after ourselves. To think on our own two feet. The heroes are all gone long ago to the hills. The great warriors do not fight for us. And God gave up on us a long time ago. In his absence the pooka make trouble and only the rain cares for us and what kind of comfort is that? Best just to get along with things as they are. Wherever you go you are. Isn't that what they always say? What I'm saying is, mind yourself.

A blackbird alights upon an ash tree and she watches it carefully, for in its flight path will lie an augury. She watches the bird take sudden flight for the south. Laughs to herself. Sure I knew that already.

How quickly a year goes out and now almost another. Already it is the autumn of 1849. So soon, she thinks, you will be nineteen. She has been a wanderer and has come to see this earth many-voiced and multitudinous and among its throng has come to believe there is not one earth but as many earths as there are people, and as many earths again to meet our changing lives. We are here under a hundred million suns and each sun dies out under the same limitless sun that burns in lasting mystery.

She has spent much of the year in south Donegal. Has seen swaths of countryside abandoned, has seen madness in the eyes of those whose fate it is to remember. And yet the lazybeds serried on every hill keep coming to green and men and women and children walk free of their shadows. They idle the corners and fill the air with pipe smoke, banter and intrigue.

In a place called Drumrat she watched an elderly horse kneel to its death and not one person rush with a knife.

She has been a maid-of-all-work in the house of a merchant six miles from Bundoran, a cooker, scrubber, washer, mender and minder of children. Has stood glad in the warmth of the kitchen. Listened to household talk of the swan-eating queen who sailed for Ireland and was met by how many steamers and such were the happy shrieks of the crowds of three cities that came to see her. Her body has grown into fullness. Her hair has captured its colour. She has grown it past her hips and thinks she might never cut it, wears it down in the private of her room and admires it in the looking glass. She has walked the twenty miles to Sligo to see a traveling circus, watched clowns teeter drunker than fools, and stared into the ocher eyes of a rhesus monkey placed upon her shoulder and what she saw in the eye of that animal, the story of a life she knew to be her own. She saw in the new year holding the good hand of the coachman Jim Collins, a man with half a left thumb lost to a berserk horse, a man who stands ample in easy kindness and still young enough, just some grey above his ears and those lovely wrinkles that corner his mouth. How in their more solemn moments he runs his hands through the sunset of her hair and smells it. He has accepted the quiet sit of her tongue and she has written to him, asking him to wait for her words, that the words will come. And now she turns from the thought that folds time and feeling upon itself, turns from a blank look and lights her pipe, watches Jim flitch wood with the ax, the way he turns then to smile at her, wipes his sleeve at his forehead. This place by the river he has built for them. This house of freestone and it is almost as if she has dreamed it, the wash of a river, the house abutting a woodland. It is a place where the old and haunting thought meets the movement of water, water that brings unceasing newness, life upon life, days that do not ask you to remember.

Then the sudden day when she hears her mother calling for her as if from afar. Hears her mother's voice in the woods. Hears her in the narrowed dark of the room. Wakes to a fluttering kick that sits her up in the bed and there beside her is the known shape of her mother.

She says, I came to see the child.

Having to slide away from Jim without waking him but he stirs anyway and whispers some confused thought and she is out the latch door into the dark and there is Mam waiting and she cannot see her eyes.

She says to her mother, the child is not born yet.

I can wait a while.

I wish you wouldn't, you are dead or long long away from here and I must be getting on with my life.

I am neither dead nor not dead. Your head is full of nonsense.

And what am I supposed to make of that?

Think of it however you like. You were always so difficult.

These nightly visits by her mother become a sorrow that increases as the child swells inside her. Sarah now an old woman, all that was once strong is quitting her body. Perhaps the child, she thinks, is growing off Mam's strength.

She says to Sarah, all right, I will care for you, but the day will come when you must go, these are the terms we must agree on.

Jim watching her with confused regard. How she sits her mother upright in the chair and listens to her grudge the world, the people she has known that are gone, the heartache that comes with the knowledge of dying. And she puts a third meal out and a third glass of water and Jim gives her a look that says, is all this for the child? Another day when he asks, what exactly is going on? And she looks at him and shrugs and she thinks, what is the difference anyhow? For she would like to say, so what if my mother comes to visit me. What is it that we really know anyhow? We cannot hold the truth of this world in our hands. And this word *truth,* what can a word measure? The truths that men hold solemn, their beliefs and their doctrines and their certitude, all of it is but smoke on the wind. And so I am happy to be as I am in this not knowing, to see things without needing to know what they are, if they come from me or they belong to the sky and the hills, my breath and your breath and the way light passes over the stillness of things. So what if my mother should visit me. Maybe she might want something.

Sarah complains for comfort, for the blanket, to be listened to, chisels endlessly at her, you are just like your father, there's a pair of you in it, never gave me a moment's peace in my life.

She tells her daughter, when I was a girl, all I ever wanted was to be a seamstress.

And then the morning comes when she wakes sudden to the sound of her mother's cry and she can feel the child in her belly kicking. Rising into the dawnlight where she finds her mother lying by the edge of the river and she goes to her and lifts her and holds her to her chest. And Sarah whispers, I am so tired, I am at my end, you must let me go, and when her body becomes still she closes the woman's eyes and sits like that a long while and then she lifts her mother up and walks her into the river, watches the water travel around her mother's body, lets her mother go, and the shout she hears belongs to Jim and then he is running and then he is alongside her and he is crying and carrying her out of the water.

In the days that follow she begins to feel a shift inside her as if a great light were shining through her, a light reaching into dark, thought like rain washing through sky, like glass that holds the world without discolour, like sunlight passing beauty through water, like sunlight passing through wind beneath the rising wingbeat. The child soon due and these are the good blue days and she knows, yes, I will speak, the words will come and I will speak of what is now, of only this, and a blue morning arrives when Jim shakes her from dream and she wakes and he whispers, you must come, and they step out of the house and it is then she sees it, the woodland held in fields of colour, a violet born of night and finding in day its fullest expression and how the trees stand hazed in the light of these bluebells and her hands go to her belly and it is then without thought the words rise and she speaks to him.

This life is light.

About the Author

Paul Lynch is the prizewinning Irish author of two previous novels, *Red Sky in Morning* and *The Black Snow*. *Red Sky in Morning* was a finalist for France's Prix du Meilleur Livre Étranger (Best Foreign Book Prize). *The Black Snow* won the French booksellers' prize, Prix Libr'à Nous, for Best Foreign Novel. He lives in Dublin with his wife and daughter.